ONE SURE THING

Raymond sat silent as Hope sipped her warm tea. She smiled over her cup and looked around the private room. "This is a beautiful restaurant. Thank you for bringing me here. I'm glad you accepted my dare."

"It's my pleasure. I'm really having a good time."

"You say that like you didn't expect to."

"Well, let's face it, Hope, you and I don't exactly have a history of polite conversation. Our temperaments are accelerants at the very least. We are anything but docile."

"I seem to remember you being completely at fault."

"Actually, I recall that you were more openly hostile."

She smiled. "You barged into my exam room."

He returned her smile. "You had me barred from the ER."

"With good cause."

"Ah, come on, you make me sound like some kind of ogre."

"Let's just say that you make a lousy first impression." She began to laugh. He joined in.

"I love that you stand up to me."

"Why wouldn't I?"

"Exactly. I'm only human."

"That remains to be seen."

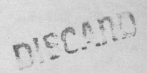

BOOK YOUR PLACE ON OUR WEBSITE AND MAKE THE ARABESQUE ROMANCE CONNECTION!

We've created a customized website just for our very special Arabesque readers, where you can get the inside scoop on everything that's going on with Arabesque romance novels.

When you come online, you'll have the exciting opportunity to:

- View covers of upcoming books

- Learn about our future publishing schedule (listed by publication month and author)

- Find out when your favorite authors will be visiting a city near you

- Search for and order backlist books

- Check out author bios and background information

- Send e-mail to your favorite authors

- Join us in weekly chats with authors, readers and other guests

- Get writing guidelines

- AND MUCH MORE!

Visit our website at
http://www.arabesquebooks.com

ONE SURE THING

Celeste O. Norfleet

BET Publications, LLC
http://www.bet.com
http://www.arabesquebooks.com

ARABESQUE BOOKS are published by

BET Publications, LLC
c/o BET BOOKS
One BET Plaza
1900 W Place NE
Washington, DC 20018-1211

All Kensington Titles, Imprints, and Distributed Lines are available at special quantity discounts for bulk purchases for sales promotions, premiums, fund-raising, and educational or institutional use. Special book excerpts or customized printings can also be created to fit specific needs. For details, write or phone the office of the Kensington special sales manager: Kensington Publishing Corp., 850 Third Avenue, New York, NY 10022, attn: Special Sales Department, Phone: 1-800-221-2647.

First Printing: September 2003
10 9 8 7 6 5 4 3 2 1

Printed in the United States of America

Dedicated to two very special people, Christopher and Jennifer, who bring humor, wit, and balance to my life. And who always remind me why I decided to write. But most of all to Fate and Fortune for your inspiration, motivation, support, and encouragement. Your love, belief, and faith continue to drive me forward.

ACKNOWLEDGMENTS

I continue to give praises and thanks for the gift, the ability, and the opportunity to bring you stories, and to share with you my love of writing.

I'd also like to thank you the readers for requesting that I write this and continue the Gates and Evans family story line. Your letters and e-mails said it all. Thank you so much for your continued support and encouragement. Also, a much appreicated thank you to the booksellers who hand sell my novels and keep them on the shelves. Thank you for your efforts and attention.

Lastly, a big thanks to my editors Chandra Sparks Taylor and Karen Thomas, for giving me a voice and letting my imagination grow and develop.

Prologue

It was late. Twilight had come and gone and so had the newlyweds. It was the perfect wedding and J.T.'s parents had done an incredible job hosting it at their northern Virginia home. Madison and Tony Gates were the ideal bride and groom and their wedding had been nothing short of the epitome of perfection. A flawless celebration of their love and devotion, they pledged their lives to one another in the presence of God and nearly four hundred guests. All of whom had retired to their homes except for three soul searching figures sitting in the darkness.

With imported cigars and snifters of brandy, Raymond Gates, J.T. Evans and Dennis Hayes sat out on the deck in the screened gazebo. Relaxed and tranquil, they watched as the lighting bugs danced across the back lawn in search of new adventures. The sky, a midnight black hue, was littered with tiny white lights that twinkled and glimmered in heavenly brilliance.

"So, what do you think Madison meant by that remark?" Raymond asked, still pondering his new cousin's less than cryptic statement. He adjusted his already loosened tie then shifted his tuxedoed clad legs down from the chair.

"You look worried," Dennis said, amused by Raymond's tense expression.

"Of course I'm worried. My neck's on the chopping block. Chances are Mamma Lou already has her picked out."

J.T looked at Dennis. Buddies since childhood, they

glanced at each other and decided to have a little fun at Raymond's expense. "Did either one of you see that woman Mamma Lou was talking to most of the evening?"

Raymond instantly sat up straighter as his eyes widened. "No, who was she?" He asked.

"Yeah, I saw her," Dennis replied. He grimaced and shook his head sadly. "If she's the one that your grandmother has in mind for you then you may have my condolences."

"What? Who? What do you mean, I have your condolences? What did she look like? Who was she?"

"Do you really think she's the one?" J.T. asked Dennis.

"More than likely. Mamma Lou was looking at Raymond the entire time she was talking to the young lady."

"Well, man, let me be the first to congratulate you," J.T. commiserated soulfully.

"What did she look like?"

"She seemed to have a great personality," Dennis noted.

"Oh yeah, but of course, she'd have to," J.T. added.

"What does that mean?" Raymond's eyes widened in complete panic. Then suddenly, he heard chuckling and laughter beside him. He realized that the two friends were only joking with him. "That's not funny."

"But seriously man, I'd get out of town as soon as possible if I were you," J.T. warned.

"I intend to. But I'm not too worried. Mamma Lou knows I'm hopeless when it comes to taking that long walk down the aisle. She's had her eye on matching me up for a long time and every time I've dodged it."

"Your grandmother's pretty spry. I think your luck's about to run out. I have a feeling that whatever she puts her mind to, she achieves."

"Not this time. Not with me." Raymond said bravely. "I have no intention of being around when she starts matchmaking again. And just to be on the safe side, I'm getting as far away from Crescent Island and Virginia as I can."

"Where are you going? Back home or to Manhattan?"

"To Manhattan, and as fast as I can. I'm leaving at the crack of dawn." Raymond stood quickly as if to make his point. He extinguished the cigar he'd been burning and picked up the empty glass. "Gentlemen, it's been a pleasure." He saluted them with his raised glass.

"Good luck man," Dennis said.

"You take care," J.T. added.

The three men shook hands. Raymond opened the screen door and walked across the deck to the kitchen.

J.T. looked at Dennis. They shook their heads at the impending doom. "Dead man walking," they said at the same time, then erupted with roaring laughter. There was no way Raymond could evade his grandmother for long. She was just too good and he was just too unmarried.

"A hundred dollars says he's married before the end of summer."

"You're on."

One

The task at hand was matchmaking. Six months after her latest triumphant union, Louise Gates was determined to succeed with her next target. It didn't matter that he objected to her intrusions into his life or protested every attempt she made. It didn't even matter that he blocked every one of her suggestions. That was to be expected. The trick was, to set plans in motion in such a way that everything would look totally natural and any incident would appear completely coincidental.

Louise smiled mischievously and watched as her grandson easily maneuvered his way through the throngs of waiting patrons. She noticed as the dreamy wanton eyes of every woman over the age of eighteen glanced, stared and ogled his way admiringly. And why not? The esteemed Dr. Raymond Gates was a handsome man with a list of credentials that would choke an elephant.

He was a doctor, surgeon, board member, lecturer and president of a non-profit foundation for children and deserving teens. And of course, there was his least favorable credential, bachelor. He exuded an abundance of class and charm and there was no wonder women loved and chased him; they just couldn't catch him.

Louise frowned then raised her brow knowingly. It was high time to remove bachelor from the list and replace it with a more appropriate description, such as devoted husband and dedicated father.

"I was about to send in the Reserves," Colonel Wheeler said as soon as Louise returned to his side. "I assume the lines were outrageous?"

"Lines in public ladies' powder rooms are always ridiculously long," she stated matter of factly. She wisely decided not to divulge the real reason for her extended delay. Somehow, admitting that she'd been listening in on a private conversation for the sole purpose of Raymond's future didn't seem appropriate at the time. So she decided to keep that bit of information to herself.

Colonel Wheeler nodded his usual understanding.

"Where's Raymond?" she asked.

"He went to the bar for refreshments. He mentioned something about needing a cold drink. He should be back any minute." Colonel Wheeler glanced in the direction of the concession stand. "After that little row you two just had, I imagine he could use a drink." Colonel Wheeler shook his head. Raymond and Louise had been at it all weekend. The lovely mini vacation had turned into a battle of wills. Each side was equally matched and just as equally determined.

Louise glowered. "I don't know why he's being so stubborn. I don't see the harm in making one simple little request."

"Louise, your one little request was for him to get married, settle down and start a family as soon as possible."

"Is that asking so much? It's not like I made it a direct order. I'm just giving him a little push in the right direction."

"Pushing him isn't working."

"Are you taking his side?" She asked of her longtime friend and companion.

Colonel Wheeler chuckled gleefully, "As usual, I'm on no one's side. I learned a long time ago never to get in the middle of one of your battles with your grandsons; I prefer to be an innocent bystander. Although, even that's becoming dangerous these days."

"Oh, you're a lot of help," she said, as Colonel Wheeler

continued laughing. Louise turned toward the bar just in time to see her grandson parting his way through the crowd. His irresistible dimpled smile greeted her as he approached. "She was attractive didn't you think dear?" Louise whispered lightheartedly to Raymond as soon as he reached her side with their drinks.

Raymond looked to Colonel Wheeler as he handed over the glass of wine. Colonel Wheeler, in turn, looked at Louise, shook his head and began his deep, throaty chuckle that quaked every part of his body. Knowing Louise Gates as well as he did, he immediately recognized her question for exactly what it was: a ploy to distract Raymond from something else.

Raymond, on the other hand, took a decidedly defensive posture. When Louise was around he rebuffed any and every woman within a mile radius just to be on the safe side. He knew what his grandmother had in mind and he wasn't having any part of it.

"Don't even think about it, Mamma Lou." Raymond shook his head, handed his grandmother a glass of wine and then leaned down to kiss the soft brown of her smooth cheek. "You promised to stop, remember?" he said, while looking and smiling back at the female bartender as she waved to him from across the room. He raised his glass of club soda and winked. The bartender instantly began to glow; as did the second woman at the bar, dressed in a skintight sequin dress and spiked heels. "You're not trapping me in one of your little matchmaking schemes. I told you before, Mamma Lou, just consider me hopeless."

"Well than, we'll just have to find you hope, won't we?"

"Okay, fine," he said offhandedly, "you find me hope, and I'll do the rest."

Raymond and Colonel Wheeler chuckled. "Go ahead and laugh. But mark my words, you're not going to be able to treat every woman as cavilerly as you usually do. Just as your father found, there's going to be one woman you won't be able to manipulate. And she'll be the one to steal your heart. I'm warning you—once you let her slip through your fingers, you're going to have a hard time getting her back."

Raymond hugged his grandmother warmly. "I have yet to meet a woman that I can't handle."

Louise nodded and smiled. "I believe your cousin, Tony, said the exact same thing just before he met Madison."

"Okay, I'll admit, it worked well enough with Tony and Madison, but it's definitely not going to work on me. I'm onto you. I have no intention of getting snared and become an unwilling victim in one of your marriage traps. Understand?" he warned pointedly.

Louise Gates's mouth gaped open in complete and total innocence. Her soft brown eyes sparkled wide with sincere naiveté. "Raymond Gates, Jr., I am truly appalled that you would accuse me of such a thing. I would never presume to interfere in your personal life. You know very well that I'm not that kind of person. For heaven's sake, you make it sound like I'm some kind of noisy, busybody with a meddling, matchmaking complex. What I do is a natural talent."

After taking a sip of his drink and hearing that remark, Colonel Wheeler guffawed and chuckled with such merriment that he nearly choked on his beverage. Concern instantly registered on Raymond's handsome face until Colonel Wheeler nodded that he was fine. Raymond then turned and looked down at his grandmother suspiciously and shook his head. The humored look he gave her spoke volumes. For the third time in as many hours, he had warned her against using her self-proclaimed God-given talent to match him with her perception of his perfect mate, which was basically every single woman on the planet.

"I don't see why you're getting so upset with me. You bring all of this on yourself," Louise admonished sternly.

"Me?" Raymond asked, so surprised by the instant reversal that his voice cracking sophomorically. "What do I do? How do I bring this on myself? I'm just an innocent bystander. You're the one who painted an 'available bachelor' target on my back and gave half the female population of New York City bows, arrows, and a detailed map of my posterior."

His comical expressions, his wry sense of humor, and the timing of a professional comic had Colonel Wheeler laughing openly and Louise snickering at the visual absurdity.

She shook her head, then reached up and stroked the smooth, clean-shaven cheek of her grandson. "You're just like your grandfather, bless his soul. Now he was a man to reckon with." She smiled, remembering the wonderful years she was blessed to spend with her late husband, Jonathan Gates. "He was a handsome devil; charming, and clever. The women went wild for him too. But, poor dears, as soon as your grandfather laid eyes on me it was all over. It was as if there wasn't another woman in the world. Mind you, I'm not tooting my own horn; I'm simply stating the God's honest truth. As a matter of fact," she nodded her head toward Colonel Wheeler, "the same thing happened with Otis here."

Otis Wheeler, a retired colonel from the US Marine Corps, had been a cherished family friend ever since he moved to Crescent Island, the Gates's family home.

Both Raymond and Louise turned to look at Colonel Wheeler. He instantly tossed his hands up in mock surrender. "Don't look at me, I'm sitting this one out." He continued chuckling until he was forced to wipe the moisture from his eyes with his handkerchief. There was nothing like Louise Gates's tenacity. When she set her mind on something, nothing on the planet could change it.

Raymond reached down and pulled Louise into the embrace of his chest. She yielded easily. "I can definitely see that, Mamma Lou. You'll always be my number one lady. So, why would I need anyone else? Who could possibly take your place?"

Louise looked past Raymond to see a tall, rail-thin woman, overdressed in a glamorous sequin evening dress, strutting in their direction. Her eyes, like the trajectory of an armed missile, were loaded and locked on the broad shoulders of

Raymond's suit jacket. "Some will try, I'd wager," Louise warned quietly.

Just then a soft buzzing sound vibrated from Raymond's inside jacket pocket. He reached in and flipped open his small cellular telephone. "Dr. Gates." The joyous levity had instantly vanished from his face as his voice took on a purely professional tone. He nodded a few times then spouted a few medical terms. Afterwards, he flipped the phone close and returned it to his pocket. He looked to the nearest exit, then back to his evening companions. The look on his face said it all. Somewhere, someone needed him.

Colonel Wheeler looked to Louise, and they shook their heads knowingly. Raymond opened his mouth to apologize as Colonel Wheeler took the glass from his hand.

"Go," Louise instructed warmly.

Raymond looked to Colonel Wheeler. He nodded assuredly, "We'll be fine."

Raymond smiled a knowing reply as he took a step back. "Don't wait up," he instructed. Then, with a sole purpose in mind, he parted the assembled crowd and disappeared through the exit doors.

Louise watched, humored by the young woman's dejected expression. Thwarted and disappointed by Raymond's abrupt departure, the targeting sequined woman stood with her mouth agape and her hands on her skinny hips. She rolled her eyes, turned, and headed back to the bar.

Louise shook her head. She had seen so many women come and go in Raymond's life. Most of them were completely wrong for him. Eventually, thankfully, he realized it before it was too late. Yes, she wanted him married and settled, but she also wanted him happy.

She herself had had many wonderful years with her husband, Jonathan. Then, several years after his death, she had been blessed to have Otis come into her life. Both men were treasures and had added to her life in a special way. It was only natural that she would want the same joy for her grandson. So, left up to her, she accepted the task of finding someone special for him.

A soft bell chimed indicating the end of intermission and the beginning of the play's second act. Colonel Wheeler took Louise's arm and escorted her back to their orchestra seats in the small plush box on the second level.

Louise settled back comfortably into her posh, velvet seat. She sat, patiently tapping her toe, while an idea began to sprout and take form in the recesses of her mind. She liked what she had overheard earlier in the powder room. All she had to do is find out where the two women were sitting and do a little investigating. Easy enough. She had friends who would be delighted to lend a hand. It was risky. It was tricky. It was perfect. A smile of sheer delight spread wide and bright across her face.

The ironic perfection of the woman being in the ladies room at that exact moment was definitely a sign from heaven as far as she was concerned. Raymond had confessed that he was hopeless. He had even challenged her to find hope, and that's exactly what she intended to do.

Smiling, she picked up the pearl-studded opera glasses and pointed them toward the stage. The red velvet curtain, still down, didn't hold her attention any longer than the assembled orchestra musicians as they re-tuned their instruments, preparing to resume play. Louise slowly fanned the small glasses around the room until they focused in on the two women she'd overheard in the ladies room. They were seated in the lower section, midway down on the far left side between two other women dressed in bright red evening suits.

Louise smiled, as she grew more confident with her choice. It was as if fate and fortune had placed her at the right place and the right time. The *who* in her plan had been found, and the careful planning had already begun. Like the evening's entertainment, the stage was set and the players were all in place. And the following week was the time she'd chosen to commence Act One.

Suddenly, Louise felt a gentle hand grasp hers. Colonel Wheeler leaned toward her and whispered into her ear. "You've already chosen Raymond's young lady, haven't you?"

Louise smiled. This man knew her far too well. "Yes, I have."

"And he has no idea." Colonel Wheeler shook his head and chuckled softly.

"Not a clue."

"I don't suppose you'd consider letting me in on the secret?"

Louise laughed openly, causing those in the orchestra box next to theirs to turn in her direction and stare questioningly. "Otis Wheeler, you know very well you can't keep a secret to save your life. Honestly, for over thirty-five years and three wars you kept some of this country's most sensitive military intelligence secrets. You detailed and planned multi-layered maneuvers and strategies with shadow teams and undercover operatives both as a reservist and civilian consultant. Then you retired. And that was the last time you kept a secret."

Colonel Wheeler, humored by the truth, chuckled as his broad shoulders shook comically. She was absolutely right. As a military intelligence officer he was sworn to secrecy, but now that he was a civilian, secrets were far too enjoyable to keep all to himself.

Moments later the orchestra began to play as the curtains slowly rose. The play was delightful. The vivid picturesque scenery and brilliant, dazzling costumes added to the wondrous evening. Louise glanced down at the woman seated between the two red bookends. The muted house lights shined down just enough to give her an added glow of beauty. Her delighted expression said it all. Louise couldn't have been more pleased with herself and her choice.

Two

Emergency room department physician Dr. Hope Adams could feel her tense body reaching the point at which no doctor should ever be. A place where pain and misery thrived daily, while happiness only visited on occasion. At this point in her career, her fill of despair had far exceeded the joys she had once experienced.

She was losing hope as the pain and suffering in the ER had begun to drain her. Unfortunately, burning out fast was an adverse fact of life in her chosen profession.

She lay in the lower, narrow bunk bed and stared up at the wire canopy above her. Her body was completely drained. The serenity and tranquility of a restful sleep had continued to elude her. Physically and emotionally she was exhausted, yet, she was wide-awake. She shifted her weight and laid the neatly folded newspaper by her side, then exhaled raggedly as she unconsciously stroked the side of her face.

A latent habit of reassurance, touching the small scar often comforted her when she was at her most vulnerable. Positioned on the side of her face just over her left eyebrow, near her hairline, it had always stirred long-ago memories of sadness and pain. The feel of the thin twist of fate had always given her the sense of a surviving victory in the face of defeat.

Tired beyond exhaustion, she was on a much needed ninety-minute break. She looked at the iridescent glow of her watch. She had just a few more hours left of a twenty-four hour rotation and, for the first time in nineteen hours and forty-one minutes, she had the opportunity to get a little shut-eye. Unfortunately, she couldn't sleep. It was the occupational hazard of long shift hours and heavy caseloads. By the time she wound down enough to relax, it was time to get back to work.

Hope looked up at the intertwined grid of metal wire beneath the empty bed above her. She had already counted the open squares, and the intersecting points. She closed her eyes again and tried to erase hundreds of flashing images speeding through her head.

She searched the room for a relaxing focal point and counted backward from a thousand. She even counted sheep, but nothing worked. Then, finally, without really trying, she drifted into a restless sleep.

A shaft of florescent light split the darkness like a hot knife in warm butter. Damn! It never seemed to fail; as soon as she drifted off to sleep some brave soul, with the audacity of a lamb strutting into a lion's den, would find some reason to awaken her.

"Hope, are you awake?" The pleasant voice of Maxine Hunter whispered in the darkness. Maxine crept further into the small room and edged forward until she was able to turn on the low table light sitting precariously on the edge of the cluttered desk. "Hope?" She moved the lamp away from the edge and adjusted the cord behind it accordingly. "Hope?"

"All right, all right, I heard you, I'm up," she said tartly, as she swung her legs over the side of the bed and arched her back in a slow lingering stretch. Forty minutes of sleep in a twenty hour time period had a tendency to make her grouchy.

Maxine turned the switch again, sending a brighter light around the room. She handed Hope the charts and clipboards she'd brought in with her, then leaned over and began to neaten the pile of newspaper, folders, medical magazines and books on the night stand.

A low, achy moan escaped from Hope as Maxine clicked the light to its brightest setting. Maxine smiled at hearing

Hope's disgruntled moan. Momentarily blinded by the bright light, Hope yawned and rolled her neck slowly.

"Somebody's not in a very good mood," Maxine said in a singsong.

"I haven't been in a good mood in close to eight years," Hope said, as she briefly read then flipped up the first two pages of the first clipboard. She initialed it, then signed her name on the third page. "And I don't intend to be in a good mood for at least another sixty years." On the fourth page she read and signed a release form that had been okayed earlier.

Then, on the last page she scanned the results of tests she'd ordered earlier for a patient. The patient came in complaining of sudden weight loss, excessive thirst and hunger, irritation and frequent urination. The tests had confirmed her initial suspicions and diagnosis. The patient was diabetic. She referred the patient to an endocrinologist on staff, then signed off. She turned her attention to the second clipboard and repeated the process.

Within minutes Hope had completed the standard sign-off forms and discharge paperwork. She placed the clipboards on the bed next to her; then sat up straighter, and fluffed and loosened the halo of flattened curls covering her head. The tiny black ringlets had always had a will of their own. She'd known that since she was old enough to comb her own hair. No matter how much she ruffled and fluffed, her hair always reformed to the same curled mass of ordered chaos.

Maxine sucked on her teeth and tsked loudly. "You have to learn to loosen up," she said with a thick Jamaican dialect that oftentimes accompanied a sarcastic remark. She picked up the white jacket from the back of the chair and held it out for Hope to slip on. Hope stood and turned to slip her arms in place. "You need to find a hobby outside of the hospital. I'm telling you this for your own good. You need to learn to relax. You're going to burn yourself out one of these days. You know of course that we're taking bets on how long before you completely lose your mind."

"I sincerely hope you woke me up for something in particular and not just for another one of your lifetime sermons. Because to tell you the truth Maxine, I'm really not in the mood."

Maxine chuckled. "I hope you were able to get a little shut-eye, 'cause you're gonna need it. The bases are loaded and we have a full house."

"Oh joy," Hope replied sarcastically.

"Don't shoot the messenger. I'm just giving you a heads up."

"I know. Don't take it personally."

"I never do," Maxine said in her perpetual blasé manner.

Hope shook her head, constantly astonished by Maxine's perpetual nonchalance. She was truly an enigma. At times, her brazen manner made most of the ER staff nervous, but for the select few who knew her well, they had a different perception of Maxine. She was kind and caring and a dedicated professional who enjoyed her chameleon-like demeanor. For added amusement, she took great pleasure in scaring the wits out of medical students, interns, and new hires.

Maxine was a fifty-something med school drop out from the 1960s with a chip on her shoulder the size of a great redwood. She'd long since burned out in ER, but refused to work anywhere else. Now, she was a talented physician's assistant with enough informal medical experience to be dangerous. Unfortunately for her, she'd been called before the administrative director on several occasions for her defiant attitude, her insubordination and her blatant disregard of medial formality.

To her credit, she had enough common sense and know-how to rival most medical professionals. They knew it and left her alone.

Born and raised in Jamaica, she was the illegitimate daughter of a British businessman and a native housemaid. She had vibrant blue eyes with specks of green that when angry, had been known to cause grown men to cry. Her high cheekbones and full lips accented her islander features. Her cream-kissed umber complexion gave her an exotic look that bespoke her layered heritage.

Banded tendrils of thick, braided and twisted dreadlocks trailed down her back like a midnight waterfall. Her frame, solid and bountiful, was Rubenesque, infused with rounded and voluptuous curves. Perpetually unhurried and unbothered, she moved around the emergency department with an assurance and aloof coolness that was legendary.

"How do you keep so detached surrounded by all of this madness?" Hope asked as she picked up and returned the clipboard to Maxine then rolled her neck, arched her back leisurely and stretched.

"I don't let it get to me."

"It's not that easy, and you know it."

"It is for me."

"Then you're the lucky one. 'Cause I think it gets to all of us eventually."

"Not if you bowl."

"Not it you what?"

"Not if you bowl. You know bowling."

"Bowling? What do bowling balls have to do with not going nuts in this place?"

"It's not necessarily the ball, it's the pins. At times, pin number one is Hugh, pin number two is Scott, pin number three is an abusive husband or parent, and so on."

"I get it, you knock the pins down instead of the actual people." Maxine nodded. "Smart. Assault and battery on a bowling pin instead of a person. Not a bad idea." Hope paused for a second then continued. "Am I ever one of those pins?" Hope asked, positive Maxine would say no.

"Sometimes. Yes."

"That's cold Maxine, even for you."

Maxine shrugged, then signed heavily. "So I've been told." Hope glanced at her friend and wondered just how much truth was in her last statement.

"Is that all?"

"No. Your favorite frequent flyer is back again. She's asking for you." Maxine handed her several more newly prepared files.

Hope looked at Maxine questioningly, then enlightenment dawned on her. Frequent flyer was a term used to denote a patient who visited the emergency department on a more than regular basis. "Leanne?" Hope asked. Maxine nodded affirming her suspicion. "Damn, not again." Hope shuffled through the files to find the patient in question. She closed her eyes and shook her head as soon as she saw the name listed on the ER report.

"Again," Maxine stated dryly.

"How bad is it this time?" Hope muttered more to herself as she looked over the initial triage exam report.

Maxine grimaced painfully and shook her head with utter disgust. "Oh, he really loved her this time. A sprained wrist to go with the broken arm from last time, two bruised ribs and a shiner that could compete with the full moon outside."

"Damn," Hope shook and lowered her head. "What is it about the full moon that drives that man crazy? He needs some serious anger management counseling."

"He needs more than that. He needs a foot up his . . ." Hope eyed Maxine and raised her brow. Maxine rolled her eyes to the ceiling. "But, if you ask me, she's the one that needs to have her head examined. She can't keep doing this to herself. How many times has she crawled, limped and stumbled in here because her husband got too drunk and decided it was a good idea to wail on her head? Month after month we've seen her staggering her sorry behind in here then twelve hours later he shows up with some pathetic half-dying flowers, a tired, lame excuse and that's supposed to make everything alright? How many times have we seen her over the last twenty-four months? Ten, twelve, maybe fifteen times?"

Hope tried hard to concentrate on the chart. The last thing she wanted to do at three-thirty in the morning was to get into a self-righteous discussion with Maxine about how someone else chose to live their life.

"Did you order the usual tests?"

Maxine nodded her head. "Yes."

"Good. Include a CAT scan and CX-R."

Maxine nodded. "I also rounded up the usual suspects: police, crisis counselor, and someone from family intervention is coming down." Hope frowned, questioning. "She said she fell down the stairs, hit her head on the rail and hurt her chest on the landing. The social service counselor is in with her right now." Maxine pronounced with more loathing and less than serious concern.

"No judgments, Maxine." Hope admonished while flipping to another file.

"I don't pass judgments. I simply state facts." Maxine looked at Hope as if to punctuate her point. "She's *STBD* and everybody knows it. She's just killing herself. The next time she comes through those doors she just might be a *DOA*. Then all we'll have to do is send her through with a pretty pink toe-tag."

Hope looked over to Maxine. Her customary affinity for using colorful euphemisms and ER jargon was infamous. Although usually looked upon as humorous by everyone in the ER, Hope often detested certain phrases. *Soon To Be Dead* and *Dead On Arrival* were two of them.

"Did the lab results come in yet?"

"No, the lab's backed up."

"Alright, I'll see her when the results are in."

"Somebody needs to have a good long talk with that woman," Maxine declared.

"I'm sure you're the right person for the job, Maxine," Hope said under her breath, just loud enough to get Maxine's attention.

"Actually, *her doctor* is the right person for the job."

"Wrong."

"I beg your pardon?"

"I've already spoken to her about spousal abuse, she knows the risk she takes. She doesn't want to hear it. She's not ready to change her life. I believe her exact words were, 'I'll die without him.'"

"At this rate she'll die with him," Maxine input sarcastically.

"She's not ready, Maxine," Hope insisted.

"Well hell, when will she be ready, when she's pushing up daisies, six feet under, with a tombstone slapped on her forehead that'll read, *She Was Finally Ready?*"

Hope looked up at Maxine. The severe seriousness in her expression was frightening. A sudden jolt of truth hit her in the pit of her stomach like a base drum. The stomach-turning bile of abuse was never long gone from her memory. She knew the scenario well.

Swelling anger would explode into a rage of fists. The uncontrolled fury would be released on its victim in wave after wave of tormented beatings. She remembered it all too well. Then afterwards, the same excuses, the same bruises, and the same pain.

Hope's eyes began to well up with dried tears she had long ago refused to shed. A part of her understood the madness it took to stay and the insanity it took to remain silent.

"No one can change someone else's life. She has to be willing to do something, to take the first step." Hope spoke as the fatigue and angst in her voice began to show. "It's not our call."

"It's her doctor's call."

"She's not ready, Maxine. You know as well as I that she has to *choose* to be a survivor." Unconsciously, Hope touched the scar on the side of her face.

"I know the standard rhetoric," Maxine admitted with little hope, "I've voiced it a thousand times myself." She went silent for a few moments as the memory of dozens of nameless faces bruised beyond reconnection appeared and just as quickly vanished before her. Maxine instantly went into a three-minute dissertation on the evils of spousal abuse.

Hope, half listening and half not, shifted another chart to the top of the pile and opened it. The discussion was getting to her, or maybe it was the memories. Either way, she'd had enough of the conversation. It was a waste of time and energy as long as the victim refused to help herself.

"What's this?" Hope interrupted intentionally, distracting Maxine from her soapbox tirade.

"What's what?" Maxine leaned over Hope's shoulder and positioned her reading glasses in place. She peered through them, over the top, then under, squinting, trying to adjust to the reality of growing older. She decided that she'd never get used to bifocals.

Hope moved closer to the table lamp. "This is a sonogram for exam room four. I ordered it earlier. But this says that the test was cancelled and the order rescinded."

Maxine pulled her glasses from her face and let them dangle from the pearl chain onto the drab blue scrub smock she wore. "Doctor Wallace cancelled it right after he reviewed the chart and discharged the patient."

"Damn!" Hope instantly sprang from the room, just missing the corner of the upper bunk bed and the edge of the table. "What is his problem? I am so sick of being second-guessed."

"He is the Emergency Room Medical Director. He gets final say on all cases. But of course, you already know that." Maxine said as she followed the quick-moving Hope down the corridor.

"There's nothing you can do. You know Hugh listens to Scott. He'll take Scott's word over yours in a New York minute. Girl, I don't know what you ever did to that man but he sure has it in for you."

Hope ignored the remark. Hugh was the least of her concerns at the moment. Her main focus was on the patient that had just been sent home. "That's not the point. This is *my* patient. He needs a sonogram, he needs to be admitted. He's got a bleeding ulcer. *Pepto-Bismol* and a *Band-Aid* aren't going to cut it this time." Hope grumbled as she punched the small blue square sending the automatic doors in motion. She burst through the Emergency Department's main doors like a cannonball in flight.

The first person she saw was Scott Wallace. He was discussing a chart with a very inattentive lab technician. Hope went directly to him.

"Doctor, may I please have a word with you?"

"Sure." He said as he dismissed the lab tech, turned and headed toward his small office.

As soon as the doors closed Hope respectfully stated her case. Scott listened attentively. It took less then three minutes for Hope to make her point. It took three seconds for Scott to decline it.

Dr. Scott Wallace, a stickler for formality, lived by the rules, particularly when it came to admitting patients. If he had it his way, no one who couldn't afford it would ever spend a night in a hospital. His most ardent rule was, *no medical insurance, no bed.*

If by chance a patient's insurance wasn't quite up to code, that patient would receive the barest attention and care, then promptly be asked to vacate the premises with a referral to the nearest state-run facility. But then again, anyone with the right insurance would be given a bevy of expensive tests, then immediately admitted for overnight observation.

Hope stomped from the office. "Pompous quack," She muttered to herself while still protesting in vain. "I really hate this part of medicine."

"It's his call, Hope. He's in charge." Maxine reminded her. "Whatever he says goes."

"Doesn't make it right." She could feel the rage still seething inside. She'd been second-guessed again. She was so tired of having someone constantly looking over her shoulder and being second-guessed in her diagnosis. She knew more about medicine than most of these so-called doctors. She made it a point to keep up with the latest technology and medical techniques.

Having completed medical school, her hundred-hour-a-week internship, two years as resident, and then as chief resident, she was now a bona fide, staffed medical professional with all the perks and student loans to prove it. But at times, the medical field insisted that the only true professional doctors were male doctors. In her particular case, it wasn't sexism, racism or any other ism. It was one man with a grudge. She knew who had sent the order down to examine every one of her cases. Dr. Hugh Wescott.

Still annoyed, she arrived at the main nurses station in the center of the large open area. She scanned the numerous charts stacked in the sleeves of the turn stand, grabbed and flipped through three charts, then moved to stand at the counter.

She briefly scanned each chart then looked up into each exam room to see the patient. Maxine stood by her shoulder giving her added information on each patient and explaining what procedures had been done so far.

Mumbling softly, she quickly read through the chart from the patient in room five. She frowned. "An allergic reaction?"

Maxine, now busy with another case, looked up and over Hope's shoulder. "Who? Which one?"

"Five. Louise Gates."

Maxine looked across to the common area to exam room number five. "She came in about half an hour ago with a serious reaction to something she ingested. She's got hives, a body rash, and red blotches and welts over fifty percent of her body. She complained about slight chest pressure so triage sent her right in. Temperature, pulse and blood pressure are elevated."

"Edema?"

"No."

Hope noted the vital signs then read the preliminary triage assessment. Everything seemed normal enough except for the outbreak of hives. "Did you give her an analgesic?"

"Just a local to relieve the itch."

Hope handed Maxine the chart. "Order a diphenhydramine hydrochloride shot." That should relieve the itch and discomfort.

"Sure," Maxine said nodding then scribbling a notation on the file page. "The pharmacy's backed up as usual. But I'll see what I can do to hurry them along."

Hope knew that Maxine had more than a little influence over most of the hospital departments. She rarely asked twice for anything.

"Thanks. Also, if you can get a list of everything she ate yesterday and late last night. That toxin came from somewhere." A puzzled expression crossed Hope's face as she looked across the open area at the woman calmly sitting up on the hospital bed with the older gentleman attentively at her side. There was nothing odd or unusual about the reported symptoms. Hope placed the chart back in the turnstile. She picked up the chart from the first exam room. "All right, let's get this party started."

Three

Louise smiled pleasantly when Hope glanced over in her direction a second time. She noted Hope's brief nod and returned the acknowledgement just before she turned and headed in the opposite direction. Louise nodded her approval, noting that by all accounts, Dr. Hope Adams was perfect for what she had in mind. And, much to her delight, the good doctor was just as lovely as she'd remembered.

Of course, gone were the satin purse, high heels and fashionable evening suit from the night at the Broadway play. But, as with any good medical professional, they were appropriately enough replaced with green hospital scrubs, a white medical coat and white-laced sneakers.

Although it was just a week ago, it seemed like it was only yesterday when she sat in the ladies room of the theatre and listened in on the conversation. Louise smiled as she remembered her earlier trepidation.

Eavesdropping wasn't exactly a carnal sin, Louise had reasoned. As long as your motives were pure, and your reasons were rational and in the best interest of all parties involved, it was pardonable. You couldn't be faulted for one small faux pas, when the bigger picture of matchmaking was on the horizon. So, with justifiable reasoning and inspired vindication, she had continued listening.

Louise sat, quietly, gently patting the soft tissue to her newly applied coral lips. She added more lipstick, then pulled another tissue from the dispenser and dabbed again. She puckered, tilted her chin upwards, and then puckered again. Smiling, she turned her face from side to side, seemingly to acquire the best lighting. Her outwardly uninterested behavior, though curious, was nothing out of the ordinary in a theatre ladies room during a twenty-minute intermission.

The busy alcove area, adjacent to the lavatory, was brightly lit with expensive chandeliers and stunning wall sconces that reflected the twinkle of light across the multi-mirrored walls. Thick plush carpet and low, wing-backed tapestry-covered chairs faded into the far background as Louise edged closer to the interesting discussion.

The two women, obviously related, were so engrossed in their conversation, they hardly noticed her. Both apparently in the medical field, they lamented over heath care providers, insurance fraud, and short-staffed facilities. Then they debated the validity of an article in the latest issue of *The New England Medical Journal of Medicine* and a comparable one found in the *JAMA*.

After a few minutes the conversation eventually veered to something more interesting, the very popular subject of finding the elusive Mr. Right. It was this last topic that garnered Louise's full attention.

Of course she'd heard this many times before. It was an age-old quandary that drifted from generation to generation, up and down through the ages. There were television talk shows, radio relationship gurus and whole sections in bookstores devoted to how-to, how-come, why-not-me, where is he, his planet-her planet, self-help books. Billions of dollars were shelled out annually to answer a very simple question.

"Hope," the younger woman said sadly, "this time I really thought it was real. He was perfect and he said that he really truly loved me."

"Faith, they say that every time."

"This time I believed it was true love."

"How can he possibly love you when he just met you, Faith?"

"Haven't you ever heard of love at first sight?"

"Sure, every other day," Hope answered sarcastically. She saw the dejected expression on her sister's face. She exhaled. "Faith, you are so trusting and men can be so cruel."

"Yeah, I know, same old, same old. But Hope, not all men are the same. They're not all like Nolan, and Hugh, and Scott, and our father and stepfather, and all the other jerks that just don't get it. There are good men out there. You just have to have a little faith and hope." She sighed heavily. "Don't you miss being in love?"

"Love is an illusion," Hope began. "Falling in love is the ultimate fantasy. That's how they trap you. Once you fall in love, your life is over."

"Oh please, not this again. Your big sister speeches are really getting redundant."

"Yes, this again. Because obviously you weren't listening the first, second or twentieth time. The perfect male, the elusive Mister Right is an oxymoron at best, and a fool's errand at the very least. Most women spend a great deal of their money, time and energy searching in vain for someone who doesn't exist, someone to fall in love with. It's not rocket science or some obscure, ambiguous quest. The hopeful search for love is an absurd impossibility. I see it everyday. There's no magical trick, love hurts, and as we well know, it sometimes kills."

"No, Hope, the trick, in my opinion," she qualified to her sister, "is to find a man suited to fit your individual personality. Then work like hell to make the relationship succeed. The problem with you is that you've lost not only your faith, but most importantly, you've lost hope. You need to find yourself again, girl."

"In a man I suppose."

"They're not all the same. One day you'll see."

"Never again."

"Never is a long time; never say never. One of these days love is going to sneak up and bite you on the butt."

Hope laughed with her sister at the image. "Then I'll just have it surgically removed."

"I refuse to believe that you're this hopeless." Faith finally relented.

"Oh yeah, Dr. Hope Adams. I'm full of hope."

Their muted tête-à-tête ended abruptly as the two exited the lady's room.

Satisfied she had heard all she needed, Louise dropped the used tissue in the wastebasket, stood and adjusted the double strand of perfect cultured pearls around her neck. She reached up to pat the secured hair at the nape of her neck.

Bravo. Mentally Louise applauded approvingly the younger woman's keen insight. She couldn't have said it better herself. Curious to see this well of wisdom, Louise pivoted in her seat just enough to see the woman's reflection bounce across the room into the near mirror. Louise smiled with added confidence. The next time she saw this woman would be the beginning of the rest of her life.

It had taken less than three days for Louise to gather all the detailed information she required for her latest venture. With the discreet assistance of a very skilled confidential investigator, she determined that Hope was just what the doctor ordered. But, she had already known that. After all, she had a gift. The gift of matchmaking. The detective's investigation was merely a formality to cross the t's and dot the i's.

When Louise found out that the young doctor's name was indeed, Hope, she was ecstatic. Raymond, who had always said that he was hopeless when it came to finding love, would finally find his Miss Right in the form of Dr. Hope Adams. She smiled at the irony; he would finally have his Hope.

Louise winced. The uncomfortable irritation had returned. Slowly, she relaxed back into the stark-white sheets on the exam room gurney. She held her arm up. The blotchy, red hive was indeed an irritant but, with any good plan, sacrifices had to be made.

She turned and smiled at her companion as he came to stand by her side. He watched her every movement. "Louise?" he asked with deep concern.

"I'm fine, Otis. It's just a little itching and minor irritation."

He gently laid his hand on hers. "We could have gone to a different hospital. Just because I've been here before doesn't mean we had to come back. You might have been seen sooner had we gone elsewhere."

"No. This hospital is just fine."

"Shall I call for a nurse?" He asked.

Louise nodded her head slowly from side to side. "No, the doctor will be here soon. She'll do just fine."

For the next few moments Louise watched intently as the young doctor moved from room to room administering to the ailing and sickly, while all the while respectfully delegating to her subordinates. Although slight in statue, she seemed substantially strong in character. When Hope spoke, however mild and tranquil her tone, she turned attentive heads. She was exactly the type of woman Louise had been looking for.

An excited shiver ran through her. The moment she'd been waiting for had finally arrived. She was about to meet her future granddaughter for the first time.

"Mr. and Mrs. Gates?" Louise looked up and smiled brightly. "My name is Dr. Adams. I'll be your attending physician this morning. What seems to be the problem?" Hope smiled at her patient with the caring warmth of a concerned healer. Putting on a good show, Louise nodded pitifully as Hope came closer.

"Good to meet you, doctor. My name is Otis Wheeler. I'm a close friend of the family." He offered his hand to shake.

"A pleasure meeting you, Mr. Wheeler." They shook hands as Hope looked at him oddly. She stared a moment. "I apologize for staring, but you look very familiar. Have we met before?"

Colonel Wheeler nodded and smiled. "You have an excellent memory. I came in a few months ago with a friend of mine, Chester Grant. He came in complaining of stomach pains."

"Of course, that's right. Mr. Grant." She smiled, fondly remembering the two older gentlemen. They were an interesting pair that kept the ER staff in stitches with their Abbott and Costello routines. "How is Mr. Grant? I hope he's feeling better."

"He's doing much better. His cancer is in remission at the moment and his doctor is very encouraged by his recent test results."

Hope smiled brightly. "That's good news. Please tell him that I asked for him when you speak with him next."

"I certainly will," Colonel Wheeler assured her, "I certainly will."

Hope nodded then turned her attention to the smiling patient lying on the hospital gurney. She picked up the updated medical chart from the end of the bed and looked it over briefly.

"I see that you have a rash."

"Yes," Louise answered calmly.

Hope grabbed a pair of latex gloves and began examining the series of red rashes on Louise's arms and legs. She focused with particular attention on the rash on Louise's face and neck. "How long have you had these?"

"Not long. A few hours maybe. They itch like the dickens."

Hope continued the initial exam while asking several questions. Unfortunately, none of the answers Louise gave added up to a definitive solution. She found herself asking more questions only to be completely confounded by the responses. She pulled the gloves off, then leaned against the metal rail at the side of the gurney.

"Have you ever been tested for various allergens? Food, chemical, abstracts, anything like that? "

"No, never," she fabricated handily.

Hope nodded and made a notation in the file. "And you've never had a reaction like this before tonight?"

"No, not that I can remember offhand." Another fabrication.

Hope, still puzzled, scribbled on the chart. She looked up at Louise again then scribbled some more. "Okay," she began, "I'm going to give you something to ease the itching and reduce the swelling. It might also make you a little sleepy, so don't be alarmed." Colonel wheeler stepped closer and took Louise's hand. "I'm also going to give you a prescription for something just in case the hives return." Hope noted the look of concern shadowed across Louise's face. "There's no need for concern. I don't think it will return. These things usually run their course as long as the initial irritant isn't reintroduced. But, just in case, you'll be prepared."

Louise nodded her understanding. "Does this mean you're going to discharge me?"

Hope smiled. "Technically, you haven't been admitted, but yes, you can go home as soon as I've completed the paperwork."

"So that's it? There's nothing else you need to do?" Colonel Wheeler asked, stepping forward.

"That's it. Mr. Wheeler, I presume you'll be driving Mrs. Gates home?"

He nodded.

"Good." Hope flipped the chart close. "That's about it, Mrs. Gates. You take care of yourself and don't forget to make an appointment to see an allergist and your personal physician as soon as you can."

"Thank you, doctor," Louise said, somewhat hesitantly.

"You're quite welcome." Hope nodded, then immediately left to attend to her next patient. She visited four patients in the next half-hour. Then, on her way back from seeing her last patient, Maxine stopped her in the nurse's station. "Number five just bounced back. She's experiencing dizziness, shortness of breath, and chest pains. You might want to check on her when you get a chance."

"Chest pains?"

"That's what she says." Maxine's expression lacked the usual *don't give a damn* luster. The relaxed smirk was noticeably replaced with genuine concern.

Hope grimaced. "That's odd." The medication she'd prescribed shouldn't have caused any type of chest pain or complicated reaction. "Set her up, and I'll be right there." Maxine nodded and quickly hurried off.

Hope sat at the nurse's station for a moment and jotted down notes from her last patient. Then, she mulled over the medication she'd prescribed and the possible side effects. She went into the computer database and pulled all related information.

The interactions were relatively straightforward as she compared the medication with Louise's chart and the medical data bank. Diphenhydramine was a standard antihistamine and a commonly issued drug used to counteract the characteristic effects of a severe allergic reaction. A physiological reaction to the cure was largely unheard of, yet still viable. Hope reread the file quickly while keying several interesting points. According to the dosage administered, Louise should have been sleepy and groggy instead of experiencing heart palpitations and respiratory difficulty.

Nothing seemed to make sense. There was absolutely no reason for her patient to have the onset of chest pains. Hope grabbed the chart and went back to exam room number five.

The exam room had magically morphed into a bevy of interconnected machines and digital gadgets all blinking and clicking simultaneously. Heart monitors scanned biorhythms as wire-connected EKG and EEG spat out narrow strips of paper-recorded data.

Louise lay still in the bed. Her eyes were closed and her breathing was labored. A precautionary oxygen apparatus had been secured and a respirator had been issued. Hope walked over to the nearest machine and read the findings. She scanned the next few machines, all coming to the same conclusion. None of this should be happening. By all accounts Louise Gates should be merely groggy from the prescribed medication.

Hope walked over and scanned the heart monitor a second time then leaned down to speak with Louise. She smiled pleasantly as not to alarm her patient. "Mrs. Gates, I understand you've been experiencing chest pains and shortness of breath." Louise nodded pitifully. Hope frowned, then lowered the chart and fixed her gaze into Louise Gates's once sparkling, brown eyes. "Tell me more about the pains. Are they sharp, stabbing pains, or more dull and achy?"

"I'm not sure. I just started to feel pains here and here." Louise pointed to her heart and chest area.

Hope nodded her head in understanding as she pulled a light scope down from the wall. "Are you experiencing any discomfort now? Any pains?" She spoke gently and softly.

Louise shook her head. "No, not at the moment. They come and go."

"I see." Hope shined the bright beam of light into Louise's left, then right eye. "When did you begin experiencing this pain?"

"About ten minutes or so after you left. It was stronger then."

"How long did the pains last?" She asked, as she continued the exam.

"A few seconds. They stopped, then they returned, stronger."

Hope nodded and continued. "Have you had these pains before this evening?"

"Yes," Louise said, then sleepily told Hope of the previous times she'd experienced the chest pains.

Hope listened attentively to Louise as she recalled the first of many occurrences. Hope frowned. Something didn't add up. Louise's eyes were as clear and sparkling as they'd been just thirty minutes ago, yet she complained of intense chest pains.

Hope removed the stethoscope from her jacket pocket and placed either end in her ears. "Did you have these pains earlier this evening, when you first noticed the hives and rash?"

"No." Hope nodded. "I mean yes." Louise said, changing her mind. "I don't really remember. We had dinner with friends last night. We went back to my son's townhouse and that's all I really remember. Everything else suddenly seems foggy."

"Don't worry about that. I'd like to listen to your chest. Just lay back and relax." Using friction to warm the metal disk, she quickly rubbed it on her green hospital scrubs then placed it on Louise's chest. After giving a series of breathing commands Hope frowned, then grabbed a pair of latex gloves and began the preliminary physical examination.

"I feel so light-headed."

"The medication is probably beginning to make you a little drowsy. Just relax." Hope picked up the medical chart. "Were you doing anything strenuous last night?"

"Oh no. We had dinner out with friends, that's all."

"And you said before that you hadn't eaten anything unusual?"

"No, nothing unusual." Louise frowned thoughtfully, then looked to Otis Wheeler.

He chimed in, as if on cue. "We ate at Spotlight NYC."

Louise continued. "I started feeling a tightness right after dessert, but I thought nothing of it. The food was really good. I presumed that I'd just overeaten. Then, a few hours later we went back to the apartment. It wasn't until afterwards, when the hives came, that I began to feel the tightness in my chest again. After that, the rash seemed worse."

"That's when we came here," Colonel Wheeler added as he stood with deep concern by Louise's bedside.

Hope put the chart down, then tugged the stethoscope from around her neck and plugged them into her ears again. She listened intently as she moved the small circular disc across her patient's chest and back.

She picked up the chart again and scribbled notes. "Well, Mrs. Gates, your vitals are all fine. I have to admit, you have me slightly puzzled. I'm not sure what's causing these chest pains." She smiled reassuringly. "Your tests are all negative. I wish I was in such good health." A chuckle from Colonel Wheeler had both women smiling.

"Maybe I have a weak heart?"

"No, I don't think so."

"How about heart arrhythmia? Isn't that when your heart skips a few beats every now and then?"

Hope shook her head. "You have no history of arrhythmia. It's not a condition that just pops up from time to time. All of your tests showed negative."

"So, are you going to keep me here then?" Louise asked, sounding too hopeful.

Hope shook her head. "I can't ethically release you knowing that you're having chest pains."

"So, you're keeping me?"

"Yes. You definitely had an allergic reaction to something you ingested. As for your chest pains, I think I'd like to keep you a little longer and run a few more tests."

She noted that Louise nodded happily.

"I see your blood pressure is slightly elevated. This might just be because of the current circumstances. Nevertheless, I'd also like to get your blood pressure down a bit before releasing you." Hope flipped a few pages in the chart. "Is this the complete list of your medications?"

"Yes."

"Doctor." Colonel Wheeler stepped forward, handed Hope a sheet of paper, then took Louise's hand. "That's the list of everything Louise ate yesterday and last night."

"Great. Thank you." Hope briefly looked over the list, not finding anything unusual. "Mrs. Gates, I'm sure there's nothing to be overly concerned about but I'd like to clear up a few questions and concerns nonetheless. Depending on the test results, I will possibly keep you tonight and tomorrow for observation."

"You want me here just twenty-four hours or so?"

"Yes. Just overnight. Is that a problem?"

"No. I don't mind staying."

"Good. I'll have someone from registration come over with the necessary forms. An orderly will escort you to your room as soon as one is available and the paperwork is complete."

"I didn't pack anything."

"No problem. A nurse will have a hospital gown for you once you get to your room. And since you'll probably only stay overnight I wouldn't worry about going home to get anything. We'll have everything you need for your stay already in the room."

Louise considered her answer. An overnight stay was a start, but she would definitely need more time. "What happens if I have pains after I leave here tomorrow?"

"As I've said, there's nothing to be overly concerned about. I don't foresee any major problems. Unless you're experiencing further discomfort, you'll be released tomorrow morning. I do suggest that you see your personal physician as soon as possible. If you experience pains again, go to your nearest hospital emergency room."

"But if I'm feeling poorly you'll keep me a few more days?"

"Yes of course, but I seriously don't foresee that occurring." Hope scanned the chart one last time and added a brief notation. "I see you have your personal physician listed, a Dr. Raymond Gates."

"Yes, my grandson."

"Do you have the phone number or a way to contact him?"

"I've already called Raymond," Colonel Wheeler interjected, still holding Louise's hand. "He was at Haven House. He's on his way."

"I don't believe I recognize the name. Is he local?"

"Yes, he practices in Manhattan."

"Fine. I'll make sure that someone is available as soon as Dr. Gates calls. If not, I'll contact him later."

Instantly, as if caught in a wind tunnel, the privacy curtains surrounding the bed blew open and a man dressed in jeans and a white cotton shirt standing six-feet-everything breezed in. "Don't bother," the deep baritone voice split the hushed tones in the exam room like an ax cutting through wood. "He's already here."

Four

Few things witnessed in the Golden Heart Medical Center Emergency Department had ever taken Hope utterly by surprise. Yet, to her complete astonishment, one such sight, in all his exalted magnificence, had just burst through the curtains of her patient's room.

Dr. Raymond Gates had arrived.

Hope blinked twice, not sure if maybe she had somehow, by lack of sleep, hallucinated him, but there he stood in all his breathtaking grandeur. Eye candy was an understatement. He was pure, mind-blowing, heart-pounding, knee-weakening, gorgeous. The white gleam of his cotton shirt accented the caramel sweetness of his rich coffee complexion and his muscular legs were long and fit his jeans as if they'd been made exclusively for him. His face, clean-shaven, angular, chiseled, and shrouded in concern was beyond devilishly handsome. But it was his eyes that became her focal point. Framed by long curly lashes, they were alight in color, hazel, with just a hint of something else. Her stomach flipped.

Without a single word spoken he looked around for a few seconds to quickly assess the situation. After a brief nod of acknowledgement to Colonel Wheeler, he moved straight to the bed and stood by Louise's side. He lovingly picked up her hand and engulfed it within his gentle embrace. Leaning down to eye-level, he stroked her forehead with his thumb, while he gently moved a few loose silver stands to the side. With heartfelt and soulful devotion, they communicated with their eyes. She assured him that she was fine and he assured her that he would make certain of it. The smile she bestowed upon him was soul-stirring.

He looked over into the curtained, empty cubical beside Louise, then took a few moments to scan the rest of the room. The condescension in his eyes was evident.

Hope stood completely flabbergasted by the man's impertinent behavior. Of its own accord, her mouth gaped open, half in astonishment and half in complete, perplexed exasperation. It wasn't until a few seconds later that she realized she'd actually been standing there, holding her breath the entire time.

Then, without missing a beat and as smooth as silk on a gentle summer's breeze, he slipped the chart from Hope's fingers and began scanning the pages.

"Who's running this?"

"Excuse me, who are you?" Hope asked, as she pulled the chart from his grasp and placed it in its pouch at the foot of the bed.

"I want a private room immediately," Raymond demanded, as he moved directly to the foot of the bed. Then with way too much familiarity, leaned around Hope's waist and took the chart a second time. After taking a second to scan the vitals, he moved back to Louise's side and observed the beeping monitors. He reached down and picked up Louise's hand, rubbing his thumb gently over it. He smiled assuredly. "Hi sweetheart, how are you feeling?"

Louise smiled brightly and nodded weakly. "Better, much better. Thanks to Dr. Adams here." She sighed heavily with just enough dramatic flair to raise Hope's brow with curious interest. "I think that maybe the trip to the Botanical Garden Flower Show yesterday, the all-day shopping at the African Bazaar, plus the dinner at Dennis's restaurant last night, might have been a bit too much for me."

Raymond picked up her other hand. "Mamma Lou, you have to learn to slow down. You've been overdoing it. You have to promise to take better care of yourself."

Louise held her head up. Her clear eyes smiled lovingly at her grandson. "Yes, I know. I promise."

Raymond nodded his reply then instantly went back into medical mode. He continued reading the chart's neatly printed notes. He frowned. "Your blood pressure's elevated. Have you been taking your medication, Mamma Lou?"

"Every day. I make sure of it. That and the cholesterol medication." Colonel Wheeler responded affirmatively.

"Are you being admitted?"

"Yes," Louise answered.

"Excuse me?" Hope said, moving closer to the gurney and pulled the chart from his hands a second time. Raymond looked up, and seemingly for the first time noticed that they were not alone in the room.

He looked at the lanyard and nametag hanging from around her neck. "And you are?" Raymond asked with sincere interest. A sly smile tipped his full lips.

"I am Dr. Adams, the attending physician. Whoever you are, you need to leave now."

Louise spoke up immediately. "Dr. Adams, this is my grandson, Dr. Raymond Gates. He's my personal physician."

Hope snarled at the need to be diplomatic. "Doctor," she nodded through gritted teeth, "as a courtesy, I'll be happy to have an orderly show you to the waiting room or the doctor's lounge. But you need to leave this room, *now.*"

With complete unwavering confidence, Raymond looked at Hope as if she'd lost her mind. He dismissed her as if she were an annoying mosquito and focused his attention back to his grandmother. "That won't be necessary, doctor. What tests have you ordered so far?" He reached for the chart again. Hope stepped back, blocking his attempt.

"I'm not accustomed to reviewing my patient's medical condition with unauthorized personnel. As a family member, you are welcome to wait in the family's waiting room. As a doctor, you are welcome to wait in the doctor's lounge. And that's it. I'll be in shortly to update you with the results of our tests."

"That won't be necessary."

"I'm afraid you have no alternative."

Suddenly Raymond laughed at the ludicrous and absurd notion of being put out of his grandmother's hospital room. Rich, jolly tones of mirth resounded through the hall as his infectious laughter continued. "You are joking, right?"

Hope placed her fist firmly on her hip and tilted her head slightly. Being the butt of laughter was the quickest way to get on her bad side. "Doctor, you are interfering with the health and welfare of my patient and I *will* have you bodily removed by security if necessary."

Raymond laughed again. This time Colonel Wheeler lowered his head and chuckled along. Louise pulled at Raymond's hand to get his attention. "Raymond dear, why don't you and Otis wait outside?" She looked over to the fuming Hope, "I'm sure Dr. Adams will be out in no time to speak with you."

Raymond held his hand up to pause his grandmother's remarks as his eyes glared into Hope relentlessly. "Doctor, I'm going to tell you how this is going to work. I am now the primary physician here. Either you can work with me or not at all, your choice. Is that understood?"

Hope smiled for the first time since Raymond had entered the exam room. "Now, doctor, let me to tell you how this is going to work," she stepped up into his face. "You will quietly leave this area now, allow me to do my job, and patiently wait in the designated area. End of discussion. Is that understood?" Her head rolled instinctively for added emphasis.

"You have no idea who I am, do you?" he looked at her in complete disbelief. His eyes sparked with a mischievous amusing glint.

"And you, doctor, obviously have no idea who I am. I am the attending physician and at the moment your worst enemy."

Eye to eye, they stood at an impasse. Both refused to back down. The intense moment lasted too long as each seared the other's image. Interrupted by the sound of an intercom page, Hope looked away, almost relieved to have the intense spell of Raymond's hazel eyes broken.

Otis looked at Louise, whose expression was that of pure self-satisfaction. A questioning expression sparked in his eyes. He'd seen that look before. It was the same smile he'd seen just six months ago when her other grandson, Tony, spoke his vows and married Madison Evans.

Suddenly, Hope realized that other patients needed her attention. She needed to end this standoff now. "Dr. Gates, a moment of your time please," she humbly requested as diplomatically as she could.

Raymond, still amused, turned to her. Her expression was so placid and so yielding. He couldn't refuse. "Yes, of course doctor," he agreed readily. "I'd be delighted."

Louise reached up and grasped Raymond's arm questioningly. Raymond turned back to her. He bent down and kissed her cheek, whispering, "Don't worry. You'll be fine," he winked at her and touched her cheek lovingly.

Louise held onto his hand and squeezed it slightly. "Be nice." She warned in a strong whisper.

Raymond looked innocently surprised by her concern. "I'm always nice." Louise gave him a warning glare. Raymond's playful dimples danced across his face, promising a mischievous adventure about to begin. He knew her expression all too well and relented. "I will, I promise."

Seconds later they left the room together. Hope led the way and for the first time noticed the attentive eyes of the nurses at the station looking her way. Apparently she wasn't the only one wowed by Raymond's appearance. She looked around to find a discreet corner in which to have a civilized discussion. But she quickly realized that it would be impossible with all eyes still glued in their direction.

Abruptly, she turned to Raymond. "We'll have more privacy in one of the quiet rooms." Smiling joyously, Raymond nodded curtly and waited for her to lead the way. Hope ushered him through the corridor, past admissions and triage. Eyes followed the two as Raymond strolled casually down the hall, she in hospital scrubs and he in a casual runway-chic outfit.

After a few turns they arrived in front of a door with its shade pulled down. Hope paused, knocked, opened the door slightly, and peered inside. Finding it empty, she turned and held the door open for Raymond. "In here."

Raymond took the weight of the door, and with gentlemanly grace waved for her to enter first. She did. Then, with questionable thoughts and a raised brow of interest, he watched the slight sway of her hips against the white medical jacket. Before she turned, he jauntily walked in and took a seat on the arm of a nearby sofa as she went back to stand by the door. He looked around at the lifeless still life prints, the drab, putty-colored walls and the basic, brown tweed furniture. It was the typical quiet room, named for the subdued reflection by family members of seriously ill patients.

His eyes roamed freely around the room then sparked again when he observed Hope's profile as she paced several times in front of the door. He tilted his head in admiration. He liked what he saw. She was attractive in a classic beauty kind of way that gave a man less than saintly ideas. He smiled openly tempted by his thoughts. The rich milk chocolate of her flawless features was set in a perfect package that made his mouth water. He smiled remembering the bright spark of anger in her soft brown eyes and the singe of red burn as their discussion heated up. Immodestly, he watched as the green scrubs gently swayed and pulled against her body. The innocent movement sent several more enticing ideas through his head. Yes, he definitely liked what he saw.

Hope continued to pace. Patiently she counted to ten, then to twenty. With each ascending number, she willed the tenseness in her neck and shoulders to dissolve. She was well on her way to thirty-five when Raymond spoke. She stopped, her back turned for fear that if she faced him she'd rip his smiling head off.

"Doctor," he began with the condescending tone that seemed to irk her, "in the future, please refrain from frightening patients with your immediate request for consultation. That's a very dear woman to me in there. I take exception to her discomfort by undo alarm, due to your bedside manner."

Unable to hold her temper any longer, Hope attacked with a vengeance. "Then maybe you should have thought about that before barging in on *my* examining room with *my* patient and second guessing *my* diagnosis. I don't know where you studied medicine, but where I studied, physicians don't behave like jerks toward other physicians. I'm sure you're reasonably competent in your field, but this is my ER and I run it how I see fit." Raymond opened his mouth to rebut, but she promptly threw her hand up to stop his remark.

"I do not appreciate your interference and in the future as long as I am in this hospital, on call, and performing my duty as a trained medical professional, I suggest you stay as far away from me as possible. Is that clear?"

Before he could answer she began again.

"This is not your hospital and she is not your patient. I realize that Mrs. Gates is a relative and therefore your concern is genuine, but that does not give you the right to burst into my exam room and take over."

A characteristically comfortable, cocked smile tugged at the end of his full lips. He had just been reprimanded, plain and simple. Hope ignored his smirk and continued. "I will, however, allow you to visit your 'Mamma Lou' during regularly scheduled hospital visiting hours, but as for her medical care, leave it up to the real professionals. I will not tolerate your interference."

"Am I to understand that to are refusing my input?"

"You need to check your medication dose, I think it may be too strong, 'cause you're just not getting it." She cited sarcastically. "Yes, doctor, I am refusing your input, turning you down, snubbing you, moving you aside. Get the idea? I don't want to hear from you. I don't need, nor want your help. Got it?"

"You can't be serious."

"As a heart attack," she assured him.

"Then I'm afraid that you and I are going to have a problem. Because I don't intend to relinquish my grandmother's health to anyone," Raymond politely assured her.

She laughed openly, "You must be kidding." She was just about to add more when her pager rang. She immediately unclipped it from her pocket and looked at the message and number. She clipped it back in place and began walking back toward the door, then she turned back to face him. She paused to stare up into Raymond's heavenly, hazel eyes. "Stay out of my way, Gates," she warned, then slammed open the door and marched out.

"I think you might have gone too far this time, Louise," Colonel Wheeler said as he neared her side and took her hand. "Those two look like they're about to do serious battle."

Louise smiled with broad self-satisfaction. "They'll be fine," she assured him.

Colonel Wheeler shook his head in disagreement. "Fine, my dear, is when you respectfully disagree. Those two are ready to go to war. I've seen that same look in men under my command in three wars, a peacekeeping mission and several police actions. That's one furious lady. I think you might have chosen someone a bit more malleable."

"For Raymond? Nah, heavens no. He's a big boy. Besides, he's been getting too big for his britches lately. He needs to be shaken up a bit and knocked down a few pegs."

Colonel Wheeler continued to shake his head. "That's exactly what I'm afraid of."

Louise thought for a moment, then smiled. Perhaps conflict was inevitable. Raymond is a very strong-willed man, but to her credit, Dr. Adams appeared to be able to hold her own. "No, dear," she took his hand, "I have a feeling that this will work out just fine."

"I hope you're right."

Louise smiled happily. "Aren't I always?"

Otis kissed her forehead. "Yes dear you are. But I have to warn you; don't get your hopes up. This time it doesn't look promising."

"Trust me."

Colonel Wheeler nodded doubtfully as he thought about Louise's last matchmaking caper. She was right about her other grandson Tony and his wife Madison. Now those two were an impossible match. But, somehow Louise found a way and everything came out smelling like a rose. Wheeler leaned down and kissed her forehead again. That's why he adored this very special woman. She had a heart of gold with just enough mischief in it to make his life interesting.

Suddenly the door opened.

Raymond strolled in. "That woman is impossible," he declared as Louise slyly looked at Wheeler. "How she successfully passed med school I have no idea. She must have gotten her degree on Riker's Island or Alcatraz. She has the finesse of a storm trooper, the temperament of General Patton, and the tact of a raging bull."

Raymond paced the floor in frustration as he continuing to rant. "Do you believe that she had the audacity to mandate my professional input on your case? Can you believe that? She wants me to sign in and out like some kind of . . . of . . . visitor." Louise looked at Wheeler. Her eyes twinkled.

Colonel Wheeler nodded his agreement and relented to her matchmaking mastery. *Yes,* he thought to himself, *she has done it again.* It was only a matter of time before Raymond would realize that he was a goner. But by then it would be too late. Colonel Wheeler chuckled to himself and wondered how long it would take for Raymond to recognize that his cleverness at eluding his grandmother's wishes had been a complete waste of time. He had literally burst right into her plan.

Five

Hope slammed the patient file on the closest desk and with pent up frustration, plopped down in the nearest chair. She perched her elbows on the armrests, closed her eyes, then swirled the swivel chair around in several complete circles. The light-headed dizzy feeling instantly distracted her.

She'd just come from having another pointless talk with her favorite, frequent-flyer patient. Lacking a sensible resolution, the conversation went around in circles much like the chair she now spun. It was useless to point out the dangerous patterns that had developed. With its potential life-threatening implications, her patient put her life in jeopardy each time she went back home. Yet, instead of seeing the potential for disaster, she merely validated her husband's brutal behavior. Hope shook her head, dismayed, as the pointless conversation rang in her mind.

"Mrs. Jackson, Leanne," Hope softened her tone and continued patiently, "it's very evident that your abrasions are not accidental or self-inflicted."

Leanne ran her fingers through her limp, mousy brown hair and looked away. She shifted her scant weight uncomfortably on the hospital gurney. "I don't understand," she stammered and lowered the ice pack from her brow.

"I think you do."

"I don't know what you're talking about," she insisted as she pulled on the blood stained T-shirt nervously.

So as not to be misunderstood, Hope reiterated slowly, "You

didn't have an accident, as you claim, you didn't do this to
yourself, and you didn't fall down a flight of stairs." She
moved closer to the head of the bed and lowered her voice.
"Mrs. Jackson, we're here to help you. If there's something
you'd like to tell me, please, now is the time to speak up. I assure you, no one here will judge you. There are people here
who will help you, protect you."

"Nobody can help me," Leanne muttered. Tears welled in
her eyes and tumbled down her purple bruised cheek. She
raised her cast-covered arm to wipe her face. She winched at
the resulting pain. Although the swelling had subsided considerably, the discoloration of the flesh surrounding the eye
could not be helped.

Leanne looked at the serene print on the far wall. It was of
a log cabin surrounded by a dense forest at the base of snow-
capped mountains. It was the most beautiful thing she'd seen
in a long time. She cried in earnest. "He," she rasped out tear-
fully. "He . . ."

"Take your time," Hope encouraged with comfort.

"He," she began again, then paused and turned to look at
Hope. Embarrassment and shame clouded the shadows of her
face. "I fell and hit my face on the doorknob."

Hope, holding her breath, eased an exhale, then nodded regretfully. "I see."

"I can't," Leanne looked away hurriedly. "I fell down."

"I understand," Hope offered truthfully. "When you're
ready, someone will be here for you. I promise you that."

Hope slowly turned away and opened the door to leave.
Just before the latch clicked she heard the sorrowful tears
begin to flow again, as her patient continued whispering, "I
can't. I can't."

The memory of their conversation swirled and mingled
into a colorless blur of hopelessness. She reached up and
stroked the side of her face. Bygone memories of a forgotten

past threatened to creep up. Frustrated, Hope spun the chair around again as her own childhood memories came in a flood of dark imagery.

"No!" It began as it always had. He was drunk, she was accessible. "Don't, please don't." She wailed, pleading in vain as he continued to strike out. The large fist swung high into the endless night. It hovered a moment in recrimination. Then it fell, leveling solidly against the side of her face. The cries of torment wailed as two young girls huddled in the corner listening to the screams of anguish.

STOP IT! STOP IT! STOP IT! She repeated over and over again in the child's desperate voice. She watched the fist raise a third, forth, fifth time.

He was drunk, she was accessible.

"Stop it!" Hope yelled from across the room. Propelled by anger she lashed out in a whirlwind of tiny fists as she jumped onto his back. She held tightly, as the bucking beast tossed her from side to side, then across the room, through the plate glass window.

She heard the voices as they shouted. Darkness engulfed her as she floated in cool white light.

Hope spun the chair around, sending the memories back to desolation where they belonged, back into the recesses of her childhood. Several nurses, who'd been standing at the counter talking, looked over briefly, then immediately went back to their conversation. Hope spun the chair several more times before she heard the familiar throat clearing of Scott Wallace.

Scott was an honored professional who had graduated at the top of his med school class, interned at Johns Hopkins, then did his residency here at Golden Heart. Yet, with all of his medical proficiency, he had little sensibility as far as doctors were concerned. In all the years as a medical professional, he had yet to learn that doctors were people too, with all the same pains, anguish and fears as the ones they attempted to help.

Scott, who's facial features rivaled the animation of Disney at its finest, was a large man with an even larger personality. Often referred to as Big Foot, he was hairy with huge bushy brows that moved in perfect synchronization as he spoke. His keen, piercing blue eyes, ever watchful, saw and observed everything in a single glance.

The butt of numerous ER jokes and pranks, he was oblivious to most and discounting of others. He was perfectly suited for his position: clinical, professional and detached. His only fault, as far as Maxine had always said, was his inability to loosen up.

Hope smiled sadistically. Her perfect justice would be to send him out on a blind date with Maxine. That would definitely loosen him up.

"This is a hospital, not an amusement park, Dr. Adams," he chastised firmly. "Surely you can find better use of your time." Dropping his voice an octave or two, he spoke with his usual deep, purposeful, commanding inflection, made more pronounced by his pompous, self-righteous attitude. Hope opened her eyes and with great difficulty, focused on her colleague.

She looked at him and smiled menacingly. Her first instinct was to lash out, but the spinning had left her more unsteady then she first realized. She glared at the overly pompous perfectionist before a broad smile spread wide across her face. Remembering an old vaudevillian response, she cocked her head to the side and said, "Don't call me Shirley."

Giggles and chuckles arose from the nurses and technicians standing at the nearby counter. Scott's mouth gaped open in stunned surprise. He expected the usual sarcastic remark. He hadn't expected a comedy routine.

Tiny gurgling sounds emanated as words choked in his throat. Hope grinned politely and spun the chair a final time before stopping with her legs neatly tucked under the desk.

Unable to articulate his displeasure, Scott looked to the nurses fiercely. They instantly dispersed.

"Dr. Adams, your unprofessional behavior with your patient's guest must be reported. Your voice could be heard all the way down the hall." Hope remained silent.

"I'm afraid I have no alternative but to inform Hugh."

"Whatever," she mumbled as he marched away in his usual rushed demeanor. She knew that another nail had just been added to her employment record. But at this point, it was the last thing she cared to think about.

Almost everyone knew that she and Hugh had a history, but no one knew exactly what that history was. As far as Hope was concerned, the past should be left in the past, but apparently Hugh had different ideas. Oftentimes openly hostile, he made it a point to have her assigned to the worst shifts and duties. He did everything within his power, which was considerable, to overtly belittle and embarrass her.

Hope was still completely amazed that of all the hospitals in the country, Hugh was assigned to this one. The irony was amazing. Apparently fate had a wicked sense of humor.

Hope sat staring at the light box. With several frustrated clicks, she toggled it on and off several times before Maxine plopped down next to her, holding a medical chart.

"You and Scott playing nicely?"

Hope looked in the general direction that Dr. Wallace had gone. "He's such a joke."

"You're playing a dangerous game. You know Scott and Hugh go way back. They even worked together at Johns Hopkins. So, if Scott catches you wrong, you can best believe that Hugh will hear about it."

Hope gave her a *do I really care at this point* expression. Maxine shook her head. "Girl, don't you know that Hugh can seriously damage your career?" Hope's expression didn't change. Maxine continued to shake her head as they watched Scott shuffle from room to room.

"Sometimes I wonder why he even went into medicine."

"I'm sure he had his reasons," Maxine answered matter-of-factly.

"With his lack of personality, he's probably not good at anything else."

Maxine chuckled. "Oh, I don't know about that. I could think of a few things he's good at." She smirked and raised her brow suggestively.

An unexpected laugh took Hope by surprise. Several heads turned in her direction as she tried to control herself.

"No way. Get out of here." Hope laughed exuberantly. "I don't want to hear it."

"That's the word." Maxine assured her.

"You've got to be kidding. The man lives by rules and regulations. I bet he doesn't have a spontaneous bone in his body."

"Spontaneity and talent are two very different things dear." She watched Scott as he walked by, completely oblivious to their conversation. "Some women might consider him a hottie."

"Scott, a hottie?" Hope whispered in disbelief.

"Why not? Particularly if he has the skills . . ."

"That's enough." Hope raised her hand to end the conversation. "I don't want that image permanently printed in my head. What are you trying to do, erase everything I learned in med school? Exactly who starts all of these rumors anyway?"

"I do of course," she said with a straight face.

Hope looked at Maxine, not believing a word she said. Maxine, a no-nonsense characterization of Mae West, was what was once referred to as a moxie broad with man-eating tendencies. It was said that she'd once had an affair with a very popular ex-governor and a New York senator. Married several times, the first at the age of fifteen, she collected alimony checks like others collected stamps.

"When do you have to leave your sublet?" Maxine asked as she motioned toward the apartments wanted section of the newspaper sitting on the counter.

"I have another few months."

"Find anything you like?" she asked as she opened the folder and made a medical notation.

"No, not yet."

"You know, I'll be happy to make room for you at Stonehenge." Maxine said, referring to several apartment buildings she owned between First and Second Avenues. Once tenement trash, she had managed to turn them into respectable housing for numerous local families.

Hope smiled at the offer. "Thank you Maxine, but I think it's time I find a more permanent place. I can't keep renting and subletting forever."

Maxine nodded her understanding, then looked up at the entrance. "Hubby's here," she said as she watched a large muscular man dressed in dirty garage clothes push through the security doors. He stood in the middle of the area and looked around. Then, he began searching out his wife by peering into all the open examination rooms.

"Crap, already?"

"Yep, and I'm sure he wants to know when his wife will be ready to leave." She scanned the appropriate page, then slid it in front of Hope.

"I seriously have to go bowling."

"You and me both girl, you and me both."

With a slight smile Hope sat back realizing that her recent battle with Raymond Gates was minuscule compared to some of the other issues plaguing the ER. Aggravated, she blew her limp curls from her brows and dropped her head into her hands. She looked at her watch. It was nearly six in the morning. "Send him home. I'm keeping her the rest of the day and overnight for observation."

"Can't do that," Maxine said.

Hope turned to face her. Her expression was quizzical. "Why not?"

Maxine reached over and flipped several pages forward in the medical chart. She tapped her pen several times at a particular form. "Her insurance doesn't cover hospitalization."

"She's stayed overnight before."

"That's before hubby dropped her from his policy. She belongs to the state now."

Hope laughed aloud out of sheer frustration. She shook her head. "You've got to be kidding. He beats her, then takes her off his medical policy?"

"Yep, that's right."

"Is there any way to get around it?"

"Nope. The state says no hospitalization without probable medical cause."

"I have probable cause. Her husband beats her. She stays."

"Scott will have a fit."

"What else is new?"

"He'll tell Hugh."

"What else is new?" She repeated.

Maxine sighed heavily. "Well, if she'd actually admit that hubby beat her we could suggest a lovely bed in a woman's shelter for the next few days. But, we both know she'd never file charges."

"True."

Maxine gathered the folder and stood. "Well?"

Hope took a deep breath and sighed miserably. "Get the admission papers ready." Maxine silently nodded and walked away. Hope followed her with her eyes until she noticed the same two nurses standing by the opening of Mrs. Gates's room. She stood and walked over to the doorway. "Is there a problem ladies?"

Both women jumped instantly, denied everything, then hurried off.

Six

"Dammit, what's taking so long?" Raymond stopped pacing just long enough to slam his fist against his open palm then pace again. He walked to the open door and glanced out, just in time to see Hope disappear into another patient's room, after speaking with a nurse. "It shouldn't take this long."

"Raymond, would you please just sit still and relax?" Louise said. "Your constant walking is making me dizzy."

Colonel Wheeler, having long since resolved himself to a lengthy wait, flipped through a golf magazine he'd found in the family waiting room. He looked up briefly, then focused his attention back to the outdated magazine. He chuckled to himself and shook his head.

Usually the cool mischievous prankster, it was purely uncharacteristic for Raymond to be so excitable. Good-humored by nature, he was known for his composed, controlled demeanor. True to his cool disposition, his surgical skills blended perfectly with his serene personality. So, to see his total lack of assurance, his less than perfect calm, was an eye-opening spectacle to say the least. The mere sight of his now chaotic bewilderment had kept Colonel Wheeler chuckling for the past hour.

"Oh this is ridiculous. It's like being in the Dark Ages again; nothing takes this long. Where is she?" Raymond stood at the door and watched Hope as she conversed with another doctor, then with a nurse. She sat at the desk examining something in front of her. Raymond frowned, then turned back into the room and continued pacing.

"Raymond Gates, Jr., would you please stay still and sit down? Your constant passing and complaining is driving me crazy," Louise finally blurted out. Raymond walked across the room and scanned the numerous monitor readouts. "Raymond, sit, now," Louise ordered firmly.

Frustrated, Raymond looked over to Colonel Wheeler. He was chuckling softly and shaking his head while still buried in a magazine. Raymond, exasperated, picked up the hospital chart, sat down in the nearest chair and read Hope's notes again.

He carefully reviewed each notation. With the available data, medical history and the various completed tests, he came to the same medical conclusion as Hope. Acute gastritis would possibly explain the chest pains. And as for the hives, she indicated it was something Louise had ingested. Therefore, she recommended a series of allergy tests.

He continued to read the extended details of her test results and prescribed treatment. Raymond agreed with Hope's basic preventive health plan. Her medical diagnosis was sound and her extended prognosis was thorough.

He was just about to close the chart when an added notation caught his attention. Possible LP macrotentioneda. He wasn't familiar with the term.

Acronyms were common in the medical profession, particularly in an Emergency Department. There, they were critical. Ray frowned. He'd been in and around the medical profession all of his life. He was unfamiliar with this particular terminology. Just as he stood to inquire as to its meaning, his cell phone rang. He'd forgotten to turn his phone off as he entered the building. He flipped open the telephone on the second ring. "Gates."

"Where the hell have you been? I've been calling for over an hour." Raymond instantly smiled.

"Let me call you back." Raymond excused himself and exited the hospital. He walked over to his car and leaned against the side door. He pressed the code to dial the lasted number called. Tony picked up instantly.

"Where have you been? I've been calling for over an hour." Tony, his usual patient, jovial self, somewhere south of fury and north of fret, blasted into the receiver. "I got a message from Colonel Wheeler. What's going on with Mamma Lou?"

"Everything's under control. Mamma Lou had an episode . . ." he began, but was instantly cut off.

"An episode?"

"Yes," Raymond answered patiently.

"What does that mean, an episode?"

"If you would calm down I'll tell you," he paused, then began again. "Mamma Lou and Colonel Wheeler were dining with some friends when she began to experiencing a tightness across her chest. The episode continued for several moments then dissipated. Then early this morning the discomfort began again. This time with a body rash. That's when Colonel Wheeler contacted emergency services and they brought her here, to the nearest facility."

"Where's here?"

"We're at the Golden Heart Medical Center in New York."

"How's she doing?"

"She was just falling asleep when I left the room."

"What do you mean when you left the room? Where are you now?"

"I'm in the hospital parking lot. Cell phones aren't allowed in the hospital."

"Raymond, is Mamma Lou going to be okay?"

Raymond nodded his head. "She's going to be fine. She's stable and resting comfortably. The attending physician gave her a mild sedative and an antihistamine that has induced sleep."

There was silence on the other end of the line as Tony processed the information. "Are you sure it wasn't a heart attack?" he asked calmly.

"I don't think so. The doctor has run a number of tests. Although the results aren't all in, it seems that she is suffering from gastritis and a severe rash."

"Speak English."

"She had an allergic reaction to something she ingested. Then possibly a gas bubble in her chest from undigested food."

"How serious is it?"

"She'll be fine."

"Are you sure?"

"Of course I'm sure."

"So what happens next?"

"The attending physician wants to keep her overnight for observation."

"Is that bad?"

"It's standard medical procedure. It's just a precaution. Her blood pressure is elevated and she has a slight temperature. But, I think those are primarily due to the circumstances. What she needs now in plenty of rest. Her body has been through a slight trauma."

"Trauma? We're on our way. We'll catch the next flight to the states and be there by tomorrow evening, give or take a few hours."

"Tony, chill out. There's really no need for you and Madison to cut your trip short and rush home. Mamma Lou's going to be just fine. I'm here and so is Colonel Wheeler. Dad is in surgery and Uncle Matthew called from the west coast. They'll both be here as soon as possible. Mamma Lou's in excellent medical hands and in a very well respected facility. If there is any change at all, I'll call you."

"Are you sure?"

"Positive."

"All right," Tony relented, "give Mamma Lou our love when she wakes up. I'll call you tomorrow to get the results of all the tests taken. Tell her I'll call tomorrow."

"Okay, talk to you later."

Just as Raymond ended the conversation, and closed the cell phone, it rang again. He spent the next twenty minutes assuring his uncle, his aunt, two cousins and several other members of the Gates family that Louise was well, getting the best medical attention, and in excellent hands.

The last call came from his father, Ray, while he was still in surgery. Having only just begun the twenty hour procedure, he had the Johns Hopkins surgical staff patch an outside communication line through into his operating room headset.

Raymond finally closed the phone, ending an extended conversation with his father. Dr. Raymond Gates, Sr. or Ray, as family members affectionately called him ever since Raymond, Jr., was born, was the Director of Neurology Critical Care at Johns Hopkins Medical. As a medical professional, he was well aware of Golden Heart Medical Center's reputation. Apparently, their newly renovated Emergency Department was renowned for it's critical care. Ray reassured his son that Louise was in excellent hands.

Raymond eventually closed and turned off the cell phone. He went back into the hospital. As he entered the ER he looked around for Hope. She was in another exam room so he continued to his grandmother's room.

He passed Colonel Wheeler on his way to get coffee. He declined his offer to bring him back a cup and continued to Louise's room. He entered to find her peacefully asleep. Raymond sat down in the seat nearest the bed. For the fist time, he took a moment to actually look around the small cubical. It was a lot larger that he'd first realized. Then he wondered why he'd never heard of the small hospital before.

His father had recognized the name immediately. He mentioned that Golden Heart Medical Center was in the process of a complete renovation of its main facility which included the total overhaul of the Emergency Department. Ray looked up at the ceiling-mounted arm that held suction, oxygen, and other emergency medical equipment, including EEG and EKG monitors. He walked over to the small cove between the two cubicles. Beside the bed, mounted on the side table, was a registration computer with hook-ups to the pharmacy, CT, and MRI labs.

He wasn't overly impressed with what he saw. The rooms were still small and cramped by his standards. Privacy was impossible and the main nurses station was right out of the Middle Ages. The technical aspects, though adequate, left a lot to be desired.

He moved back to his grandmother's bedside. She slept in a peaceful, restful slumber.

Raymond marveled at the beauty she still possessed. It was hard to believe that she'd just turned eighty almost a year ago. Her even, mocha complexion, virtually wrinkle free, was still extremely smooth. The only telltale sign was the brilliant glow of soft, thick, silver-white curls haloed around her head.

Her even-tempered demeanor was misleading to most, while a complete mystery to others. She had all the charm and style of a sitting queen and enough feistiness to behead you if you got on her wrong side.

By all accounts, she was the matriarch of the extended Gates family. With three younger brothers and a younger sister, she was used to getting her way in all matters. Especially when it came to matters concerning her two grandsons.

Recently she'd begun a new whim, turned hobby, turned pastime, turned full-time occupation. That whim was matchmaking. After her success with his cousin Tony and Madison, she'd seriously began turning her not-too-subtle attention in his direction.

Although Raymond had been quite apt at averting her many advances, he was certain that she wouldn't give up until he was walking down the aisle with a new bride on his arm, as the minister pronounced them man and wife.

Raymond shuddered at the thought. Married life was definitely not for him. He was a confirmed bachelor and nobody, not even his beloved Mamma Lou would change that.

At least he didn't have to worry about her doing any matchmaking while she was in the hospital. After all, who in their right mind would plan and scheme while lying in a hospital room?

Seven

Raymond stood and paced around the room a few more times.

"Why don't you go grab yourself a cup of coffee?" Colonel Wheeler suggested. "There are a few vending machines in the small area next to the family waiting room." He walked over to stand by Louise's side, a place he'd grown very comfortable being over the years. "I'll be here," he looked down at Louise lovingly. "If she awakens before you get back, I'll call you."

Raymond looked over to his grandmother. She was still sleeping peacefully on the narrow gurney. He watched as Colonel Wheeler wrapped his large, loving hand around her petite hand. He sat down in the chair nearest the bed, leaned over, and then gently stroked her cheek with their hands still intertwined. He gazed tenderly at her face, then seemed to still his thoughts.

Without reply, Raymond quietly walked from the room and silently closed the door behind him. He stood just outside the door for a second thinking of the deep love and devotion his grandmother and Colonel Wheeler shared. Theirs was a loving affection of understanding and compassion. For a split second he wondered if he'd ever find that kind of enduring companionship.

A concerned grimace of deep thought creased his knitted brow. Then, slowly, it was replaced by an easy, knowing smile that steadily crept across his face. The bizarre thought of finding a devoted relationship had taken him by surprise. But now he was back to his old self again.

He shook his head to clear his strayed musings. He refused to be betrayed by his own thoughts. Mamma Lou, with all of her matchmaking talk, was beginning to get to him. This wasn't the first time he'd wondered about his romantic future. But he would certainly make sure that it would be the last.

Now, for the first time since crossing the threshold of Golden Heart Medical Center did he actually take the time to look around at his surroundings. Feeling like the misplaced Dorothy in Oz, he was definitely not at Manhattan Medical, nor any of the other uptown facilities for which he was associated. Compared to them, Golden Heart was more like a poor, sick, pathetic stepchild in need of major support and an even more major influx of cold, hard cash.

The main nurses station was surreally still, as if stuck in a time warp. The ridiculously outdated, florescent lights gently radiated a luminescence of serenity down onto an enormous circular workstation. Home to a bevy of chairs, charts and cabinets, the workstation was virtually devoid of human contact.

He walked over and stepped up into the ER nurses' station. He glanced around for any sign of Hope. Several nurses attentively looked up from their designated tasks with interest. He declined their assistance, then questioned Dr. Hope Adams's whereabouts. He was informed that she would be back within the half-hour. He nodded and walked away more disappointed then he should have been. He told himself that he was solely interested in the test results, but a part of him knew better.

He briefly glanced into each of the eight exam rooms as he passed, only three of which were occupied. Yet, seeing that Hope was nowhere to be found, he continued through the large circular area until he came to triage. Instinctively, he looked in. It too was empty except for a duty nurse who'd been cleaning and restocking the area of supplies. She politely asked if she could assist but again he declined her offer and instead asked for directions to the cafeteria.

"Dr. Gates."

Hearing his name called, Raymond turned around. "Yes?"

"Dr. Gates, excuse me. Might I have a moment of your time?"

"Yes, of course," Ray responded automatically.

Scott Wallace extended his hand to shake. "Dr. Gates, I am honored to meet you. It's truly a pleasure. Your reputation precedes you. I've followed you and your father's work extensively. As a matter of fact, I did my internship at Johns Hopkins and spent quite a few hours watching your father operate. He's a brilliant surgeon."

Not particularly surprised by the sudden pep rally, Raymond thanked him for his compliment. "Thank you, Dr. . . . ?"

"Wallace, Dr. Scott Wallace. I'm the Emergency Medical Director. First off, I'd like to offer my sincere apology for the appalling treatment by my staff. Dr. Adams was completely out of line, and totally unprofessional. Her behavior was unwarranted and completely uncalled for. And I assure you, she will be suitably reprimanded."

"That's not necessary. Dr. Adams was just doing her job. She is the attending physician."

"I'll discuss this with the hospital administrator and have her removed from the case at once."

"That's a bit extreme doctor, don't you think? After all, we were both at fault."

"Dr. Gates, you needn't concern yourself. I assure you, this isn't the first time that Dr. Adams has overstepped her bounds."

"Ultimately, my only concern is the welfare of my grandmother."

"As am I, I assure you. It will be my honor to personally take over the case."

Ray wasn't completely comfortable about changing doctors in this mannor. "I'm sure Dr. Adams is quite capable. And I appreciate your interest but . . ."

"No need to thank me. I assure you, it's my pleasure."

Scott spent the next ten minutes relaying the accolades of

Raymond Gates, Sr.'s illustrious career at Johns Hopkins, while simultaneously boasting about his own career at Golden Heart.

"Dr. Wallace, I do have one question. I haven't been on an ER medical staff since my intern rotation, I'm unfamiliar with the term LP macrotentioneda."

Scott grimaced. "Acronyms like those are why we would rather not use them."

"What does it mean?"

"Actually, I'm not familiar with that particular term, but I'll be happy to find out for you."

"I'd appreciate that doctor, thank you."

Seconds later Raymond pushed the large, blue square panel on the sidewall and waited a second or two for the automatic doors to swing open. When they were completely ajar, he stepped through into another world.

The outer area, the waiting section, was almost completely empty. Raymond glanced around, getting his bearings, mindful of the directions he'd just received. He turned right and passed the main information and sign-in desk where two nurses, an orderly, and a police officer talked quietly amongst themselves.

A young man, in his mid-twenties, sat nearest the desk watching the television as he waiting patiently. On his lap was a sleeping child, obviously exhausted from the extended wait. Propped up next to him was another sleeping child, older, maybe four or five, with his head leaned awkwardly against the man's arm.

In the far corner, there was a much older man sitting beneath a perfectly peaceful picture of a child playing in the sand. He was hunched inward, bundled up in a too-small sweatshirt and too-large jeans. Now he was fast asleep, his hands still gripping a newspaper he'd been reading, as his slowed, rhythmic snoring wheezed with little difficulty.

A continuous blast of air from the air conditioning vent directly above him kept the unread newspaper flapping in his stilled hands. Gruff and grimy in appearance, his matted hair was a disastrous crop of brown and gray, seemingly unkempt and uncombed for many days. He had a large suitcase near to his dingy, socked feet, which were very comfortably planted next to his pair of very new, very chic, very red, three-inch patent leather pumps and matching purse.

Raymond shook his head, not completely surprised by New York's finest. Often referred to as "toons," "loony-toons" or "bags of peanuts," hospital waiting rooms were notorious for bedding the homeless and mentally challenged nightly. Often shooed back out onto the streets by security, they returned dutifully. But, instinctively craving safety, humanity and the kindness of the medical staff, they would more likely than not return, having nowhere else to go.

And yet, far be it for him to pass judgment on anyone, the same could be thought of him as he walked around dimly lit hospital corridors at five o'clock in the morning. It wasn't the oddest thing, but also not exactly the usual.

With continued, relative ease, Raymond followed the directions exactly, but instead of finding himself in the cafeteria, he was led directly to the doctor's lounge. Hoping to find a hot cup of coffee, he pushed through the doors and entered.

She had her hands cupped over the top of her head, with her head bowed low into her chest. Soft, gentle sobs of pain emanated from her obvious distress. In an instant her head bobbed up, displaying the anguish of her life's treatment across her face. Her gasp of surprise was as heartbreaking as her still gently falling tears.

With little thought to the appropriateness of the situation, Raymond found himself by her side within seconds. He embraced her lovingly, and protectively wrapped his arms around her.

He leaned her head onto his chest. She conformed easily, allowing his strength to still her. Raymond drew her closer and inhaled the sweetness of her scent. She smelled of clean, fresh cotton and jasmine.

"I'm sorry," Hope said, as she tried to move away before

she thoroughly embarrassed herself. She had misjudged his compassion. "This is totally unprofessional of me. I'm sorry." Utterly and completely mortified by her outbreak of humanness, she continued to apologize.

"What's wrong? What can I do? How can I help?"

"Nothing's wrong. I'm sorry," she hiccuped and swallowed a sob while continuing to edge away from him.

"There's obviously something wrong. Tell me; what is it?"

"Nothing," she sniffed away a falling tear then turned to the anxious man beside her. "Your grandmother will be fine."

"I know that," Raymond said indignantly. He was slightly insulted by her assumption that his only concern at that moment was for his own well being and that of his family. "My concern is for you. How can I help?"

Hope stared at Raymond for an instant. She was taken aback by his genuine concern; his ardent, almost passionate plea to assist. He was actually concerned about her feelings and her discomfort. *Why?* She wondered to herself with dubious curiosity. What possible difference could her distress make to him? Then, suddenly, an overwhelming sense of attraction swept through her. Hope gasped. She sat back and shook her head, as if to dispel the odd feeling of enticement and fascination that had somehow snuck up on her.

Raymond watched closely enough to notice a sudden change in her facial expression. The uptight, embittered medical professional had turned from a sobbing innocent to an awed sophisticate right before his eyes.

"Listen," he said, speaking in the barest whisper, "whatever it is, whatever the problem, sometimes talking about it, talking to someone else, a friend maybe, makes a difference." Raymond reached up to wipe the last fallen tear from her cheek. Her skin was soft, too soft. He smiled, openly assessing. "Sometimes even talking to someone you barely know, can't stand, and just met after a major argument in the hospital quiet room can be helpful."

Hope suppressed the smile for as long as she could. But

eventually, it forced its way free. It crept from a single corner, than spread wide across her full mouth, until her entire face was lit by her radiance. Raymond's touching, slightly comical remark had somehow sparked hope into a dismal memory.

Perilous in its contagiousness, the infectious smile was all Raymond Gates. Hope easily succumbed, yielding to the charm he so naturally exhumed. Surrendering to this man would be too easy.

"I'm sorry for this, this . . ." she paused to consider her wording, "unprofessional . . ."

"Why do you keep apologizing?" Raymond questioned, still sincerely concerned. "There's no need to apologize."

"It was unprofessional."

"To show emotion is unprofessional?" He said as she remained silent. "Do you want to tell me about it?" She slowly shook her head no. "Okay." He acknowledged her simple statement with accepting understanding.

Suddenly the stilled silence of the room and the close proximity of their bodies drew an instinctive reaction. Wrapped in the protective strength of Raymond's arms, Hope looked up into his heavenly hazel eyes. Drawn by an unseen force, their lips met in a crush of passion. He held her and she wrapped her arms around him. The kiss, as necessary as the air they breathed, seemed natural and comfortable. There was no awkward positioning or clumsy hesitation. Giving and taking, their lips joined in perfect harmony as she parted and he entered. Passion soared and desire grew in a kiss that left their bodies aching for more.

Then Hope pushed away. The intensity of the moment reflected in both of their eyes. Something had just passed between them and it wasn't just the kiss.

She looked around the small room uncomfortably. Suddenly being this close was too close, and she needed breathing room. She stood up suddenly, taking Raymond by surprise. "The final test results came in. Mrs. Gates experienced a serious allergic reaction to something she ingested."

"I see. Do the tests indicate the catalyst?"

"No, I've ordered a comprehensive allergy test later today. I've already contacted registration about an available room."

"So you're recommending she stays here?"

"Yes, her blood pressure is still elevated, her cholesterol is borderline dangerous, and her heart rhythm is erratic. I'd like her to stay at least the day for observation."

Raymond walked over to the pot of newly brewed coffee on the side desk. He poured rich dark coffee into a Styrofoam cup. "I can have her transferred to Manhattan Medical within an hour."

"Transferred?"

"Yes." He took a timid sip of the hot brew then pulled his telephone from his jacket pocket and prepared to dial. Then closed it and looked for a landline.

"Why would you want to disturb her rest by transferring her to another facility?"

"Because it's a better hospital and it's my hospital."

"Are you implying that Golden Heart is less than adequate?"

"I'm saying that I want my grandmother at Manhattan Medical, a hospital with which I am associated. A hospital where I can be sure that she's receiving the best care and attention."

"And exactly what do we admister to our patients here, doctor, chopped liver?"

"That's not what I said. I merely inferred that Manhattan Medical has doctors who are experts with this particular issue. Geriatric care can be complicated. Manhattan Medical's staff is extremely well trained and have an extremely high level of expertise and experience. Their principles and morals far exceed the norm, while the level of professionalism exceeds most large hospitals, let alone the smaller ones, like this one. The doctors are less," he paused to consider his wording, "constrained."

"That's extremely impartial of you, doctor," she said sarcastically.

"Hey, I'm only speaking the truth. This facility is sorely lacking in many respects. Even my brief time here has shown me that."

"So, not only are you questioning our Hippocratic oath, but you're also degrading our facility."

"You're twisting my words."

"You're twisting your own words." She replied sharply, as she walked over to the door and angrily swung it open. "When you decide to come down off of your golden pedestal, you let the rest of the world know. Until then, stay out of my face." She stormed out of the room without a glance back.

"How can anyone be so damn arrogant and pigheaded?" She mumbled, as she breezed through the empty halls. "And to think," she added, "I was just beginning to see him as a regular guy, then he goes and acts like a complete jerk by opening his mouth and speaking."

Her mind still buzzed with Raymond's remarks. She ranted and raved with each step, pounding her footsteps harder and harder as she went. Within minutes Hope rounded the corner that led her back to the ER. Just as she breezed through the main doors her arm caught and held. She looked down, and then whipped around to face Raymond, his hand gently gripped around her arm.

Raymond let go instantly. "I'm sorry."

Hope looked at him coldly. "For what? Your honesty?"

"It's obviously now that some of my remarks were uncalled for. My behavior was unconscionable."

"You could say that."

"Look, I only want what's best for my grandmother and her being in Manhattan Medical, with me, is what's best."

"Maybe you should ask her."

"I don't have to. I know what she needs."

Hope took a deep breath and let it out slowly. "You are a piece of work, aren't you?"

"Maybe you should get to know me better and find out for yourself." His brow rose ever so suggestively.

A proposition? Hope questioned silently. She looked at him oddly. *He's serious.* Disbelievingly, she smirked, shook her head, and looked toward the nurses' station.

"You are an arrogant jerk." She moved to walk away from him.

Raymond stepped in front of her. "Name calling is a bit childish, don't you think, doctor?"

"Get out of my way." She said through gritted teeth.

Raymond smiled the genuine smile that always got him his way. The fire in her eyes had sparked something deep inside of him and he was enjoying every bit of it.

"I've got this uncontrollable urge to kiss you again."

Hope's eyes grew wide with shock. She was utterly speechless. She blinked twice, blew out a deep completely exasperated breath, turned and marched back to the nurse's station.

Raymond couldn't help but smile. His off-handed proposal and suggestion had taken the confident Dr. Adams completely by surprise. The expression on her face was priceless. He looked over to the nurse's station before entering his grandmother's room. There was something about Hope. The indomitable spirit that came along with those sexy lips and that wicked tongue that made her a very interesting prospect.

Raymond paused by the open doorway a few seconds before entering. He turned, and looked toward the nurses' station. Hope looked up. They stared at each other a moment. His dimple winked and she quickly glanced away.

Raymond entered the exam room, surprised to see his grandmother awake and smiling happily. She and Colonel Wheeler were talking quietly. "Come in, dear. The orderly just left. My room is ready." Louise looked up and smiled when Hope entered, seconds later. "How am I doing, doctor?"

Hope smiled and checked the monitors. "Your admittance paperwork is complete. An orderly will be here in a few moments to take you to your room. Do you have any questions?"

"No."

"Good. Sit back and relax." She helped Louise lay back in the bed. Cautiously, she looked up at Raymond who had been silently staring at her the entire time. Uncomfortable from his intense look, she looked away quickly, and began to fidget with the machines.

Just then the orderly arrived with the gurney. Hope breathed a sigh of relief and made a speedy exit. Thank God her shift was over.

Eight

Dr. Hugh Wescott stood at the window of his comfortable office and looked down at his domain. Trash, broken bottles, abandoned cars, and dilapidated houses met him at every turn. He hated this view, and he hated everything associated with his quarantined detention.

He had been assigned here because of one reason. He was being punished for his lack of foresight. Due to events beyond his control, he had inadvertently lost a lucrative position and had therefore been reassigned to this isolated wasteland of a prison.

He looked far off into the distance. On the outskirts of a bustling metropolis, the Golden Heart Hospital complex was composed of a single six-floor building that connected to the four-tier parking lot and was situated on twenty-two acres of less than prime real estate. Surrounded by poor, lower, middle and working class neighborhoods, it was more than slightly rough around the edges. It had all the class and charm of a derelict.

Yet, what it lacked in neighborhood charm and public acclaim, it more than made up for in heart and soul. With all of its distinction, it rose above the area's level of poverty with a dignity befitting an elder statesman.

Built in the early 1950s, it was a medical marvel in its heyday. Patients came from all over the island to seek medical expertise at a level unparallel to most area hospitals. But, like most in its era, it fell on hard times during the tumultuous extremes of the sixties, seventies and eighties.

It had taken nearly fifteen years for Hugh's predecessor, Bartholomew Gibson, to get Golden Heart back to some fraction of its former grandeur. It had been an uphill battle at best, but he had done an excellent job. Golden Heart had begun reaping accolades and praise for its bootstrap victory.

Then, as with most newly successful businesses, hospitals were just as vulnerable to take-over. Listed as an available public facility just before the turn-around, the recent surges in cash flow and revenue had made it even more attractive to investors.

There was an aggressive strategy to get the facility into a private program. Golden Heart had finally gotten the attention and was instantly purchased by The Barclay Medical Corporation.

After a healthy settlement with the county, Golden Heart had become a member of *Barclay Med,* as it was sometimes affectionately called. Shortly thereafter, Bartholomew Gibson suffered a massive, fatal, heart attack. Hugh Wescott, an influence-seeking professional who had recently joined Barclay Med and was eager to advance with the company, was enlisted to take Bartholomew's place until further notice. Then, as with most smaller acquisitions, Barclay Medical had lost interest.

Barclay Med was a large conglomerate of private hospitals run with the proficiency and competence of a military boot camp. Unfortunately, the uniformity of the program had taken its toll on the professional population. Due to restrictions, Golden Heart had lost a fair number of gifted professionals. But, those dedicated to the health and welfare of others, remained strong.

Still, Golden Heart's medical services, as far as most were concerned, were the best in the county. Their doctors, nurses, and supporting staff were the finest. The problem, unbeknownst to many, having been stigmatized by the label *public hospital* for so long, Golden Heart lacked the serious interest by its newest private facilitator.

Regulated to the extreme and scrutinized for every penny issued, the privately held Golden Heart was in just as much turmoil as the public one, making the health and well-being of its patients nearly last on the priority list. Although Golden Heart legally held the distinction of being *A Barclay Med Private Hospital,* it was considered a poor stepchild in comparison to other, more prestigious facilities.

Hugh was determined to change that image. He needed Barclay Med to see him as a no-nonsense bureaucrat that applauded the HMOs, heath care system and pharmaceutical companies for their courage to lead this country forward. So what if a few crybabies went without heath care? In all great undertakings, some sacrifices had to be made.

In his nearly forty years in hospital administration, he had been challenged with every dire dilemma and critical crisis a hospital could face. Golden Heart was in serious trouble.

Unfortunately, under the new Barclay Med régime, devotion to the sole purpose of healing the sick wasn't always good enough any longer. Due to extreme budgeting, HMOs, and the high cost of medical insurance, Golden Heart was literally on its last financial leg. Having come close on numerous occasions, Hugh was familiar with the corporate procedure. Money talked and he needed an instant infusion.

Adding to its troubles, lately the hospital had been plagued with its fill of lawsuits, malpractice litigation and wrongful-death proceedings. But, it had always managed to remain standing with its doors open to the needy.

Hugh sighed heavily as he looked up at the sky. The sun hung low in the sky, just above the distant trees in Wellington Park. He smiled openly as he refolded and placed his silk handkerchief back into his jacket pocket. He adjusted the already perfect knot at his throat and creased the tie's silk dimple.

His clear brown eyes, the color of a shallow mud puddle on a rainy day, sparkled in continued anticipation as he spontaneously broke out in a chorus of deep chuckles. His thin, narrow face, littered with wrinkles, was pinched in delight. This day just kept getting better and better. He couldn't believe his luck. Of all people to be admitted to ER, it was Louise Gates. He smiled, remembering his early morning conversations with her.

She was all that he'd imagined and more. But, the most important thing was, she was in his hospital, under his supervisory care. And Dr. Raymond Gates was on his way to his office at this very moment.

Not one for whimsy, daydreams, and fanciful yearnings, Hugh preferred to remain in the realm of reality. Practicality was his mantra. He made a point of knowing exactly what he had and how to use it to gain maximum serviceability. Yet, for a brief moment, Hugh let his fantasies roam wild. Having Raymond on staff would be a dream; having both him and his father, Raymond, Sr. on staff, would be nothing less than euphoric. With their prestige, Barclay Med would give him practically anything he wanted. He could even have Golden Heart rebuilt from the ground up.

After another moment or two, his riotous chuckles turned to a mild snicker, then slowly faded into a broad grin. Not even the routinely ponderous duties as Hospital Administrative Director had weaned his exuberant mood. Ever since he received the early morning telephone call, nothing could extinguish his enthusiasm. Still, at times they came close.

Hugh rubbed his neatly-trimmed beard, then pulled on the tiny diamond in his ear lobe. After a miserable start to a deplorable day, this was indeed going to be an excellent finish.

He began his day with his usual morning stroll through the ER. He always enjoyed the hectic pace of battling life and death. Scott Wallace's usual long-winded reports consisted of usual complaints about Dr. Adams's performance and inability to lead the staff as ER medic. Thankfully, their conversation was interrupted by an urgent call.

Next, he was cornered outside of his office with the typical hassles with doctors about petty patient problems. He was then forced to listen to the nurse's rep whine about cut hours and additional work. Afterwards, the Hospital's Community Relations Representative unburdened herself with a list of possible demands for additional funding.

Then, in ordered sequence, a train of staff paraded through his office as if it were Grand Central Station with tales of woe, misery and tribulation. This was immediately followed by an unannounced visit by a Barclay Med representative.

Hugh smiled with each proceeding crisis. After receiving the phone call earlier, nothing could dampen his mood.

Now, grateful to have a moment's peace before his appointment arrived, he sat down at his desk and cleared the open files to a waiting out bin. He looked at his watch again. He smiled as the tiny sliver of gold ticked off another minute. Usually, he'd be well on his way home by this time. But, when he received a call requesting an immediate appointment, there was no way he was going to postpone it to make it more convenient. Not after he'd been actively pursuing this man for the last two years.

It was exactly six o'clock. His appointment would be arriving at any moment. A slow, easy smile creased his thin lips as the buzz of the intercom sounded.

He pushed the button and leaned in excitedly, "Yes?"

"Dr. Wallace is here to see you."

"Tell him I'll speak with him tomorrow."

She covered the telephone for brief moment than returned, "He says that it's urgent. He'd like to talk to you before he goes on shift."

Hugh rolled his eyes; everything was urgent as far as Scott Wallace was concerned. "It will have to wait until tomorrow."

"He says it's regarding a disturbance in the ER last night."

"Send him in," Hugh stated and blew a heavy, exasperated sigh, rolling his eyes to the ceiling. Scott Wallace was an excellent doctor with credentials that included interning at Johns Hopkins under his personal tutelage. Unfortunately, emotionally, he hadn't gotten past the third grade. He had the sometimes annoying knack for prying, spying, and tattling like an eight-year-old.

Wallace hurried in with his usual rushed demeanor. And, within five minutes outlined the general gist of the early morning ER altercation. Hugh sat quietly, listening with his usual disjointed interest.

". . . Dr. Gates and Dr. Adams . . ."

"What?" Hugh asked with interest. "Who did you say?"

Scott repeated his story as Hugh's thoughts drifted to two little words, damage control. He barely even noticed when Scott ended his tirade and left the office.

He had his assistant leave a message on Hope's beeper that he wanted to see her as soon as possible.

So, crestfallen, Hugh guessed that Raymond Gates was probably irate at his treatment last night and was here only to lodge a formal complaint. So much for pipe dreams and wishful thinking. Although he was curious that Raymond hadn't mentioned the altercation when they spoke on the phone earlier.

Hugh relaxed back in the cushioned, leather chair with his arms resting comfortably on the armrests. He decided that he liked his office's recent decorating job. With rich tones of navy, mahogany and tan, it suited the prestigious title of Hospital Administrator.

He pivoted slightly to glance up at the impressive wall of diplomas, citations and awards which were prominently positioned behind his desk. This was his masterpiece, his showpiece, his wall of homage, and a prominent self-serving display of gratuitous bravado.

It had taken years to amass, but it was well worth it. It was imposing to say the least, giving everyone who entered the office the opinion that they were in the privileged presence of a highly regarded medical professional and distinguished statesman. They were always impressed.

Hugh nodded approvingly after standing to straighten a tilted award bestowed upon him from the board of directors two years ago. They had honored him for his administrative contribution in attaining a grant for a much needed addition to the radiology department. It was a small token of their gratitude that was given at the annual hospital fundraiser.

Recently, Hugh had been unofficially given the tasks of recruiter and fundraiser. Up to this point he had risen to every challenge, going beyond the call of duty, outdoing even his own expectations. But he needed just one major achievement to gain a seat on the distinguished Barclay Medical Corporation board of directors.

Adding Raymond Gates to his staff of surgeons would be the biggest accomplishment of his career since he angled a one hundred thousand dollar grant from the Bo Watson estate. After literally months of phone calls, Raymond Gates had called him and finally requested to meet with him. Now, all he had to do was secure Gates permanently and he'd be sitting on easy street. With Gates on board, a monetary endowment from his notable family would be inevitable. The hospital could easily be looking at a remarkable influx of revenue. And he could write his own ticket to any hospital in the country.

Hugh quickly made a mental list of the items he wanted immediately, the items he would wait on, and the items he would have to reconsider. With everything neatly listed, he decided to scratch the last list, shoot the works and get it all. The buzz of the intercom broke his thoughts. "Yes."

"Dr. Gates has arrived."

"Thank you."

Hugh stood, straightened his tie again, then excitedly hurried across the room. He opened the door and burst through with ecstatic zeal to greet his distinguished guest. The smile on his face was endless as he extended his hand to shake exuberantly. "Dr. Gates," he said, with a sigh of admiration, as if he had just met a long honored saint. "Please come in." He stepped aside, allowing Raymond to pass through easily.

"Thank you," Raymond replied, breezing into the inner office. "And I appreciate your seeing me on such short notice."

"Oh, think nothing of it. I'm always available for a fellow physician."

Hugh briefly nodded a pleasant goodnight to his secretary, then turned back to follow Raymond. He found Raymond standing in the center of his office, glancing at his wall of homage.

"Very impressive."

"Oh, they're simply tokens." Hugh smiled proudly. "Dr. Gates, please have a seat," he offered with exaggerated charm. "May I offer you a cup of coffee or tea, or perhaps something stronger?"

"No, thank you," Raymond responded automatically.

"I must say Dr. Gates," he began smoothly, "it's indeed a pleasure and honor to finally meet you. Your remarkable skill and reputation precedes you."

Raymond nodded, not completely unfamiliar with the verbal accolades. He took a seat across from the large, neatly ordered desk. "Thank you, and please, call me Raymond."

Hugh nodded, smiled, then slowly circled his desk but didn't sit down. "And I insist that you call me Hugh. I must admit Raymond, I was both intrigued and excited to receive your call this morning. As I'm sure you're well aware, we've been trying to get you on board at this hospital for some time. But, first of all and most importantly, I'd just like to say that I have only recently been informed of your problems in our ER last night. I am truly appalled. And on behalf of the entire Golden Heart staff, I'd like to formally apologize." He lowered his eyes, expecting the worst.

"Dr.—" Raymond began, than altered his appeal, "Hugh, I didn't come for an apology from you. I came to offer an apology to you and your commendable staff."

Light-headed with sudden exhilaration, Hugh nearly passed out. He listened to Raymond's point of view about last night's incident, which was totally different from Scott's. His head spun with joy, as his smile nearly eclipsed his face. Suppressing the urge to dance a jig, Hugh nearly leaped to

Raymond's side to shake hands. "So, the events of last evening are barely worth mentioning."

"Exactly." Raymond added.

With a new surge of confidence, Hugh instantly began his pitch as he circled back behind his chair. "Raymond, our medical resources here at Golden Heart far outweigh Manhattan Medical in many ways. Our facility, although small in stature, offers a tremendous range of medical services. Of course, we don't have the monetary resources of an uptown medical facility, but I'm sure if you give us a chance, you'll find we are every bit as efficient."

He paused briefly to come around front, perching on the edge of his desk with extreme confidence. "We would greatly benefit from your medical expertise, as you will of course benefit from our wonderfully abundant surroundings."

Raymond, first taken off guard by the sudden pitch and employment offering, continually smiled assuredly. He had no intention of leaving Manhattan Medical Center. "Thank you for your very generous offer, Hugh, but I'm quite satisfied with Manhattan Medical at the moment. But, should my circumstances change, you'll be the first to know."

Hugh smiled, not completely assured by the reply, but accepted it nonetheless as a questioning look replaced his accommodating expression.

"Actually, the reason I'm here is that my grandmother was admitted to this hospital very early this morning."

Hugh hung his head in compassion. "Yes, I was deeply sorry to hear about your grandmother's ill health. But, I assure you, everything is being done to make sure that her stay with us is calming and relaxing. And, of course she has the medical attention of some of the state's foremost physicians.

"As a matter of fact, I met with Mrs. Gates earlier this afternoon, and I must say she is a very remarkable woman. I don't believe I've ever seen so many flowers, telegrams, and phone calls for a single patient."

Raymond nodded. "She is extraordinary."

Hugh almost giggled with overwhelming glee. "I actually received a phone call from the governor of Virginia's office this afternoon. Not to mention several congressmen and a senator. I believe one of the congressmen actually referred to her as a national treasure. I can surely see why she is so admired. She is incredible."

"She is that," Raymond agreed readily, then changed the subject to get to the point. "About my grandmother's attending physician, Dr. Adams. Although extremely capable, I'm sure, she seems detached."

"Yes, Dr. Hope Adams. I assure you, she is one of our most promising physicians. But there is such a tragic past. You see, as a child she was present when her mother was brutally killed. That's how she got the horrid scar on her face. She fell through a window." Hugh smiled sensitively and nodded with complete assured confidence. "But, she is a very talented and experienced medical professional by all accounts."

"That's terrible. I'm very sorry to hear that." Raymond said sympathetically. He paused, remembering the brief moment they shared in the doctor's lounge. "Be that as it may, I'd like to arrange for my grandmother's transfer to Manhattan Medical, where I can more closely monitor her progress."

Hugh nearly choked on his panting tongue. "Manhattan Medical! There's no need to transfer your grandmother. We are every bit as capable as Manhattan Medical."

"I have no doubt that this hospital is extremely capable."

Hugh nearly fainted. He couldn't believe what he was hearing. There was no way he was going to have Raymond's grandmother transferred to another facility as long as he was administrative director. "Raymond, there must be another solution. You of course know that transferring a patient mid-treatment can be damaging to the patient's recovery."

"I'm sure that won't be the case in this instance. As you say, my grandmother is extremely resilient."

"Yes, but sound medical advice would strongly recommend that a patient remain in the host facility until fully recovered."

"I would agree in most cases but not in this particular case. And not with my grandmother."

"Is she receiving the best medical attention?"

"Yes, of course. I'm certain she is."

"Is the standard of our medical care as high as or above the level of Manhattan Medical?"

"Yes," Raymond admitted honestly.

"Then I don't understand why you'd like to have her transferred."

"Having my grandmother uptown, where I'm already on staff, would be more convenient for all parties involved."

"Well," Hugh began, greatly relieved, "if that's all that's concerning you, why don't I simply add you to our staff? Temporarily, of course," he added as an afterthought. "Now, don't get me wrong, I completely understand your deep concern. After all, it's your grandmother's health we're talking about. But, I might also add that Dr. Adams is one of our most talented, young doctors. Her record is impeccable."

"I'm sure she is. But . . ."

Hugh held his hand up to pause Raymond's added concerns. "If I might," he began diplomatically, "as I said earlier, I spoke to your grandmother at length this afternoon. She is truly a delight. She seemed very comfortable with her surroundings and had nothing but praise for Dr. Adams. As a matter of fact, she even requested that Dr. Adams continue as her physician of record. You see, here at Golden Heart Medical Center, when a patient is admitted to the hospital from the emergency room, the attending physician isn't always the same. Our ER is like a separate entity. Seldom do our ER doctors continue with hospital care. But, since Mrs. Gates insisted, I readily agreed."

Raymond's brow rose with interest. "Insisted? Really?"

"Indeed. It's not necessarily a common request, but we do make the rare overture on occasion. Particularly when the patient is such a lovely woman."

"Uh-huh."

"Plus, I personally reviewed Mrs. Gates medical chart and I completely agree with Dr. Adams's diagnosis. I believe that under our roof, Mrs. Gates is receiving the best medical care possible."

"I'm sure she is."

"I also noted that she's scheduled for a forty-eight hour discharge, or after the final test results have come in." Raymond nodded. "So, since she'll only be in this faculty for another twenty-four-plus hours, isn't it preferable to have her discharged home rather than taken by ambulance to another hospital?"

"Nevertheless, I still prefer that my grandmother be transferred." Raymond said.

Hugh sighed anxiously. This wasn't going as he anticipated. For the first time in almost fifteen minutes he began to feel as if he was losing the battle. "Raymond, talk to your grandmother, and if at that time you still want her transferred, I'll deliver the papers myself."

"Fair enough, as long as Dr. Adams is her primary physician."

"Of course, I'm sure you'll find there will be no problem with Mrs. Gates staying with us a bit longer. And, for your convenience, I will add you to our consultant file immediately. As of this moment, you have all the rights of a Golden Heart staff physician."

Raymond nodded. "In that case, I'd like to meet with Dr. Adams to discuss my grandmother's case as soon as possible."

"Of course. Although, I don't believe she's on call until later."

"I'll be at my office until late this evening."

"I can have her meet you at your office, at let's say, eight o'clock tonight?"

"That would be fine," Raymond said as he pulled two business cards from his holder and gave them to Hugh. "I appreciate that. And thank you for your time, Hugh." Raymond stood and extended his hand to shake. But instead of receiving Hugh's hand, he received a white linen envelope.

Hugh had grabbed the envelope from atop his desk and thrust it at Raymond. "As a newly staffed physician, this is your invitation to our fund raiser this weekend. It's a twelve hour event so feel free to come and go at your pleasure."

Raymond opened the envelope and instantly noticed the location of the event. *"Spotlight NYC."*

"Yes, it's supposed to be the hottest place in town I hear. I understand from the committee that the proprietor is donating his time and the restaurant, free of charge.

"Dennis Hayes is a very generous man."

"Oh, do you know Mr. Hayes?"

"Yes, Dennis and I have met from time to time. He's a good friend of my cousin's family."

"Good, great, then you'll be there?"

"I'm afraid I have plans this weekend."

Hugh was visibly disappointed. "Oh, that's too bad. I am sorry to hear that. I'm told it's going to be an outstanding event."

"If I know Dennis, he'll certainly outdo himself." Raymond extended his hand to shake. Hugh grasped it firmly. "Again, thank you for your time, Hugh." Raymond said before turning to leave. Then, Raymond pivoted and turned back to Hugh. "Question. Will Dr. Adams be attending this weekend's event?"

Hugh looked questioning at first, then realized that Hope's attendance might be the catalyst to get Raymond to attend. "Yes," Hugh chirped louder than intended, as he instantly decided for her, "as a matter of fact, I do believe she will be attending."

Raymond nodded his head, adding an interesting smile. The telephone began to ring, drawing Hugh's attention. Raymone held up the invitation and shook Hugh's hand again. "Thanks again for your time doctor." Hugh waved and went back to his desk to get the ringing phone.

As soon as Raymond opened the door, Hugh picked up the phone.

Nine

Hope ripped the taped, pink announcement from her locker door. She read the note, balled it up, and jammed it into her jeans pocket. It was starting out to be another miserable day. She looked up onto the top shelf of her locker. Neatly pressed scrubs and a white jacket were stacked, folded and waiting for her. It was too early to change. So she clipped her ID badge onto her jeans pocket and slammed the locker door closed.

The only good thing was that she was still scheduled to work during the twelve hour fundraiser tomorrow. She shuddered outwardly. Awkward conversation, small talk, toe-crunching dancing, and overly inebriated colleagues embarrassing themselves weren't what she considered a fun time, even if it was at the hottest nightclub and restaurant in Manhattan.

She went over to the coffee station and poured a cup of dark, rich, Columbian, mud-like liquid. Like cold molasses, it oozed from the carafe and plopped into the thick paper cup. *Yuck!* She trashed the cup and took the decanter to the sink.

With a distasteful grimace on her face, Hope drained the abhorrent brew and rinsed the pot, intending to brew more coffee. Yet, as with most, the often-mindless chore sent her mind wandering in dangerous directions of disjointed logic. Thoughts that didn't normally come to her, where now oozing like smelly, burnt coffee, forcing their way from her subconscious to her conscious.

Money, power, influence, style, class: Raymond Gates was without equal. As far as men went, he was in a class all by himself. Still, it took more that good looks and a healthy bank account to make a doctor. She was all too aware of that fact. She smiled, remembering that mischievous dimple and how it winked the more irritated he became. She had to admit, she liked the way he moved. A lingering smiled widened across her face as she recalled their kiss.

The hot passion of his playful tongue sent a sizzling wave of heated desire coursing through her even now. Her stomach did a somersailt and her cheeks flushed warm. The impromptu kiss had stayed in her thoughts all day long. Each time she closed her eyes to sleep, she smelled his spicy cologne and felt his chest pressed against hers. The man obviously knew how to please a woman.

Then, just as the thought of him pleasing a woman entered her mind, the image of Raymond's hands on her slowly seeped into her fantasy. A seduction scene played out in tantalizing slow motion, the ER exam room, curtains drawn, a stationary gurney, his body, her body, and a kiss. She smiled, enjoying the scintillating daydream.

Stop it! She suddenly demanded of herself. *What am I doing? Damn.* Ever since that man breezed into her life early that morning, all she could think about was the illustrious Dr. Gates, those stupid, adorable dimples, and his hazel eyes. *Oh, brother. This is it. I've finally lost it.*

Hope flopped, then slouched back against the comfortable leather sofa, resting her feet up on the wooden coffee table of the doctor's lounge. She maneuvered the brand new throw pillows behind her head and leaned back, preparing for a long, comfortable pause. Just as she closed her eyes, her pager sounded.

She looked at her watch; she was two hours early. No one should have been paging her; she hadn't even changed into her scrubs yet. She stood, looked at the LCD numerals and picked up the telephone on the side table. While preparing her newly brewed coffee, she waited impatiently for the message to play in completion. It was Hugh's assistant; she'd been summoned by the great and powerful Hugh.

Dressed in well-worn blue jeans, a University of Pennsylvania sweatshirt and sneakers, she left the lounge and headed to the elevator.

On the way to Hugh's office, Hope decided to make a brief stop at Louise's room. She got off on the fifth floor and proceeded to her room. Hope knocked and entered. She was surprised to see that Louise wasn't lying in bed. Instead, there was a very attractive man standing at the window. Hope immediately assumed that he was another handsome grandson.

"Hello," Hope said looking directly at the stranger. The man turned and smiled openly. Her questioning expression was obvious. "I'm Dr. Adams."

Dennis looked down at the sweatshirt, blue jeans, and sneakers and nodded after seeing the staff ID badge and lanyard dangling from her front pocket. "So," his smile broadened, "you're the guardian angel Mamma Lou's been talking so much about."

"I wouldn't exactly call myself a guardian angel." She came further into the room. "I was her ER physician. And you are?"

Dennis slowly strolled around the side of the bed towards Hope. Needing only a few steps, he approached with a broad, welcoming smile that widened, putting an instant spark into his dark, smoldering eyes. He extended his hand eagerly. "Dennis Hayes. I'm a good friend of the family."

Hope nodded and shook his hand. "Hello, Dennis."

"The pleasure is truly mine, I assure you." His charming, suave reply was anything but innocent.

He held onto her hand a second longer than necessary, and Hope instantly recognized Raymond's kindred spirit.

Dennis had the same mischievous glint in his eye and similar, devilishly handsome features that obviously brought dozens of interested glances from admiring women. Laid back to the point of perpetually casual, he was everything a woman could ask for. But he wasn't Raymond.

Distracting herself, Hope looked around the room. It resembled a mini flower shop. The sweet scent of flowers surrounded them at every point. Bouquets of every imaginable description sat on the windowsill, desk and dresser. A large floor bucket was pushed into the corner by the window.

"Looks like Mrs. Gates is a very popular woman with the local floral delivery shops."

Dennis looked around. "Actually, I'm surprised that there are so few. Mamma Lou is an extremely well admired woman."

"I'm learning that fast. Where is she?"

"Mamma Lou and Colonel Wheeler went for a walk, down to the gift shop. They'll be back soon. In the meantime, why don't we get better acquainted?"

Hope smiled and shook her head. The charming Dennis Hayes offered her a seat, then perched on the end of the bed. Hope sat on the chair near the dresser. Within minutes Dennis had Hope laughing with his outrageous sense of humor. In the middle of another humorous story, the door opened. Louise and Colonel Wheeler had returned.

"Hope, dear, what a pleasant surprise."

"Hello, Dr. Adams," Colonel Wheeler said, as he closed the door.

Dennis instantly hopped up and dashed across the room to aid Colonel Wheeler in assisting Louise in returning to her bed. Bookended by two handsome gentlemen, Hope just shook her head. Louise Gates was truly a unique personality.

Hope stood and moved closer to the bed after Louise settled in comfortably. "Hello," she said then said to Louise, "you look much better."

"I feel much better," Louise said. "Hope, this is a dear friend of the family, Dennis Hayes. Dennis, this is Dr. Hope Adams. She's my physician."

"Yes, we've just met," Dennis said. Louise couldn't help but notice the smile her doctor exhibited when she looked at Dennis. He had returned her smiled with equal relish. "Hope and I were getting more acquainted when you returned. I see why you raved about her so, Mamma Lou. She is quite a rare gem."

Hope nearly blushed. To her amazement, Dennis Hayes was every bit as charming and charismatic as Raymond. As they all continued to talk, Hope shook her head, and wondered if Louise Gates was associated with every handsome man in New York City. She stayed a few more moments, then grabbed her now-cold coffee and excused herself in order to attend the meeting in Hugh's office.

As soon as she stepped outside of the room, she paused to make note of Louise's jovial spirits. She was spry and lively. Hardly the sickly patient she'd seen just hours earlier.

Her thoughts continued to wonder about Louise, as she entered Hugh's outer office and was instructed by his assistant that he would be right out. The door was closed and she could hear him speaking loudly. She assumed it was to someone on the telephone since she only heard Hugh's voice.

Hope looked around the office seeing that Hugh's assistant had packed up and prepared to leave for the day. They said their good-byes as Hope took a seat on the sofa and picked up a medical magazine. She began to flip through the pages while sipping her chilled coffee, an occupational taste she'd grown used to.

After a few minutes, the door began to open slightly as the telephone began to ring. Hope stood up. Assuming it was Hugh, she stepped closer, knowing that he'd open the door then walk away to get the ringing phone, leaving her to enter and close it. She grabbed the knob and pulled as the door was being pushed from the other side.

Raymond, looking back while walking out of Wescott's office, bumped full force into Hope. Her coffee accidentally spilled down the front of her sweatshirt. The stain of the cold, dark liquid splashed everywhere, including her jeans and sneakers. She was a mess.

She looked up at him. Her aggravated expression said it all, until that pain-in-the-neck dimple winked at her. She stiffened her resolve, ignored it, then looked down the length of her, as did Raymond. Wordless, she began shaking her head at this man's latest intrusion into her once peaceful, uneventful life.

"Are you all right?" He quickly asked.

"Yeah, great, covered with coffee, but uh, doing real good. Thanks for asking. How are you?" Her sarcasm was obvious.

"I am so sorry," he said, with a smile broadening from her rye humor.

Hope looked up at him. "Yeah, I can tell."

"No, really," he began to chuckle at the absurdity of the fateful moment, "really, I am very sorry. I guess we just don't have our timing together yet."

"Gee, yah think?"

Suddenly realizing the coffee spill down the front of her, Raymond pulled a bright white handkerchief from his pocket and began gently rubbing the coffee stain from the large University of Pennsylvania letters. After a few seconds exactly what he was doing dawned on them both. Whoops.

Hope snatched the handkerchief from his hands and continued to wipe the front of her shirt and jeans. "Look, I'm really sorry. What can I do to make it up to you?"

"Nothing. You've done quite enough," she said too quickly, then breathed deeply, aware of Raymond's closeness and thankful the heavy sweatshirt hid her aroused nipples. "Don't worry about it really, it's okay."

Raymond reached out and steadied her busy hand. "But, it's not okay. Please, allow me to pay for it."

"It's just an old sweatshirt, no big deal."

"But it *is* a big deal, and I'm sure it holds a lot of wonderful memories of your time in Philadelphia." He spoke softly.

Hope refused to look at him. That inkling of sensitivity and sincerity had peeked out again. She was instantly mindful of their meeting in the doctor's lounge earlier that morning. The kiss. "It was just as much my fault. I should have been watching where I was going." She looked into those hazel eyes, rimmed with dangerous thoughts. Big mistake.

A moment of comfortable silence passed between them as they smiled and observed the stillness of their colliding worlds. "We really do have our moments, don't we?" Raymond offered.

"I guess we do," she agreed.

The gentle softness of their voices drew a familiar feeling. Slowly Raymond leaned closer. Hope tilted her head up slightly. Their lips parted in anticipation as their eyes met and held. The memory of the kiss washed over them and pulled them closer.

The door suddenly opened wider, forcing them to proceed in their intended directions, then causing them to bump back into each other again. They spared each other a last needed glance, then parted unimpeded.

Wescott, who had emerged from his office to witness the two stumble into each other, opened his door wider to allow Hope to pass through. Then he got the final glance at Raymond turning back to watch her walk away. Raymond's eyes on Hope spoke volumes, yet he played it off with tremendous ease. But it took an interested man to know one. Raymond was apparently very interested in Hope, and Wescott was very interested in getting Raymond on his hospital staff.

Wescott closed the door soundly. Lacking the barest pleasantries, he didn't even offer her a seat. He made one brief statement. "You will attend to your ER duties this evening and tomorrow morning, but I am also putting you on temporary loan to the fifth floor recovery ward, until further notice."

"Excuse me?" Hope said.

"Please don't interrupt. I've rescheduled your time. As of tomorrow, you are solely responsible for the health and wellbeing of a single patient, Louise Gates. And, I expect her and her family to receive the best possible care this hospital and its staff have to offer."

"You've gone too far this time, Hugh. I've put up with all of your crap since you came here. You put me on graveyard shift, you extended my hours, and now you're adding to that by assigning me to the fifth floor until further notice? You have absolutely no grounds."

"I can, and I have."

"I didn't spend eight years of my life in med school, interning and doing my residency, to be considered a glorified babysitter and handmaiden for anybody." She stood and moved to the door, then paused, turned, pointed her finger, and rolled her head in a typical home girl manner. "If Mrs. Gates needs constant attention, I suggest she hire a private nurse. And you can tell her family for me that they have some nerve."

"Please, sit down, Hope, and let me finish." She hesitated and glared at him, then finally moved back to the chair. He waited patiently until she relented and sat down. "This is not a request from Mrs. Gates, nor any member of her family. This is a request from the hospital administrative offices and Barclay Medical."

"I'm sure Barclay could care less about Louise Gates or any other patient for that matter."

"That's where you're wrong. Barclay Medical is very interested in Louise Gates." He noted her reluctance. Then contemplated altering his approach. "A few extra hours of your time to care for a very sweet, very dear, older woman, who thinks the world of you, isn't overburdening is it?" Hugh knew the moment he had her.

"Why?"

"Mrs. Gates is a very important patient and we'd like to keep her happy."

"Aren't all of our patients equally important?"

"Yes, of course they are." He lied easily, annoyed by Hope's persistence.

"So, why the special treatment for Louise Gates?"

Hugh, never one to be daunted, rose to the occasion with a spectacular team spirit pep talk that could easily shame the entire Collegiate Eastern Conference. His long-winded dissertation bordered on political fillerbuster and lasted nearly just as long.

"Actually, none of this matters because Scott took me off of her care. He's Louise Gates's physician now. So you'll have to talk to him, not me."

"Consider yourself back on." Her expression never wavered. "I'll release a few extra hours in exchange."

"I'm not playing *Let's Make a Deal* with you Hugh. Patients' lives are at stake. ER is already short staffed. No, thank you."

"This isn't a request doctor. It's a direct order." Her expression remained the same. "I can, however, make this more difficult for you. I can assign you to the fifth floor permanently."

Hope was more than a little surprised. Something was up and she wanted to know what.

The implication was obvious. It was a threat. Blackmail had always been Hugh's weapon of choice. She had experienced it several times in the past and each time she had relented. This time was no different.

"All right, fine. I'll do it," she huffed.

Hugh stood and extended his hand to give her Raymond's business card and address. She looked away purposefully. "Thank you, doctor. Your commitment and generosity to this hospital will not be forgotten."

"Whatever," she muttered too low for Hugh to distinguish. She stood and turned to the door. As she reached for the knob she paused. Hugh called to her.

"Oh, and Hope, your presence has been requested at the fundraiser this weekend."

"What?"

Hugh walked over and handed her an invitation. She took it, staring, as if it were a foreign object. He turned and went back to his desk, closed his briefcase and prepared to leave for the day.

"What?" Hope asked a second time, still staring at the

envelope in her hand. "Are you kidding? I can't go to this. I have plans to work a double shift."

"You're off this weekend. It's already been arranged."

A slow burst of halted nervous laughter erupted as Hope walked back to the desk and placed the envelope on Hugh's closed briefcase. "I still have other plans."

"It might be in your best interest to alter your plans. If you need a few hours to do it, fine. I'll have someone cover for you." Hugh picked up the telephone and began to dial.

"No!" Hope shouted and nearly lunged across the desk to stop him before he completed the connection. Hugh stopped dialing. "No, I just don't do parties like this. My plans were to spend the time on an additional shift in the ER."

Hugh placed the receiver on the cradle. "Oh, well, then it's settled. For the time being, you're no longer solely in ER," he said cavalierly, as he picked up the envelope and offered it back to her. She inched away, as if it were the forbidden fruit of Eden.

Hugh picked up his briefcase and came around to the front of the desk. "Hope, no excuses," he placed the invitation securely in her hand. "I'll see you at the fundraiser this weekend. Oh, and before I forget, you have a meeting with Dr. Gates at his office later this evening. Eight o'clock, don't be late."

She went numb as she looked at the white envelope, then slowly sat back in the chair. Her mind flashed thoughts of jumping out of the window, but she figured Hugh would probably still make her attend the function, broken legs and all. She looked up, hearing him call her name a second time.

"Hope, have a good evening and I will see you this weekend at the fundraiser, and don't forget your meeting with Dr. Gates this evening. I left his business card on the desk. Remember, eight o'clock. Don't be late."

Ten

Raymond smiled as he jauntily took the stairs down to the fifth floor. He was in a good mood. The smell of coffee on his hands brought a quick and easy smile to his face. Stray thoughts of Hope had made him smile a lot lately.

Seeing her nicely-tight jeans walk away from him brought an interesting thought that he quickly expanded on. He readily agreed that hidden beneath the drab blue scrubs, she had a nice body. Not skeletal-skinny or anorexic-thin, but full and balanced with just the right touch of curves that could drive a man wild. She had a heart-shaped bottom that moved like bottled heaven. Curved to voluptuous perfection, her rounded hips begged to be caressed.

Raymond savored a sly smile at the direction his thoughts had taken. A refreshing departure from the women he most often encountered and was usually attracted to, Hope was a breath of fresh air. There was something about her that made him want to smile a lot in the past few hours.

Her decidedly foul temper and distant demeanor had only added to his budding attraction. She'd put a smile on his face that was quickly becoming impossible to erase. Each time he thought about the way she lit into him, made him laugh openly.

As he walked down to the nurses' station on the fifth floor, he introduced himself and asked to use the phone. As he dialed, he requested and received Louise's chart.

He called his office, his answering service, then a good

buddy of his at the University of Pennsylvania. After brief and successful conversations, he headed for his grandmother's room.

As he approached her room he realized that the joyous laughter he heard was coming from his grandmother's room. Pouring out like bubbling champagne, he entered the room to see what looked like a late afternoon tea party.

Several nurses and an orderly surrounded Louise, while Dennis Hayes and Colonel Wheeler were right in the middle of a tag team–like rendition of a comedy routine. They detailed, in every laughable aspect, the joys and horrors and sometimes riotous efforts of running profitable eating establishments.

Raymond joined in, while curiously watchful of his grandmother. Except for the persistent red rash, she didn't appear to be sick at all. If he didn't know any better, he'd say she was up to something. But, since being in the hospital her matchmaking had been temporarily put on hold, so he presumed that he was just imagining it.

Eventually, the impromptu party broke up. Dennis and Colonel Wheeler excused themselves to attend to business issues, and the nurses and support staff went back to their duties and workstations.

Raymond smiled down at Louise, then looked closer to examine her face and eyes. They sparkled and shined with renewed vigor and energy. Dressed in a pastel-lilac robe adorned with dainty flowers and lace, trimmed at the neck and cuff, she looked as if she could have been lying in her chaise longue at home. "You look great Mamma Lou. How do you feel?"

"I feel much better than I did earlier this morning."

"You look much better. I see the hives are beginning to fade."

She nodded. "Yes they are, thank the Lord. The itching has almost completely ended as well. After Hope gave me that last shot this morning I fell right to sleep. Otis tells me that I pretty much slept all morning. I woke up just a few hours ago. He and Dennis were discussing restaurants, as usual." Louise yawned and stretched lazily.

"Looks like you had a few deliveries."

Louise looked around the room at the generous display of flowers. "Aren't they lovely?" Raymond nodded. "I've collected all the attached cards and telegrams to make sure I send thank you notes when I return to Crescent Island. Unfortunately, I ran out of floor space, so I sent most of the flowers to the maternity ward. I think they'll brighten up someone's day, don't you?"

"When was the last time you saw Dr. Adams?"

"She came up from the ER shortly after you left this morning to give me another shot, then again just a few minutes ago. Just before you came in as a matter of fact. She and Dennis were having a good old time when Otis and I returned from my walk."

"Oh really, she and Dennis?" Raymond's interest was piqued as a troubled grumble echoed though his body. "I didn't know they knew each other."

"Oh, they just met. Hope is such a nice young woman. I thought maybe I'd have Dennis ask her out sometime."

"Dennis? Dennis Hayes?" Raymond nearly fell off the chair. "No!"

"Sure, why not? Dennis is a fine young man, good family, polite and successful. He and Hope seemed to really get along earlier. I think they just might make a wonderful couple."

"No," he said definitively. The stern grimace on his face was all the encouragement she needed to continued with her original plan. Apparently she'd been right all along. Raymond and Hope were perfect together.

"Well, if you're so sure, maybe I'd better rethink it."

"Mamma Lou, we talked about this matchmaking thing of yours before. Just because it worked once, doesn't mean it will work every time."

Louise smiled knowingly. He had absolutely no idea that she'd been matchmaking all of her life. Including matching his father with his mother years ago.

"Yes, I know dear. I promise to stop." She continued to smile, as Raymond nodded with his small victory. The fact that she never mentioned *when* she would stop never occurred to him.

Raymond, once visibly shaken by the thought of Dennis and Hope together, breathed a relaxed sigh of relief. Louise continued to smile happily as she changed the subject. "How was the rest of your day?"

"Busy, as usual. I had a few morning consultations, along with several minor procedures. I just had a meeting with the foundation."

"How's the new building?"

Raymond nodded his head. "It's looking good. It's right on schedule. It should be ready on time."

Louise smiled, thinking of the foundation Raymond had founded several years earlier. It had begun primarily as a mentoring program, then evolved into a scholarship and teaching organization that assisted achieving African-American teens further their education in the medicine and research fields.

In the span of four years the Foundation had succeeded in sponsoring several promising students at MIT and other institutions of higher learning.

"What are your plans for this evening?"

Raymond shook his head. "I have a consultation at the office in an hour and another meeting after that."

Louise looked up at the clock. "That's awful late isn't it? It's already six o'clock. This must be a very special patient."

Raymond thought about his patient and shook his head with exasperated irritation. "If you mean special in an annoying way, yes. She insists on having a particular procedure done. It's dangerous and risky even under the best of conditions. I refused to do it, but she insists. She's threatening to go to someone else."

"Raymond, if this patient decides to go elsewhere, even after you've repeatedly warned against it, it's no longer your responsibility. I know it's frustrating when others don't listen, but in this case, you've done your job."

Raymond walked over to the window and looked out at the dilapidated buildings in the far distance. The area seemed to be consumed with decay and blight. As a cosmetic surgeon, his job was to correct deformities and enhance beauty. From this vantage point, there was no beauty. He turned back to Louise who was flipping stations with the television remote control.

"Mamma Lou, I don't get it. Why here?" Raymond asked simply, changing the subject completely.

Louise relaxed back in the hospital bed, one arm casually tucked behind her head, still holding the television's remote. She looked at Raymond questioningly. "Why where?"

Raymond smiled and moved closer to the bed. "Why this particular hospital? You left midtown Manhattan, surrounded by numerous hospitals, to come to this? He waved his arms around toward the window. Why?"

"The paramedics felt that I should seek medical assistance as soon as possible."

"You were already at dad's brownstone on the Upper West Side, near several private facilities. Why not ask to be taken to Manhattan Medical? It was the closest. There's also St. Vincent's on 11th, or St. Luke Hospital Center near Columbia University. Any one of them would have sufficed. Why would you choose to come here?" Raymond's suspicious tone was evident.

"It's very simple, Raymond. I asked to come here. So the paramedics brought me." She dramatically placed her hand on her forehead and closed her eyes. She waited a second, then peeked through to see the results of her performance. Then, with barely a second's breath she added, "Have you consulted with Hope yet?"

Raymond poured water into a small glass and handed it to

his grandmother. "Actually, I've just come from an appointment with Dr. Wescott, the Hospital Administrator. I was going to see about having you transferred to Manhattan Medical."

Louise nearly choked on her water. "What?"

"I want to have you transferred to my hospital."

"Don't be ridiculous. This hospital is just fine." She looked around the sparse room filled with flowers. "I rather like it here. The people are wonderful."

"Mamma Lou, you'll be better cared for at Manhattan Medical. Besides, I'm there. I can care for you personally."

"Nonsense. You have enough on your plate without worrying about me. No, I'm staying right here."

"Mamma Lou," he began, but stopped when the nurse walked in the room. She announced that she needed to take Louise to have tests run. "This isn't over," he warned.

Louise smiled brightly, "Of course it is. Now you go on and get back to work. I'll talk to you later."

Louise had a way of dismissing that made Raymond feel like he was seven years old again. He dutifully kissed her cheek and promised to return the next day.

Eleven

After her horrendous meeting with Hugh, Hope proceeded to the ER. Her dark mood prompted those around her to steer clear.

At seven o'clock Scott approached her. "I understand that your shift is up. Isn't about time you got going?"

She looked at him, her eyes blazing with renewed annoyance. "Excuse me?"

"I received a phone call from Hugh. He informed me that you were leaving early. He also wanted me to make sure that you left in time for your downtown consultation. I believe Dr. Gates is expecting you at eight o'clock."

"I won't be attending," she said defiantly. After all, what could Scott possibly do to her if she refused to go?

"In that case, Hugh asked me to mention to you that the temporary arrangement on five could be permanent."

Forty-five minutes later Hope stepped off the elevator and followed the hall to the only suite on that floor. She came to the end of the corridor and stood before double frosted glass doors. She looked at the business card that Hugh had given her and sighed heavily. The etched and engraved name on the frosted glass door read simply, DOCTOR RAYMOND GATES AND ASSOCIATES, COSMETIC SURGERY. She pushed the door open and walked inside.

The room, brightly lit by overhead spotlights and several table and floor lamps, was completely empty. Hope looked around the splendor of the open office. With the doors closed behind her, she realized that the room, larger than she originally thought, was shaped like a huge semi-circle.

The room was comfortably decorated in classic chic with
muted earth tones and large-leafed green plants. Cool, clean
marble and deeply-polished wood accented the remainder of
the room. Hope shook her head as she looked around in
amazement. Apparently cosmetic surgery did even better than
she'd imagined.

She walked to the center of the room and stood, looking
side to side. Like mirror images across from each other, there
were two seating areas complete with a cozy sofa, loveseats,
wingchairs and coffee tables. It resembled a cozy living room
that could have been found in the average upper-middle-class
home.

The far wall was made up of perfectly arched panels of
frosted, plate glass bricks. In the center of the dynamic, crystal display was trickling water.

The waterfall was a sheer, tapered stream of steadily flowing water, pouring down the glass wall. The effect was
stunning. Hope walked closer to the glass and peered over the
desk to see the water gently puddle into a long narrow receptacle. The unexpected waterfall in the center of the
business environment and the gentle soothing sound of flowing water brought a smile to her face.

Backlit from behind to create a soothing glow, the waterfall was framed to the ceiling on either side with several
oversized palm trees and a number of smaller tropical plants.
Beyond the foliage were walkways that led to the rear offices.

She heard a woman's laughter from behind the glass wall
and called out a greeting to get someone's attention. She
heard Raymond's voice as he approached. He came up from
behind the waterfall, walking with firm, determined steps.

Wearing metal-framed glasses and a friendly, detached
smile, he was all business. The crisp whiteness of his shirt
against the dark navy of his pants made the silhouette completely professional.

His clean-shaven face and soft, caramel complexion made her heart stop. The soft, hazel tint of his eyes had kept her awake practically all day long. Tired and still reeling, her less-than-pure thoughts continued exactly where they'd left off.

Gorgeous men, although usually smug and stuck-up, were one of the greatest delights walking the earth. Often, they had only one redeeming quality: they were pure eye candy. And, if you were very lucky and had the opportunity to do more than look, the pleasure was sheer heaven.

All day long, Hope had delved into those possibilities. Raymond's casual style was too comfortable, while his charm was too irresistible.

"Hi, how are you?" he said. Hope nodded her cautious greeting as he continued. "Thanks for coming. Have a seat. I'm in with a patient at the moment. I'll only be a few more minutes." She nodded again, then took a seat as Raymond disappeared back down a narrow hall, presumably to his office.

Hope noticed a fan display of magazines on the side table. She walked over and read through the titles. There were the typical doctor's office reading material: *Family Circle, Women's Day, Time, National Geographic, Sports Illustrated* and *Black Enterprise*. She chose one and began flipping through it, agitatedly. She tossed it down and then picked up another magazine, a medical publication. It was actually a special edition of the *JAMA*. It was entitled *Plastic Surgery Today*. She absently flipped through the magazine then stopped when she saw a byline. An article entitled "The Risks of Before and After" caught her attention. It was written by Dr. Raymond Gates, Jr.

She turned to the page and began scanning the article. Growing more interested, she decided to read it from the beginning. The editorial suggested some provocative challenges to the recent deluge of instant facelifts and at-home injections. With her interest piqued, she settled back on the sofa and read more.

The article suggested that with a series of local anesthetics, hairline incisions, sutures, stitches, and up to ten to fifteen days recovery, anyone could feel revitalized and rejuvenated. He advocated the use of smaller, more exacting procedures, rather than the more commonly prescribed, full face lift.

He added that, although the stated procedures were extremely effective in the removal of facial wrinkles, reducing a percentage of body fat deposits, and minimizing the visible signs of aging, they should not be considered by themselves to be miracle workers.

He went on to warn against fraudulent claims of wonder-techniques and at-home remedies. He also suggested that board certified practitioners with the American Board of Plastic Surgeons should always have access to hospital facilities, even if the procedure could successfully be performed in the office.

The following pages gave exacting details of the aforementioned procedures in a step-by-step manner. Hope continued to read, gaining a better understanding of Raymond's medical world.

Raymond closed the door of his office and walked back over to his desk. He turned to see Mimi standing against the wall looking at her reflection in the mirror. Raymond shook his head. He was amazed by how similar mother and daughter were. Like her mother, Laine was stubborn, bull-headed and vain. And, he had just had the same, endless argument with Laine earlier, on the telephone. Mother and daughter were a lethal pair who could get on any man's last nerve.

Laine Herrington was a cheap knockoff of her mother. She had the wanna-be nature of a lioness, but not the heart. He feared she'd forever be on the yellow brick road in search of the "Land of Oz" and the illusive "Great and Powerful Wizard," for which she whole-heartedly searched. But, unlike her mother, she finally relented.

On the other hand, Mimi Woods Herrington Carter Brown

wasn't just a potential client; she was an old family acquaintance who'd long ago staked her claim on his time and patience. Yet, unfortunately, she had the tenacity of a pit bull, and the fortitude and determination of a marathon runner.

Raymond sat back behind his desk and massaged his temples. He'd been trying to talk Mimi into not having a paralytic drug injected into her forehead to reduce unsightly wrinkles.

Seeing that Raymond had returned, Mimi went back to her seat. Her newly silicone-injected lips, still slightly swollen, protruded with added annoyance. "As I was saying, if you don't do it, I'll simply hire another plastic surgeon to do the job."

Raymond stood, leaned back against the front of the desk and shook his head. As usual, he wasn't getting anywhere with Mimi. When she made her mind up to do something, there was very little anyone could say to change it. "That, of course, is your prerogative Mimi, but I strongly advise against it. I have to be candid about this Mimi. The procedure only lasts up to four months before having to be repeated, plus it can be very dangerous if improperly done."

Mimi stiffened her resolve. "But, you leave me no other choice," she said. Raymond remained silent as he went back behind his desk. "For heaven's sake Raymond, it's been approved by the Food and Drug Administration and it's not like I requested another eye-lift." She looked over to the mirror across the room, then back to the small, three-sided mirror on his desk.

"An upper blepharoplasty is also out of the question."

"Why are you being so difficult?" She looked at him pointedly as she returned to her seat.

Raymond examined Mimi's face carefully. The incisions he'd made had nearly faded, leaving no visible marks at all. Over the last few years she had requested, and he had performed, a number of very expensive mini-surgeries. Raymond had initially suggested those procedures instead of a painful, full face lift. He had targeted specific areas of her face: she'd had eye, cheek and neck lifts.

Her last procedure, a cheek lift, had gone better than he had expected. Over time, as with most, Mimi's facial fat had begun to sag due to the universal dynamics of gravity. Raymond had suggested a cheek lift. The procedure had restored her narrow profile, softened the shape of her mouth, and had given her a more youthful-looking appearance.

Just last month he had ended the six-month microdermabrasion treatment which had literally sandblasted the outer layer of skin from her face, removing age spots and surface wrinkles.

Raymond smiled broadly. "Mimi, I'm not deliberately trying to be difficult, I assure you. It's just that at some point you have to realize that enough is enough."

"That's not what I hear," she insisted.

"Mimi, I'm telling you, the procedure is unsafe. Botox is just an inexpensive facelift using a paralytic drug. In essence, a toxin is injected under the skin."

"Then why is everybody doing it? Hell, they even have Botox parties. I've even been invited to several myself."

Raymond tossed his hands up in surrender. "Mimi," he began again, "do you realize that the drug is actually a poison? Have you ever heard of botulism?"

"Yes, of course I have," she stated indignantly.

"Botulism is a deadly food poisoning that is caused by botulin being absorbed into the blood system. The resulting effect is oftentimes permanent damage to the body's nerve tissue. But, before that, the body is racked with a number of unpleasant side effects such as nausea, impaired vision, diminished muscle capacity and vomiting. Not a pretty sight, I assure you." He paused to gauge her reaction. She was muted, but steadfast. "Botulism can be fatal."

"I know the risks, Raymond. That's why I came to you instead of going elsewhere."

"Mimi, we've discussed this at length on numerous occasions. I won't change my mind. I will not perform the procedure."

"You are so damn stubborn. I don't know why you're making such a big deal out of it. How on earth do you make a decent living? No one turns down an opportunity to be paid," she said, as she stood, gathering her purse and wrap from the chair next to her.

"I do."

"Well, that's just ridiculous. And to think, I gave my approval for my daughter to date you."

Raymond smiled, shrugged, and nearly bit his tongue off. Laine, the spoiled, flighty, ever unstable, ninety-pound nightmare with delusions of grandeur, was a walking horror show. Her obsessive attachment to his cousin Tony a few months ago was borderline psychotic and had nearly cost him his happiness.

But Raymond knew that he was in no real danger of attracting Laine's affections. She never really considered him as a viable suitor because she often said she could never be the wife of a boring doctor. It wasn't until recently that she seemed to have changed her mind.

"Thanks, but no thanks. That really wasn't necessary."

Mimi smiled knowingly, "I understand that my daughter called you recently."

"Yes, she called."

"And?"

"And, I was unavailable."

Mimi began wiggling her finger. "I've heard about your reputation, Raymond."

"Mimi, Laine and I are friends. That's all."

"Oh please, that's exactly what your cousin said before he broke my daughter's heart."

"Tony didn't break Laine's heart."

"He did. I was there."

"I thought Laine was in California, living with some aspiring actor."

"It didn't work out. She's at my home in DC. Why don't you give her a call, or better yet, stop by sometime."

"I'm usually very busy, particularly since Mamma Lou is in the hospital."

"What? Louise is in the hospital and no one informed me?"

"It's nothing really."

"Don't be ridiculous. Louise is a dear friend. She's been like a mother or grandmother to me. What hospital is she in?"

Raymond reluctantly gave her the information. She wrote it down quickly, then went back to her conversation.

"I'll make sure to have Laine call you."

"That's really not necessary, Mimi. As a matter of fact, I already have my eye on someone."

"Really?" Mimi sauntered up to Raymond. She arched her brow in a particularly interested way that made Raymond shudder. "I take it by that remark that you're interested in someone in particular?"

"Yes. I am."

Mimi ran a long, brightly colored fingernail down the open v-neck of her low cut dress. Her newly fashioned breasts, thanks to Raymond's talent, nearly burst from their scant confinement. "And who might that be?" She licked her lips seductively.

"You don't know her."

Offended by the slight, her eyes instantly glazed. This was so typically Mimi. A newly divorced Washingtonian, she was a woman of means, with the social calendar of a debutant and the brazen moxie of a streetwalker. Few people turned her down. She went through men like a submarine through water.

Having been married three times, it was obvious that she had no intention of staying single for long. Her creed, borrowed by a great statesman, *by any means necessary,* was how she lived her life. As per the society pages, she was currently dating a US Senator and had all intentions of making him lucky Mr. Four.

"You realize of course, that I will have this done elsewhere."

"Mimi, I can only give you my ardent warning. You're a

very attractive woman; I've already preformed as much work on you as I intend to do. Stop now."

She tossed her wrap over her shoulder. "I'll think about it." Raymond walked over to open the door for her and escorted her to the lobby.

As soon as Mimi laid eyes on Hope she recoiled and grimaced. She turned back to Raymond and leaned in to kiss him. Raymond turned his head, leaving her to kiss his cheek. "I see your next patient has arrived." She reached up and stroked his face seductively. "Goodnight, Raymond. I'll give Laine your best." She turned, eyed Hope, then proceeded through the door.

Raymond stood, slightly stunned by Mimi's performance. He shook his head then escorted Hope into his office.

"I apologize for having you wait. It was unavoidable. I intended to be finished by now." He held the door to his office open and watched Hope as she breezed through gracefully. She smelled of jasmine and lilacs. He loved jasmine and lilacs.

"I'll be brief so that you can get back to your evening," Hope declared as soon as she entered the office. Without sitting, she leaned her backpack on the arm of the closest chair and pulled out several test result reports. She handed them to Raymond as he came up and stood beside her.

"That's not necessary. That was my last appointment. And I have no other plans for the evening. Do you?"

She looked at him, then at the carpet. Her heart beat a mile a minute as the sudden gasp and intake of oxygen burned her lungs until the barest whisper was released. "No."

"Good, so, before we get started and you say anything," he began, as he removed his jacket and laid it across the back of the chair, "I'd like to say something regarding our earlier conversation." She turned away and continued looking in her bag as he continued. "I still believe that my grandmother should be transferred to Manhattan Medical. This has nothing to do with you professionally. You're an excellent doctor. It's just that I would rather be more in control of her care."

"Sure. I understand." Hope said without looking up.

Raymond stepped closer and placed his hand on her arm. "Doctor," his voice was soft and caring as he loosened his tie. "Hope, I didn't go over your head." She stopped to look at him. His sincerity was overwhelming. "I just wanted you to know that. I've spoken to Mamma Lou. She's staying until you're ready to discharge her."

"Thank you." She paused a second, looked at him, and decided to change the subject. She looked away. "Your office is beautiful."

"Thank you. We work very hard to make a comfortable environment for our staff and patients."

"So you have other doctors working with you."

"Yes, there are three of us. With a five-person staff."

"I wondered why . . ." she began, then stopped suddenly.

"Why what?" he asked.

She continued hesitantly. "You seem to be at Golden Heart quite often. I just wondered what kind of caseload you have. You must not be very busy if you can spend so much time elsewhere."

"My caseload can be lightened at any time by distributing my patients to my associates. If a patient requests to see me personally, then it's usually late in the evening, like tonight."

"Oh, I see."

"Anything else?"

"No."

"Wouldn't you be more comfortable sitting down here, or on the sofa?" He offered as he brought her attention to the oversized sofa by the side wall.

"No," she stated and pulled the last report from her bag.

Raymond took the file, walked over to the sofa and sat down. He spread the papers out on the coffee table and focused on them in detail.

Curiosity won out. Hope glanced over at Raymond. He looked like a schoolboy studying for midterm exams. With his wire frame glasses perched on his nose, his focus was unwavering as he turned the page, then turned back to reread a notation.

Attempting to concentrate was nearly useless. He had actually reread the same paragraph three times. He had to turn back to the first page to remember exactly what test he was reading about. The woman had him twisted in a knot without even knowing it. "They all came back negative," he said, finally looking up to Hope. "There's got to be a reason for the rash and hives. We must be missing something."

"I assure you, Dr. Gates, we were extremely thorough."

"I don't mean to imply that you weren't." Immediately sensing Hope's annoyance he moved to her side. "Hope, if we're going to work together on this, I'd like you to trust that everything I say isn't a direct snipe at your ability as a physician. I don't make a habit of second guessing my colleagues." She remained silent and looked away. "When I agreed to have my grandmother remain at Golden Heart, it was with one stipulation: the understanding that you would be her physician. Believe me when I say, I would not trust every doctor with my grandmother's care."

"I realize that, Doctor," she said, still looking away.

"Raymond," he insisted.

She nodded and looked at him. Big mistake. The warmth and sparkle in his eyes were trusting and soothing. They seemed to draw her in, welcoming her tenderly. Her instinct was to reach out to him. She forced her hands to remain still at her sides.

A pregnant silence fell between them as they realized they had a stalemate. Raymond, his usual charming self, spoke first. "Truce?"

She nodded. "Truce."

He sighed heavily with a dimpled grin of relief. She smiled also, releasing an abundance of pent-up tension and frustration.

With that out of the way, she felt relaxed enough to sit down and seriously converse with him about Louise's puzzling case. With no previously known allergen revealed, and no prompting factor discovered, they looked at the medication and the possibility of a previously obscured side effect. But, everything came up negative. Finally, they came to the conclusion to run another series of tests. They also agreed to put Louise on a strictly controlled diet.

"There is one other possible cause I've considered, but hesitated to mention earlier." Raymond looked up, extremely interested. Hope took a deep breath knowing that what she was about to say would most likely bring their fragile relationship back to square one. "Macrotentioneda."

Raymond frowned. "Yes, I remember seeing that you had jotted that in your notes the night Mamma Lou came in." He quickly scanned the notes. "Here it is: 'possible LP macrotentioneda'. I'm not familiar with that term. Exactly what is it?"

Hope hesitated a moment, then looked into his trusting eyes and sighed deeply. "It's a term used in some ERs. It actually means nothing but it implies that the patient is seeking attention from either family, friends, or the medical staff. Thus the words 'macro' and 'attention'." She waited for the inevitable blow of hostility.

"Actually, I thought about that too. Mamma Lou can be a piece of work, even on a bad day. But lately, she's been visiting so many friends; she and Colonel Wheeler have been here with me in the city. They're constantly out enjoying themselves, so I tossed that notion. But if you think it's still a viable possibility, we can delve into it deeper."

Hope was stunned. She expected no less than a tirade. But, instead, she listened as Raymond seriously dissected the possibility. "No, as long as you've already considered it, I think we can move on."

After twenty minutes, their conversation shifted to a number of medical topics including plastic surgery.

"But it's such a trivial vanity," Hope insisted, her tone condescending and arrogant. "It's like being on the sidelines while someone else does all the important work."

"You mean it's fluff."

"Exactly, although I wouldn't have put it so bluntly."

"Sure, some of the work I do is pure and simple vanity," Raymond said.

"Precisely. For instance, the woman that just left. Her profile is obvious: rich and vain. That's your typical patient, correct?"

"Not everything is as it appears."

"But this is. I can plainly see that she's had some work done and here she is, back again. I bet she wanted something else done, right?"

"Cosmetic surgery can be just as addictive as caffeine, nicotine and heroin. Although it's obviously not a chemical substance, it can be just as dangerous an obsession for some people."

"Doesn't it ever bother you that you're not making a substantial difference in the lives of others? I mean look around; all you do is add silicone and suck out fat. You cater to the rich and super rich. What about the disenfranchised and indigent? Who helps them? Don't you ever want to do something more to help people? Like for instance, your father. His work has changed so many lives. I don't see plastic surgery having the same effect."

"There are many aspects to my work. Yes, there is the traditional pampered debutant, socialite, or corporate exec with a bucket of cash wanting a quick fix nose job or liposuction. And that's fine. I'm delighted to help someone feel better about themselves."

Hope's expression showed the haughty, self-righteous disdain she felt.

"But," he continued, "there's also the child, who's been burned on over ninety percent of her body, and whose life will forever be altered by a tragic accident. Who'll never be asked to the prom because she looks like her body's gone through the wrong side of a meat grinder. Whose face and hands would have been better off going through a blender than enduring the twisted, mangled mess she's been left with. The young boy who just wants to die because the loneliness is just too much to bear. The young girl who sits alone while others go to the parties or the mall.

"Or what about those born lacking the simple standard of which we take for granted. By the stroke of a single, obscure gene, fate has left them a twisted defection, an abnormality in a normal world. They're society's throwaways, the ones we turn away from. They just want a little something to make their lives better. I offer them a chance.

"It's been my experience that sometimes the smallest scar carries the biggest burden. So, to answer your question, no. I don't strive be like my father and heal the masses. I simply try to touch one person at a time."

Tears threatened to fill Hope's eyes as she nervously held her hand over her scar. It was as if he'd gone into her soul and pulled out her inner most thoughts. So often, she felt turned away because of the scar. Although small to most, it was the barrier she used to push the rest of the world away.

Raymond gathered Hope in his arms. "I didn't mean to make you sad. I just needed you to understand my work. It's important to me that you do."

"Why?"

"Why what?"

"Why is it important that I understand?"

Raymond smiled. His dimples deepened with effect. A playful glint sparked in his eyes. "Truth or dare?" he asked.

"What?" she asked, completely confused.

"Didn't you ever play truth or dare as a child?"

"Yeah, I guess so."

"Okay, truth or dare?"

"Truth," she chose.

"Why did you come here tonight?" he asked.

"I had no choice. Dr. Wescott insisted that I come here tonight to discuss your grandmother's case."

"No, I don't buy that. You could have gotten out of it and you know it. You don't seem like the kind of woman that would do something she really didn't want to do."

Hope went silent. This was getting too complicated.

"Well?" Raymond prompted.

She bit at her lower lip. As the game required, she had answered truthfully, but not necessarily completely. "I already answered the question. It's your turn. Truth or dare?"

"Truth."

She eyed him slyly. "Why did you ask me to come?"

Raymond smiled, expecting the question. "Because I need you to know me outside of the hospital."

"You use the word *need* a lot. You *need* me to understand your work; you *need* me to know you. Why?"

"You and I are connected. We have been since the very first moment we laid eyes on each other. You knew it and so did I. There's a strong emotional attraction that's been building between us. I'd like to do something about it. My turn; truth or dare?"

Hope didn't want to play the game any longer but she was too curious to stop. Truth had gotten too dangerous, so she decided to change. "Dare."

Raymond smiled with all the glee of a triumphant victor. "Kiss me."

A whirlwind of images went through Hope's mind. Kissing Raymond again would be like heaven, she had no doubt. But, like the addictive drugs he mentioned earlier, she wasn't sure she could stop with just one.

Stone-faced, she took his hand and slowly leaned in, just inches from his mouth. Then she stopped, brought his hand to her lips and kissed the inside of his palm. Raymond smiled, enjoying her aversive act. His unexpected humor was definitely worth the suggestive display.

"Truth or dare?" she asked.

"Dare."

She looked at him, wanting to follow his lead. But she knew that if she dared him to kiss her, he would. And that would be the beginning of something she wasn't sure she wanted to start. Unconsciously, she licked at her suddenly dry lips. Suddenly the room grew smaller, closer, and warmer. He sat too close and he looked too good. She gazed into his eyes. Sparks of rich, smoked crystals gazed back at her. Her heart told her everything she needed to know. He was right, there was an attraction between them. So, she did what any hot-blooded woman would do.

Twelve

Hope looked around the beautifully decorated room. She'd never been inside a traditional Japanese restaurant before. She'd never even tasted Japanese food until today. It was everything she'd imagined and more.

Designed for optimum usage, the restaurant was sectioned off by tissue paper–thin room dividers, while scroll-like makimonos of intricate calligraphy hung horizontally on the more solid walls. The exotic decorations suited the space well.

Several large bonsai trees with decorative porcelain figures and inset waterfalls adorned each room. Hope was amazed at the intricate design and detailed perfection of nature's miniature treasures. Reflecting off the black marble floor like a mirrored image, the foliage of the fully-grown trees, the size of the houseplants, was a stunning accent.

Greeters and servers, dressed in elaborately decorated traditional Japanese kimonos with obis, moved silently through the space, catering to the needs and wishes of their patrons. In stealth procession, they dutifully performed their assigned tasks, while all the while smiling and bowing gracefully.

As they first entered, they passed through an open area where a number of patrons were seated along a counter, being served delicate sushi delights being prepared right in front of them. Hope watched in awe as the head chef, wearing a tall, white chimney hat, spooned a large amount of steamed rice onto a thin layer of black seaweed. He evenly spread out the rice, adding more where needed, while constantly wetting his hands in a dish of water.

When the rice had completely covered the seaweed, he secured it by patting it down firmly. Then he picked it up and flipped it onto a small tray of reed-thin wooden sticks. With the rice now on the bottom, he began to add a number of ingredients to the small masterpiece. Salmon, wasabi, tender, green sprouts and thin slices of avocado comprised the inside. Then carefully, the chef rolled the ingredients tightly with laced bamboo skewers. When he unwrapped the skewers, he rolled the ingredients into a dish of sesame seeds. Then, he began cutting the roll diagonally into one-inch pieces.

Hope watched in admiration the skill and precision as the eager patrons sitting along the counter waited anxiously to sample his colorful masterpieces.

Beyond the sushi bar, Hope watched as flames burst into the air while a chef stood at a cooking surface surrounded by seated patrons. Their awed expressions of delight and wonder said it all and pulled a smile from her lips.

Hope and Raymond were eventually led to a private room where they removed their shoes outside and were escorted through tissue paper–thin sliding doors. Once they entered they were served a meal of lobster, shrimp, and scallops with sprouts and seasonings.

Raymond sat silent as Hope sipped her warm tea. She smiled over her cup and looked around the private room. "This is a beautiful restaurant. Thank you for bringing me here. I'm glad you accepted my dare."

"It's my pleasure. I'm really having a good time."

"You say that like you didn't expect to."

"Well, let's face it, Hope, you and I don't exactly have a history of polite conversation. Our temperaments are accelerants at the very least. We are anything but docile."

"I seem to remember you being completely at fault."

"Actually, I recall that you were more openly hostile."

She smiled. "You barged into my exam room."

He returned her smile. "You had me barred from the ER."

"With good cause."

"Ah, come on, you make me sound like some kind of ogre."

"Let's just say that you make a lousy first impression." She began to laugh. He joined in.

"I love that you stand up to me."

"Why wouldn't I?"

"Exactly. I'm only human."

"That remains to be seen."

The spicy repartee was perfectly timed and superbly delivered. Raymond sat back and nodded his head, having enjoyed the saucy wordplay. "You're not too bad at all, Dr. Adams," Raymond admitted freely.

Hope tilted her head and nodded. "You're not too bad yourself, Dr. Gates," she returned the volley, her voice deep with added inflection.

"I'm glad we can laugh about it now."

"Me too."

"Seems we tend to have a very passionate association."

Hope chose to remain silent. She sipped from her cup again as Raymond began to stare. "What?"

"Nothing," he replied as he continued staring at her.

"What? You're staring at me again. Why?"

"Because you're so beautiful," he said matter of factly. "Why else would a man stare a woman? He's overwhelmed by her beauty."

"That is such crap. Does that pick-up line actually work for you?"

"First of all, I'm way past pick-up lines. Secondly, I never say anything I don't mean. And lastly, you are beautiful."

Her cheeks immediately began to warm. "Don't say that."

"Why not? It's true." She looked away quickly, hesitantly. Her heart began pounding rapidly as the knot in her stomach twisted tighter. "I didn't mean to embarrass you. I was just stating fact. You have a loveliness, a beauty that's tender and caring. You hide behind this tough exterior, hoping no one sees the beauty inside. But I see it. And usually when I see an attractive woman I say something."

"Raymond, look, I'm flattered by the compliment and the attention, but I'm going to have to be up front with you. I don't like wasting time, yours or mine. This isn't going to happen."

"What isn't?"

"This thing, between you and me. We're colleagues, that's all. As soon as your grandmother is discharged you'll be gone."

Raymond smiled, his dimples playing havoc with Hope's stomach. "Are you so sure about that?"

"Yes."

"What else do you see in your crystal ball?"

Hope laughed, not expecting the odd remark.

Raymond watched her face as she laughed. It was a nice face. A face he could grow to love. "You feel it too, don't you?"

"Let it go, Raymond."

"I don't think so." His voice was low and sexy.

"I think we should keep this strictly business." Her nervousness was obvious.

Raymond reached across the table and grasped Hope's hand. "Hope, I didn't mean to upset you."

"I'm not a distraction, Raymond."

"I know that."

"We're from two different worlds and I learned a long time ago that those two worlds never come together."

"Looks like I have my work cut out for me."

"What do you mean?"

"I'm going to do everything within my power to prove you wrong."

Hope watched the determined glint in his eye. She had no doubt that he would, as he said, do everything within his power, but the problem wasn't his. "That wasn't a challenge."

"I'm very attracted to you."

"I'm attracted to you, too."

"So what are we going to do about it?"

"Nothing. We're going to be adults about it and do absolutely nothing. You and I are like oil and water. Nothing good can come from it." Raymond opened his mouth to rebut as Hope interrupted and continued. "And before you say something else, let's change the subject."

Raymond laughed riotously as their server entered the little room, and the meal was served.

The conversation during the remainder of the evening was kept light and easy. Unfortunately, by this time Hope's insides were in turmoil. She listened to Raymond as he excitedly discussed his foundation and the building he was having constructed. She held onto every word as he described a delicate surgery, while all along chastising herself and suppressing the building desire she continued to feel.

No excuses; she just wanted him. The realization was staggering. She knew that she was attracted to him. She just wasn't aware of the extent.

The meal ended with the splendid treat of Raymond conversing easily in the owner's native tongue. As they prepared to leave, Hope leaned over to him. "I didn't know you could speak Japanese."

He helped her up from the floor. His easy smile broadened. "Neither did I."

Hope burst with laughter until she realized that as Raymond helped her up from the low table, her body pressed provocatively against his. She took a deep breath, but remained in the warm place.

Raymond looked down into her soft brown eyes. The reflection of her desire met him as he leaned down to touch her lips. The kiss was gentle and complete, then continued as wanton need drove them both with lustful yearning. Fitting with perfect accord, they held the embrace for a lifetime. As their lips slowly parted, breathlessly she held onto him.

Hope reached up and touched his face. This was the face

in her dreams, the face that had haunted her since the moment they had met. Clean-shaven, the soft angles of his strong jaw were silky smooth to the touch.

Hope drew her hand away suddenly and headed to the door of their private room. She turned back to him. "That was probably not a good idea."

"You're right," he followed her through the restaurant, "that was a great idea."

As soon as they stepped outside they realized that a storm had reared up. Lightning lit the sky as bright as day, while the sound of thunder rocketed through the streets.

Raymond handed the valet the car's stub and the young man instantly ran off around the corner as they waited under the awning. A few moments of pregnant silence passed between them.

Within a few minutes Raymond's car pulled up in front of them. "Thank you for dinner, I had a really good time," she said. She couldn't help but smile.

"You're very welcome. I had a good time too."

"I'm gonna get a cab." She began looking down the street for the familiar bright yellow glow in the darkness.

"I don't think so," Raymond said, as he opened the passenger side door. "I'm taking you home."

"That's not necessary."

He gave her a no-nonsense expression as he held the door open. She conceded and got in. Raymond handed the valet a healthy tip and slid behind the wheel. He asked for Hope's address and pulled off into the night.

The drive to Hope's apartment was too short as far as Raymond was concerned. He tried to focus on the light evening traffic and torrential rain, but his eyes roamed too often to Hope, sitting next to him. They arrived at her front door much too soon.

Raymond gathered an umbrella from the back seat and escorted Hope to her brownstone. Lined with oak trees and flower-boxed windows, the street was clean and neat. He looked up at the tall building. Its wide double door was welcoming. "This is nice," he said.

"I'm subletting for the moment, but the building is going condo. I either have to buy it or leave."

"What have you decided?"

"I'm still weighing my options."

As they approached the front door Raymond held his hand out for her keys. Hope hesitated then relented. He slid the key into the door's lock and held it open for her. Once inside, they walked up to the second floor to her apartment. She stopped at her front door and he repeated the action, then handed her the keys.

A moment of silence swelled between them as they stood and looked at each other, almost trancelike. "Well," they said at the same time, then stopped. "I'd better go now," they said again in unison then stopped. "You first," they spoke together again. "No after you," they said again comically. Then out of nowhere, he kissed her. His lips were soft, gentle and calming. Neither embraced the other, making the kiss almost sweet and innocent if not for the rage of surprised passion they both felt at the touch. The end came too soon.

"What was that for?" she asked when he leaned back.

"Every first date needs to be sealed."

"This wasn't a first date."

He smiled knowingly. "Are you sure?" She chose to remain silent as they stood at the open door in uncomfortable ease as a disquieting silence slipped between them. Raymond stared down at her. She looked away, refusing to look into his eyes. He reached down and took her hand. He brought it to his lips and kissed it. "Good night, Hope."

"Good night, Raymond." He turned back to the steps. She stepped back, but remained at the open door. He walked down four steps, then stopped. He turned to meet her eyes, then slowly walked back to her. He leaned down to kiss her gently. The kiss was chaste. He turned and walked back to the steps a second time.

Hope closed her eyes and reveled in the feel of his mouth. She smiled, realizing that she hadn't stopped smiling and laughing since she left Raymond's office. Spending time with him was just what the doctor ordered.

It was an incredible evening and the most perfect almost-maybe-date she'd never been on. Because in all actually, it wasn't a date, was it? It was two colleagues getting together to discuss and diagnose the condition of a patient.

So why did it feel like a date? Why did she want to reach over and touch his hand at dinner? Why did she need to laugh at the silly jokes he made? Why did she hang on every word he uttered as if he'd spoken oracles?

Lightning flashed and the low rumble of thunder shook the building. She wanted to call out his name, but she knew that if she did, she'd want to call it out all night. She touched her lips. The kiss was still richly pressed there.

What am I doing? Raymond was charming and thoughtful and attentive. He laughed and listened as she amusingly relayed comical events in the ER, and he relayed his own outrageous experiences in private practice. He made her feel like she was the only woman in the universe. So, why was she letting him go? "Raymond," she called out before realizing it herself. He stopped midway down the steps. She heard the footsteps of her destiny returning to her.

Within seconds he stood before her.

He reached out and touched the side of her face. She backed away slightly when his hand fell upon the small scar. He smiled at her sensitivity and leaned in and kissed the tiny mark. Hope nearly fell from the tender act.

She backed up, allowing him passage into the apartment. Raymond stepped inside and slid his arm around Hope's waist in one smooth move. He kissed her with all the passion he'd been feeling.

Breathless, she backed away and held her hand up to him. "I don't know what to feel when I'm with you. I'm off balance." She looked up at him and shook her head. "You confuse the hell out of me."

Raymond smiled. "You do the exact opposite to me. Suddenly everything in my life is crystal clear. I know exactly what I want." He stroked her brow lovingly. "I want you in my life, Hope."

"Where is this going?"

He smiled easily. "All the way." Raymond began gently kissing the soft planes of her face.

Hope shuddered as butterflies took flight in her stomach. "What am I going to do with you, Dr. Gates?"

"Love me."

"I can't."

"You already do."

Hope took Raymond's hand and led him through the darkness to her bedroom. Her heart beat faster than it had ever beaten. She wanted this, she wanted Raymond. But the apprehension she felt vanished at his first touch. She closed her eyes and reveled in the feel of his hands on her.

Raymond stopped as soon as he reached her bedroom. He stood in the doorway. Hope turned to him and slowly removed his suit jacket and undid the loosened tie's knot around his neck. She pulled at one end, slowly drawing the other end from his collar.

She willed her hand to remain steady, unbuttoned his shirt and pulled the ends from his pants. When the shirt was completely undone she ran the palms of her hand over his bare chest, feeling the powerful muscles beneath his deep honey-toned skin.

Slowly, with newly skilled fingers, she released his belt buckle and unzipped his pants, sliding them down his legs. Her hand brushed against the reflection of her handiwork. She trembled inside as anticipation eclipsed her hesitation. She reached up and pulled his mouth down to hers. The kiss joined their souls as the hot sweetness of his mouth made her bolder.

She slipped her hand between their bodies and felt the stark firmness of his arousal. Raymond muttered something inaudible as her hands, finding a new talent, began an exquisite torture.

With a steady stare, she stepped back. Swiftly, Raymond drew her body into his arms and carried her across the room to the bed. Hope's body quivered in anticipation. Raymond felt the slight tremor and stopped with her still wrapped in his arms. "If you're not sure . . ." he began.

She placed her finger to his lips. "I'm very sure."

Raymond laid her across the bed and, taking his time, unbuttoned her shirt as she had done to him. He pulled the fabric away, exposing the lacy swell of her breasts. He leaned in to gently kiss the lace covered tips, then, using his stiffened tongue taunted her until she moaned aloud.

He unsnapped the front clasp and released the mounds of tender flesh. Relishing one and then the other, he tormented her until her body writhed with need. She watched in awe as his skilled mouth suckled, taunted and teased her hardened nipple to maddness.

Purposefully, his hand came to the waistband of her jeans. He unsnapped, unzipped and lowered them to just below her hips. Then a sharp intake of air sent a shiver through her as he stopped to admire her black-laced thong. The knowing smile that crept across his lips spoke volumes. "Thank you," he rasped huskily and ran his finger along the thin black band of the one material separating him from his treasure. Her stomach somersaulted when his hands circled behind her and toyed with the elastic lace then grasped the firmness of her buttocks sending a bolt of breathless rapture through her.

"Do you have any idea how much I want you right now?" he whispered in her ear as his tongue teased her lobe.

She smiled her answer. "Ditto."

He leaned back and looked at her face. The hot passion of his desire reflected in her eyes. He removed her wayward bra and jeans then laid her face down on the bed. He placed her arms at her side then moved up beside her body. With just enough pressure and tender strength, he began massaging her neck and shoulders.

Hope closed her eyes and reveled in the sensational feeling of his hands caressing her body. He moved to her back, to her buttocks, to her legs. Then she felt the tender kisses sending a swell of ecstasy on overload. She rolled over and pulled him down to her. Their mouths connected sending a burst of heated passion through her body. "Come inside," she whispered.

He smiled. "Soon," he promised.

His kisses increased as he traveled down her stomach and across the thin, banded lace. Teasingly, he nipped at the elastic band sending wave after wave of writhing desire through her. "Raymond," she moaned, as his skilled hands pleasured her body. The rapture of his touch entranced her with wanton need. Gradually he entwined their bodies, lifting her to kneel as his equal.

Face to face they touched, kissed, caressed, and embraced. She stroked his chest feeling her way down to the band of his boxers. In turn, he taunted her with reckless kisses that set her body burning.

"Take this off," she commanded brazenly, as she ran her finger around the band of his boxers. Raymond smiled, did her bidding, then reached over and pulled a small circular packet from his wallet and protected them. Now together, freed of all but one hindrance, she laid him back onto her bed and straddled his body. With the slow teasing deliberance of a burlesque artist, she removed her thong.

Looking down, she leaned in and kissed him. His hand came up and grasped her waist, holding her in place. She lifted her hips and lowered herself onto his hardness. She gasped with the exquisite fullness as her body swayed. Arching back, Raymond's hands covered her beasts, massaging and kneading her tenderly. As she began the slow ride to ecstasy, he sat up, taking each breast into his mouth. Her nails bit into his flesh.

In rhythmic rapture they rocked in cadence to an undulating swell. Moving up and down in slow steady waves they felt the surge of passion pulling them closer and closer to the pinnacle of pure bliss. Building endlessly as their pace quickened, each wave of passion yielded abundant currents until the ultimate quake shattered in blinding white lights, taking them over the edge. Climatic spasms exploded in repeated brilliance.

Their bodies stiffened as the last remnant drained, leaving them weak and worn. Raymond gathered Hope into his arms and laid back, bringing her down on top of his body. She lay there for what seemed like an eternity. "Sleep," he said as he stroked her back. And she did, with as much peace and calm as ever before.

Thirteen

Raymond was feeling good, although he had broken both of the only two rules he'd always lived by; rule number one, never have a romantic relationship with someone you work with, and number two, never forget rule number one. But he didn't care. He had found Hope.

He smiled just thinking about their evening together. They had made love, slept, then awoke in the middle of the night and made love again. She was so giving and loving, he could have laid there with her all day. But regrettably, he had an early meeting in town.

With his top down and an early morning disc jockey joking on the radio, Raymond headed south down Broadway with a broad smile on his face. He had the perfect day planned. First, a meeting on the Lower East Side, then a quick stop at the hospital and finally, back to the office to clear his desk of month-long, piled-up paperwork. Then, a quick visit with his grandmother and finally, a nice quiet evening meal with Hope.

Thankfully, it wouldn't be the usual glamour-filled day, with affluent socialites seeking silicone injections, tummy tucks, liposuction, and various implants. Raymond shook his head, always amazed as he recalled the endless line of men and women, all in search of the fountain of youth via his skilled scalpel.

Breezing quickly, he darted in and out of traffic like a professional New York City cab driver on a five-minute lunch break. Never missing an opportunity to further his advance, he cautiously maneuvered his 1956 Jaguar Roadster with the precision and accuracy of his surgical blade. He veered into the left lane, avoiding the frequent stops of an early morning trash truck. Checking his rear mirror, he instantaneously swerved to the right, and zipped two blocks nearly traffic free.

Then, hearing the familiar tire screech and accompanying crash of metal, the once quickly breezing traffic was now a bottleneck of congestion. Raymond slowed to an almost crawl as the traffic stopped dead in front of him. He ventured a squinted glance to the next block. It was the typical New York City accident.

Two cars, both taking the right-of-way, met the hard way, connecting with each other's bumper. And, instead of maneuvering their cars out of the flow of traffic, both men, apparently uninjured, jumped out of their vehicles to instantly begin the ritual argument of fault and blame. Raymond shook his head in mock amusement. This was the one thing he detested about Manhattan traffic: the total lack of skilled drivers.

Stalled for no apparent reason, Raymond took a moment to observe his surroundings, something rarely done by busy New Yorkers. Often taken for granted, Broadway was one of the most legendary and rightfully acclaimed streets in the world.

Famous for its lavish theater productions and its extravagant stage shows, this was the heart and soul of Manhattan. Drama, musicals, comedies, and revivals all found a cheering audience on the glitzy glamour of the Great White Way. Between 41st and 54th, the streets beat to the pulse of live performance. Often starring the cream of Hollywood, nearly ten blocks between 6th and 8th avenues was the world's center stage.

Patrons of the arts and lovers of theatre, dressed in evening formal or matinee finery, came faithfully to witness the splendor of the latest Broadway offerings.

With the extravagant Lyceum Theater being its matriarch and the modern Majestic its babe, the revitalization of the stage-era hadn't seen such excitement since the Ziegfeld Follies days of the 1920s.

But at this hour, the glittering lights of the night before had long since been turned off. The Great White Way was now dimmed and desolate, yet numerous people still mingled about. Dawn was on the horizon and downtown traffic was already heavy.

After creeping along at twenty miles an hour for the last ten minutes, Raymond finally found a window of opportunity and accelerated around a slow-moving car whose driver gawked blatantly at the minor fender-bender. He wheeled his car around a slow driver, then accelerated to make up for lost time.

With the cell phone's wireless attachment in his ear, Raymond finally found time to patiently listen to a message left by his office assistant the day before. He smiled when he heard the exasperation in her voice while relaying a message from Laine Herrington and Mimi Brown. Apparently, they had called several times yesterday and were very insistent on speaking with him.

Knowing exactly what Laine wanted, Raymond shook his head automatically. He was in too good a mood to deal with Laine. They'd had the same conversation before. Obviously, just like with his cousin Tony, she wasn't going to take no for an answer.

He also knew what Mimi called about. Just five months earlier, using a series of collagen injections, he had already enhanced her thin lips to give her mouth a fuller, more sensuous appearance. Now she wanted him to redo the procedure in order to make her lips even fuller.

Nevertheless, true to Mimi's nature, she still hadn't taken no for an answer. But, unfortunately, she'd have to this time. What she wanted done was not only ethically questionable, but totally unnecessary and dangerous, even in the best and

most skilled hands. He made a mental note to call Mimi back
with an even firmer answer.

Raymond continued listening to the messages. In great detail his assistant reviewed his morning meetings, then
continued to list his afternoon appointments. Raymond listened while making mental notes to reschedule certain
appointments and cancel others. When the message ended, he
auto-dialed his office to leave his changes.

Snagged in another early-morning traffic jam, Raymond
used the time to dictate added notations to a proposal he was
making to the board of directors of his foundation.

Since the new building would be complete in a few
months, he had to come up with a name. After last night, he'd
decided on the perfect name. He smiled again as his thoughts
centered on Hope. She was indeed the hope that his life had
been waiting for. He openly laughed at the thought of
Mamma Lou telling him that he needed hope in his life. Then,
his laughter ended suddenly, as he wondered if she had anything to do with their meeting. But how could she have, right?

As traffic slowed again, Raymond instantly returned to
thinking about Hope. She was the most sensuous and sexy
woman he'd ever met and his body hardened just thinking
about their night together. He smiled as the memory of her
body fit and formed to his perfectly, giving their union an
ideal bond. He found that he loved to watch as she reached
her climax. Giving her pleasure was the most erotic sight
he'd ever witnessed. His brow raised and his smile broadened thinking of spending the next eighty years giving her
pleasure.

He stopped at a traffic light as a woman crossed the street
with a baby in a stroller and a young child in tow. He thought
of Hope. He smiled thinking of the children they'd have and
the life they'd share together. He was on cloud nine knowing
that Hope would be his future.

When the traffic freed, he turned the corner to see the magnificent sight and all questions faded from his mind. Beneath

the awesome shadow of the Brooklyn Bridge, it stood just as strong and just as determined. Comfortably located between the Lower East Side and the East Village, the as-yet-unnamed building stood in an uncomfortable state on a cobblestone street, somewhere between total disaster and complete ruin.

Four stories high, with a columned entryway, double-hung antique windows, and ornate moldings, the edifice was magnificent. Having held up for over half a century, it remained stately and regal. It was originally constructed in the post-war era of the early 1950's. A peacetime boom in the national advancement had re-energized the building industry. Developed with modern advancements and progressive technology, the structure was a modern-day marvel in its time.

But, now, the forward achievements were a crumbled mass of debris, overflowing in the huge trash receptacles stationed beneath the massive, windowless openings. Levels of wooded scaffolding framed the outer façade, as workmen busied themselves removing layers of grime to refurbish the original brick front.

Raymond looked up at the once-great Baroque-style building, shielded behind the scaffold. It dwarfed its surroundings. Distressed but not undaunted, from the outside it still looked every bit the stately manor it once was. Of all the location sites he had visited, this one had immediately caught his eye. He knew that this structure would alter his life, as he transformed the once-condemned structure into a place of hope.

Surrounded by vacant buildings, artist's lofts, and the hopes and dreams of thousands, it was the perfect location. Situated on a quiet street, recessed and unassuming, it was close enough for comfort, yet far enough away to heal.

Never having been an elegant establishment, it was a far stretch of the imagination to see it as anything other than what it was. To most, this dilapidated structure would never be more then a shell.

But Raymond saw it differently. When he looked up at

the five-story structure, he saw a building filled with possibilities. A place that could be called home. A place where daunted refugees could go and rest from the misery of their life's trials. He saw a shelter to those in need of hope.

Construction had begun nearly four months ago. He had hired the best. And, backed by several well-established professionals, both in and out of the medical field, he gained the financial support needed to complete his dream.

Raymond looked up at the renovation site as he approached. It was progressing even more quickly than he had hoped. He wanted the building completed and fully operational by the middle of summer. It was the end of spring and although there was still a lot of work to be done, it was certainly taking shape.

It was nearly six o'clock in the morning and the construction crew had already arrived and had been working steadily. Busying themselves, the workmen labored tirelessly to transform this relic into his dream.

Trash and debris littered the once-elegant front yard as the stoic, iron gates gapped open, extending their arms wide. Raymond passed through the open doors and nodded to several workmen as he entered. The entrance hall, soon to be the reception area, had already been electrically wired and dry walled. A number of workmen were standing on ladders and wooden platforms using a thick plaster compound and sealer to join the sheets of drywall. The concrete floor was still littered with the remains of degraded ceiling tiles and scrapped plaster.

Raymond stepped over the piles of trash, turned around, and eyed the open, airy space. The fifteen-foot original windows had been reset and scraped clean of the layered paint they once had. Brilliant sunlight streamed in, giving the area a whole new radiance. He could easily envision its transformed beauty. He nodded approvingly at the progress made since his last visit.

He turned and passed through the inner doors to the next

area. Once inside, he looked around at the cavernous space of the enormous, hulled shell. This area was far less complete. The walls had been gutted and remained open to electrical wiring, as did the ceiling. Secured beams crisscrossed the ceiling, giving the space an exposed, warehouse feel.

Although the foundation stood strong, the inside walls had to be completely gutted and rebuilt. He watched as several workmen, using sledge hammers, pounded their way through plaster and wood-framed walls.

Raymond walked over to the foreman's worktable and began flipping through the numerous blue prints scattered about. He settled on one floor plan. Taking time to read the particulars, he held it up against the far wall. Pleased that everything was done to his specifications, he placed the blueprint back on the table just as the foremen arrived.

"Hey, Doc. How are you? Sorry I'm late." Greer removed his jacket and loosened his tie. He reached out to shake Raymond's hand.

Raymond extended his hand and smiled his usual good cheer. "I just arrived myself." He looked around the immediate area and nodded. "It's really starting to take shape."

Greer followed Raymond's gazed and nodded in agreement. "Yep, the place is really coming along." He reached down and grabbed the hardhat that had Raymond's name printed on it. He handed it to him, then picked up his own hardhat and slipped it on. "Why don't we start at the top and work our way down? I think you're going to pleased with the results." Greer grabbed the rolled blueprints and led the way.

Raymond put on the hardhat, removed his jacket and followed the foreman back out into the foyer area. From there they took the suspended staircase to the second level and continued in the elevator to the top floor.

The two men began talking as they went, with Greer pointing out details and specifications of note. Raymond asked inquisitive questions regarding particulars he'd noticed.

Greer, well aware of Raymond's limited knowledge of construction, spoke with distinct detail, laying out the finer points of the engineering and construction.

"We're still waiting for the building inspector's report, but I don't foresee any problems. If anything, they should pay you for raising the neighborhood's standards. I tell ya," Greer looked around admiringly, "when this place is complete, the real estate market will go through the roof. It's a good thing that you purchased the adjoining property for phases two and three. In another five years the property values will be sky high. You bought in at the perfect time."

"Timing is everything."

"Just let me know when you're ready for another partner. Although, I'll have to work on trade. Your guys are too rich for me."

Greer referred to the partnership that Raymond had with his family and close friends. With their backing and support the project moved smoothly.

"How's Martha?" Raymond asked. Greer and his wife Martha had been Raymond's Connecticut neighbors since he had moved in six years ago. High school sweethearts, Greer and Martha had been married for over thirty-five years and were still hopelessly in love.

"She's fine. She's dying to get that new botox thing done to her face. But frankly, injecting one's forehead with botulism sounds like trouble just waiting to happen."

"I'm with you on that one. That's why I don't offer the service in my offices. It hasn't been clinically tested to my satisfaction. I don't know if it ever will be."

"Man," Greer began to chuckle, "some of the faces I've seen . . ." he chuckled again letting the statement trail off with humor.

Raymond shook his head with the levity. "No matter how many warnings you hear, and no matter how many botched procedures, people still insist on getting it done. I spend at lest three hours a week talking patients out of having it done and ten hours correcting the mess that was made after they've had it done."

"You know my brother had it done?"

"Paulie?"

"Yep, Paulie. He said it was a boost to his acting career. He got a nice sized part in a local television cop drama and he says he owes it all to botox."

"What about the thirty-five years of acting classes, parts in small productions and all those television commercials he did? Doesn't that count for something?" Raymond asked.

"Nope. He says it was botox that made him young again. He says, it made him a star."

The two men shook their heads, both trying not to laugh aloud. "So," Raymond began as the elevator doors cranked opened, "since Paulie had some work done, are you ready for me to do a little work on you?"

Greer guffawed and nearly dropped the rolled blueprints back down the elevator shaft. Raymond laughed at his stunned expression. It had been a running joke between them. "I won't even justify that with an answer."

As Raymond stepped off of the elevator, he was amazed by what he saw. The top floor was completely done. The space had been divided into several rooms and each room was complete. The two men walked from room to room, examining each in turn. Greer unrolled the blueprints he'd been carrying and pointed out several things to Raymond. Afterwards, the two continued the assessment on the next floor down.

They took the newly refurbished stairs to the fourth floor. "I have the modified blueprints from the architect, ready for your signature downstairs." As soon as Greer began showing some of the particulars on the blueprint, Raymond's cell phone rang. He excused himself and answered. It was the office, calling to check in, and to review and confirm his revised schedule. As soon as he closed the phone and Greer began speaking again, the phone rang a second time. Raymond excused himself again and answered. This time he turned and walked away. Greer's brow rose with interest. The conversation he'd overheard sounded serious. Whatever was happening didn't sound good.

Raymond flipped the cell closed and spun to confer with Greer. "We're going to have to postpone this until later," he said as he headed to the elevator, then impatiently turned to take the stairs.

"Sure, just give me a call." Greer wanted to ask if there was anything he could help with, but not being in the medical profession, decided that would sound strange. So, he simply offered to have the blueprints hand-delivered to his office that morning. Raymond nodded and disappeared through the stairway doors.

By the time Greer walked over to the large row of windows at the front of the building, Raymond was darting across the street to his car. Whatever was going on must have been major.

Fourteen

Something was wrong, Louise was sure of it. Hope had come in earlier, angry. Raymond had called repeatedly asking if she'd been in. Something was going on. Somehow, something had happened and it was up to her to put it right. And if that plan included getting sick again, so be it.

Louise opened another candy packet and took a bite of the chewy, nutty candy. She laid back and reminisced back to when she'd first decided to embark on her current endeavor. Raymond, her grandson, proudly stood at his cousin's side. Overwhelmingly pleased, he dutifully pledged to bear witness to Tony's marriage to Madison. At that instant, Louise noted a certain glint in Raymond's eyes. That glint had immediately sparked her creative, matchmaking juices.

Matchmaking, Louise had learned from past experience, although richly rewarding, was an extremely tricky enterprise. Each plan's undertaking, no matter how complicated and complex, had to be fine-tuned to perfection. Plus, and most importantly, she needed to consider the two individuals involved. Added to that was the awesome responsibility of successfully blending the unique personalities of the participants while encouraging the delicate union.

So, when you decide to change a person's life for the better, you undoubtedly had better have a dammed good plan. Particularly when that person suspects something and watches every move you make. Without a doubt, Louise had the perfect plan. As a matter of fact, she'd had the perfect plan for the last six months. Unfortunately, implementation wasn't as straightforward as she anticipated. She had the means, she had the know-how, and she had the when. The only thing missing was the who. Herein lay her dilemma.

Even though the qualifications were uncomplicated, finding Miss Who wasn't. After dozens of blind leads and failed attempts, Louise realized that finding the elusive Miss Who was more difficult than she anticipated. Each time she'd thought that she'd found the perfect woman for her grandson, the woman turned out to be Miss Totally Wrong, Miss No Way, or Miss Not On Your Life.

Perplexed, Louise had never imagined that it would be so difficult to find a woman of style, grace and integrity. One with a sharp intellect, a pleasant personality, and enough inner fortitude to easily match wits with her grandson. And, since lowering her standards was out of the question, Louise had concluded that a change in venue was in order.

So she broadened her horizons.

While traveling in the guise of impromptu visits, she innocently queried friends and associates about available relatives. Within the span of four weeks, she'd met dozens of women, but all to no avail. Thus, before desperation took over, she decided to head to the big city. After all, she reasoned, how hard would it be to find the perfect single woman in New York City.

To her grandson's delight, she was spending time with him in his hometown. He had often begged her to come and enjoy the awesome pleasures of the "City of Lights." But his overly suspicious nature proved too sensitive. He watched her like a hawk and balked at every tiny suggestion she proposed. So, just when Louise had about given up hope, fate and fortune stepped in. But, now there was trouble.

This was the perfect match and she was going to see Raymond happily married even if she had to eat every candy bar in the gift shop. Louise, with annoyance, took another bite of the sweet, chewy bar.

* * *

"Unbelievable." Hope slammed her tray on the table and plopped into the seat across from her sister and next to the large, corrugated box. Her coffee spilled on to her French fries but she barely noticed.

Faith looked up at her sister as she returned to the table. Then, she focused her attention on the large box she'd deposited on the chair before getting her coffee. "Hope, what's really going on?"

"The man is unbelievable."

"So you've said." She leaned over and curiously opened the box as Hope continued to rant.

"He's just unbelievable."

"You're repeating yourself."

Hope glared at Faith and gritted her teeth in defiance. Then she went into a seemingly endless rant. "I just can't believe his nerve. He's so, he's so . . ." She searched in vain for the appropriate wording.

Completely forgetting about her own food tray, Faith reached into the box and grabbed a sweatshirt. She unfolded it and held it up to her chest, admiring the fit. She placed it back into the box and grabbed another shirt. "Unbelievable. I believe that's the word of choice," she offered dryly.

Hope looked at her sister and squinted her eyes with warning, finally breaking from her rant. "Yes, that it. He's absolutely unbelievable. He wanted me to come to his office last evening to discuss his grandmother's case. Apparently *Mr. I'm Too Important* is too busy to meet here so I have to go to him."

"So, why didn't you just say no and not go?"

"It wasn't that easy. It was a mandatory request from Wescott."

"Okay, since when do you care about what Hugh wants?" Faith asked with added inflection. "Well, did Mr. Unbelievable at least spring for dinner or something?"

Hope looked at her sister strangely. "Dinner? Faith, are you listening to me?

"I heard you. But did he take you to dinner afterwards?"

"Yes, we ate afterwards. So what?"

Faith, only half satisfied with her sister's answer, smiled and took out another sweatshirt. "Dinner is always a good start."

Hope's brow rose. "It was just one simple dinner, Faith. No big deal."

"Where'd you go?"

Hope took a deep breath and looked at her sister. "It was some Japanese restaurant near his office."

"Did you have a nice time?"

"Yes."

"Did he drive you home?"

Hope paused to consider her answer. "Yes, he took me home," she answered testily.

"Then what happened?"

"He got up and left me."

"What do you mean he got up and left you?"

"It was storming outside, so he kind of waited until the stormed passed then left."

"Uh huh," Faith nodded. "What did you do in the meantime?" Hope went silent and looked away. Faith's mouth opened wide in shock. "You slept with him."

"I don't want to talk about this anymore."

Faith instantly broke out in a bright grin. "He got up this morning and left without saying anythiing, didn't he?"

"That's not the point. The fact remains that man's attitude is unbelievable."

Faith smiled mischievously. "Actually, that's exactly the point. Why don't you just admit it? You're angry because you slept with him and he left."

"I admit nothing."

"Suit yourself," Faith said, innocently folding the shirt and placing it back into the box.

"What does he think? Am I supposed to be impressed or something? So what if he has connections? So what if he has influence?"

Faith continued folding the last sweatshirt. The bold, blue lettering of the University of Pennsylvania sweatshirt lay on top of the pile. She adjusted the sweatshirt and placed it back in the oversized box. "Hope, even you've got to admit, the man is impressive. Look at all of this."

"I am not impressed. So what if he can have a few university sweatshirts delivered the next day. Anybody can do that."

"No, I don't think so. And actually it was the next morning," Hope looked at her, totally stunned by her betrayal, "to be exact."

"He probably just went on-line."

"Since when does anything arrive just hours after it's ordered on-line? Please, girl. Just admit it, the man is good."

"Big deal. The University of Pennsylvania is just in the next state over."

Faith reopened the box and began shuffling through the various colored sweatshirts. "Princeton University, Harvard University, Yale University, California Institute of Technology, Duke University, Massachusetts Institute of Technology, Stanford University, Dartmouth College, Columbia University, and of course, the one that started it all, University of Pennsylvania."

"Are you quite finished?"

Faith giggled in spite of Hope's stern expression. She applauded herself for making such an unshakable case. "Yeah."

Hope ignored her completely. "He went to Westcott first to have his grandmother transferred to Manhattan Medical, then had my entire life rearranged to suit himself. I spend half my time in the ER and half on the fifth floor. Can you believe that?" She rambled for another few moments uninterrupted.

Then, finally, Faith shrugged her shoulders innocently. "Manhattan Medical is a great facility. They have every major, modern medical convenience imaginable. I don't blame him for wanting the best for his grandmother."

Hope looked at her sister with annoyance. She wasn't supposed to agree with him. She was supposed to stay loyal to Golden Heart. "So what are we, chopped liver?"

"No, of course not. Golden Heart is wonderful. But Manhattan Medical is arguably the best private hospital in the area. Their trauma unit alone generates over twenty thousand patients a year."

Exasperated by the lack of solidarity, Hope looked at Faith as if she'd grown two heads. "What?"

"Hope, you're getting all worked up over nothing."

"I am not," Hope crossed her arms over her chest defiantly.

"So, take a few days to hang out with a nice older woman. Read a book or two. Get some rest. What's the harm?"

"I don't like my life being altered and mandated to me. Did I tell you that I have to go to the fundraiser this weekend?"

"Repeatedly," Faith added dryly, as she picked up and sipped the last of her tea.

"Well, it bears repeating."

"You know, you should seriously think about reducing your caffeine intake. You're getting way to upset over something so small," Faith said mockingly. Then, with a suddenly knowing smile, she added, "What's really going on with you and Dr. Gates?"

"What? Nothing!" she nearly shouted. Then, she hushed her tone and looked around the emptying cafeteria. "Nothing."

Faith began laughing. "I can't believe I didn't see it earlier. He fits your profile perfectly, doesn't he?"

"What profile?"

"He's a wealthy plastic surgeon, apparently gorgeous, probably lives in an ivory tower, has a dozen women after him, and is completely unavailable."

"Oh, please." Hope tossed her hand up to dismiss the notion quickly.

"You are attracted to men that are totally unattainable."

"I am not."

"Oh, please. Every man you ever dated was either some

tragic figure or some lost cause. They either went back to their ex-wife or"—she paused for added interest as Hope glared at her—"or they were rich jerks who were cowardly, daddy's boys and not man enough to stand up for themselves."

Hope looked at her through slits of threatening eyes as she continued. "For example there was a certain ex-husband whom you helped through med school because his father had cut him off financially. You marry the fool then he up and divorces you 'cause his daddy threatens to cut him out of the will. And on top of that, he marries some knucklehead that his dad picked out for him."

Hope went still as Faith continued. But to her surprise, the raw anger was gone. It was true; Nolan had no intention of keeping his vows and standing up to his father. It took him six months just to admit to his father that they'd even gotten married.

"Why don't you just admit that Dr. Gates is someone special?"

A pause of hurt slipped in, then just as quickly slipped out. Hope was surprised by her reaction. Usually, the mention of those eighteen months of marriage instantly brought tears to her eyes. But now, other than a passing annoyance, she felt nothing.

"Raymond's nothing to me," she stated coldly, feeling the same anguish she felt when she awoke to a cold, empty bed. The same feeling she had when Nolan left her without even a note.

"Doesn't sound like nothing," Faith assured her.

"Nothing," she reiterated, then paused and began again. "He actually had the audacity to accuse me of being self-righteous. Can you believe that? Me, self-righteous?"

"Well Hope, you do have a tendency to come off a bit preachy."

Hope's mouth dropped open. "Excuse me? Preachy? Since when have I ever been preachy?"

"Oh please, since when are you not?"

"I presume that's a professional opinion."

"No, a sisterly observation. I've known you all my life, that makes me an authority. I'm your younger sister, that makes me an expert." Faith smiled sweetly at the grimacing Hope.

Suddenly, they laughed out loud until Hope accidentally hit the box with her knee and began her rant again. "And another thing," she began with a deep breath, intending on another long speech about the unfairness of her current situation. "Day shift? I haven't been on day shift in over two years," Hope blew out exasperated. "All of this because of one man."

"Ah, but what a man." Faith said in dreamlike state.

"What do you know? You've never even met him."

"I don't have to. Rumor has it that he's gorgeous with a capital 'G'."

"His grandmother just checked in the other day. How can there be rumors about him already?"

"Your little performance yesterday morning was all around the hospital by yesterday afternoon."

"Oh please."

"Girl, you know the rumor mill gets to grinding quicker when gossip is this juicy. So tell me, did you really kick him, you know where?"

"What? No."

Faith sucked her teeth loudly and looked overly disappointed. "I didn't think so." She shook her head silently at the misinformation. "So what's he really like? Everybody's dying to know."

"He's an arrogant jerk, typical blade. He thinks that because he's a surgeon, the world should revolve around him."

"He's not just any surgeon, Hope. He's a well-known cosmetic surgeon. He was even featured on the Discovery Channel."

"Faith, baboons are featured on the Discovery Channel. I don't think that Raymond being on is any big deal."

"You know, Hope, I don't believe I've ever heard you protest so much."

"Meaning?"

"Meaning, what did ye old Shakespeare say? Oh yeah, me thinks thou doth protest too much."

"Well, me thinks thou has lost thy mind. 'Cause there's nothing remotely appealing about that man. He's the biggest snob I've ever met."

Faith smiled, knowing her sister too well. If she truly disregarded someone, she wouldn't even acknowledge that they existed much less talk about them for half an hour straight. "So what you're saying is that we just spent my entire break talking about a man that you care nothing about? And all those rumors about how handsome he is, how generous he is, and how skilled he is, are just that, rumors?"

"Yes, well, no, well . . . he's kind of cute in a handsome sort of way. He's got these dimples that wink at you when he smiles or laughs and he's got hazel-colored eyes that have yellow-green flecks." Hope looked off with a dreamy expression, then bit at her lower lip with a slightly tilted, wicked grin. "He's sweet and caring with his grandmother. And he's tall with broad shoulders and graceful hands that . . . and his body . . ." She trailed off as Faith's already wide grin expanded.

"What?"

"Girl—"

"Don't even try it. He and I just have to work together until his grandmother is discharged, which will be as soon as possible."

"Sounds like there's a lot more to the rumors than meets the eye."

"I have to go. My shift starts in fifteen minutes." Hope stood and picked up her tray. "I don't know who started all of these ridiculously childish rumors floating around this place, but it's gotten totally out of hand."

"Hey wait a minute, what do you want to do with this box of sweatshirts?"

Hope paused. She'd forgotten all about the special delivery

she'd received first thing this morning. She came back to the table. "What am I supposed to do with them?"

"They were a gift. Keep them and wear them."

Hope picked up the hefty box, then began her tirade all over again. "Unbelievable . . ." Just then her beeper sounded. She put the box down and looking down at the code, panicked. "Louise Gates just relapsed." She instantly ran from the cafeteria.

"I'll put the box in your car," Faith called out after her.

"Thanks," Hope replied before disappearing through the open doors.

Faith sat and watched as her sister ran out of the cafeteria. She shook her head with concern, hoping that Louise Gates would be okay. Then, she looked at the cumbersome load and chuckled. Hope wasn't fooling anyone but herself. She had a thing for Dr. Gates even if she refused to admit it to herself.

Faith placed her empty tea mug on the tray. She stood and went to the kitchen bin. She came back to the table and picked up the box. She thought about Hope and Raymond Gates, then decided to make a point of introducing herself to Louise Gates before she was discharged.

An Important Message From The ARABESQUE Publisher

Dear Arabesque Reader,

I have some exciting news to share....

Available now is a four-part special series **AT YOUR SERVICE** written by bestselling Arabesque Authors.

Bold, sweeping and passionate as America itself—these superb romances feature military heroes you are destined to love.

They confront their unpredictable futures along-side women of equal courage, who will inspire you!

The **AT YOUR SERVICE** series* can be specially ordered by calling 1-888-345-BOOK, or purchased wherever books are sold.

Enjoy them and let us know your feedback by commenting on our website.

Linda Gill, Publisher
Arabesque Romance Novels

Check out our website at www.BET.com

A SPECIAL "THANK YOU" FROM ARABESQUE JUST FOR YOU!

Send this card back and you'll receive 4 FREE Arabesque Novels—a $25.96 value—absolutely FREE!

The introductory 4 Arabesque Romance books are yours FREE (plus $1.99 shipping & handling). If you wish to continue to receive 4 books every month, do nothing. Each month, we will send you 4 New Arabesque Romance Novels for your free examination. If you wish to keep them, pay just $16* (plus, $1.99 shipping & handling). If you decide not to continue, you owe nothing!

- Send no money now.
- Never an obligation.
- Books delivered to your door!

We hope that after receiving your FREE books you'll want to remain an Arabesque subscriber, but the choice is yours! So why not take advantage of this Arabesque offer, with no risk of any kind. You'll be glad you did!

In fact, we're so sure you will love your Arabesque novels, that we will send you an Arabesque Tote Bag FREE with your first paid shipment.

Call Us TOLL-FREE At 1-888-345-BOOK

* Prices subject to change

THE "THANK YOU" GIFT INCLUDES:

- 4 books absolutely FREE (plus $1.99 for shipping and handling).
- A FREE newsletter, *Arabesque Romance News*, filled with author interviews, book previews, special offers, and more!
- No risks or obligations.

INTRODUCTORY OFFER CERTIFICATE

Yes! Please send me 4 FREE Arabesque novels (plus $1.99 for shipping & handling). I understand I am under no obligation to purchase any books, as explained on the back of this card. Send my **FREE Tote Bag** after my first regular paid shipment.

NAME _____

ADDRESS _____ APT. _____

CITY _____ STATE _____ ZIP _____

TELEPHONE ( ) _____

E-MAIL _____

SIGNATURE _____

Thank You!

AN093A

ARABESQUE

Accepting the four introductory books for FREE (plus $1.99 to offset the cost of shipping & handling) places you under no obligation to buy anything. You may keep the books and return the shipping statement marked "cancelled". If you do not cancel, about a month later we will send 4 additional Arabesque novels, and you will be billed the preferred subscriber's price of just $4.00 per title. That's $16.00* for all 4 books for a savings of almost 40% off the cover price (Plus $1.99 for shipping and handling). You may cancel at any time, but if you choose to continue, every month we'll send you 4 more books, which you may either purchase at the preferred discount price. . . or return to us and cancel your subscription.

* PRICES SUBJECT TO CHANGE

THE ARABESQUE ROMANCE CLUB: HERE'S HOW IT WORKS

THE ARABESQUE ROMANCE BOOK CLUB
P.O. BOX 5214
CLIFTON NJ 07015-5214

PLACE
STAMP
HERE

Fifteen

With coordinated flight arrivals, Raymond Gates, Sr., usually called Ray by his family and friends, and Matthew Gates arrived at the hospital within minutes of each other. As scheduled, they met in the hospital lobby. The greeting was brief but loving. They shook hands, then embraced. After the initial catch-up they turned their attention to their mother.

"I've been thinking," Matthew began. "Is it me, or does this sudden allergic reaction sound too familiar?"

"It's not just you. It sounds very familiar," Ray added. Matthew referred to the sudden, unexplained rash and hives Louise came down with just a few months after Ray began working at Johns Hopkins Medical Center. While visiting Baltimore, she suddenly came down with a similar condition, and was treated by a bright, young chief resident by the name of Dr. Joy Alexander.

After several very passionate battles over the diagnosis and treatment, Joy and Ray finally concluded that Louise's sudden reaction was an anomaly. But, by the time they finally concurred with her condition, the seed of love had been planted. They were married within six months. "Either she thinks we've forgotten, or she doesn't think we'll interfere with her plans."

"My thoughts exactly," Matthew added. "Chances are, since Tony's already out of the way, and since she's gone to so much trouble, I'd have to say it's Raymond this time."

"I agree."

"Do you think he has the slightest clue to what he's in for?"

"I doubt it. Our mother can be very persuasive when she puts her mind to it. And if he's anything like I was, he'll be completely blind-sided."

"Medically speaking, is she in any real danger?"

"No. I don't think so. I asked the Emergency Services Administrative Director to e-mail me a copy of her chart. Her primary is a Dr. Hope Adams. She and Raymond are working together. Their prognosis is sound. She'll be fine."

"I presume Hope Adams is the intended?"

"I'd say so."

"Have you met her yet?"

"No."

"What do you know about Dr. Adams?"

"Not much. So far, that she's an excellent physician and that she and Raymond get along like fire and water."

"Sounds like a perfect match so far. What do you suggest we do about it?" Matthew asked.

Ray shook his head slowly then looked at his brother. They could end their mother's charade instantly or do nothing and see what happened. "Let it play out. But just to be on the safe side, she stops ingesting the allergen today."

Matthew nodded his agreement as they boarded the elevator to the fifth floor.

Louise smiled brightly when she saw both of her sons walk through the door. They kissed her cheek warmly. Then, Matthew stood back and looked around the room as Ray scanned her medical chart. Matthew picked up a discarded candy wrapper and held it out for his brother to see. Ray took another candy wrapper from the trash can and read the ingredients.

As idle small talk about the weather and travel continued, Louise watched carefully as her sons seemed to have come to an unspoken agreement. "Mom," Ray began, but was interrupted.

"I know what you're going to say," Louise said. "But I had to get his attention somehow. He's as stubborn and pigheaded as his father. I gave him every opportunity to handle this on his own."

"Mom, that's not what . . ." Ray tried again.

Louise looked at Ray pointedly and continued. "I refuse to have my grandson, your son, continue his apparent quest to break every heart on the East Coast." She crossed her arms over her chest defiantly. "Somebody had to do something."

"Mom," Matthew said when Louise stopped talking.

"Don't you two 'mom' me," she said as she turned her attention to Matthew. "If it weren't for me, Tony would be the same way. Thank goodness I found Madison in time."

"Mom," Ray began again, "listen, Matt and I just wanted to let you know that we're not going to interfere with whatever you're doing, this time. But if this scheme you've devised doesn't work, you have to promise to let it go and back off."

"Mind you," Matthew added, "we don't necessarily agree with what you're doing, but we won't interfere, yet. Okay?"

Louise looked at her sons with a warm and loving smile. This was just what she wanted to hear. She knew they'd remember and recognize the same scenario from when she matched Raymond's father and mother years ago. And since it worked so well back then, she decided to use the same circumstances.

They stood on either side of the bed. She reached out and took their hands. "I promise."

"Oh, one more thing," Ray added. "No more of these." He held up the empty candy wrapper. "You made your point. You got their attention. If they haven't figured it out by now, let it go." He looked at her face neck and arms. "As soon as the hives leave, you're discharged, understand?"

She nodded regretfully.

"So," Ray began, "when do we get to meet my daughter-in-law to be?"

Just then the door opened and Hope walked in with a

bright, cheerful smile. Matthew and Ray looked at each other and nodded approvingly. "Perfect."

Hope looked at her watch as she closed the door behind her. She was surprised by how late it had gotten. She'd stayed much longer that she had intended, but she had to admit, she had a wonderful time. The Gates men were incredibly charming. She was surprised by how open and friendly they were. It was as if they'd wanted her to know everything about their family as soon as possible.

At first she felt uneasy being confronted by the two Gates men, particularly Dr. Gates, Sr. His esteemed reputation as a neurosurgeon was exemplary. Meeting him was like an artist meeting Rembrandt or Cézanne. He was the best in his field and she had always admired his work.

When she first entered the room he seemed to look at her oddly, as if assessing her intentions. Then, his intense questioning of her professional and personal background completely took her off guard. He wasn't exactly intrusive, but he was purposefully curious. If she didn't know any better, she'd think that she was interviewing for a position on his staff. He seemed distracted and uneasy at first, but soon he relaxed and enjoyed the conversation.

As Hope pushed the button and waited for the elevator to arrive, she continued to think about the time spent with the Gates family. She smiled remembering the wonderfully funny stories they told of Raymond as a young boy. She shook her head and quietly laughed to herself. Between him and his cousin, Hope wasn't sure who was worse.

Apparently, in their unstated arrangement, Raymond usually thought up the mischievous schemes, Tony added the logistics, and together they implemented the most riotous pranks imaginable. It was typical Raymond. With that ever-present mischievous glint in his eye, she could definitely see him getting into all kinds of trouble and evidently they had all of Crescent Island at their mercy.

Hope sighed dreamily. Crescent Island must truly be a wonder. Louise and her sons talked about it as if were a slice of heaven. She knew that Louise lived in Virginia. Hope just didn't recognized where, having never heard of Crescent Island before. The incredible stories Louise and her sons told of the historical presence were fascinating.

Having practically spent her entire life within a forty-block radius of where she stood, she couldn't imagine growing up on an island as historically significant and ideally beautiful as Crescent seemed to be. Although Louise had invited her to the island on several occasions, it wasn't until Ray and Matthew made the request that she actually consider going.

A slight grimace shadowed her face as she realized that Raymond had never mentioned Crescent Island to her. Even over dinner the night before, they had talked about, discussed and sometimes disputed just about everything under the sun. But in all that time together, he'd never even mentioned his home. It was as if he didn't want her in that part of his life. Suddenly she wanted him to invite her.

Hope stepped into the elevator and pressed the button for the first floor. Her mind still buzzed with thoughts of the Gates men. As passengers got on at every descending floor, she stepped further and further back. Now, secluded in the back of the elevator, she began to think about the one Gates man that truly interested her: Raymond.

His open smile and sparkling eyes often delighted her at the oddest moments. The deep, sultry tone of his voice repeatedly sent a thrill like butterflies in flight in her stomach. His gentle, humored chuckle made her want to giggle like a schoolgirl, and when he touched her, she felt as if the floor had dropped from beneath her feet, sending her stomach in free fall. A slight chuckle went through her when she thought of his expression when she dared him to take her to dinner.

Hope closed her eyes and remembered how tenderly he

held her. The solid strength of his arms as they wrapped around her; the cooing words of desire still sending a shudder of want tingling through her even now.

Then, her thoughts turned to the night they'd spent together. As the fierce storm raged outside, their passion raged inside. They'd made love with their hearts: with tenderness, fire and passion. Each time their bodies came together their hearts melded as one. At least that's what she thought, until she awoke this morning in an empty bed.

As the elevator reached the first floor, she realized that Raymond was beginning to become a habit. A habit she couldn't afford to have because once Louise Gates was discharged there'd no longer be a reason for them to continue seeing each other. So, no matter what she felt, she had to stop. This was a heartbreak in the making. And, no matter what her heart said, she had to keep her distance.

She stepped out of the elevator, determined to set thoughts of Raymond aside. The lighthearted distraction had to end. She steeled herself against any lingering desires. Her resolve had to be strong. And the ER was the best place for her to get her mind off of Dr. Raymond Gates.

Just as Hope pressed the blue square for the ER staff entrance, she heard the static emergency announcement over the two-way band radio. She hated that apparatus. Though medically invaluable, it always brought pain, suffering and anguish to the department.

Hope walked over to the nurse's station and looked into her friend's worried face. Maxine shook her head confirming the worst, then leaned down and whispered in Hope's ear. "Police, fire and paramedics are on site," she began. "We're waiting for the complete report from the on-site paramedic."

Hope frowned and nodded.

The sound of cracked static drew everyone's attention. "Okay, here it is: automobile vs. sport utility vehicle vs. motorcycle, seven casualties total. Victim one: motorcycle primary is a twenty-year-old male, no helmet, possible severe head trauma, multiple injuries to arms and legs. He looks really bad. Victim two: motorcycle secondary is a nineteen-year-old female, head trauma, critical, still trapped beneath the SUV. Fire and rescue approximate extrication in less than thirty minutes."

There was a loud crack as communication was momentarily halted. Everyone looked around. Eyes blinked and heads shook slowly. It was another tragic scene that they'd all seen too many times. The battle to save lives became the focus.

"Victims three and four were in the SUV: two males in their mid-teens, driving while apparently under the influence. Police have already done a sobriety test. They have bruises and contusions, minimal injuries at best, for both. Oh, God, hold. Victim one just went critical code." The radio transmitter cracked with static, then went completely silent.

Hope looked over to Maxine who shook her head, troubled. Critical code, cardiac arrest, either way it wasn't a good sign. Scott stood nearby, spouting general orders to the receiving trauma team that was already in the process of readying themselves for the arrivals.

Suddenly there was a crack of static again as the EM tech continued. "No pulse, we have a flat-line on number one, CPR is being performed, hold . . ."

Maxine held the receiver in her hand while others circled, listening to the emergency medical technician list the remaining patients' vitals. The bodiless voice continued his list of multiple fractures, contusions and abrasions. Then he stopped when his partner hollered something in the background.

"We're continuing CPR on victim one, still no pulse, blood pressure is nil. I think we're gonna have a DOA coming your way." There was a slight pause as the room held its collective breath.

"Pulse!" cracked the voice through the radio speaker. A sign of relief sparked through the assembled few.

"Okay, victim five is already en route to Children's Medical and victims six and seven are braced and stable with complaints of back and neck injury."

"What's your ETA?" Maxine asked.

"Estimated time of arrival, seven minutes," came through the speaker as high-pitched squawking. Scott nodded pointedly and the trauma team instantly swung into action. Hope hurried off right behind them.

Minutes seemed like hours when calls came in through an EMT team radio. The anxiety of what was to come shadowed the faces of those hurrying to prepare for an inevitable situation.

Then, sure to their word, seven minutes later three ambulance gurneys burst through the receiving doors. In ordered chaos the dance of preparation had commenced.

The gurneys rolled in with two paramedics each running alongside them. A third paramedic was straddled atop the patient on the first gurney, continuously pumping his chest. "Victim one," the EMT shouted breathlessly above the clamor. "We lost the pulse again, while in transit." She continued CPR. "Still no pulse," she yelled as she burst through the doors.

One minute later the doors burst open again and a fourth gurney rolled in. The battle had begun.

The balance of life and death hung precariously in the capable hands of the medical professionals. In skilled practicality, the hopeless became the possible and the undoable became the achievable.

In delegated procession, the critical patients were ushered directly to the OR, the stable were comforted and assured, while the guarded were watched with added caution.

Hope, the calm in the center of the maelstrom, was a consummate professional. She maneuvered through the tense moments with a certainty of knowledge and a composed and unflinching assuredness. Her steadfast conviction was inspiring in its unfaltering focus.

With confidence and certainty, she dispensed, with grace and agility, she saved, and with gentleness and compassion, she healed. She had won many wars, but a single lost battle was always the most difficult to accept.

The battle continued for others, the rooms loud with medical chaos. Hope's room went silent. Masked faces looked up as exhausted eyes were drained of emotion. They stared at each other feeling nothing. "Call it," Hope said. The nurse made ready. She looked up at the wall clock as Hope pronounced the time of death. The young man lying still on the gurney would never see another birthday.

She pulled the blood-soaked gloves from her suddenly frail hands. The inadequacy of modern science could not save him. A second's glance at the patient was all she could afford. She had to remain distant and detached.

Then, just as suddenly as it had begun, the hours of chaos and insanity vanished, as a stagnant calm hovered over the ER. Hope had emerged bone-weary and mentally drained. She had lost. Death had visited and taken her patient. All the skill at her fingertips could not delay the inevitable.

She pulled the wrap from her head and took the lonely walk to the family waiting area. She looked at the quiet room door. The patient's family had assembled and were eagerly awaiting favorable news. She entered. She knew the screams well, and had heard them many times before. It was the silent pain that had always singed her soul. The quiet weeping and prayers for understanding tore at her.

Hope walked over to the nurse's station and gathered her charts. While getting a quick update she looked over, surprised to see Raymond standing there. He was looking directly at her. She frowned, picked up the charts then walked in his direction. She nodded curtly and walked past him into the nearest exam room. It was dark and empty. Raymond followed her inside. She turned to see him blocking the doorway.

Raymond looked into her eyes. The spark of life had long since been extinguished. For a brief moment he wondered what had smothered the flame in her heart. Then he knew, remembering the look from his early years. "I'm sorry about your patient." He spoke in hushed tones, barely audible to anyone passing by.

She nodded her head, slowly accepting his sincere condolences. "Yeah, so am I. His skull was crushed. There wasn't a whole lot we could do." She looked away. "Kinda makes that case for mandatory helmet laws, doesn't it?"

His heart propelled him forward. She stepped back and looked away, then looked back at him.

"Is there a problem, Dr. Gates?" The pure sadness and exhaustion in her eyes was heartbreaking. She had been beaten and had lost to the ultimate player, death.

"No." He looked at her strangely. "Hope," he moved closer as she backed away.

"Last I checked your grandmother was feeling much better. I still have no idea what brought on this new attack of hives."

"Hope." After the evening they'd had he was surprised by her purely professional attitude.

She looked at him oddly. "Why are you still here?"

"What's wrong with you?"

"Nothing."

"I wanted, I needed to talk to you."

"About?"

He produced a small, powder blue box with the Tiffany logo notably printed on the top. He offered the box to her. "I saw this and thought of you." She backed away.

"Dr. Gates." She looked at him sternly. "Raymond, please don't buy me any more gifts. It just complicates things." She began to walk away.

"What things?" He asked.

She reached up and touched the scar, uneasy with the direction of the conversation. "You know the drill, doctor-patient gratuities. I'm sure you discourage your patients from any gifts, presents, or personal contact."

"I'm not your patient, Hope. And last I'd heard, personal contact is allowed between two consenting adults." He took her hand and held it gently in his, then brought it up to his lips and kissed the two fingers that had just stroked the scar. She looked up at his face just as his mouth began to descend. He kissed her, gently brushing his lips against hers, barely touching, yet passionate enough to leave them yearning for more. The sudden and intense heat they generated could have set the room on fire.

After a few seconds, Raymond leaned back, not knowing what to expect. Hope looked at him but didn't speak. Moments passed, then finally she opened her mouth. "You do that again without permission, and I'll personally perform my first lobotomy on you."

Raymond smiled. His dimples danced as his tender laughter brought a smirk to even Hope's stern expression. Still holding her hand, he gave her the small blue box. "You're a hell of a woman, Dr. Adams. I have a feeling that I'm going to enjoy our time together. I'm on my way to the fifth floor. I'll see you later." He kissed the hand that held the box, then he turned and walked out of the room and down the hall. Hope stood in the dimly lit room pondering what had just happened. She shook her head as if to clear away the laced cobwebs recently placed there by Raymond.

She was just making out with a doctor in the ER exam room. What was she thinking? Someone could have easily walked by and—Hope slapped her hand to her forehead and closed and covered her eyes—she'd be dealing with rumors for the rest of her career. Her mind began to whirl with explanations and justifications.

It's a full moon. I was traumatized by the accident. No. I hadn't eaten and my glucose level was low. No. Momentary insanity? No. The man gives me fever and knocks my socks off and every time I see him I want to rip his clothes off. Yes. She leaned back against the bed.

After five solid minutes of chastising self-dialogue, Hope walked out of the room. She stopped briefly to look in on several patients and to get updates on others. On automatic-pilot, she followed the necessary tasks to complete her responsibilities.

She crossed the nurse's station and headed for the small triage office. It was empty. She closed the door behind her and tossed the blue box and her stethoscope on the desk. She looked at her watch; less than two hours remained in her shift. Slowly she collapsed in the wheeled chair. She felt the swells of frustration and aggravation beginning to reach their peek for the day.

Life in the ER at Golden Heart had a tendency to do that to a person. Life on the graveyard shift was even worse. As the dregs of society stumbled, crawled and rolled in, her joy had exited.

"Hope?"

She looked up instantly. "Yes, Maxine."

Maxine smiled broadly. "I stopped by earlier to tell you that Mr. Jackson is looking for you, but you and Dr. Gates were," she smiled even broader, "preoccupied."

Hope rolled her eyes to the ceiling. Of all the people in the world to see her in a compromising position. "Maxine, it wasn't what you think."

"Oh, I doubt that."

"Okay, it was. But I can explain."

Maxine snickered and leaned back against the counter. "This ought to be good."

Hope raised her hands, repeatedly diagramming various scenarios without saying a single word. She took a deep breath and began again. Her hands moved wildly, her face was animated, but she never spoke a word.

Finally, Maxine couldn't take the excruciating punishment any longer. "I'll tell you what, since this is obviously going to take the better part of my middle age, why don't I explain to you what happened."

"By all means."

"You and Dr. Gates have been attracted to each other since the first moment you laid eyes on each other. The smoke-screen arguments you've been having merely hid what neither one of you wanted to admit until about fifteen minutes ago, if not before. And that is that he rocks your world and you rock his. So, the passionate kiss I witnessed was merely a prelude to passion yet untapped or revisited. And, in the next few minutes, hours, days, weeks, months or years, you and the good doctor will experience a love so divinely perfect as to reach the apex of human experience."

Hope was speechless and simply threw her hands up in defeat. Maxine walked out, her usual joyous laughter even more high-spirited.

Hope shook her head, smiling to herself as she touched her lips. It was nice, she admitted, turning the wheel chair around to the desk and curiously opening the blue box. Two beautifully scripted charms hung from a gold chain. She pulled the sparkling gold from the box and held it up. As the charms spun around against the play of light from the hall, she read the inscription aloud. "Truth. Dare."

The man was truly unbelievable. She returned the jewelry to the case and placed the box in her pocket. Then, with determination, she opened the first file and devoted the next thirty minutes to her caseload.

"Yes?" she asked, without looking up.

"You took my wife. I want her outta here now."

Recognizing the low, raspy voice and the heavy scent of mechanic's oil and cheap beer on his clothing, Hope looked up to see Wes Jackson standing in the doorway. The comical word, *sleazoid* came to mind. "This area is reserved for authorized personnel only. You'll have to leave."

"You kept her away from me all night long. I want my wife outta here now," he demanded roughly.

"Mrs. Jackson was admitted for overnight observation."

"It's been longer than overnight."

"Upon further observation, we've found that her injuries require further tests. She'll be discharged as soon as medically feasible."

"That's bull. Why you keeping her? You think you smart, don't you. Fancy doctor. Ain't nothing wrong with her."

"She needs rest and quiet. And, a black eye, bruised ribs and a sprained wrist aren't exactly what I'd call nothing."

He quickly averted his eyes. "She's clumsy, always has been."

"She's being physically abused."

Wes looked back to Hope. His eyes narrowed threateningly as he glared at her. "She tell you that?" Hope looked at him as he turned into a coward. " 'Cause if she did, then she's lying. Ain't nobody touch her."

"No. She didn't tell me that. She didn't have to. It's obvious that she's being abused by someone. Got any idea who that person might be?" Hope's glare hit the mark, making a very definite point. Wes understood all too well. He'd been found out and Hope wasn't going to cover for him.

"You got something to say, doc, say it."

Hope opened her mouth to put Wes in his place and bring out the coward that he was. But she realized that whatever she said, he would eventually take it out on Leanne. And she didn't want to put her in any more jeopardy than she was already in. "I don't have anything to say to you, Mr. Jackson," she sneered out.

Wes nodded his head knowingly. As usual, he'd gotten the last word. He puffed his chest out and turned to walk away.

Hope picked up a chart and began to speak out loud. "Coward, abuser, bully, jerk."

He whipped around and looked back to Hope. "What did you just call me?"

Hope continued reading the chart. "You talking to me?" She looked up stubbornly.

At that moment Maxine came to the triage doorway. She looked from Hope to Wes, feeling the thick tension. "Excuse me, Dr. Adams, your patient in exam nine would like a word with you before they leave. Also, you got a call from the fifth floor."

Hope nodded and stood. She folded and closed the file and tucked it neatly under her arm. As she walked out she glared at Wes, making her animosity unmistakably clear.

Sixteen

Louise was smiling victoriously as she sat up in bed, flipping through the stations of the television suspended from the ceiling, across the room. She was delighted with the news she'd just heard.

Apparently, Raymond and Hope were back on track to becoming quite the couple. The rumors were already all over the hospital. And if even a remote part of the rumors were true, she would be elated. Of course, neither Hope nor Raymond would admit anything, but they didn't have to. All she had to do was mention the name of one while in the presence of the other, and their eyes would tell her everything she wanted to know.

So, Louise waited patiently for Raymond to return. A knock on the door drew her attention. The door opened just a bit, then widened. She instantly brightened as soon as Hope appeared at her bedside.

"Hope," she exclaimed with animated delight as she turned off the television to give Hope her complete attention. "How sweet of you to stop by. How are you, dear?"

Hope smiled and flipped open the chart as she approached the bed. "Shouldn't I be asking you that question?"

"You will."

Hope came closer to the bed and looked down into Louise's bright, sparkling eyes. "I was on my way home when I received a message that you wanted to see me. How are you doing this evening, Mrs. Gates?"

"Please call me Mamma Lou. I feel absolutely wonderful,"

Louise said with exuberance. She had been more than delighted with the way things were going between Raymond and Hope.

"Good. That's wonderful. It looks like all of your tests are coming back negative and your blood pressure is dropping nicely." She looked up and examined Louise's face, neck and arms. I see your hives have diminished considerably. Looks like we'll have you out of here in no time."

"What do you think about my grandson?"

Taken completely off guard by the blunt question, Hope began to stutter, "Your grandson? Dr. Gates?"

"Yes, what do you think about him?"

"Fine. Fine. He's fine," she said with as much detached emotion as possible.

Louise smiled knowingly. Hope looked at her questioningly. "The whole hospital is buzzing about a budding romance between you and my grandson."

"Really? Mrs. Gates . . ." she began.

"Why don't you call me Mamma Lou?"

"Mrs. Gates," Hope reiterated more professionally, "rumors circle around this hospital like buzzards on rotten meat. I wouldn't take whatever you've heard too seriously."

The knock on the door drew both women's attention. "Hello, Mamma Lou."

Louise beamed brightly, "Raymond, you're back. We were just talking about you," Louise said, as Raymond came into the room and paused by the bed. He leaned down to kiss Louise on the cheek then leveled his gaze at Hope and kept it there. He placed the magazines Louise had requested from the gift shop on her lap.

"So how's the doctor business?" Louise asked, breaking the thin line of tension swirling around the room.

"Good," Raymond replied, his eyes riveted to Hope. "Hello again, Hope."

Hope blushed for no apparent reason. "Dr. Gates." Hope cleared her throat uncomfortably. "Well, I'm going let you two have some time to visit." She turned to avoid Raymond's piercing stare. "I'll be back tomorrow." She nearly ran from the room. Her knees wobbled, her palms moistened and her heart pounded. *Get a grip girl,* she warned herself as she hurried down the hall to the elevator.

The Great Escape was all she could think of. Images from the movie flashed before her eyes as she repeatedly pressed the elevator button. Seeming to take forever, the elevator eventually arrived and she hurriedly jumped on.

Just as the doors began to close, Raymond stepped on.

An inner groan escaped.

"Did you see your gift?"

"I thought we'd already discussed giving gifts."

"You discussed it."

Hope sighed heavily, obviously exasperated by his logic. "It's very beautiful. But then, you already knew that." He smiled happily as she pulled the blue box from her pocket and held it out to him. "I can't accept this."

"I can't return it. It's already been engraved."

The elevator stopped on the next floor down and several departing visitors got on. Raymond and Hope stepped back as others piled neatly to the front. He stepped closer to her than necessary.

"Then give it to someone else. I'm sure there's no end to the number of women for whom this might be appropriate." She whispered, trying not to draw attention to their personal conversation.

Raymond gasped playfully. "Are you implying that I play our game with other women?" A woman standing in front of Hope turned briefly and smiled.

Hope side-glanced, seeing Raymond smile easily. His dimples creased as Hope's heart fell. "I'm not implying anything," she hissed. "And, it's not our game. You can play with whomever you chose. It's none of my business."

"Sounds an awful lot like you're jealous."

"That's absurd," she whispered louder than she had intended.

The woman directly in front of Hope stepped back further as more people got onto the elevator. She glanced back at Hope a second time. This time smiling openly.

"No," he said emphatically, "now it definitely sounds like you're jealous." His smiled widened.

"Well I'm not." Hope insisted. "I just thought that you might want to give it to someone whom you're interested in and care about."

"I just did."

The elevator stopped on the first floor and all of the passengers exited. Hope and Raymond were the last to leave. Slowly she stepped out, her mind still trying to process his last remark.

"Hope."

She stopped and turned around. Raymond stepped out of the elevator as a number of other people got on. He walked over to her as the doors closed behind him. The smile in his eyes was suspiciously like that of a man who had just opened his heart.

Hope looked away. The twitching, shuddering spasms in her stomach grew worse. Looking up into his eyes had been a mistake.

"We should talk."

"I'm on my way out."

"So am I."

They walked out together.

Smoke blew out of the open window. Watchful eyes observed Hope and Raymond coming out of the hospital and walking toward the parking lot. He flicked the lit cigarette from the window and got out of the car.

With added haste, he hurried across the open parking area and pulled his shirt down over his belt to conceal the large leather covering. He slipped easily around the side of the building and hurried up the steps.

At each level he stopped, opened the door and glanced around the parking level. On the third floor he grasped the door's handle and prepared to pull when he heard a woman's voice. He stopped and flattened himself against the door to listen.

He heard a car start and slowly opened the door to see Hope drive away. The man with whom she was talking stepped back into the elevator. He smiled. Perfect.

Seventeen

This was the day that Louise had dreaded. Today she was going to be discharged. Raymond and Hope had come in together and informed her of their decision to allow her to go home this morning. Although they came in together, she could tell that there was still an uneasiness between them.

Louise sat on the edge of the bed wondering what to do next. As far as she knew everything had been progressing just as she'd planned. Now all of a sudden, nothing. Raymond and Hope seemed to have stalled. She needed to jump start this relationship as soon as possible.

Her blood pressure was perfect and her cholesterol was back down to normal. There was no way she could develop another case of hives; Matthew and Ray had seen to that. They had taken her stash of chocolate candy and made her promise not to eat any more. It was just her luck that years ago Ray and Joy had figured out her little secret. Right now she need someone else to take her place as matchmaker. But who?

Louise was continuing to think when she heard a soft knock at the door. "Come in."

The door opened and a woman peeked in. She smiled eagerly and asked to come in. Louise recognized her instantly.

"There's no way that you're related to Hope Adams."

Faith came into the room and closed the door. "Hello, Mrs. Gates. My name is Faith Adams. Hope is my sister."

"I knew it. I just knew it."

"I hope I'm not disturbing you."

"Of course not, sweetie. Come on in and have a seat." Faith sat down in the chair next to Louise's bed. Louise raised her eyes in a silent prayer of thanks. She knew that her prayer would be answered, she just didn't know it would be this soon.

The two women settled into an easy conversation that centered around music, food, travel and the weather. Faith told Louise all about her nursing career and how happy she was to be working in the maternity ward at the hospital.

Eventually, the conversation turned from maternity and babies, to children, to hers and Hope's childhood. Faith told Louise how much they loved being raised by their grandmother.

"She sounds like a delightful woman. I'd love to meet her someday."

"She is wonderful. You remind me a lot of her."

"I take that as a true compliment. Tell me about your parents." Louise already knew some things about them because of the file she'd received from her private investigator.

Faith took a deep breath and poured her heart out. She was open and candid in her recall of the events leading up to their mother's death. Louise was touched by Faith's love of her sister and equally impressed by their devotion to each other.

Faith told Louise that Hope had been married before and was gun-shy when it came to romance, particularly with men of means. Louise's brow rose with added interest. This was definitely not on the detective's report she'd received.

"Was it a messy divorce?"

"The worst. Hope's ex-father-in-law accused her of marrying his son, Nolan, for his money because they had eloped and Nolan didn't have a pre-nuptial agreement. Hope was devastated. She had a lawyer who told her that according to the law of the state, she could conceivably ask and receive half of Nolan's belongings."

"How long were they married?"

"Eighteen months. But actually they were only together for about a year. As soon as Nolan's father found out about the marriage he threatened to cut his son off financially and re-move him from the will."

"That's horrendous." Louise said in disgust. "I do hope that young man stood up to his father."

Faith shook her head, no. "Nolan wanted the money too badly."

"Then I say good riddance to him."

"Anyway, in the divorce settlement Hope only requested enough money to send me through nursing school. She didn't even want her medical school loans paid off. The only thing she thought about was my future and happiness. So you see Mrs. Gates, Hope saved my life more than once. I owe her everything." Faith stopped and glanced out of the window.

She cleared her throat and continued. "That's why I'm very concerned about Hope's relationship with your grandson. Al-though I haven't actually met him, I understand that he's very nice, but I also understand that he has a reputation." Faith took a deep breath and continued. "I don't want Hope to get hurt. So if he just wants to play around, I was hoping that maybe you could suggest he look elsewhere."

Louise smiled at Faith's attempt at courage. It was touch-ing to see a younger sister protecting her older sister so faithfully. "Faith, I assure you, a lot of Raymond's reputation is very well founded. I'll be the first to admit that my grand-son isn't an angel. He has had his moments. But, in his defense, he is a very responsible man and he would never in-tentionally hurt your sister. If you're asking me if his intentions are honorable, I would say yes. Raymond seems very fond of Hope."

Faith smiled, nodded and stood. "Although," Louise con-tinued gaining Faith's full attention, "I would like nothing better than for Hope and Raymond to be together perma-nently, they seem to have some wedge between them at the moment. Do you have any idea what that might be?"

For the next fifteen minutes Faith and Louise put their heads together, planning, plotting and scheming. They developed what most military minds would consider a blueprint for a treaty.

With their heads together and their coalition sealed, the two prepared by discussing the best way to handle the reluctant pair. Faith informed Louise of Hope's mandate to attend the fundraiser and of her pending three-day vacation. Louise immediately assured Faith she would make sure that Raymond attended the upcoming event.

They had concluded their discussion, having decided on the best strategy to get Hope to Crescent Island. Louise relaxed back happily, assured that Faith would be an excellent ally. "So, Faith, tell me, have you met my dear friend Dennis Hayes yet?" Just then the door opened and Raymond walked in. Both heads bobbed up. Raymond grimaced; guilt was written all over their faces.

Raymond walked into his grandmother's room expecting her to be anxiously anticipating her trip back home. Both he and Hope had signed off on her discharge paperwork and this morning he had arranged for an orderly to wheel her to the exit. When he arrived on the floor, he looked around for the orderly and was informed that he was delayed and would be available as soon as possible. So, Raymond went directly to Louise's room.

He walked in and to his surprise, instead of his grandmother waiting excitedly, he was astonished to see her talking quietly with a nurse.

The nurse looked up and Louise turned around. Raymond did a double take. The last time he'd seen two women look so much alike was when he'd first met Madison's sister Kennedy. This woman was the spitting image of Hope.

He looked to his grandmother. She smiled broadly and held out her hand to him. Raymond went to her side. He kissed her cheek and looked into her clear eyes. "How do you feel today, Mamma Lou?"

"Wonderful. Couldn't be better."

"Good. I'm glad to hear that."

Louise, still smiling, looked over to the woman now standing by the foot of her bed. "Raymond, this is Faith Adams, Hope's sister. Faith, this is my grandson, Dr. Raymond Gates."

Raymond came around to the side of the bed to greet her. "I've heard a lot about you, Dr. Gates." They shook hands while Louise added to the conversation by telling Raymond of Hope's interest in visiting Crescent Island.

"Please, call me Raymond. It's wonderful to finally meet you, Faith. Hope has told me some very impressive things about you. Hope should definitely come to Crescent Island. I'd love to show her around. I'm sure she'd love it there."

Louise and Faith eyed each other slyly.

"Faith works in the maternity ward; she's a nurse."

Raymond looked impressed and asked questions about her career choice and background.

"Louise, I'm glad I had the opportunity to meet you before you left. Take care of yourself. I promise to stay in touch. And, the next time you're in the area and would like to spend a little time volunteering in the nursery, let me know."

"I certainly will. Good-bye dear," Louise acknowledged as Faith left the room. Raymond walked to her overnight bag. "We have a few minutes, the orderly hasn't arrived yet. Do you have everything packed?"

"Yes. Where's Otis?"

"He's downstairs with the car."

"Good. I can't wait to get back to my begonias."

Raymond picked up the television's remote control and turned to the hospital news station. "So," Raymond said, as Louise looked at him with innocent interest, "how long have you known Faith?"

"Oh, we've only just met."

"Really? You two seemed very friendly."

"She's a very nice young lady, just like her sister."

Raymond walked over to the window and looked down. "So what else did you two talk about?"

"Nothing much, this and that," Louise answered, seemingly distracted as she watched the hospital administrator talk about Golden Heart's newly implemented programs.

"Did you have an opportunity to catch up with your father and uncle?"

"Yes, I spoke with Uncle Matt on the phone. He was having dinner with some business associates. Dad and I grabbed a bite at Spotlight NYC."

"That's nice. It's a shame that you two don't see each other as often as you should."

"Dad's busy. He's always been busy." A thread of resentment piqued Louise's attention.

For years Raymond and his father had experienced a strained, often forced relationship. Only recently did Raymond begin to understand his father's complete and total loss and the trauma it caused, leading to his decision to have Louise raise his only son.

"He loves you."

"I know."

"I wish you two had more time together."

"I dropped Uncle Matt and Dad off at Kennedy Airport earlier. They said that they'd call you later this evening at Crescent."

Louise smiled and nodded her head.

Raymond looked at her suspiciously. "You look particularly chipper today."

Louise couldn't help but smile. "I guess I am in a pretty good mood."

"Any particular reason?" Raymond looked up at Hugh's smiling face as he proudly described how Barclay Med has been a beacon in the community.

"Of course," Louise said happily. "I'm going home."

Raymond nodded, not completely sure he believed it. For the first time in a long time he had the feeling that his grandmother was up to something. "Have you seen Hope today?" he asked as he turned back around.

"Yes, she stopped by earlier to say good-bye. Did she need to speak with you before we left?"

Raymond frowned and took an overly long time to answer. When he did the disappointment in his voice was painfully obvious. "No." Hugh was now excitedly talking about the hospital fundraiser. Raymond looked away from the television screen.

Louise nodded her head knowingly. She'd never seen Raymond look so disheartened. He had the definite look of a man who was miserably confused or maybe, hopefully, in love. "The hospital is having a fundraiser this weekend," Louise began cautiously, as not to make him suspicious.

"Yeah, I know. I received an invitation from Hugh Wescott."

"Are you going?"

"I doubt it."

"Pity. I hear it's going to be quite wonderful. Faith was telling me all about the planning. She told me that she and Hope would be going."

"Oh?" Failing miserably at the art of deception, Raymond couldn't mask his apparent interest. Louise patted herself on the back for making such a perfect match.

"How was dinner with your father last night?" she asked, changing the subject.

"Fine. I guess you've heard that the fundraiser is a twelve hour event," Raymond added, changing the subject completely and suddenly losing interest in television. He stood at the window after pacing the length of the room several times in a feeble attempt at gaining more information from her.

"Yes, I heard. Faith told me." She decided not to give him a break.

"So, I guess Faith also told you when Hope was going?"

"Yes," Louise said as she watched the television.

Raymond stood with his back to her. She could tell he

wanted to say more but was hesitant. "You know it's being held at Dennis's place."

"Yes, I heard."

Raymond whipped around quickly. "You're not still thinking about trying to get those two together, are you?"

Louise looked up. "What two? Oh, you mean Dennis and Faith? I might, I don't know just yet."

Frustration began to nip at Raymond's last nerve. "No, not her sister. Hope. You're not still thinking about matching Dennis and Hope, are you?"

"Well, I've already introduced them, so it's really not up to me anymore."

"Wait a minute, when you matched Tony up with Madison, you did more that just introduce them, didn't you?"

"Well, that was different. They already had a spark."

Raymond turned to the window and looked out at the parking lot. He scratched his head repeatedly, sighed several times, then turned. "So, did they have a spark?"

"Who, dear?"

"Hope and Dennis. Did they, you know, spark, like Tony and Madison?"

"Hope is such a lovely woman, don't you think? She does have that little scar on her face. I wonder how she got it? But, I don't think any man worth his salt would have a problem with the scar, do you?"

"It's a beautiful scar," he said, too lovingly for his own good.

"Yes, I think so too." Louise decided that she'd tortured him enough. "Faith told me that she and Hope plan to get to the fundraiser around six or seven o'clock. And no, there was no spark between Hope and Dennis."

Raymond looked at his watch, then hurried over to Louise's side. "Mamma Lou, I've got to make a quick phone call. If the orderly arrives before I return, tell him to wait for me. I'll be right back."

"Is there a problem?"

"No."

"Oh, have you decided to attend after all?"

"Well, yes, well, I guess I should maybe stop by. I mean, after all it is for a good cause. Dennis will be there. Hope will be there. Oh, and her sister uh—uh—Faith." He kissed her cheek and began backing out of the room. "So, I'll be back in a few moments." He disappeared instantly.

Louise could barely contain her laughter. Tears streamed down her face at the thought of Raymond trying to justify going out. Her poor, lovesick grandson had been reduced to a confused adolescent. She laughed harder and harder until finally a nurse stopped by her room.

"Mrs. Gates, are you all right? Can I get you anything?"

"No, dear. For the first time in a while I'm doing just fine." She chuckled again as she picked up the receiver and asked to be connected to the maternity ward's nurse's station. Faith would love this.

Ten minutes later Raymond came back to the room slightly out of breath. The orderly was sitting on a chair talking with Louise. A wheelchair was sitting in the center of the room.

"All set?" Louise asked, still amused by Raymond's sudden dash out.

"Yes, Colonel Wheeler is parked out front. Shall we go?"

Louise sat down in the wheel chair as Raymond gathered her overnight case and the orderly positioned himself behind the chair. Minutes later and after a myriad of good-byes, Louise was being wheeled through the hospital's front doors. Colonel Wheeler's Cadillac was waiting there for her.

She climbed in easily as Raymond and Colonel Wheeler said good-bye. He got in and started the car. Louise rolled her window down as Raymond came around to her side. She kissed him good-bye, then cautioned him to behave himself.

"Oh, you won't forget to give those beautiful flowers a good home will you?" She called out to the orderly.

"No, ma'am, I'll get right on it."

"Thank you, dear."

She blew a kiss and nodded sternly to Raymond. He winked back. She couldn't help but laugh. As Colonel Wheeler pulled off she hoped that she'd done enough. She watched Raymond in the side view mirror. He turned and went back into the hospital. She smiled as Colonel Wheeler took her hand.

"He'll be just fine. Are you ready to go home?"

Louise took a deep relaxing breath. "Yes, my work here is done." She sat back and closed her eyes, letting Colonel Wheeler take her back to Crescent Island.

By six-thirty Hope had completed her rounds in her usual quick and efficient manner. She made a point to see all of her patients, even those currently assigned to other doctors for more specialized medical attention. She sat at the nurse's station beside Maxine and completed her notes.

"You had a visitor."

"Who?"

"Dr. Gates. He said that he'll catch up with you later."

"Whatever." Hope said, as her heart sparked brightly.

"You're not on duty are you?" Maxine asked as she picked out another chart and made a notation.

Hope continued to write, but paused just long enough to look at her watch. "Actually, I'm just getting off duty."

Maxine looked at her strangely. "Day shift?"

Hope nodded absent-mindedly and pulled an invitation from her pocket. She showed it to Maxine, who instantly began chuckling.

"I thought you might find that amusing."

"Hugh?" Maxine speculated.

"Yep, I got the request the other night. Report to day shift, then present myself at the fundraiser. Since the board will be there, he probably wants as many people in attendance as possible to make the hospital look efficient."

"Wouldn't that logic work better if you weren't at the

fundraiser? That way, at least the board would think that you're dedicated to your profession." Hope shook her head and continued writing in the chart. "If I didn't know any better, I'd say you were being punished."

"I am."

Maxine's head shot up like a bullet. "What?"

Hope shook her head and walked away. Maxine dropped the chart back in the bin and quickly caught up to her.

"Punished? You? By Hugh? For what?"

"You said yourself, it looked like Hugh was punishing me. I'd say that he probably is."

"But why you?"

Hope looked around and waited until a couple of technicians walked past. Maxine stepped in closer. "Hugh and I have a history."

"Oh, everybody figured that. Rumor his it that you two were lovers at one time." Maxine's smile was wide and curious.

Hope held her stomach. "That would be positively insulting, if it weren't so nauseating. No, not that kind of history," Hope sighed. "Years ago, when I was still in med school, I was married to his son, Nolan. My married name was Wescott, but thankfully I never took it. Hugh was my father-in-law.

"Of course, now it all makes sense. That's why Hugh is so hostile toward you, because you divorced his son."

"The other way around. Nolan divorced me."

"Get out. Why?"

"Hugh didn't approve of the marriage. He felt that Nolan could do better."

"Then he underestimated you."

"He always does."

"So he's insisting you go to the fundraiser just to drive you nuts." Maxine pondered the plausibility of Hugh's warped logic. It was completely unreasonable and seriously flawed. And definitely sounded like something Hugh would dream up. Maxine began laughing. "Go to the fundraiser and have a great time, for me."

They walked back to the station. Hope picked up the folded paper she'd been reading.

Maxine looked on. "Find anything yet?" she motioned to the neatly folded newspaper lying beside the pile of folders.

Hope looked over to her, then back toward the newspaper. "No, not yet." She pulled an x-ray from the large manila jacket and attached it to the vertical light box. She switched the light on, then carefully scanned the fibula's tiny bone fracture, barely visible to the naked eye. Confirming the patient number, she pulled a second film out and attached it, beside the first. Studying the film intently for discrepancies, she reached into the empty envelope for the third ordered film.

"How long do you have?"

"A few more months." Hope picked up the telephone and dialed the radiology department. After a brief conversation about a missing x-ray from a set of films she ordered, she hung up and continued writing.

"Why don't you just buy it?"

"Rent it, yes. Lease it, maybe. But buy it, no way."

Maxine reached over and fingered through the newspaper. It was haphazardly marked with tiny red dots and circles, resembling a measled child more than the New York Times. "How many today?"

"Four. And before you ask, no. I haven't found anything yet."

"Patience."

"Yeah, I know." Hope stood to leave.

"You leaving now?"

"No, I want to check on an x-ray before I go. It's not ready yet. I'm heading to the cafeteria. Beep me if radiology calls." Maxine nodded, as Hope pushed through the doors.

It was seven-thirty P.M., midway between evening and night. It was too early to go home and too late to go on duty. Since she wasn't particularly tired, Hope decided to go to the cafeteria. She squinted her eyes against the bright neon cafeteria lights as she looked around. Their bland nakedness gave the room an empty, hopeless feel. A row of vending machines lined the far wall. The room was empty except for a few visitors and several cafeteria workers sitting together, quietly talking. Hope nodded her acknowledgements, then moved on to sit alone near the side window. Dusk was just beginning to settle across the city.

Hope slid in and slouched down comfortably in the plastic formed chair. She propped her feet up in the seat across from her. Then, after a slow, easy neck roll, she yawned lazily and let her head fall back until she was staring at the cafeteria ceiling. "One, two, three, four . . ." She counted the perforated holes in the ceiling tile. Something she'd done hundreds of times before. "Twenty-seven, twenty-eight, twenty-nine . . ."

"May I join you?"

Hope jumped. Then, seeing Raymond standing above her, she sat up straighter in her seat and dropped her feet to the floor. "I'm sure you must have something better to do."

"Not at the moment," he continued to stand, holding two small, steaming cups. "May I?"

She looked at him for a moment, then barely noticeably, nodded her head, tilted her chin upward, closed her eyes and moaned. "Great, I hoped you'd be happy to see me."

"Mamma Lou was discharged. Why are you still here?"

Raymond placed the Styrofoam cups on the table then took a seat across from her. He smiled infectiously, but Hope refused to submit to the addiction. "I came to see you, of course." She looked away deciding not to answer. "I never got the opportunity to thank you for helping my grandmother."

Hope still remained silent.

"I also want to apologize for my behavior. I shouldn't have kissed you in the exam room like that."

Raymond reached out and stroked her cheek. It was just as soft and inviting as he remembered.

Hope sighed and leaned back, suddenly aware that she'd allowed him to touch her face, her scar.

"I'm sorry," he said.

"No, it's me." She looked away then shrugged her shoulders like an embarrassed teen. "Listen, I'm not looking for anything right now. I just got out of a very difficult relationship and I—"

"I understand."

She looked away again.

"Are you on duty?"

"Just getting off."

"Want to grab a bite to eat?"

Still she debated. "That's probably not a great idea. That last time . . ."

They both smiled remembering the Japanese restaurant and the rainy night. "I can't promise you what will or won't happen tonight, Hope. You know how I feel about you."

"Sure. Dinner sounds wonderful. I have to check an x-ray first. I'll meet you out front."

Raymond nodded. "I'll see you soon."

Hope stood to leave. Suddenly, her thoughts were interrupted by an all too familiar call: code blue to the ER trauma unit. Instinctively, Hope hurried as if propelled by an unseen force. She arrived at the doorway where a battle cry for life had begun.

Like a blender abruptly set to hyper-speed, the once placid nurse's arena had transformed into a montage of juxtaposed images in dramatic chaos. Hope, its leading lady, took center stage and looked perfectly at home in the erratic madness.

The drama, an acrobatic race for life, began in a burst of blurred images hastily descended on a single room. She spewed out a rhythmic montage of procedure, orders and demands. The patient was out of time and she refused to let the Reaper win this battle.

Pleading for relief, the child looked up into her eyes. Hope connected instantly. His pleading stare was empty, on the verge of lifelessness. Hope spouted new orders. *You're not dying, not today, not on my watch.*

Maneuvering closer, Raymond smiled at the absurdity of the life and death struggles being waged and the battle between Hope and the Grim Reaper. She'd won this round.

When the pace calmed down to a manageable level, Hope looked up into Raymond's eyes. She shrugged, he nodded his understanding. They held their gaze for a moment. Until her attention was drawn back to her patient. Raymond walked away.

Eighteen

The hospital fundraiser, a twelve-hour event, began at high noon with the warmth of the sun peeking down at a garden party at the famous Spotlight NYC. It was the perfect day and the perfect place. As the sun hovered high in the sky, so did the high spirits of all those involved.

As soon as the minute hand struck twelve, the first guests began arriving at the restaurant. Then, en masse, they arrived, expecting a day of wonder. And, true to the organizers' promise, that was exactly what they received.

Touted as the event that couldn't be missed, the entire day was one long who's who of power, privilege and influence. A continuous swell of attendees flowed comfortably throughout the day, the most prominent being the prestigious Barclay Medical Corporation's board of directors.

White-haired old men, they had skin so leathered with age that detailed road maps had fewer lines, rivaling that of Methuselah. Their appearance did little to dissuade the tender, young, token charms solidly attached to their arms. Draped in diamonds and designer fashions, these women purposefully regaled in their prominence.

The surrounding, unending hype and the promotional machine did a fantastic job promoting the prestigious event. They had lined up prominent public figures that would make the Oscars' red carpet jealous. Everyone who was anyone made an appearance at some time during the day.

The affair was basically four separate events that contrived to allow all hospital employees, that wanted to attend, ample opportunity to do so. The Garden Gathering was the first event held in the courtyard. It was followed by an English tea party at four o'clock in the main dining hall. Afterwards, an elegant dinner at dusk was served in the courtyard. And finally, the showstopper, was the Nightlight Extravaganza.

The garden party commenced at exactly high noon. With lavishly designed floral bouquets and radiant centerpieces on each table, the open courtyard was the perfect setting for the first event.

Through the open French doors, the garden guests proceeded into a wonderland filled with visions of grandeur. The tent-covered courtyard was furnished with large, linen-topped, circular patio tables with an open umbrella in the center of each. They circled the open pavilion making the area look like a movie set from the Great Gatsby era. Symmetrically set to surround the fishpond, each table was topped with a glass hurricane candle and freshly cut flowers.

The outside setting was completed with a patio arbor, set above and between the courtyard and main dining hall, hung heavily with vines of concord grapes, ripe for the picking. There were miniature lemon trees atop Italian slate pedestals. Honeysuckle bushes completed the look. The air was scented with the tangy, tart citrus of lemons and sweet fragrant honey. Rows of white rose bushes in white-boxed urns lined the walkway as seven-foot trellises paraded along the brick, basket weave walkway at the entrance.

Soft, delicate classical music played as delighted attendees were greeted by a buffet of garden party favorites. In straw hats, brightly colored floral print dresses and white linen suits, the guests enjoyed a light luncheon of turkey, roast beef, and carved ham with all the trimmings. Salads of every imaginable type, breads from around the world, and extraordinary desserts lay beneath a huge ice sculpture depicting a vase filled with dozens of crystal-iced budded roses.

By three o'clock the sculpture had melted and the garden

party had dwindled down. Some remaining guests went inside the main dining room for English tea. Served at exactly four o'clock, it began when a small chime sounded. Then, dozens of waiters emerged from the pantry with porcelain pots of Earl Gray tea. Elegant, linen tables decorated with English ivy topiaries centered each table.

Within minutes of the tea, silver multi-tiered platters covered with tasty treats were placed on each table, as beautifully flowing classical music surrounded the social gathering.

Tea sandwiches of every imaginable type delighted the guests as a stately parade of watercress, salmon, cheese, crab and chicken shaped in triangles, twists, circles, pockets, and puffs, continued to flow from the kitchen. Soon after, roulades filled with appetizing cheese and meats were served. Scones with clotted cream, curd and sweet apple-rum jam disappeared as soon as they were presented. Lastly, lighter-than-air almond macaroons, sugared shortbreads, delicate fruit tartlets, sponge and pound cake, and frosted petit fours completed the meal. Each platter was generously decorated with miniature marzipan morsels.

Then, at six o'clock the white, gossamer, silk drapes that lined the closed French doors opened. The awed assembly waited impatiently at the door until their turn to enter arrived. The third gala had begun with an exaggerated flourish.

Sparkling with tiny, white lights that twinkled like diamonds beneath a muted, crystal sky, the atmosphere in the newly recreated courtyard was elegantly charming and stylish. Dinner at dusk had moved back outside to the courtyard, which had been redesigned to resemble a Parisian outdoor jazz fête.

Sophisticated and suave, the savoir faire was enhanced by a quartet of piano, saxophone, bass, and percussion. The pianist, a dead ringer for Louis Armstrong, played the piano like he was born with ivory in his veins. Completing the small ensemble was a sultry songstress with the vocal range of an angel who performed ballads from throughout the ages.

The atmospheric mastery continued through the evening as

the musicians tickled the ivory, slapped the skins and blew hot tunes from the days of big band crooners and jazz.

The evening's meal, a masterpiece of edible, sensual and visual enchantment, had been served buffet-style. Laid out like a royal offering, the guests stood in line with bone china and silverware, anticipating the delights. Mouths watered at the aromatic scents of roasted lamb with mint marmalade chutney, chive and parsley twice-baked potatoes with cream, grilled, succulent pork slices, marinated in port wine and topped with a tangy, spiced barbecue sauce, and chicken covered with spiced herbs and bread crumbs, steeped in Marsala wine and seasoned vegetables.

Then, at long last, the evening's main event began. Special guests, from hip-hop to Latin to rhythm and blues to country and western, had arrived. To the surprise and astonishment of the publicity machine, the extended A-list offering rivaled most Hollywood premieres. Touted as "a night to remember," it certainly was.

"This place is incredible," Faith said, in awestruck wonder, as she looked up at the building. The outside of the tall building was lit up with a huge spotlight that fanned the night sky. Roped off and lined with a deep blue carpet, the entrance to the club was announced by a beautifully penned sign. A tall, wide man with a thick neck stood outside the frosted glass door and asked to see invitations as attendees approached. "Can you imagine coming here every night?"

Hope nodded her agreement. "It is beautiful." Faith and Hope stood in line behind several familiar faces.

"I hope you're gonna be in a better mood than that all night."

"There's nothing wrong with my mood."

"Ever since you and Raymond had your little date, you've been grumpy, rude and cranky."

"I have not. And it wasn't a date."

"Do you think he'll be here tonight?"

"I have no idea and could care less."

"Uh huh, that's why you're looking around so much."

"Faith, I'm warning you, if you don't . . ."

"Hope," Dennis crooned in his rich baritone. Both Hope and Faith turned around to see Dennis standing behind them.

Hope smiled instantly as Dennis's eyes went from face to face. The resemblance was evident. With his eyes glued to Faith, he took Hope's hand and brought it to his lips and gently kissed it. "A pleasure to see you again, Doctor." Then, he turned to Faith and smiled seductively. "I don't believe we've met." He took Faith's hand and repeated the action.

"Faith, this is Dennis Hayes. He owns the Spotlight. Dennis, this is my sister Faith Adams. She's a pediatric nurse at the hospital."

"The pleasure is all mine, I assure you." Dennis brightened as his eyes remained on Faith. "Both in medicine, how delightful. Your parents must be very proud." He stepped between Hope and Faith, placing their hands in the bend of his arm, and escorted them to the front door. He nodded at the security and continued inside. "Shall we?" Dennis escorted the two women through the foyer area and up to the main reception area.

Dennis had pulled out all the stops.

Spotlight NYC, the newest and hottest restaurant and nightspot on the Island, was the perfect location for the hospital fundraiser. Centrally located, it offered an eclectic mix of uptown cultural ambiance and downtown chic, melding both together in a unique fusion of hot music and sophisticated style.

Unlike most hot clubs, Spotlight NYC catered to no one. Here, everyone was equal, much to the surprise and horror of some. Often frequented by Hollywood's elite, it was soon well understood that as soon as you paid and entered the glass doors you could expect the same treatment as the most in-demand superstar.

With a simple plaque at the door that read, *Check Your Ego Here*, the word had quickly gotten out, that at Spotlight NYC anyone could enjoy anonymity and have a good time without suffering the crush of notoriety. And they came in droves: from uptown, downtown, the east side, and west side, Spotlight NYC was the place to be.

Situated on intersecting corners with two separate entrances, Spotlight NYC was a three-story building with a huge open space divided into two separate but complete areas. A club within a club, each section had it's own entrance and dining hall.

The courtyard terrace was composed of several deck-like platforms stair-stepped around a rectangular pond and fountain filled with carp and large goldfish. Bordered by a series of wooden columns that seemed to grow from large slabs of terra cotta, Italian marble and moss-tinted limestone, the openness resembled a stage production set in the middle of Babylon's hanging garden. It was truly a wondrous sight to behold.

Above, the entire area was covered by tinted glass, wooden beams, and completely surrounded by teak wood and live greenery, including full-grown trees. Large baskets of floral bushes sat beneath the trees while smaller hanging baskets held decorative floral vines. Each tree sparkled as tiny, white lights twinkled on a thin wire intertwined throughout the branches.

Frolicking sprites and fanciful fairies of brass and marble perched on feng shui–designed ornamental boulders, situated in the garden scene. Whimsical, miniature, metal sculptures dominated the area set behind the buffet table, giving the whole scene a humorous, light-hearted atmosphere.

The continuous swell of attendees had been manageable and flowed rhythmically all day. For comfort's sake the gala, crowded to the rafters, had opened only the top floor for private diners of the restaurant, leaving two levels plus the courtyard for the fundraiser.

By nine o'clock that night, in the city that never sleeps, a hot, pulsating club called Spotlight NYC had managed to host the most exciting party of the year. With the atmosphere ripe with merriment, the club, complete with DJ and mirrored disco ball, had become a mecca for enjoyment.

* * *

The dance floor was packed solid. Faith returned to Hope's side after several dances with Dennis. She fanned her face with her fingers as Hope handed her a cocktail napkin.

"This place is incredible," she yelled above the loud music, then leaned in closer. "Guess who's here?"

"I'd rather not," Hope said indifferently.

"That's right," she sang out, "he's right over there surrounded by about a dozen women."

"Drop it, Faith."

"Girl, why didn't you tell me before that you knew Dennis Hayes?"

Hope shrugged her shoulders. "We actually just met a few days ago."

"He is so cool. I wonder . . ." Hope noticed that Faith smiled in a way that told her that she was very interested.

"Don't you dare," Hope warned.

"What?" Faith asked innocently.

"You know exactly what. Don't you dare go after him."

"I wasn't even thinking about it, but, now that you mention it," she began, then burst with laughter as her sister's face exhibited the frank knowledge of her raised brow and amorous smile. "Oh my God, you are not going to believe who just walked in." Hope attempted to turn expecting to see Raymond. "No, don't look, wait a second."

Hope stood still, yet she was eager to see Raymond. She waited until Faith glanced back in the direction of the front entrance. "Okay, hurry up, look."

Hope turned quickly, expecting to see Raymond. Instead, she saw someone entirely different. "What is he doing here?"

Faith shook her head "Good question. I thought he was in California with a wife, two point five kids and a white picket fence."

"Apparently not."

Hope turned back around. "There's no way I want that man to see me here."

"Why not?"

Their conversation was interrupted.

Recognizing the voice, Hope turned around nonchalantly. Her eyes sparked seeing Hugh Wescott's son.

"Hello, Hope, Faith." Hope eyed him as Faith rolled her eyes, turned her back and walked away.

Hope nodded her greeting. "Nolan."

"You haven't changed a bit." He smiled through thin, pressed lips. "How've you been?" She didn't answer so he continued. He looked around the room. "I assume you're here alone?" His smirk was evident.

"Can we drop the pleasantries?"

"Hope, it's been years. Can't we at least be civil and drop the hostilities? The past is the past. Let it go. You'll find someone, just as I have."

"If you expect friendship, I suggest you look elsewhere. If you're looking for forgiveness, tough luck."

"Forgiveness for what? You knew the marriage was a farce, just as I did. It didn't take a blind man to see that it was a mistake."

"You're right, it didn't take a blind man. It took your father." She turned to walk away when he reached out a took her arm.

"That was petty and completely uncalled for."

She seethed with enough malice to spoil acid. "I don't usually use this kind of language, but I think I'll make an exception. I'd advise you to take your hand off me and leave me the hell alone." He removed his hand when she gave him a warning look.

She turned around and came face to face with Raymond's very forbidding face. "Here's your drink, darling." He handed Hope a wine glass, then leaned down and kissed her briefly.

Nolan's mouth gaped open.

Raymond glared at Nolan as he wrapped his arm around Hope possessively. Suddenly nervous, Nolan extended his hand to shake as Hope introduced them. "And you are?" Raymond asked of Nolan.

Hope, not sure who she was more annoyed with made the introductions. "Dr. Raymond Gates, this is Nolan Wescott."

"Dr. Wescott," Nolan corrected. Raymond nodded, shook hands appropriately, then turned to Hope. "Shall we dance darling."

"Dr. Gates?" Nolan asked. "Are you by any chance the plastic surgeon?"

"Yes."

Thoroughly impressed, Nolan's demeanor completely changed. "Of course, my father is Dr. Hugh Wescott. He mentioned that you were on staff at Golden Heart. It's an honor to finally meet you. Your work is very well received in California and I am constantly amazed by your father's work."

"Thank you."

Nolan turned to Hope. "So, Hope, I'm glad to see that you're finally going to get the thing on your face removed like I suggested."

"I beg your pardon?" She hadn't been listening to him, but suddenly realized what he was implying. She made a motion to walk away when Raymond took her hand and held her to his side.

"Dr. Wescott," Raymond began in his most condescending tone, "although our relationship is none of your concern, I'm going to let you in on a little secret. A man, a real man, looks at Hope and sees beauty in its purest, most perfect form." He turned to look at Hope admiringly. "If I could, I would stop time for this woman. I treasure every second, every moment that I am blessed to spend with her."

His gaze locked with hers alone. "A lifetime with you will never be enough for me. I would gladly give everything I possess for just a smile, a touch, a whisper." He picked up her hand and gently caressed it, kissing each finger. "I am yours for eternity." He turned back to Nolan. "There is nothing on this perfect being that I would dare touch. Her beauty is beyond my meager skill." He turned his back to Nolan and guided Hope to the dance floor.

Nolan stood with his mouth agape for some time. It wasn't until someone bumped into him did he realize that he was still standing in the same spot, staring at the loving couple on the dance floor.

"What are you doing here? Tickets were sold out months ago," Hope asked as Raymond held her too close.

"I was invited."

"By whom?"

"Dr. Gates, Raymond." Hugh Wescott hurried across the room. "I'm delighted you could clear your schedule."

The song ended and Raymond and Hope parted. "Hello, Hugh," Raymond said, as Hope turned away to look around the crowd. The men shook hands.

"Good evening, Hope."

"Hello, Hugh." She turned to Raymond. "Thanks for the dance," she said pointedly. He knew her exact meaning and nodded assuredly. "If you'll excuse me," Hope said, having her fill of Wescott men for the evening. She found Faith talking to several members of the pediatric ward with Dennis at her side. Hope spent the remainder of the evening as far away from Raymond, Nolan and Hugh as possible. And since Hugh and Nolan barely left Raymond's side, it worked out perfectly.

After the longest hours in recorded history, Raymond was finally able to lose the Wescott doctors. He searched for Hope. He found Faith and Dennis just as they were about to disappear into his office. The two of them had been completely inseparable. But Hope was nowhere in sight.

Raymond began to wonder if she hadn't left while he was being tormented by Hugh and Nolan. Then he spotted her talking outside on the terrace.

Later that evening, tucked away in a secluded nook, Raymond had finally been able to talk Hope into sitting down with him. "I called you several times."

"I know."

"You obviously got my messages. Do you want to tell me why you've been avoiding me?"

"Do you want to tell me why you snuck out in the middle of the night like that?" Raymond honestly had no idea what she was talking about. "You could have at least said good-bye or left a note."

"What? Oh, Hope, I'm sorry. I didn't mean to hurt you by leaving like that. I had an early morning meeting and I didn't want to disturb you. You were sleeping so peacefully that I didn't want to awaken you. But, you're right, I should have left a note. I'm sorry."

Hope looked away, more angry with herself at this point. Due to past experience, she expected a more sinister excuse. Had she just communicated with him, she would have known that his slight wasn't intentional, as Nolan's had been.

"Are we okay?" He took her hand and held it to his lips. "I would never do anything thing to hurt you. I hope you know that."

"I do."

After that Hope and Raymond sat for most of the late evening discussing everything from medical malpractice to New Orleans cuisine.

"I'd love for you to see Crescent Island."

"I can't believe I've never heard of it. Exactly where is it again?"

"A few miles off the coast of Virginia. There's a ferry that'll take you across. It's one of the most beautiful places in the world." He held her hand lovingly. "You really have to visit one day soon."

"I might surprise you and just show up one day. How often do you go down there?"

"Unfortunately, not as often as I like. I try to visit at least once every two months. I usually drive down and visit my dad in Baltimore, then keep going to Virginia."

"Wow, the way you describe the island, it sounds incredible. The history is so unique."

"It is."

Hope spotted Faith on the dance floor partnered with Dennis. She smiled at how much fun they seemed to be having. "They look like they're having fun."

Raymond refused to take his eyes off of Hope. "So tell me about you and Faith. Is there a Charity also?"

"No, it's just the two of us."

"Tell me about your mom and dad. Were you raised in the city or elsewhere?"

Hope took a deep breath. She hated this part. The questions, the getting to know each other part. "My dad deserted us when we were young. My mom remarried, then she died a few years later."

"So you grew up with your stepfather?"

"No."

"What happened to him?"

"He's in the state penitentiary doing a life term for first degree murder." Raymond began laughing until Hope's expression didn't change.

He instantly stopped. "You're serious aren't you?" She nodded slowly. "Hope, I'm sorry. That must have been extremely difficult for you and your sister."

"Faith and I were raised by our mother's mother in Harlem. She's a retired seamstress. We haven't seen or been in contact with my stepfather in over twenty years."

Raymond went silent, then, as if speaking his thoughts aloud, he continued. "It's hard growing up without parents." Hope gave him a *how would you know* look. Raymond saw her skeptical expression. "My mother died of breast cancer when I was young."

"But you still had your father."

"No, I didn't. Not really. He was so devastated when my mother died that he couldn't care for me. I was sent to live with Mamma Lou on Crescent Island. My cousin Tony's mother had died the year before, so he was already living there. We grew up together."

"What about now? I know your dad is still at Johns Hopkins Medical Center, right? Are you two close?"

"Yeah, we are now. He's the Director of Neurology at Johns Hopkins. After my mother died, he threw himself into his career. I hardly ever saw him. It was like not even having a father."

"What about your maternal relatives?"

"I never really knew my mother's family. They kind of slipped out of my life when my mom died." A moment of heavy silence hung between them until Raymond continued. "So it looks like we have something in common. We were both raised without parents."

"But, with a lot of love," Hope added.

Raymond nodded, agreeing completely. "Definitely, a whole lot of love."

"She's such a sweet lady."

"Mamma Lou is something else. Lately she's been driving me crazy."

"What do you mean?"

"Mamma Lou thinks she's a matchmaker. About a year ago she matched my cousin Tony up with his now-wife, Madison. Ever since then, I've been her next target."

Hope began laughing. "Get out of here, really? She's so sweet."

"Don't let her fool you. As a matter of fact, she wanted to match you up with Dennis over there."

"Me? With Dennis? I thought you said that you were next?"

"I was, but that was before she checked into the hospital. Since she's been there, she's left me alone."

"So how did I get involved?"

"Oh, it doesn't take much. Once Mamma Lou decides that she's found the right person, she's impossible to stop. She'll do just about anything to make a match."

"Well, I'm sorry to disappoint her. Dennis is a nice guy and all, but he's really not my type." She glanced over at Dennis and Faith, still on the dance floor partying. "Although, I think he definitely might be Faith's type."

Raymond finally glanced toward the dance floor. "It looks like they're having a great time." He looked around as the music slowed to a soft romantic tune. He took Hope's hand and stood up. "Would you do me the honor of having this dance?"

Hope opened her mouth to decline but closed it just as quickly when Raymond literally whisked, then twirled her up and into his arms. He led her to the dance floor, found a nice spot and embraced her gently.

The dance seemed to go on forever. All Hope knew was that Raymond was the smoothest man she'd ever met. He was firm, but strong, and he moved and glided her across the dance floor like liquid silk. She melted into each step he took. Hope closed her eyes and reveled in the tenderness of his touch as he stroked her back, nuzzling closer.

Her breasts tingled as she was pressed tightly against his chest. Her stomach lurched and quivered each time he maneuvered her closer. The music didn't stop and the evening never ended. To her surprise she didn't ever want it to.

After a while she was sure that she was floating since she didn't remember much of anything else until they stopped walking and entered a small café and bookstore. Open until four in the morning, they sat and talked until it closed. Then, the blur of the evening broadened until she vaguely remembered saying good night at her front door and him turning to leave. Then he stopped, turning back to her. And with purposeful steps he came up to her and waited.

"Is this the part where I ask you to kiss me?"

Raymond smiled openly. "May I?"

Hope looked into his soft, hazel eyes. There was nothing she wanted more at that moment than to be wrapped within Raymond's embrace. "Yes," she said before even finishing her thought. With that simple response he kissed her until she saw stars.

Nineteen

What in the world was I thinking?

Hope yawned sleepily and leaned the back of her head against the sofa cushion as she half-listened to Hugh's assistant talk endlessly about what a great time she had at the fundraiser. She was completely exhausted. Staying up until four in the morning, talking with Raymond at a little coffee shop was totally uncharacteristic. And now she was paying for it.

She yawned again and tried hard to focus on the in-depth report. But unfortunately, all she could think about was the last twelve hours and her wonderfully magical evening with Raymond Gates.

She admonished herself for staying up all night. She should have known better, but she couldn't help herself. She was having such a wonderful time. Raymond was intelligent, charming, and funny. It was the best time she'd had with a man in a long time. She didn't want their time together to end. And best of all, it seemed like he was also having a good time.

But, she didn't want to read too much into it. After all, she was talking about Raymond Gates, a notorious flirt and terminal bachelor. Between him and Dennis Hayes, they had just about every woman at the fundraiser eating out of their hands.

Hope remembered seeing them as they walked through the room. It was truly remarkable. It was as if every female head in the room turned on cue, instantly drawn to the two men.

They talked together, laughing about something only the two of them knew. Raymond's dimpled laugher was addictive. Women couldn't help but fall in love with him. He was breathtaking and completely mesmerizing, clad in a designer suit created to enhance every inch of his firm body.

A continuous line of women stood by his side most of the time. Who could blame them? Vying to get his sole attention became the newest Olympic challenge. To be by his side, dance with him, or just exist in his space was heaven. She remembered the heated stares she'd received toward the end of the evening, as Raymond had stayed by her side.

"Dr. Adams?" Hope looked up from the magazine she barely registered holding. "He'll see you now."

She blew out exasperatedly. These visits to the office were beginning to feel like being sent to the principal's office in grade school. She stood and walked to the half-open door. A smile tugged at her lips when she remembered her University of Pennsylvania sweatshirt and the last time she stood here with a cup of coffee. She pushed open the door and entered the room.

Hugh looked up from his desk with annoyance. "Sit down."

She stood defiantly.

He looked up again seeing that she hadn't moved.

Leaning his elbows on the desk, he folded his long, thin fingers under his chin and got right to the point. "I am told that you attended the fundraiser."

"You saw me at the fundraiser, remember?" She spoke slowly and patiently as if he were senile.

"What is your relationship to Dr. Gates?"

She didn't respond.

"I asked you a question. What is your relationship to Dr. Gates?" he repeated.

"We're colleagues, obviously."

"Are you romantically involved?"

"That's none of your business, is it?"

"It is when it could damage this hospital's reputation and

the Barclay Med Corporation." He slammed the flat of his palm on the desk. "I will not stand by and have you ruin someone else's life like you tried to ruin my son's."

"And I will not let you, nor your son, try to control my life. You did it once, which was enough. What I do, and with whom I do it, is none of your damn business."

"Everything in this hospital is my business, young lady. That includes your selfish behavior."

"What?"

"Everything you do is a direct reflection on this hospital and I will not have it." He slammed his fist down this time. "You will not destroy my work here by embarrassing me with your gold digging."

"My what?"

"At first I thought that you were simply interested in getting that disgusting mark off of your face, but now I learn that you've actually been romantically involved with Dr. Gates," Hugh spat out. His contempt was obvious.

"Oh, I see. Nolan." It had dawned on her that Nolan had told his father of Raymond's passionate remarks the night of the fundraiser.

"Yes, that's right, Nolan. And don't think for a minute you'll be getting him back."

She laughed. She couldn't help herself. Her laughter blurted out like a bursting damn. Hugh's expression was livid, which made her laugh even harder. As tears began to well, she forced herself to get it under control. "There is no way that I'd want your pathetic son back in my life. He's so attached to your apron strings that I'm surprised he had the balls to move to California. He hasn't made a single decision on his own since the day he decided to marry me. Thank God you made him divorce me. I can't imagine spending the rest of my life living with a spineless coward for a husband and having you as a control freak father-in-law."

"I beg your pardon?"

"You should have."

"My son is the best you'll ever know. And as for my fatherly instinct, I knew exactly what you were the moment he brought you to my door. Do you think I hadn't already checked up on you the moment Nolan told me that he was dating you? Yes, I know about your family, your mother and your murdering father. The only reason you married my son was for his inheritance. Don't deny it."

"My murdering stepfather and the two of you would get along admirably. You're exactly the same."

"If you think that a man like Raymond Gates truly wants you in his life, then you are pathetic. He only wants one thing from you."

Her eyes narrowed into slits of fury as she smiled. "Jealous?"

"You're out of line."

"No, I'm out of here." She turned to walk away.

"This isn't over," he demanded, as she opened the door.

"It is for me." The door closed soundly as her name was called.

Hope immediately went back to the ER. As she approached the nurse's station she saw Raymond standing at the counter, conferring with Scott and Maxine. She looked at the three oddly.

Scott and Maxine remained, as Raymond walked over to Hope. She eyed him suspiciously. "What are you doing here?"

His face looked different, tired and peaked. She presumed he was just exhausted like she was, due to their late night and lack of sleep.

"I needed to see you, or rather, to speak with you."

"Regarding Mamma Lou's care?"

"No." Raymond looked around anxiously. Eyes stared from all around the nurse's station. "In private." Hope didn't move. She held the suspicious expression on her face. "Please."

She turned to the nearest nurse. "I'll be right back." Then she turned and went to the ER doctor's lounge. Raymond followed. Moments later, she pushed through the door knowing that Raymond would enter right behind her.

As soon as he entered, he swooped her up in his arms and kissed her. Her arms instantly encircled his neck, drawing him closer. The kiss, hard and demanding, ended in a bevy of nibbles along her neck and shoulder. Breathlessly, they parted.

"I've wanted to do that all day today."

Her eyes were distant and steady.

"What is it?" Raymond asked.

"I'm just tired and busy." Hugh's words rang in her ears.

"Not good enough. What's going on?" She turned away in silence. "Hope. Last night wasn't a fluke was it? We have something very special. Talk to me."

Raymond spun Hope back around to face him. "Talk to me, doctor, answer the question."

"To what end."

"What?"

"We'd be together for a few more days, weeks, months, then what?"

"Then we'd allow the natural progression of a relationship to develop."

"Oh, please. We both know this isn't going anywhere."

Raymond kissed her gently. Taken off guard, Hope's stomach trembled. She drew back, sending her head spinning. "You do that again and I'll remove your spleen."

Raymond smiled, laughed, and watched her walk to the door. "It just might be worth it." She smiled. "Have a little more faith in us."

"I have to get back to work."

"I'll call you later," he promised.

Hope headed back to the ER. Between Hugh's accusations and Raymond's persistence, her head was spinning.

Twenty

"Hey. Are you okay?" Maxine asked, as she walked up to the nurse's station. She placed her hand on Hope's shoulder.

Hope lifted her head from the counter and squinted against the bright lights above her. "What?"

"I asked if you were okay," Maxine repeated, bending down to look into Hope's eyes. "You look a little washed out. Are you coming down with something?"

"No, I'm fine. I'm just tired and I've got a headache, that's all. I guess I've been overdoing it lately."

"There's that summer flu bug still going around. You'd better take care of yourself. Use your downtime to get some rest and recoup."

Hope used two fingers to slowly massage her temples, then she cradled her head in the palms of her hands and leaned back down on the counter. "I definitely intend to."

Maxine looked at her again. A concerned expression covered her face. "Are you sure you're all right?"

"Yeah, I'm fine," Hope said as she reached over to pluck a patient's chart from the carousel. She opened the chart and scanned the first page for effect.

"All right, if I don't see you before you leave, have a good one." Hope nodded, as Maxine walked away. As soon as Maxine disappeared into a patient's room, Hope slid the chart back into its sleeve. She was in no mood to play twenty questions. She looked around the station. She was in an overlap shift, so her presence in the ER was a mere formality, since her relief had already been on shift for close to an hour.

Hope looked at the iridescent glow of her watch. She had just thirty minutes left in her shift. She breathed a sigh of selfish anticipation. Thanks to Hugh, it had been a long time since she'd been granted several, consecutive days off. She intended to take full advantage of each and every second.

First, she intended to sleep for at least twenty-four hours straight. Then, she thought she'd consider grabbing a bite to eat. Afterwards, she'd take a nice long nap for ten to twelve hours. After that, she'd really get some serious rest and relaxation.

A sly, satisfied smile eased its way across her full lips. The sheer selfishness of thinking only of her own needs made her almost giddy. She got light-headed just thinking about it. Five whole days of nothing but sleep, eating and more sleep. She could seriously get used to that.

She had intended on spending some time with Faith, but ever since the night of the fundraiser, Faith and Dennis had been inseparable. They were practically joined at the hip. Dennis even rearranged his schedule so that he could spend some time in the nursery as a volunteer.

Hope checked her watch. Unfortunately, getting herself energized for the last thirty minutes was close to impossible. The ER was unusually slow and she was stuck filling out paperwork and jotting down notes for the physicians taking her caseload.

Tedious, mindless work that had to be completed before a shift ended always made her crazy. It was at that time her mind wandered the most. And, as of late, it wandered more and more in the direction of a certain plastic surgeon.

Hope frowned. She hadn't heard from Raymond in nearly two days. Could she have been right? Could Hugh have been right? Maybe this thing between them was just a distraction on his part. It was beginning to get ridiculous. Of all of the men on the planet she couldn't seem to keep her mind from wandering to Raymond. Sure, he was gorgeous, but looks faded. He was wealthy, but money could be lost. That left his tremendously toned and incredibly agile body. Plainly put, he was built like an Olympian god. But, in her line of work, she'd too often seen how quickly the human body could deteriorate.

That alone should have detoured any further musings. But instead, she mused about the ultimate attraction as far as she was concerned. Raymond Gates was a brilliant surgeon and an undeniably gifted doctor. That, she couldn't deny. The ingenious way his mind worked with unwavering focus was astonishing. There was no wonder he was recognized as the foremost expert on reconstructive surgery and regenerative tissue.

Still, beyond even that, it was Raymond the man that had her so captivated. His warm, loving personality, his giving nature and his overwhelming concern for others, along with his wry humor, were just too hard to resist. She enjoyed being with him. And the way he looked at her made her feel like the most beautiful woman in the world, scar and all.

Blushing, she often remembered how many times she focused on his hands. Strong, tender, and talented, they were the hands of a healer. Suddenly Hope's thoughts wavered to a place she'd long avoided. She knew first hand just how talented his hands actually were.

Drifting further and further into the musing of Raymond, Hope remembered his hands on her. Proficient and capable, he'd rub and knead her tender muscles. In her mind's eye he'd manipulate her body with expert precision and practiced perfection. Endowed equally with strength and gentility, she remembered his hands as they moved from her shoulders to other needful parts of her body.

"That must be some kind of daydream."

"What?" she asked, barely audible.

"Girl, you need to take that look off your face before you get yourself in man-trouble."

"I have no idea what you're talking about."

"Uh huh, I bet you don't." With that, Maxine continued strutting to the nurse's station. "Did you get your page?"

Before she had the opportunity to respond, she was paged again. She quickly grabbed the nearest phone and dialed the central number. She listened to the recorded message, jotted down the phone number, then hung up. She looked at the unfamiliar number again. Who in the world would be calling her from California? Tagged as urgent, she got an outside line and dialed the number. She didn't recognize the area code, but dialed the number anyway. Within seconds a familiar voice answered.

"Dr. Adams? Hope?"

"Yes, speaking." She paused to mentally confirm the voice she half recognized. "Mrs. Gates?"

"Yes, dear and please, call me Mamma Lou."

"What can I do for you?

"I understand that the fundraiser the other night was a huge success."

"Yes, it sure was."

"Did you have a good time?"

"Yes, I did." Hope frowned, not sure where the conversation was going.

"I'm truly sorry I wasn't able to attend, but I heard all about it."

"Well, maybe you'll be healthy enough to attend next year's event."

"I'm sure I will." Then, without missing a beat, she continued. "The reason I called, Hope, is that I need a favor. I need your medical assistance. I'm afraid I'm quite desperate and you're the only one I can turn to."

Concern instantly gripped her. "Are you okay? Are you having chest pains again?"

"No, nothing like that, dear."

"Is it Mr. Wheeler? Or his friend, Mr. Grant?"

"Oh no, dear. We're all fine. What I need is a favor of a very personal nature."

Oh boy, Hope thought to herself. *Here we go.*

"What I need," Louise continued, "is to have someone with medical experience make a house call."

"A house call?"

"Yes."

"Mrs. Gates—" she began, but was cut off.

"Mamma Lou," Louise reiterated more firmly.

Realizing she had little choice, Hope relented momentarily. "Mamma Lou, no one makes house calls anymore. Whatever the problem, just go to your local ER."

"Oh, it's not me, dear. It's my grandson."

Hope's heart lurched, then bottomed in a split second. "Raymond?"

"Yes. I'm afraid he's terribly sick."

"Where is he?"

"At his apartment."

"Where is his apartment?"

"In New York."

"No, I mean where exactly?"

"Oh, the Upper West Side. He's been laid up for the past two days. I'm afraid he's not doing very well at all and I'm unable to get there for another few days. You see, I'm on the West Coast, visiting my son."

"Mrs. Gates—"

"Mamma Lou," Louise corrected her.

"—Mamma Lou, if he's that sick, you need to have an ambulance take him to the nearest hospital."

"I'm afraid that's not possible."

"Why not?"

"He wouldn't go. You see, he's quite stubborn."

"No kidding," Hope said, louder that she intended. *Like, tell me something I don't know.* She'd run into Raymond's stubborn nature several times in the past. They'd gone toe-to-toe and head-to-head on several occasions. Unfortunately with no definite end, they'd often compromised for the better.

"Obviously you're familiar with my grandson's temperament."

"You could say that."

"Then you'll help him?"

"Exactly what's wrong with him?"

"The poor dear, I'm afraid that he has the flu, or a twenty-four hour bug or something."

"The flu this time of year is rare, but I'm sure he's had his flu shot. Just give him a few days. If it's just a virus, that too will pass. He'll be as good as new in no time."

"Well that's not the only problem. He's all alone in the apartment, without a single thing to eat."

"What do you mean, without anything to eat?"

"Exactly that. Raymond always eats out. As a matter of fact, I don't even think his apartment has any pots and pans. I've already spoken to his doorman and he'll let you in with no problem."

"Mrs. Gates, I didn't say that I'd do it."

"You're a healer, dear. It's in your blood. You couldn't allow anyone to lie suffering any more that I could have a begonia go without water. Healing is part of you and there's no way around it."

"Mrs. Gates," she sighed heavily, "Mamma Lou—"

"The doorman's name is Jimmy. He's expecting you. He'll be on duty until midnight, so take your time. You might want to stop at home and pack a few things. There's no telling how long that nasty bug will last."

Realizing that saying no to Louise Gates was not possible, Hope surrendered. "Okay, Mrs. Gates, I'll stop by when I get off work. But that's it. If Raymond needs serious medical attention, I'll make sure he gets to Manhattan Medical and have them contact you."

Louise smiled happily. "Whatever you see fit to do, dear. I trust your judgment." She gave Hope the address and the alarm code. "Thank you, dear. Good-bye."

Hope hung up the telephone and looked at it as if it were

from outer space. "What just happened?" She asked, out loud, as she folded the paper and put it into her jeans pocket.

Hope arrived at Raymond's Upper West Side apartment ninety minutes later. She looked up at the very recognizable building. Somehow she wasn't surprised that it was one of the most renowned apartment buildings in New York City.

Jimmy, the doorman, escorted Hope to Raymond's apartment and handed her a sealed envelope. "Mrs. Gates said that I should give you this. It's the office's key to the elevator and Doc Gates's apartment. She said that you already had the security code."

"Yes I do, Jimmy, thank you." Hope took the envelope and turned it over, reading her name neatly printed on the front. "Excuse me, Jimmy, when exactly did you speak with Mrs. Gates?"

"She called early this afternoon and told me to have the keys ready for you to pick up."

"Mrs. Gates called you early this afternoon?"

"Yes, just after noon. She said that if you need anything, I should help you out. So, if you need anything just call me. I'm on the intercom."

Hope nodded her head knowingly. She'd lived in New York City too long not to know when she was being played. And this set-up reeked of a scam. She opened her purse and reached for her wallet. She pulled out a large bill. "Thank you, Jimmy. I appreciate your help."

"Nah, don't worry about that. Doc and his grandmother always take good care of me and my family," he said, as his head bobbed up and down. He tipped his hat to her and stepped back into the waiting elevator. "Don't forget, use the intercom if you need anything. The number should be by the kitchen phone. I'll be here 'til midnight."

The doors closed, leaving Hope standing in the posh hallway, staring at her reflection in the polished chrome of the elevator doors. Standing there with her medical backpack slung over one shoulder, she finally looked around. The lavish corridor, larger than her living room and dining room put together, was complete with ornate mirrors, decorative wall prints, two high-back chairs and a beautiful, silk, floral display. It was breathtaking, torn right out of the pages of some opulent interior design magazine. "What am I doing here?" she wondered out loud at the empty space.

She walked over to the gilded mirror and looked at herself closely. Her starched, white cotton shirt was buttoned to the top and tucked neatly into her blue jeans. She looked down at her white sneakers. Dressed as she was, she looked more like a college student then a seasoned professional.

The only clue to her true age was on her face. What little makeup she had used had long since vanished and her tired eyes betrayed a long, hard day. She fluffed her curls and subconsciously ran her fingers over the scar. *What am I doing here?* she questioned again, as she opened the sealed envelope and dropped the key ring into her hand.

She gathered up the short chain and eyed the cast metal several times before tilting her head in wonder. *What are you up to Louise Gates?* Her inner voice, naturally suspicious, sang out, loud and clear. There was something else going on, she was sure of it. Louise Gates had an agenda. The question was, how did she fit into it?

Hope turned to the front door, rang the bell and waited. There was no answer, so she rang it again. When there was still no answer, she inserted the key into the lock, turned it and stepped inside.

Twenty-one

A soft, buzzing sound alerted her as soon as she entered. Hope instantly remembered the security code Louise had given her. She dug into her backpack and realized it wasn't there. Her heart began to pound faster. The buzzing had become louder and more pronounced. Jamming her hands into her jeans pockets she came up with a folded piece of paper. She unfolded the pink paper and keyed in the series of numbers. The noise instantly stopped, leaving only silence.

Darkness instantly engulfed her. As her heart continued to pound, she called out. "Hello?" There was no answer. "Terrific," she muttered. She looked around slowly, adjusting her eyes to the darkness. She noticed a dim, muted light glowing from somewhere beyond the open space. She sat her backpack down by the door and looked around for a light switch. Squinting, she found a control switch near the front door. She flipped the switch, bathing the area with muted, overhead track lighting. Overwhelmed by the sight, she let out a joyous laugh.

The apartment was huge. The apartment was empty. She stood for a moment, pondering the sight. The spacious rooms were enormous, yet there wasn't a single piece of furniture anywhere. The whitewashed walls and perfectly-polished parquet floors were spotless and bare.

Hope walked further into the center of the vacant space. She turned around slowly to confirm her first impression. There was no doubt about it. The rooms were completely empty. Not a sofa, chair or table occupied the stark openness.

She moved through the living room to the dining room. A sparkling, crystal chandelier hung down from the center of the completely empty space. She turned back to the living room, seeing the one exception.

A large, as yet unhung painting leaned up against the far wall. Hope walked over to the canvas, bending down to get a better look. The overhead lights illuminated the tranquil scene. It was a lovely, detailed oil painting of a waterfront house with a small cottage behind it, surrounded by massive trees and colorful gardens. In the foreground were two young boys playing, as large, blown bubbles floated gracefully above their heads. The vibrant hues and impressionistic style added to the warmth and charm of the tender scene.

Smiling, she stood, turned, and moved along to the row of curtainless windows that extended along one side of the living and dining rooms walls. She stood at the bare windows. Dusk had settled quickly. The twinkling sparkle of Manhattan's nightlife was just beginning. The windows glowed with a soft, warm, sapphire-blue tint that gave the cityscape below an almost dreamlike look of perfection.

Hope walked toward the back of the apartment. A dim light shown beneath a cracked door at the end of the hall. *Okay,* she said to herself, steadying her resolve, *if he's in here with someone, just turn around and walk out.* With her plan firmly planted in her mind, she pushed the cracked door open and went inside.

She traveled through a short hall with a recessed light set into the ceiling. The hall light was bright enough that she had to squint against the sudden intensity. The four doors were all closed. Methodically, she checked them all. "Hello," she called out, as she grasped the first knob and turned. The room was empty, exactly as the rest of the apartment. The same was true for the next two rooms. The third was a bathroom. She readied herself for the last door, turned the knob and entered.

The room was dimly lit, except for a bright shaft of light coming from a second, cracked door across the room. It split the muted darkness like a knife through a birthday cake. In the soft glow of its illumination, Hope was able to make out that this room was very different from the others. It was larger, cozier and most surprisingly, it was completely furnished.

Perfectly outfitted, including what looked like knick-knacks and photos on the fireplace mantel, this was the master bedroom.

Dark walls of forest-green perfectly matched the mahogany-accented ceiling and chair rail, circling the room. Two large armoires, in a matching mahogany wood, stood side by side like attentive soldiers, guarding what looked like the entrance to a walk-in closet.

Perfect balance was attained with the large television wall unit, the desk, bookcase, sofa and two armchairs. Calculated to precision, each piece countered and complimented the others in explicit, meticulous balance.

Across the room the drapes were still open, even though the dusk of evening began to set, exposing a wondrous view of the season's evening haze. Then, diagonally set, as if looming from the two corners on a raised platform, a sleigh bed broke the room's idyllic symmetry.

She walked over to the bed. She saw a manly form lying atop the tousled bed sheets. Hope eased around to the side of the bed and switched on the nightstand lamp.

She looked down at the heap lying across the bed. He was completely clothed and face up. The two-day-old beard made her smile. He looked more like a dangerous desperado than a sleeping man. "Raymond?" she said softly. He didn't budge. She moved closer. Seeing sweat beaded randomly across his forehead, she reached down to touch him. He was on fire. "Oh my God, you're burning up."

She quickly looked around and found another door leading to the bathroom. She hurried inside and grabbed several towels. She tossed two into the sink. Then she took the third and ran to the kitchen. She held a towel beneath the refrigerator's ice dispenser, gathering a mound of ice cubes. She ran back to the master bath, dropped the ice in the bathroom sink and poured cold water over the towels.

She reached into the iced water and gingerly squeezed the towel damp, then went back into the bedroom. She placed the towel on Raymond's forehead and slowly maneuvered it across his face, down his neck and over his arms. The fever's heat immediately warmed the chilled cloth.

She repeated the action several more times. Then, as the towels were soaking in the iced water she went back to the bedside and began removing his clothing. Now semiconscious, Raymond rolled over with her assistance. Half awake he mumbled, "Hey, what are you doing?"

"I'm taking your clothes off," she whispered seductively, as if she were undressing a lover. She unbuttoned his shirt to the waist and spread it open. "You're burning up. I need to cool you down."

He smiled and muttered, "Good idea." He shifted his shoulder out of his open shirt. She tossed it on the floor next to the bed, then unbuttoned the pants waistband and pulled the pant zipper down. He mumbled something barely audible then drifted back into darkness. She pulled his pants down, sliding everything down as they went.

After she'd completely undressed him, she hurried to the bathroom and returned with a less-chilled, damp towel. But, as she walked to the bed, even in his unconscious state, a primal urge struck her. Suppressing the impulse, she immediately cleared the wayward thoughts. Medically speaking, it wasn't professional. But she couldn't help herself. Womanly desires tugged at her. The memory of their night together made her stomach quiver. She needed to focus.

She swallowed hard, then shook her head, clearing the less-than-medical thoughts. She began gently rubbing his body with the cool towels. He lay there, still as death, while she worked busily to reduce his fever.

After several moments she stopped and returned to the bathroom and placed the towels back into the sink. She placed her chilled hand on her face. She felt the sudden flush of cold instantly. She opened and looked through the cabinets for a thermometer and a fever-reducing medication like ibuprofen or acetaminophen.

Finding neither, she went back to the living room, grabbed her backpack and headed back to the bedroom. She pulled out the thermometer and took his temperature. It was, as she'd feared, just above one hundred. If it were any higher she'd have immediately called an ambulance. She continued with the chilled towels to reduce the heat of his fever.

As Raymond began to cool, she allowed the towels to come to room temperature and laid one across his forehead. The small nightstand light she'd left on by the bed barely illuminated the large room. She walked over to the bed and looked down at the peacefully sleeping Raymond. She smiled. He was pure man-child. The adorable honesty of boyish dreams melded with the hot, sexual intensity of a vital man. She draped the silk sheet over his body.

Hope sat on the other side of the bed and examined her surroundings. The soft dimness of the bedroom held him in perfect stillness as he slept peacefully, unaware of her presence. Deep shadows staggered around the room. Suddenly, she felt as if she were an intruder, invading the sanctum of his inner-most privacy. She watched as his bare chest raised and lowered while his slow, even breathing sang in the stillness of his haven.

His tranquility had bewitched her. She reached out her hand to touch him, but stopped, afraid she would awaken from her own dream. This wasn't the man who had stormed into her patient's room and this wasn't the man who had made love to her that stormy night. This was someone different. This was a man of strength and power. A man who soared with eagles and ran in the company of panthers. This was the man she loved.

It was easy to see how women fell for him. He was everything a young girl was raised to believe in and everything a woman fantasized about. Suddenly she wanted to care for him. He had drawn her into his web of seduction and she had gone willingly.

Resisting temptation, Hope stood up, then walked back to the kitchen. She hung the damp towels on the rim of the sink and looked in the cabinets for a glass. She found a neat row of large wine goblets hanging from an overhead shelf. Having grabbed a glass, she went to the refrigerator for water. The inset dispenser gave her both ice and water. She poured her water, took a sip, then leaned back against the counter.

She looked around the large kitchen. Terra cotta earth tones dominated the wall and floor tiles, while cobalt-blue and sage-green accented the counter and island top. Of a modern design, the lines were clean and stylish. With a classic triangle-style floor plan, it was a perfectly designed kitchen. It looked as if it had never been cooked in.

Hope shook her head, amazed by how easily Louise Gates was able to manipulate her into being here. Absent-mindedly she opened the refrigerator in hopes of finding something to nibble on. To her surprise, the inside was as the rest of the apartment, completely empty, except for half a jar of green olives.

She opened the bottom crispers and found them empty. She went to the cabinets and discovered them just as bare. Then she remembered what Louise had said earlier about Raymond's eating habits, or lack thereof. But, unfortunately, she was hungry and wanted something besides olives.

She looked around and found the number Jimmy had spoken about earlier. She called. He answered on the first ring. "This is Jimmy," he chirped happily.

"Jimmy," she began timidly. "Hi, my name is Dr. Adams. I'm staying with. . ."

"Yeah, Doc," he interrupted. "How ya doing? How's Doc Gates?"

"Jimmy, I wonder if you can give me the name of an area grocer and a pharmacy that delivers."

"Sure Doc, make a list of what you need and I'll have it delivered."

"Oh, okay," she said, surprised by the simplicity of the arrangement. "I'll have the list and a prescription in a few minutes."

"Gimme ten minutes and I'll be right up," Jimmy assured her, before hanging up.

Hope quickly jotted down a brief list of ingredients and some juices. She pulled her medical pad from her backpack and wrote out a prescription to help bring Raymond's fever down. Then she grabbed her wallet and pulled out several twenty dollar bills.

Nine minutes later Jimmy stood at the front door. He took her short list, prescription and cash then promised to have everything delivered within the hour.

Sure to his word, in less than forty-five minutes he had returned with two grocery bags from the local store and a small white bag from the pharmacy.

Hope was stunned when she opened the door to the smiling Jimmy. "Hi, Doc. I got everything you needed."

"That was quick." She stepped aside as he walked into the apartment and went directly to the kitchen. He deposited the two bags onto the counter. He pulled the white pharmacy bag out and handed it to Hope, along with the twenty dollar bills.

"What's this?" she asked.

"Oh yeah, I had the grocery store and pharmacy put everything on the Doc's tab. He'll catch 'em later." Hope was amazed and offered to at least give Jimmy a little something for his troubles. "Nah, that's not necessary. Doc's cool and Mrs. Gates always takes good care of me and the family." He started back to the front door. "Thanks anyway, Doc." He opened the door and stepped out into the hall.

"Thank you again, Jimmy. I'll make sure to mention how wonderful you've been."

He smiled wide, tipped his hat and disappeared onto the waiting elevator. "See you, Doc. Call if you need anything else."

Hope closed the door and walked back into the bedroom.

Raymond was still asleep. She rousted him awake, just enough for him to swallow the two pills and drink some water. Afterwards, he went right back to sleep and she went back to the kitchen. She unpacked the two bags leaving a number of items on the counter. She washed her hands, pulled out a large pot she had seen earlier and began to work.

After boiling for fifteen minutes, the brew of chicken broth bubbled on the stovetop as she completed her last pile of chopped ingredients. Carrots, onions, celery, parsley, a pinch of basil, a dash of thyme, and other herbs sat on the cutting board next to the diced chicken breast. She seasoned the brew and stirred the pot, sending an aromatic cloud wafting through the kitchen.

One at a time she added the remaining ingredients, giving each the opportunity to meld and blend with the seasonings. After all the ingredients had been added, she let the pot cook. Then gradually she added the cooked cubed chicken and egg noodles. She covered the pot and lowered the heat, allowing the soup to simmer until the vegetables were tender and the noodles were done.

In less than ninety minutes' time she was savoring the aromatic concoction. She found an oversized mug in the cabinet and helped herself to a serving of chicken soup. It was perfect. She put the rest of the soup in the refrigerator, then cleaned up the kitchen. Afterwards, she went back into the bedroom to check on her patient. He was still asleep, so she relaxed in the chair beside the bed.

Half an hour later, Hope looked up just as Raymond began to stir. She watched as he looked around then found her sitting in the chair next to the bed. She smiled down at him. "Hi. How do you feel?" Her voice was thick and husky.

His dimple, barely noticeable beneath the silken hairs of his beard, slyly winked at her. "How do I look?"

She lowered her eyes not wanting to show the inner turmoil she was going through, just from seeing his half-naked body lying there.

"That bad, huh?"

"You look like you have a virus."

Ever the jokester, he muttered slowly. "Good, 'cause that would explain why I feel like I have a virus."

"I see that you haven't lost you sense of humor."

"Always the last to go. How long have I been asleep?"

"I don't know, but I got here about four and a half hours ago. Did you take anything before falling asleep?" He shook his head from side to side. "Good, then take this." She reached into a white paper bag and pulled out a medicine bottle. She unsuccessfully twisted at a small white cap several times. She stopped, then twisted again. "I hate these bottle tops. They never open when you want them to. Although, just give it to a four-year-old kid and voila, the cap pops right off."

"Give it to me." Raymond rose up on his elbows then reached out to take the bottle from her.

She chuckled. "To do what?" She looked down at the bottle, reread the directions, then tried twisting it again. "You can barely sit up. You're as weak as a babe."

"Ah, that's where you're wrong. I'm not as weak as I appear. I'm saving my strength for"—he paused to leer at her—"later." She laughed at his attempt at seduction. "Come on, give me the bottle."

"You don't have the energy to argue with me, so just shut up, lay back and do as I say."

"You're loving this, aren't you?"

She nodded with an impish grin.

Raymond plopped back onto the pillows. "You need to work on your bedside manner."

"So I've been told." She finally opened the bottle. She dropped two pills into her hand and picked up a glass of water from the nightstand. Raymond took the pills, swallowed, then sipped the water.

"I assume I'm no longer delirious and hallucinating. So, tell me," he breathed heavily, "what exactly are you doing here?"

"I'm apparently making a house call."

"How did you get in?"

"Jimmy. Your grandmother left the key with him."

He nodded and smiled. "So that's what you're doing here. Mamma Lou sent you."

"She was concerned, so she asked me to stop by."

He nodded his head slightly, then placed his hand over his eyes. "Is it bright in here or is it just me?"

Hope looked around the dark room as she came closer to the bed. "It's just you."

She reached down and placed her hand on his forehead. He was warm but not as hot as he was earlier. "You still have a fever."

"Thanks, Doc."

She picked up a cold glass of water again. "Here," she placed the glass to his lips. "You're dehydrated. You need to drink more of this."

Raymond caressed her with his eyes, drawing an instant blush from Hope as she looked away. "You look tired."

"I am," she answered, still holding the glass to him.

"Lie down."

"I will, as soon as I get home."

"No. Lie down here, next to me."

"Raymond, my being here is a professional courtesy. I don't lie down with my patients in the ER and I have no intention of lying down with you here. Understood? Now, finish your water."

Raymond smiled as he half sat up and took a few more sips from the glass. He collapsed as she placed the glass back on the nightstand. "You need to rest."

"I intend to rest. I have the next few days off. I am going home to sleep for at least twenty hours."

"You can sleep here."

"You have one bed in a four bedroom apartment. So much for sleepovers." She gasped silently. "I'm sorry. I didn't mean that. Your personal life is none of my business."

Raymond smiled weakly. "Dr. Hope Adams, frazzled. I

kind of like that. And, I believe that now you are my personal business."

"Drink," she demanded, softly holding the glass closer to his mouth.

"You're not being very nice."

"I know, drink." He did, until the tall glass of water was empty. She placed the glass on the nightstand and sat down on the bed next to him. She placed her hand across his forehead and nodded approvingly.

"Still warm?" he asked. She nodded. He reached up and stroked the side of her face just as he had in the cafeteria. This time she didn't pull away. "You are so beautiful sitting there like that."

"You're delirious."

"True. But you're still beautiful." She blushed.

He peeked under the sheets seeing that he was completely undressed. The dimple winked again. "One of us is entirely overdressed. See what you can do about that." He yawned, laid back, then promptly fell asleep.

Raymond's tender words echoed through her mind as she stood and went into the bathroom. She turned on the faucet, took a washcloth from the basket, and then dipped it into the cool, running water. Slowly she held the cloth to her face and let the coolness refresh her. After wringing the cloth dry she looked up at her reflection in the mirror.

Detached, she moved her face from side to side. She never considered herself as anything special. She had an average face with average features and an average body. Suddenly she smiled as naughty thoughts skipped through her head. *He said I was beautiful.* She dampened and puckered her lips, then yawned. She looked at her watch. It had gotten late, she was exhausted and going home at this hour would be ridiculous.

She walked back into the bedroom. She looked down at Raymond, asleep, then to the opposite side of the bed. She decided to lie down on top on the comforter, next to Raymond. The silky, satiny softness was just what she needed to relax her. She rolled over and watched the slow rhythm of his breathing. She closed her eyes and fell right to sleep.

The dream was divine. Soft, warm and floating, she snuggled deeper into the curve of the comfort. Breathing serenely, she drifted on a pool of still water, troubled only by the molding of her body to the gentle waves. In luxurious self-indulgence, she bathed in lavish comfort. With a sigh of contentment, she snuggled deeper and closer to the source of her pleasure.

Soon, her soothing solace became an aroused yearning as she felt the tender whispers of a tantalizing embrace. Against a caressing curve she murmured, keeping her eyes closed for fear that the illusion would vanish. "What are you doing?" she moaned, still half intoxicated by the feel of his body intimately pressed against hers.

"Kissing you," he said as he continued to shower tiny kisses onto her shoulder. She savored the feel of his mouth.

"You can't do that," she moaned, half-audibly.

"Can't do what?"

"That."

"Oh," he continued. "Why not?"

" 'Cause."

" 'Cause isn't a valid reason." Raymond attested.

" 'Cause," she began, then sighed deeply, and began again. Her voice was thick with emotion. " 'Cause it wouldn't be right."

"Why wouldn't it be right?" Never moving his hands from his side, he continued kissing her, tracing a burning trail of desire along the curve of her neck and shoulder. Hope squeezed her eyes tighter. The ember of desire made her body tremble.

"Because of the situation," she barely rasped out.

"What situation?"

"Me, here, lying in your bed like this, with you. You're still sick."

Raymond didn't answer, so Hope opened a single eye. She turned. When she saw the expression on his face, she opened the other eye and looked at him. She looked into his face and instantly saw the difference. "You shaved."

"Don't tell me that you prefer the beard?"

"What are you smiling about?"

"Technically we've just slept together."

"Technically, I fell asleep on the opposite side of the bed while you were incapacitated. So, nothing happened."

"The evening is young," he smiled seductively.

She sighed pleasantly. "All that proves is that you were unconscious and I was exhausted. But now that we're both"—he began kissing her shoulder again—"in our right minds we can," she moaned when he nibbled her earlobe, "we can, we can—" Raymond's kisses drizzled to the hollow of her neck, causing a series of tantalizing sensations to erupt. She shuddered, loosing track of her thoughts.

"Yes, we can," he readily agreed.

"Think more clearly," she quickly added. Unfortunately, thinking more clearly was the last thing on her very clouded mind.

"I am thinking clearly," Raymond assured her.

"Your temperature is close to 102 degrees. You're hardly capable of a roll in the hay."

"My temperature is 99.2. I'd hardly qualify that as critical." Her expression questioned how he knew his exact temperature. "I got up while you were asleep."

She looked down the length of him. He had slipped into a pair of sweatpants. "Be that as it may, you're still sick."

"You obviously don't know me very well. I'm a man of many talents. That, you will learn." He ran his finger down the length of her arm.

Hope quickly sat up and slid her feet to the side of the bed. "Since you're obviously feeling much better, I'll leave." She stood and turned away.

Raymond reached and captured her hand. "Hope."

She went still. Her heart pounded in her chest. There was nothing she wanted more in the world at this moment than to make love with this man, but she knew it wouldn't be enough. She refused to turn around, knowing that if she did, she'd be lost in his eyes forever. She turned further away to face the opposite side of the room. She looked at the armoire, the dresser, the paintings, and the sitting area, anything not to look at him.

"Hope," he repeated, softer.

"You're vulnerable right now, Raymond. You don't know what you're saying. You're going to wake up tomorrow morning and be glad that I didn't stay. Believe me."

"I feel so much for you, it scares me. I've never felt this way before. I love you, Hope."

"No. You don't mean that." Hope shook her head repeatedly. Nervously, she placed her free hand over her scar to soothe her aching heart.

"Yes, I do," he whispered softly as he sat up and gently pulled her back onto the bed beside him. "Ever since that night I saw you in the doctor's lounge. You were crying. You were so beautiful, so fragile and delicate. I wanted to climb the tower, slay the dragon, be your hero and rescue you. I wanted to save you from whatever demons troubled you. At that moment I knew that there was something special about you. I needed to know you. I mean really know you, know everything there is to know about you. I still do. But one thing I already know that is you're someone I need in my life." His declaration was heartfelt.

Boldly she turned to face him. "Your chivalry is commendable, Raymond, but I don't need your protection, your pity, or to be rescued."

"Pity? You? Are you kidding?" He chuckled slightly. "You, Hope, are the strongest, toughest, most indomitable woman I've ever met. You're also the sexiest woman I've ever met. I crave you. And I know that you're just as attracted to me as I am to you." Their eyes locked: his, painfully sincere, hers, undeniably tempted, but still on the brink of denial.

In her heart, there was no denying her feelings for him. He was right. She was attracted to him. But she knew that there was more. She was in love with him. She closed her eyes, muted against the truth.

"Kiss me and prove me wrong." He leaned in, his mouth just inches from hers. "Kiss me." She didn't move. He kissed her lips gently.

"I can't."

"But, you want to."

Looking at him was her undoing. One night with Raymond was all she had ever imagined. Tonight, a second night, would only cement her feelings. She knew that. She also knew that in their very different worlds, they could never share anything more than a brief moment in time. But, one more moment was all she needed to fulfill a fantasy. So, with all the urgency and passion she had locked up inside of her, in loving infatuation, she dived off of the highest cliff into the shallow stream called love.

She kissed him.

Surrendering to his taste, she reeled dizzily, feeling the force of his mouth on hers. Her thoughts, a clouded mass of colors and images, swam in an endless pool of passion. She floated on the very real possibility of making love to him again. Her body soared, anticipating more of his aroused urges. She closed her eyes and soaked in the heavenly rapture of the moment.

The sound of his moan edged her further into the solidness of his embrace. Intoxicated with wanton passion, her mind whirled with desire. The splinter of need that had been planted the first night she saw him, now emerged at an uncontrollable force, consuming all that she was.

Deepening in intensity, the kiss consumed both of them. Then, slowly the intensity faded into gently, pleasing passion. His lips pressed tenderly until she felt a mere whispered caress.

Raymond leaned back, his eyes riveted to her face. He soaked in every loving inch, memorizing the moment to immortalize for an eternity. He smiled, his eyes loving and adoring. "You are so beautiful." His allure beckoned her.

He drew her closer. She fell onto his bare chest. Her heart pounded riotously as she held tightly to his firm body, a body designed in heaven and made to please a woman. She spread her hands wide over his chest, entwining her fingers in the gentle hairs. His nipples hardened instantly as a low, rumbling moan purred from him.

Hope closed her eyes. This was far better than any fantasy she could have imagined. His body grew hot as the fire within raged. He laid her back, positioning himself on top of her. He braced her hands up against the overstuffed pillows. His hands drifted over her shoulders, down her arms and over the flat of her stomach. Slowly he unbuttoned her white shirt and spread the ends wide revealing a white, lace bra. A crooked smile of satisfied pleasure spread wide as he unsnapped the front hook and released her.

Hope inhaled quickly when his mouth covered her. Her moan quaked him, prompting an increased intensity. She bit at her lower lip, holding in the scream begging to be released. Without breaking his rhythm, his hands slipped beneath her waist and lifted her up. He pulled her closer against his body as he slowly rolled. She sat up, looking down on him, her legs comfortably straddling him. She instantly felt the hardness of his desire through the soft material of his pants.

Holding her firmly, he tantalized each breast. The teasing torture sent a shock wave surging through her body. She quaked, arching forward, allowing him full access. He lifted her upwards, kissing and caressing his way to the flat of her stomach. She floated precariously until he rolled over gently, lying next to her, on his side.

Silence.

He stopped.

Something is wrong. He changed his mind. He doesn't want me. Hope opened her eyes with a flinch. Her chest heaved rapidly. The split-second of panic lasted an eternity. It ended when she looked up and saw Raymond smiling down at her. "You are so beautiful." Erotically, he ran a single finger across her lips, down her neck, encircled each breast then delved lower to the waistband of her jeans. Her breathing increased instantly.

Still smiling, he took each of her hands and placed them above her head. "I just want to look at you." He was nearly begging. Hope began to lower her hands to her face. "Don't. Let me see you. All of you." He took each hand, kissed it, then placed them back above her.

"I. . ."

"Shh. . ." his dimple winked at her playfully. "You undressed me, so it's only fair." She squirmed when he slowly unbuttoned her jeans and pulled the zipper down. The metal ripping sound lasted longer then she had imagined.

Enticingly, he rubbed her stomach, sending a scalding blast of heat through her. Her quick intake and low throaty moan was his provocation. He freed her from her pants. "I like these," he said toying with the thin elastic lace of her panty waistband. He drew a finger around the elastic, pulling just enough to peek at her possibilities. She squirmed. A low, guttural groan emanated from his primal need.

His hands traveled down the length of her, eliciting the desired response. She surrendered. Then, she felt the moist wetness of his mouth as he tasted her soft brown thighs. He kissed her knee while caressing the form of her legs.

The torment of his body so close and her need so strong was torture. "Raymond. Now," she commanded.

He shook his head from side to side. "Not yet, my love. I've only just begun. We've got all night. I'm not going anywhere this time. I want to memorize every inch of you by dawn, then start all over again."

The unimaginable possibility of his assertion sent a shot of fire to her core. "Raymond," she called out.

He kissed her softly. "Shh. . . let me love you," he whispered in her ear as he leaned over her. His detailed promise gripped her in a dizzying state, sending a swirl of images through her mind. He intended to make love to her all night long.

His talented hands began the fateful promise of his words.

He sat back, observing her every reaction. "I want to know what pleases you. Does this please you?"

She gasped, her eyes blinked closed. A bright flash of light blinded her at his touch. The medical profession had surely taught him well. He truly knew how to bend the female body to his will. "Do you like that?" he asked as his hand dipped between her thighs and found the core of her pleasure.

Hope had no idea if she answered or not. Her mind was a total wash. She could only bend to his skillful touch.

The surging, hot burn intensified. She was on the verge. "Raymond, now," she demanded, as his torment escalated.

"Yes, now," he said increasing the sensation of her pleasure point. "Does this please you?"

She raked her lower lip between her teeth. Her body writhed in quickening anticipation. She moved against him. Faster and faster. She held her breath as she soared blindly, higher and higher. Her body jerked, spasmed, and rocked as she screamed and cried out his name. He had fulfilled his promise, yet his torturous skill continued.

She spasmed again, writhing on the wings of her pleasure. He took her to that wondrous place, again and again. Each time she soared higher and higher, never ceasing to reach the pinnacle of pleasure.

Breathless and panting, she reached for him. He accepted her hand as he reached over to the nightstand for a foil packet. He opened it and prepared himself. Hope opened her eyes and smiled seductively. It was her turn to please him.

He leaned over her. The weight of his body was held at bay by the strength of his muscular arms. She looked down the length of him. Toned muscles rippled against her. She reached out. He pulled away. His muted expression was easily readable. *Yes.* She nodded. Wholeheartedly.

He came just to her and paused a fraction of an inch from where she needed him to be. He looked down into her eyes. She quivered, seeing the familiar sincerity.

He entered her fully. The engrossing feel of him inside of

her made her gasp, then sigh. Her eyes fluttered closed as she raised her legs to surround his waist.

Raymond intended to remain still and savor the moment. He'd always known that Hope was special. But he had no idea that she was special for him solely. The desire he'd felt for her gave way to something more cherished. It was as if he had found his destiny, his hope. He had reached the place where he would forever belong.

Hope developed a rhythm. She moved her hips, thrusting to meet, capture, release then recapture him. Eyes wide open, their faces masked nothing. Eye to eye, mouth-to-mouth, they gave fully, bonding together in the primal dance. Firmly entwined, the rhythm increased as he led. Deeper and deeper, faster and faster, they gyrated until the lustful tension blinded them with unrestrained resolve. Pulsing, pounding and throbbing, the dance quickened.

A tsunami of abandoned pleasure sent them soaring as one. She screamed in blinding release. He tensed up and held her even tighter, calling out the primal roar of perfectly sated pleasure. After several moments of earth-stopping, mind-blowing spasms, they drifted back, settling comfortably in each other's arms. There was no way she could make love to another man after him. Raymond had seen to that.

Silently, they lay in each other's arms. Words weren't needed and could never adequately express their emotions. With a mix of playful teasing, Raymond firmly massaged her bottom. "You realize, of course, that you've branded me. You're stuck with me now." He rolled over bringing her to his side.

"Really?" she said, comfortably settling along the length of his body.

"Um hum. It's an old African proverb. When a man has gold in his hand, and diamonds in his pocket, he puts his hands in his pocket and never lets go."

"That makes absolutely no sense."

"Okay, how about this one. When a man finds Hope, he never lets go."

"That's worse than the first one."

"Okay what about. . ."

"Truth or dare?" she interrupted.

"Truth."

"Where do you see this going?"

"All the way."

"What does that mean?"

"Uh, ah, ah, only one question. My turn. Truth or dare?"

"Dare," she responded bravely.

Raymond smiled, satisfied with her choice. "I dare you to marry me."

"What?"

"You heard me." He leaned up on his elbow and looked into her eyes. "I realize that this isn't the most romantic setting and I promise that once I choose the perfect ring, I'll get down on bended knee and do it right. But, for the time being, will you marry me?"

"How can you ask that? You don't even know me."

"Answer the dare, Hope. Marry me."

Hope sat up and swung her legs off the side of the bed. "This isn't funny. I don't want to play anymore."

"I'm not laughing. It's not a joke. I'm asking you to marry me."

"Then my answer is no." She paused and waited for it to come.

Raymond smiled and pulled her back by his side. "Your mouth says no, but your eyes say yes. I'll accept your answer for the time being, but as soon as I get the ring, you'll say yes to me."

Hope snuggled comfortably beside him. "Your money can't buy me and your prestige doesn't impress me."

"In that case, I'll just have to try harder."

Twenty-Two

Hope got up slowly and gathered the remnants of the tousled sheets around her. She stood and looked around the room for her clothing. She hadn't seen them in almost three days. She found her jeans and shirt hanging in the closet and the rest of her belongings neatly cleaned and folded on the dresser. She gathered everything and hurried into the bathroom to get dressed.

When she came out she saw Raymond still asleep in the bed. She walked over and reached down to touch him. Her soft gentle strokes were loving and tender. This was how loving should be. In Raymond, she'd found everything she had ever wanted in a man. He was sweet, charming, kind, loving and tender. And each time he called her name or touched her, it was as if the world grew brighter.

She had spent three wondrous days and nights in his arms doing everything from playing Scrabble to watching old movies to discussing medicine and of course, making love. Her stomach instantly twitched at the thought of their union and her skin flushed hot with sensous memories. He was an incredibly inventive lover who had indulged and satisfied her every whim. Every desire and every fantasy she'd ever imagined, he had fulfilled. She smiled at the silk tie still wrapped around his wrist. It wasn't going to be easy walking away from him, but she knew she had to. She grabbed her backpack, socks and sneakers, then quietly hurried out.

She stood at the window looking out at the darkness of the

city before her. Dawn had just reached out across the night's sky, pulling with it all the hopes and dreams from the night before. Hope watched as daybreak slowly inched from behind the buildings and trees, beginning to make its ascension, bringing with it the promise of a new day and the memories of a past one.

Dreamingly, she stood remembering the childlike fairy tales from long ago where everything was perfect, hope found a way and love always worked out in the end. Cinderella found her Prince Charming, Snow White found her Prince; even Miss Piggy found her Kermit and lived happily ever after. Hope turned and looked back to the bedroom. A part of her had always longed for the happily ever after scenario, where the loving couple happily walked off into the sunset, but she knew that it was impossible. She'd seen too many times when love had caused hurt and destruction. She would never let it happen to her, not again.

"There you are," Raymond smiled as he walked up behind her. "Woman, you have this strange effect on me." Hope squirmed anxiously as he moved closer.

"What effect is that?" she asked, unable to think clearly. Raymond moved even closer, then averted his direction to stand beside her at the window.

"I would have thought you'd have figured that out after three days and nights," he said, almost breathless, as his dimpled winked seductively. "I want you in my life."

"For how long?" Hope asked without turning to him. She couldn't bring herself to look at him just yet. A whirlpool of confusion swirled around in her mind. Attraction intermingled with confusion as lust readily gave way to desire.

"For as long as we can be together. How about forever?" he whispered gently into her ear. The warmth of his breath tickled her, making her squirm away. He stepped behind her and placed his hands on her shoulders and dipped his head into the curve of her neck. He pecked tiny kisses at her earlobe, then trailed down her neck and across her shoulder. A series of chills ran through her. This man had the Midas touch when it came to her body. Thoughts of their nights together sent a thrilling spark through her. Hope shook her head as she watched their reflection in the window.

"Are you all right?"

She nodded her head anxiously.

"Liar. Come on, tell me what's wrong."

"Nothing," she moaned.

Intuitively she melted into the curve of his body and he gathered her closer. An unconscious moan slipped from her lips as his magic continued. She closed her eyes, weakened by the feel of his body behind her. His desire was evident as his arms encircled her.

"Hope?" Raymond asked.

She suddenly jerked away, and then spun around. "Aren't you gonna asked me how I got it?" She stared into his eyes, waiting for the inevitable flinch. It didn't come.

Raymond reached out and gently touched the scar on her face. "Trust is something you don't ask for. When you're ready, you'll tell me."

"Why are you being like this?"

"Like what?"

"I have to go," she barely rasped out.

"No, you don't. Stay here with me."

"I can't." She stepped away, only to be drawn back into his embrace.

"Of course you can. We have everything we need right here."

"What do you want from me, Raymond?"

"What?"

"Why me? Why did you choose me? I'm not exactly your type."

"What's my type?"

"Thin, beautiful, graceful, obedient, submissive, well-behaved," she paused for a single breath then continued, "unscarred."

"What kind of list is that?" He backed away, staring at her oddly. "It sounds more like requirements for adopting a puppy. Is that the type of man you think I am?"

"Oh please, that's what every man wants in a woman. Perfection."

"Where is this coming from?"

"Every man wants a woman that he can dominate, with the coldhearted, masculine blade of control. Wielding the ultimate power: fear. My father left us as soon as Faith was born. You see my mother wasn't perfect because he only wanted boys. My stepfather controlled my mom until the day he killed her. Nolan controlled my past, and Hugh controls my future," she said with tears in her eyes. "There doesn't seem to be anything left. So, what do you want to control?"

"I don't know what kind of men you're used to dealing with, but they all seem to have a serious testosterone problem. That's not me. You of all people should know that by now." His smile was all she needed to see that he wasn't like the others. She knew in her heart that he wouldn't take advantage of her or deliberately hurt her. "You, Hope, are my perfect gem. You sparkle and shine beyond anything I've ever experienced."

Hope looked away. "Your gem is flawed."

Raymond tipped her chin back to his direction. "You're one of a kind, Doc, and I can't keep my eyes off of you. I can't stop thinking about you. I admire you and I adore you. I love you."

Hope turned. The twinkling light of New York awakening sparkled behind her. "Love is a trap and I'm not a fixer-upper. I don't want to be healed or saved or cured or rescued. I come exactly as you see me. I control me."

"You do need to be healed and if you'd let me, I can heal you." She turned quickly, expecting to finally hear the words. Raymond reached down and touched her heart. "In here." She looked at him. His sincerity was overwhelming. "I wish you could see yourself as I do. You are so beautiful."

"Stop saying that!" She nearly screamed. "I'm not beautiful. Look at me. Now. Look at me exactly as I am, scar and all. Even your skills as a plastic surgeon can't heal this."

"Hope," he began.

She threw her hands up to silence him. "I don't need your pity."

"Is that all you think this is about? Pity?"

"Tell me it's not."

"I didn't think I had to. I thought you felt something for me. I thought this was going somewhere."

"I have to go."

"Hope."

"Thank you so much for your hospitality."

"Hope. Don't run from this."

"I'm not running."

"You've been running all your life. It's time to stop."

Hope turned around, stunned by the truth in his words. "I don't know what are you talking about."

"Hope, I already knew what happened to your mother."

Her mouth gaped open in stunned pain. The anguish of someone else knowing and pitying her was abhorrent. "How dare you pry into my private life?"

He moved closer. "I didn't pry. I didn't have to."

"Who told you?"

"It doesn't matter. I have to go to Crescent Island tomorrow. Come with me. I want you to meet everyone. They're going to love you as much as I do." He reached for her, she backed away.

She looked at him and shook her head. "Good-bye, Raymond."

Twenty-three

Raymond and Tony walked down the path toward the small deck that extended out into the Chesapeake Bay. They stood in silence as each contemplated the explosion of beauty laid out before them. Raymond smiled watching a butterfly dance across the water's edge in search of refreshment. It was the perfect scenery. It was God's Garden.

Aptly named, Crescent Island was considered by most to be the picturesque perfection of God's creation. In its awesome beauty, it was unparallel. A favorite vacation destination to camera-toting vacationers and weekend retreats, it was considered one of the most desirable locations on the East Coast. The tourist brochures boasted that the island charmed over two million visitors each year. That was easily attested to by the hundreds that flocked to the small, moon-shaped island each day, throughout the peak seasons.

Located in the Chesapeake Bay area, just off the coast of Virginia's mainland, it was surrounded by numerous smaller islands. But none was as lovely and charming as Crescent. Those who adored history relished the historical aspects of the island, which had been settled by freed slaves on a quest to return to their motherland, Africa.

The brochures told of several hundred freed slaves who boarded many small vessels and sailed toward the rising sun, in hopes of returning to their homeland. They never reached their homeland; instead, they landed on a beautiful crescent-shaped island in the middle of the Chesapeake Bay. The island became their new home.

That was over a century ago. Now, visitors journeyed there for a different reason. Some came to follow the historical journey of the freed slaves: to see their grave markers, their church and their home sites. Others came for the sheer pleasure of resting and relaxing, away from the hectic pace of the big city rat race. And, still others came to enjoy the excellent seafood, fishing, classic gardens and small-town elegance. But, more were drawn in by the wonderfully quaint shops, and the simple peace and quiet of nature.

Raymond's thoughts centered on the peace and harmony of rejuvenation. He needed the comfort and solace that Crescent Island had always offered. He needed the serenity of spirit to know that all would be right in the end. Deep down he knew that he and Hope would have a long, full life together. He just had to be patient and have hope that she'd realize the same.

The sound of nature sang in splendid form, as did the lilting sound of Madison and her sister, Kennedy, laughing and talking in the distance.

This was Kennedy's first trip back to Crescent Island since Tony and Madison had wed. Madison was insistent on showing her every nook and cranny of the island she had grown to love and call her second home.

They had all just returned from a morning outing, visiting tourist retreats and experiencing private haunts from Raymond and Tony's youth. It was interesting to revisit the places he had taken for granted, now seeing them through Kennedy's eyes. He anxiously wanted to show his home to the one person in the world he couldn't yet: Hope.

This was Tony and Madison's first real opportunity to see everyone since their extended honeymoon, which included a lengthy stay in Egypt for Madison's research and a extensive sojourn to Eastern Africa for Tony's antique stores.

As if reading his mind, Tony broke into Raymond's

thoughts. "No matter where I go in this world, there's nothing like coming back here to Crescent Island."

Raymond nodded his head in complete agreement but remained silent and pensive.

Crescent Island would always be his second home. He was raised here and, like Tony, would always call it home. Wistfully, Raymond's thoughts went to Hope. She would love this place and also call it her home someday.

It had been just two days, but already it seemed like a lifetime. Hope's absence from his life, the emptiness he felt, and the desire to bring her home to Crescent instantly brought a brooding scowl to his face.

Tony looked over at Raymond. "I know that look," he simply stated. Raymond responded by kneeling down and picking up a small pebble. He rolled it around in the palm of his hand for a few moments, then looked out across the Bay to the bright red sun, setting in the west. Tony smiled patiently.

Raymond was a tortured and troubled man. He tossed the stone and watched it skip across the stilled water until it finally sank deeply, mirroring the depths of his own sorrow. He watched as the rippling circles expanded until they reached the outer banks, disappearing into the lapping water on the sandy beach. He shook his head, as if to surrender to the weighted emotions within his heart.

"Married life must agree with you and the news of your pending fatherhood is wonderful. I couldn't be happier for you."

"Thanks, man. It was a big surprise when Madison told me. I just hope I can be half the father our fathers are."

Raymond nodded his head in agreement. "I must say, cuz, I've never seen you look so deliriously happy."

Tony turned to watch the sun sparkle around Madison as she walked to the gardens with Kennedy and Mamma Lou. She was as beautiful now as she had been the first moment he'd laid eyes on her. "I truly am. Madison is still the most incredible woman I've ever met. I can't imagine my life without her."

"Well, you almost had to."

Tony thought back to the time leading up to their relationship. He was a fool and because of his arrogance, had almost missed out on the most precious thing in his life. "I still can't believe what a fool I was."

"I can," Raymond joked, as Tony swung at him playfully.

"All because I refused Mamma Lou's matchmaking." Tony shook his head at the near-missed possibility. "I don't know what I would have done if Madison had turned me down."

"You would have persisted until she accepted your proposal."

Tony nodded. That's exactly what he would have done. "So, what's Mamma Lou been up to with you? Has she been driving you crazy with dates?"

"No, not me." Tony's brow rose.

"That's odd. I thought surely you were next in her sights."

"Mamma Lou met a woman when she was in the hospital. She was her ER physician. Dr. Hope Adams. I think she's been concentrating on matching her up."

"Really?"

"Yeah, really." Tony's brow rose at hearing Raymond's disturbed tone.

"You don't sound all that pleased with Mamma Lou's latest quest. I would think you'd be ecstatic that she's concentrating on someone else and not trying to hook you up with someone." Tony looked at Raymond. His expression betrayed his troubled thoughts.

Raymond scratched at his head roughly. The annoyance of hearing those words did little to assuage his feelings. It was a true oxymoron. On one hand, Mamma Lou wasn't after him to marry any longer. But, on the other hand, she was after Hope to marry. "The thing is, Hope is an incredible woman. She's a brilliant doctor: compassionate, caring, and attentive. She's funny, graceful, and classy, in a down-to-earth kind of way. She's patient, generous, and she cries when a young man dies in her arms. And," Raymond smiled, remembering his time with Hope, "she's got a laugh that could brighten up purgatory."

"She sounds like the perfect woman."

Raymond laughed openly. "She's far from perfect. She's also stubborn, persistent, pig-headed, and won't listen to a word I say without at least fifteen minutes of heated debate."

"So she doesn't take any of your crap. It sounds like she's got you pegged already."

Raymond looked at his cousin in warning then shook his head, smiling. "In a New York minute."

"So, why hasn't Mamma Lou tried to match you up with her?"

"I told her that I wasn't interested, so she's been pulling every available bachelor out of her bag. She pinpointed her focus on Dennis for a while, but he was more interested in Hope's sister, Faith. So, she talked Madison's brother, J.T., into coming to New York to meet her."

"Did he meet her?"

"No, I called and asked him to cancel."

"Oh really? And why was that?"

"I don't know."

"Yes you do."

"Yeah, I do. Sometime, somewhere, somehow, I changed my mind, okay? Are you happy?"

Tony nodded his head. "I think the question is, are you happy?"

"No."

"So, do something about it. Tell her."

Raymond shrugged and looked out into the Chesapeake Bay. The crystal water sparkled like fine jewels tossed across the water's surface. Raymond bent down, picked up another small, smooth stone and tossed it as far as he could. The stone hopped, skipped, and jumped across the surface a few times before plopping in with a splash. Raymond stared out at the troubled water. "How did you know that Madison was the only woman for you?"

"I didn't. At least not for a while." Tony bent down, picked up a stone and mirrored Raymond's actions. "I didn't want to admit it to myself. But, I guess I always knew."

"Can you get any more cryptic?"

Tony smiled at the remark. "Love is cryptic."

"Oh, this keeps getting better."

Tony laughed. "You're attracted to her, that's obvious. The question is, will she hold your interest. You know, when it comes to women, you don't have the longest attention span."

Raymond smiled, thinking of his last evening with Hope. "She is well worth the effort. I can't stop thinking about her. Sometimes she drives me crazy. Other times," he paused to reflect, "I can't imagine my life without her."

Tony smiled knowingly. "That sounds about right." He smiled remembering his early, rocky relationship with Madison. They'd had a tumultuous beginning, but now he was in heaven. He looked over to see Madison waving at him. He waved back with a smile as wide and as broad as the state of Texas. "But it's worth it in the long run."

Raymond looked over to Tony, understanding the smile on his face. "It's not the same as with you and Madison. Hope despises me."

"You think Madison didn't detest me?" Tony laughed openly. "They all say that, but they don't mean it."

Raymond laughed. "Believe me, this one means it. She hates everything I am and everything I stand for. The money, the prestige, everything."

"So you gotta ask yourself, is she worth it?"

Raymond looked back out over the bay. A slow, easy smile spread across his face that matched Tony's exactly. Tony began laughing. "I'll take that as a yes."

"Hell, yes."

"So, what are you doing here? Go get her."

"How?"

"Surely this can't be the great and powerful Dr. Raymond: healer of the sick, defender of the weak, champion to the underdog. Man, I thought you could leap tall buildings with a single bound and were able to bend every woman to your will."

"As I said before, not this one. She's different."

"So you be different. Be everything she wants in a man."

Raymond looked over to his cousin. "You mean change who I am?" The bitter taste of disdain soured his mouth.

"No, of course not. Just let her see the real you. The you that we see every day."

"Easier said than done."

"How badly do you want to be with her?"

"Badly enough to propose marriage."

Tony smiled, accepting the news with a hearty slap on Raymond's back, an exuberant handshake and bear-like hug. "That's great man. So she's really the one? When are you going to pop the question?"

"Don't congratulate me yet. I already asked her to marry me."

"You what?"

"You heard me. I proposed."

Tony grabbed Raymond and whooped loudly. "That's fantastic."

"It would have been, if she'd accepted."

"She didn't accept?"

Raymond looked out over the water and shook his head. The once troubled surface had now stilled to its original facade. Raymond smiled, reflecting on the turbulent relationship. Although his calm demeanor portrayed his control, inwardly he toiled. "It's over."

"Maybe not."

Raymond half smiled. "The funny thing is that Mamma Lou once said that once I find hope, I should make sure to never lose it. Looks like I finally did. For once in my life I found the perfect woman for me and I lost her."

"You know what, I've always found that hope is never very far from our hearts and that when you need it, it's always there."

The two men remained silent, each pondering distant thoughts.

"I need to get back."

"To Haven House?"

"Eventually. But, I need to stop at the apartment first. I promised Kennedy I'd give her a ride since she's staying at J.T.'s place."

"That's right, I forgot that you two were neighbors."

"Yeah, he's on the next floor up. Kennedy's staying at his place for a few days. She has a conference at the Metropolitan Museum."

"How's the new building look?"

"Great."

"Is it ready for the grand opening?"

"Yeah, but I still need to finalize some of the details. Are you and Madison still coming to the opening?"

"Yep. Kennedy's also coming. Also, J.T. said he might stop by. He's still in Europe working on some new software deal. He's supposed to be back in the states by then."

"That man had better learn to relax."

"He said it's on his schedule. Since he'll be in New York, he promised Madison he'd find time to stop by."

"Great. The more, the merrier." Raymond sighed heavily and took one last look around. He held out his hand to shake, then the two grabbed each other in a comforting embrace.

"Drive carefully." Raymond nodded and walked back up the winding path to the house.

"Mamma Lou!" he called out as soon as he reached the sliding, glass door off the veranda. He looked around the large, open-style kitchen. "Mamma Lou! Mamma Lou!" he called out, louder.

"Boy, if you don't stop that yelling in my house, I'm going to put you over my knee and take a paddle to you."

Taken off guard, Raymond burst with laughter. His day had just instantly brightened. The sternness of her expression increased his laughter until he was wiping tears from his eyes. After a minute or two more of laughter, Raymond finally calmed down.

He looked into the sweet serenity of his grandmother's

eyes. There, he found the strength of century-old valiance. The determination that drove those first, freed men and women to call Crescent Island their home was the same fortitude that flowed through his veins. He was a descendent of their intrepidness and strength.

"Hope and I. . ." he began until she interrupted.

"I know, dear." She gently stroked his face as he bent down to kiss her cheek. "Kennedy's already waiting out front. Drive safely."

He winked and hurried out.

Twenty-four

"New life," Hope smiled as she and Faith stood side-by-side at the shielded, glass window. She pressed her hand against the glass, then drew a happy face. She couldn't help but smile. The nursery was filled with little bundles, swaddled in pink and blue. One infant, donning a blue cap and blanket, wailed at the top of his lungs. Eventually he incited a riot of random cries, joined by the entire brood. Hope laughed joyfully. "They're so precious," she added, then turned to look at her sister.

"Yes, they are. Life is so fragile," Faith lamented woefully.

Hope nodded. "Life is a continuous circle. A time to be born and a time to die."

Faith took a deep breath and walked away slowly. Hope followed. "How sick was she?" They turned and walked down the corridor.

"Very. Her mother is a drug addict. She was born addicted to crack." A tear slid solemnly down her cheek. "She was only seventeen days old. We tried everything, but there was nothing anyone could do. I only knew her for a few weeks, but she was a remarkable little lady. I just wish she had more time. She should have had more time."

They entered the chapel.

"Faith, listen to me. We're only human, we're not God. We can't give life. The best we can to is to ease suffering. That was the oath we took: do no harm. Our purpose is clear."

"Yes, yes, I know all that. It doesn't make it any easier." Faith said, as tears slowly drifted downward.

Hope reached out to her sister and pulled her into her loving embrace. "I know. The death of an innocent is always insufferable," she said, her voice thick with emotion. "Life is too short."

Fully weeping, Faith laid her head on her older sister's shoulder. "She died without ever being loved. Her mother is still so cracked and coked up and in detox. She has no idea what a precious gift she lost."

"That will be her cross to bare. When she recovers, she's going to have to live with this for the rest of her life."

"She died alone." Faith looked up at Hope, her face damp with emotion. "All alone and unloved."

"No, she didn't, Faith. She died with you at her side. She died with faith, right?"

"Right. Okay." Faith sat up and wiped the tears from her eyes. "I'm okay now. Thank you, sis. I guess we all need a shoulder to lean on from time to time." She took Hope's hands. "I'm glad I have you."

"Me too."

"Did I ever say thank you?"

"For what?"

"You divorced Nolan and sank your settlement into my education. I'm a registered nurse because of you. What would I have done without you? You saved my life."

"No, I didn't."

"I was so small. He would have killed me if you hadn't jumped on his back."

"Some cavalry I turned out to be. I went flying through the plate glass window."

"It stopped him."

"But it was too late." The sisters looked at each other. The memories they shared would always be there. In time, the pain would diminish.

"How's Dennis?"

"Perfect. I love him."

"I'm happy for you, Faith."

"What, no lecture, no sermon on the evils of falling in love? What's wrong with you?"

Hope had to smile; Faith knew her too well. "No lectures, no sermons. Only my best wishes for your happiness." She hugged her sister. "Be happy."

"I will." Faith took a deep breath and stood. "I have to get back to work."

Hope smiled. "I'm going to stay in here a bit. I'm not technically on duty until eight. I'll call you tomorrow."

Faith nodded and quietly walked out.

"Excuse me, is Dr. Wescott available?" Raymond asked.

His assistant looked up. "I'm sorry, Dr. Wescott's been in a meeting all day."

"Do you know if Dr. Adams is in yet?"

"Which Dr. Adams?"

"Hope Adams."

The woman opened a computer window and scanned the screen. "Yes, she's here. She checked in an hour ago. You might want to try the ER."

"I already have. She's not on duty yet."

"Then you might want to ask her sister. She might know."

"Faith?"

"Yes, Faith Adams. She's in the pediatric ward on four."

"Thanks."

Raymond took the elevator to the fourth floor. He entered the pediatric ward within minutes and looked around for assistance. "Excuse me," he stopped a man passing with a hospital nametag attached to his shirt. "Have you seen Dr. Adams?" The technician shook his head then pointed in the direction of the nurses' desk. Raymond stepped up to the counter. "Dr. Adams?"

"Yeah, I just saw her. She's with Faith. I think they went to the chapel down the hall, fourth door on the left. There's a plaque on the wall."

"Thanks." Raymond walked down the hall and followed the signs to the hospital chapel. When he arrived at the door, he pushed it open slightly.

He entered. The room was subdued by darkness, but was comforting. He allowed his eyes to adjust to the sharp light contrast, then he looked around. The front of the chapel was a backlit, stained glass window depicting a peaceful sunrise over a meadow. He saw the sisters sitting near the front alter. They were talking softly, but with the excellent acoustics, he could hear every word.

He took a seat on the last pew and waited patiently. Mamma Lou went to church every Sunday and then twice during the week. Looking back, he realized that he hadn't been to church in years. Maybe it was time to renew his faith and hope in the world.

He watched as the sisters embraced, then Faith stood to leave. He stood as she passed his pew. They smiled at each other as he held out his hand. Faith took it as she passed. They squeezed hands affectionately as she eyed him knowingly. Raymond nodded. He'd understood perfectly.

Hope focused on the colored glass as her mind flashed back to her unannounced trip to Raymond's apartment. She had gone over to apologize for her behavior and to confess her feelings. But as soon as she walked up the street she saw them together. She couldn't believe her eyes. He was there with another woman. A beautiful woman. He helped her carry in several bags as if she was staying with him for a while.

She first felt anger, then rage. Now, only sadness was left. She had scolded herself over and over again. She never should have fallen in love. Love was painful. Love hurt. She vowed never again.

"I missed you." She remained silent; her eyes still focused on the sunrise on the glass panes. "Have I done something wrong?"

Hope looked up at him. "What?"

"Have I upset you?"

"No."

"I call, I leave messages and nothing. Silence."

"I've been busy."

He smiled, his dimple deepening. "Liar."

Hope looked away. The memory of their night of passion was always just a blink away. She loved him and it hurt.

"I think we moved too fast," she confessed.

"Too fast for what?"

"We had a fling and now it's over. You're seeing someone else."

"What?

"I went to your apartment building the other day. I saw you with another woman. She suits you perfectly. She is beautiful."

"When? What woman?" Raymond began to think back. The only woman who had been to his apartment building lately was—"Kennedy?" Hope looked away. "Hope, you saw me with Kennedy. She's like a sister to me. She wasn't staying with me; she was staying at her brother's apartment. We live in the same building. I gave her a ride home. Is that why you haven't returned my phone calls?"

"Raymond, please understand. I'm not ready for you, for this, for us."

"I love you. What are you afraid of?"

"Winding up with a man like my father. He left and divorced my mother because he said he fell in love with someone else. Just like that. He has four sons now."

"That would never happen."

"How do I know that?"

"I know that."

"We both know that this isn't going to last."

"Why wouldn't it last?"

"Oh, for two to three weeks it'll be great. But after that, reality will intrude. It always does. What happens after that?"

He produced a beautifully square-cut diamond the size of a toaster. Even in the dimly lit room it sparkled radiantly. "This is what happens." He got down on one knee and took her hand in his. "Hope Adams, I love you with all of my heart. Will you do me the honor of becoming my wife? Will you marry me?"

Hope sat in shock. Her eyes blinked like flashing lights at a train stop. "I have to go." She got up and left.

Raymond smiled. "At least she didn't say no this time."
Still on one knee, he looked up at the ceiling and gave thanks
to an answered prayer.

After Hope left, Raymond stayed in the chapel for a few
more moments. He sat on a pew and enjoyed the quiet serenity
of the moment. When he finally left he went back to Hugh's office. The door was open and Hugh was sitting, talking with his
son. Raymond frowned as he knocked on the door and entered.

"Come in, my boy," Hugh said as he leaped from the desk,
hurrying to open the door wider. Nolan stood and followed
his dad foot-for-foot.

"I got your message. I don't have a lot of time. You said it
was urgent."

"Yes," Hugh motioned for Raymond to sit and he did.
Nolan sat beside him as Hugh took his place behind his desk.
"Raymond, I feel like I must give you some fatherly advice. I
know if my son were in your place, as he was not too long
ago, I would have prayed that someone talk to him before he
had made the worst mistake of his life."

"What are you talking about?"

Hugh took a deep, exhausted breath. "I'm talking about
Hope Adams." Raymond's brow furrowed as a menacing
scowl appeared. "You see, my son here was once married to
Hope. And, don't get me wrong, I'm sure she's a nice person
in her respected circle, but she has a history of throwing herself at financially endowed bachelors. She did the same to my
son while they were in med school together."

"I see. And now you're warning me, sort of like my father
would do if he were aware of the situation."

"Exactly." Hugh nodded. Nolan nodded.

"Thank you for this interesting development." Hugh
glanced over to his son and smiled with an, *I told you he'd
be grateful,* expression on his face. "But," Raymond stood,
"my father already knows everything there is to know about
Hope, as do I." Hugh's mouth gaped open. "Yes, we are well
aware of Hope and Nolan's marriage as well as his recent
medical malpractice court proceedings in California."

Raymond reached into his pocket and pulled out the enormous diamond ring and showed it to father and son. "Not that it's any of your business, but I've asked Hope to marry me several times already. She's turned me down each time. I love her and I'm not giving up. So, in the future when you speak about Hope, be mindful that you're talking about the future Mrs. Raymond Gates, Jr., with all the perks and privileges that come with that title." He sighed heavily. "Now, if you'll excuse me, my future wife is waiting." He walked out of the door leaving Hugh and Nolan to stare after him.

The black and white film easily confirmed what Hope had suspected. The arm was fractured. She studied the thin hairline crack and traced it along its path down the ulna. She made a notation on the chart, and then clicked off the light screen. It had taken her fifteen minutes to do that simple task.

But, she couldn't help it; her mind was saturated with thoughts of Raymond. For the last two days all she thought about was him and his marriage proposal. She had finally convinced herself that he wasn't serious then he showed up in the chapel with a diamond the size of a subway car.

Maxine came up and sat down beside her. "I heard an interesting rumor this evening." When Hope didn't answer Maxine continued. "Hugh's son, Nolan, just settled an out of court injunction in the California Board Medical Review. Seems young Dr. Wescott was cited for wrongful death, negligence and gross incompetence."

Hope wasn't at all surprised. She always knew that he didn't have the knack for medicine. She was just sorry that someone had to suffer for his incompetence.

"It's also out that he was once married to someone on our ER staff. You."

The cat had been let out of the bag. "Yes, Nolan and I were married for eighteen months. We got married right out of med school."

"Everyone's stunned that Hugh is your father-in-law."

"Ex-father-in-law," Hope said emphatically.

"That really explains a lot."

"Explains what?"

"The animosity and the resentment."

"I guess it was pretty obvious?"

"Oh, please, you can cut the hostility with a hacksaw."

"That was us, one big, happy dysfunctional family."

"I also heard that Nolan is coming here to practice."

That got the reaction Maxine expected. "Here where?"

"Hugh was in meetings all day to have Barclay Med contract him in administrative services."

"There goes the neighborhood," Hope said dryly.

Maxine walked away laughing.

Hope kicked her chair back and spun around several times. Scott walked by, looked at her sternly, and kept walking. Hope delved back into her reports. Ten minutes later Maxine came back and stood by her side. "Whatever it is, I don't what to hear it," Hope said, before Maxine could open her mouth. She'd had enough bad news for one day.

Maxine didn't budge. She looked up as Maxine sat down beside her. She smiled broadly.

Hope looked at Maxine, and then did a double take. Maxine was smiling. There weren't a lot of things to cause Maxine to smile, so when she did everyone took notice.

Hope looked at her watch. "I have one hour left on my shift. I'm afraid to even ask," Hope said.

"Leanne Jackson is here."

Hope moaned inwardly and buried her face in her hands. "Not again, she's only been discharged a few days." Hope had just gone mid-shift, so the last thing she wanted to deal with was a self-destructive enabler. Suddenly, Hope looked up. "How bad is she?" Maxine smiled and Hope realized that Maxine hadn't used her usual euphemism. And more importantly, she actually seemed pleased to deliver the news of Leanne's arrival. Hope looked at her suspiciously. "Why are you smiling?"

"Mrs. Jackson would like a moment of your time."

"Mrs. Jackson?" Hope winced. She'd never heard Maxine refer to Leanne as anything other than *frequent flyer*.

"She's in one."

"I'll be right there. I have to take care of a hairline fracture in seven."

"I'll take care of seven. You need to get to one. Now, before she changes her mind."

The cryptic remark was more bewildering than confusing.

"What are you talking about?" Hope asked, standing up.

"Just go to one." Maxine reached down, grabbed the x-ray and chart, then headed to examine room seven.

Hope went to one and curiously opened the door. She had no idea what to expect. She peered into the room. The lights were dimmed. She looked around. Not seeing anyone sitting on the gurney, she turned to leave, then caught a glimpse of someone sitting in the back corner. "Leanne?"

"Dr. Adams?"

Hope opened the door wider and stepped inside. She pulled her stethoscope from around her neck, folded it and put it in her pocket. "What can I do for you?"

"You said that you'd help me."

Hope walked over and sat in the chair next to the visibly broken woman. "Are you in pain?"

"No."

"Do you want to tell me what's going on?"

Leanne sat quietly for a long time. She stared out into the distance, seeing things only she could see. For the first time in a long time she was at peace. She sat still, soaking up the harmonious quiet.

"Leanne? How can I help you?"

"I . . . I . . . I left him," she stuttered bravely. "I need a shelter or something, someplace to stay." A tear crept down her face in slow motion, as the clarity of her decision sparked her to continue. "You said I could come to you when I was ready. I'm ready. I need help."

Hope sank back into the chair. Words of that magnitude

needed to be savored and relished. Hope reached over and placed her hands on top of Leanne's. A slow, solemn tear crept down the side of her face. She was overjoyed by Leanne's bravery.

"I can have someone from *Women's Intervention* come down to meet you and take you upstairs." Leanne instantly hesitated and backed up. Her fearful expression broke Hope's heart. "Or," she pause a moment, "would it be okay if I went with you to *Women's Intervention* and stayed for a while?" Leanne nodded her head nervously. Hope smiled and took her hand. "Come on, let's get you safe." Together they walked to the crisis intervention center on the next floor up.

Since visiting hours had ended hours earlier, the hospital halls were practically empty, except for medical and custodial staff. Hope made small talk as they took the elevator up. As the doors opened, Leanne jumped, seeing a man dressed in a blue work uniform attempting to get on the elevator, unaware that they were getting off. Hope placed her arm around Leanne's shoulder and steered her forward.

"It's okay," she muttered into Leanne's ear. "Hi, Angelo, how's your wife?" She said aloud to the confused-looking electrical technician.

"Hey, Dr. Adams. She's getting bigger and bigger. They say no twins this time, but I don't know. I'll tell her that you asked for her. Be careful down the hall, I need to put in a couple of new fluorescent bulbs."

"Thanks, Angelo." The elevator door closed as Hope and Leanne walked down the hall. Hope explained that Angelo and his wife, who had already had two sets of twins, were expecting another child. Leanne actually smiled when Hope mentioned the hospital pool he had started to raise money for their education.

Hope stopped at a closed door with a small plaque on the wall that read, INTERVENTION SERVICES. "Shall we?" Leanne nodded. So Hope opened the door and they stepped inside. Several women milling around glanced up when Hope entered.

"Is Dr. Murray here?"

"I'm here," she called from the back office. "Hope? Is that you?" She asked as she came around the side of the partition. She smiled heartily until she saw the terror in Leanne's face. She also saw the victory in Hope's. "Come on back," Dr. Murray said.

The three women walked to Dr. Murray's office. "Have a seat." Leanne sat, as Hope stood by her side.

"Dr. Murray, this is Leanne Jackson. She would like to seek shelter in a women's center as soon as possible."

Both doctors smiled and nodded at the victory of Leanne's newly discovered freedom. "Hello, Mrs. Jackson."

"Hi, Dr. Murray," she said timidly.

"Please call me Charlene. May I call you Leanne?" She nodded. "Good." Charlene took a seat next to Leanne on the comfortable sofa. She smiled welcomingly, easing Leanne's fears. "First of all, Leanne, would you prefer to stay with your family or at a friend's house?"

"I don't have any family and I don't have any friends. Wes saw to that."

"Well, you do now, honey. You do now. Let's talk a bit and get to know each other. I'll start if you'd prefer." Leanne nodded again. "Okay, first of all, I want you to know that I understand your pain. I know exactly what you've been going through and I know what you're feeling right now. I was right where you are now, not too long ago."

Leanne seemed to brighten when she realized that she wasn't alone in her suffering. Charlene continued with her story as Leanne listened with open emotion.

After ten minutes or so Hope excused herself and quietly left the room. She'd just closed the door when she heard a great deluge of joyful, unused tears begin to flow. Leanne was welcomed with open arms to a safe place where she could be cared for, protected, and have her spirit healed.

As Hope returned to the ER, her thoughts centered on her mother's pain and the suffering she had endured for so long. In silent reflection she prayed that peace had finally found its way into her heart, as her soul rested in final freedom.

The sadness of knowing that there were women all over this world who were in the midst of this horror prompted her to quicken her step. With purpose and determination, Hope began to realize her calling.

The struggle for freedom wasn't always a victory won by the mighty and the brave, by countries and armies, nor with guns and knives. Sometimes the tiniest victim won the greatest battle. And that small victory was the sweetest.

Hope pushed through the ER doors as an uproar turned to pushing, shouting and fighting. A blast of obscenities instantly turned in her direction.

Wes Jackson was livid. The simple, victorious smile on Hope's face told him what he had already suspected. Leanne was here and Hope knew where she was.

"Where is she?" he yelled, pointing across the room at Hope, as soon as he saw her enter the area. "What did you tell her?"

"Get him out of here now!" Scott instructed. The security guards, who had recently arrived, instantly jumped into action. They blocked him, grabbed his arms and tried to restrict his aggressive actions. They held him back securely. But his strength propelled him forward, with all three guards in tow.

"I want to see my wife now!" Foul-mouthed and belligerent, he screamed as the guards restrained him and dragged him from the treatment room. "You can't keep me from her. Where is she? I know she's here. Leanne?" He roared at the top of his lungs. "Leanne?"

"I'll be back!" he screamed, then pointed across the room at Hope. "I'll get you! I warned you to stay out of my life! I told you to stay out of my business!"

As the doors solidly closed behind him, the echoing sound of his taunts and threats still drifted in the fouled air. Everyone turned to look at Hope. Her expression was that of disgust and exhaustion. She was just plain tired of abuse, threats and fear. She walked over to the nurses' station as everything slowly went back to normal.

Twenty-Five

The graveyard shifts were getting more strenuous, or maybe it just seemed that way. Hope stood at her locker after slamming the door close. She collapsed on the sofa and tied her sneakers. She sat back and looked across the room at the small space. The walls were lined with blue painted lockers on one side and a single, barred window on the other. They seemed to close in on her.

Each day became harder and longer, made even worse by Raymond's recent absence from her life. *This is ridiculous,* she bemoaned. She gathered her belongings and passed through the empty halls with one destination in mind.

She waited a split-second before the automatic door opened with the familiar swoosh. She looked up at the musty sky. It was early, not quite dark, yet past dusk. The city was alive, preparing for the exciting evening ahead. It was the weekend and life in the Big Apple was filled with thrills. Everything was as it should be. But in the ER, nothing was ever as it should be.

She had just completed another long shift in the ER, filled with the usual dregs and misfits of society. It was mankind at its worst, devouring everything in its path. She walked through the back lot, toward the parking lot. The small elevator door opened instantly and she walked inside. She pushed the button for the third floor and went on autopilot as the doors closed and the elevator began to move.

Hope leaned back against the rear wall, closed her eyes and

stretched her neck from side to side. She had somehow managed to complete another insufferable shift. She walked through the parking garage, her thoughts centered on Raymond. Faith was right; she needed to resolve the rift between them. Raymond had done nothing but be the man he was. What did she expect?

She was the one that couldn't handle his love. She was the one that had thrown everything away just as she'd always done. She reached up and stroked the scar on her face. She had worn it like a badge of pity, never allowing another man to get close enough to her heart to do her harm.

She knew that men weren't all like her deserting father and abusive stepfather, just as women were not all like her accepting mother. She didn't have to live the rest of her life waiting for some man to hurt her, either emotionally or physically. She could choose to bury the past.

The sudden crash of glass against the brick wall got her attention instantly. "You need to mind your own damn business," Wes Jackson slurred, barely comprehendible. "I told you that before. But you wouldn't listen, would ya? Now ya gonna haveta pay." With a mean-spirited cackle, he laughed loudly. The obnoxious shriek reverberated against the parking garage walls, producing an echo of hollow madness.

Hope closed her eyes and lowered her head in loathsome dread. She'd recognized the voice even before he finished his mindless ramblings.

"Turn around," he commanded forcefully.

Hope didn't speak. She looked up over her car's roof at the security camera, then averted her eyes and stared out at the distant memories. Although she had always had strength, the pain and misery of memories had drained her of hope. She was determined not to relinquish her spirit. She stared at the far-away images straight-on, refusing to back down. Slowly they receded, fading into the nothing that they were always meant to be.

"I said, turn around," he commanded again, louder and more forcefully. The determination in his voice was evident.

She decided at that moment that he had no power over her. She turned away from her car to face him. Unflinching, she looked at him, staring him straight in the eye. Her blatant audacity staggered him. Then, she saw it, disbelief first, then hesitation. For a brief instant, uncertainty shadowed his brow. For a split-second power had shifted, and he had no idea what to do.

Unshaven and dirty, his wide mouth was drawn even wider when his smug grin wavered. Then, he steadied himself. As far as he was concerned, he was still in control. And, since power was his ultimate addiction, he needed to regain it.

He pulled a small, brown bag from his back pocket. "Who do you think you are?" he asked rhetorically, as he unscrewed the top of the second bottle he held in his hand. He lowered the brown paper bag just below the rim and quickly tipped the bottle up to his mouth. He tossed his head back, taking a long and hard drink. Hope watched, repulsed, as alcohol clumsily dribbled down his jaw, neck and hand. When he had finished his swig, he tossed the bottle against the wall, breaking it beside the first.

She flinched.

Satisfied that he'd properly frightened her, he nodded with a leering grin, exposing his yellow teeth. "You need to be taught some manners." He unloosened his belt and slowly, methodically pulled it through the loops of his pants. For the first time, she noticed a sheathed knife attached to his belt. "Your man don't seem to be doing his job, so, it looks like I'm gonna haveta."

With a menacing swagger, he inched closer, making the dramatic scene look like a bad B-movie. He stuck the knife in his waistband, then wrapped the belt buckle around his fist and began slapping the thick leather against his leg. He stared at her face, centering his blurred vision on her scar. "Looks like I'm gonna have to finish what someone else already started."

Hope spoke softly. "Is this the part where I'm supposed to be afraid and beg you not to hurt me?" Both Wes and Hope looked startled. The courageous words came out of her mouth before she had even realized she'd said them. "I don't think so," she added defiantly.

"You think just 'cause you're some fancy doctor, you can control my wife. *I* run my household. *I* run Leanne." Like a jungle primate, he beat his fists against his chest in an attempt to show superior strength. "*I* tell her want to do, not you. You understand me? She belongs to me."

"She belongs to no one. Least of all you."

"You have a lot of mouth for some about to get beat down."

Hope, finding a surge of power from deep inside herself, continued to stare. She never realized how pathetic he actually was. "You do what you think you need to do."

Hope watched cautiously for Wes's next movement. That's when she first noticed movement behind him, over the cement barrier, on the third level. Several hospital security guards were now pointing and running in their direction, with the intention of sneaking up on him. Hope glanced away quickly, not wanting to draw Wes's attention to them.

Wes's mouth dropped open, agape, shocked by what he was hearing. He was completely taken off guard by her barefaced nerve. No one had ever spoken to him like that. He wasn't sure what to do. He needed a drink. Drinking gave him courage and courage made him a man. He looked over at the two broken bottles smashed against the wall. His mouth salivated with desire.

He took a step toward the broken glass, and then staggered backward. He turned back to focus on Hope, then began yelling obscenities. The smell of his alcohol-induced rage permeated the air, leaving a vile stench. As his crazed rampage intensified he began waving his arms wildly, threatening to hit her with the belt in an instant.

Hope looked toward the security force running toward them. They would never make it in time. It was up to her to protect herself. She lowered her backpack, wrapping the elongated straps around her fist.

Wes lurched toward her, his arm raised in attack. Hope heaved the backpack upward and swung it across his face. The force knocked him against the wall. He stumbled, then lurched again, this time attempting to swing the belt bucket at her face. She ducked, swung, and knocked the belt from his hand.

Wes pulled the knife from its sheath. He smiled menacingly, assured of his victory. He leveled the blade and swung a wide arch. Hope jumped back, the knife missing her by inches.

Before he could regroup, she swung the backpack at his legs, sending him crashing to the ground. The knife fell free, as the side of his face scraped against the broken glass. He screamed in stunned agony.

Hazed by alcohol, pain, and rage, Wes staggered to his feet. But, instead of lurching again, he fell back against the wall. Hope watched, then raised the backpack again. She steadied herself in a defensive stance, waiting for his next move. There was none. She jerked the backpack at him again. He flinched, screamed and covered his face.

In a heap of pathetic wails, Wes rolled on the cold cement, screaming for help. He gripped his face as streams of blood trickled through his fingers. Hope dropped to her knees and opened her backpack. Donning latex gloves, she tore open a sterilized, gauze packet and drenched it with an antiseptic gel. She hurried over to Wes, kicking the knife further away. With brute force, she pulled his trembling hands away from his face.

Within minutes she was completely surrounded by hospital security, police, and Raymond. In the midst of chaos, calls of alarm and assistance screeched over the two-way radio as the police officers pulled her away and picked Wes up.

Raymond immediately went to Hope's side. He grabbed her face and kissed her with all the passion he had locked inside. Fear had propelled him to latch onto her for dear life. Once he'd been assured that she was fine, he turned his attention to Wes.

The fire in Raymond's eyes blazed. Without warning he lurched at Wes, knocking him down along with two security guards and a policeman. They unsuccessfully tried to pull him away from the screaming man until Hope grabbed him and held him back. Raymond reluctantly allowed her to separate them. Raymond stayed by her side as the police and security guards handcuffed Wes and took him to the ER.

Against Hope's will, she and Raymond were escorted to Wescott's office. Maxine and Faith met them there. The three of them stormed around the office like caged animals, each wanting to get their hands on Wes for a few moments. Hope looked at them in astonishment until she realized that she was no longer frightened. The memories she'd cleaved to for so long were gone.

She didn't cry; she couldn't cry. She'd been silently crying her entire life. Having been too young to help her mother and too old to forget, she was forever stuck with the inner turmoil and continuous cycle of reliving the pain of abuse.

The haze of the next two and a half hours faded into a blur of jagged emotion. Wes had been treated then escorted to prison on charges of assault and attempted murder.

A police officer escorted Leanne to Hugh's office. Raymond, Hugh and the officer waited outside while discussing the official police report.

Leanne walked into Wescott's office and looked at Hope. She looked dazed, drained and twisted, like a discarded washrag left to dry and harden. She'd obviously heard the news that Wes had attacked Hope in the parking garage. She didn't weep, she didn't cry.

A knowing smiled creased both of their faces as the pain they'd each suffered for so long had ended and the burden they'd silently carried had been removed. Hope stood as Leanne approached. Then, without saying a word, they wrapped their arms around each other and surrendered the burden. The healing had finally begun.

Maxine and Faith looked at each other. They couldn't help but smile. For Hope and Leanne, the nightmare was finally over. The four women gathered in a small circle, cheered, and rejoiced at the newfound freedom.

Hugh barged into the office in the midst of the tender moment. The quizzical expression on his face at seeing all four women laughing and smiling was humorous. Maxine took Leanne back downstairs to *Women's Intervention* to gather her things. They had instructed her to go directly to the police station, file assault charges and petition for an emergency restraining order against her husband. Maxine had volunteered to go with her.

Raymond and Faith sat by Hope's side as Hugh detailed the charges brought against Wes. When he had finished, he produced an official complaint report. Hope signed it as Faith looked on.

"I've asked Dr. Murray to make herself available to see you as soon as possible. She'll be in her office all evening," Hugh said.

Hope frowned. "Why?"

"Hope, you know that it's procedure to see a counselor in these matters," Faith insisted.

"But I'm fine, really I am."

Raymond took Hope's hand. "This was a traumatic experience. What happened to you was horrendous. Taking some time to talk with a counselor might be prudent."

"But I assure you, I've never felt better."

Both Raymond and Faith looked at Hope with concern. Then, Faith saw a light sparkle in Hope's eyes. She hadn't seen that spark in years. It made Faith smile. She had never seen Hope so calm. It was true. She was all right.

"Are you sure?" Hugh asked.

"Completely." Her eyes sparkled. "I've never been more sure of anything in my life."

Hugh nodded reluctantly. "Okay, I'll have to take your word for it. I've spoken to several members of the board and we feel that it would be prudent for you to take tomorrow off."

"That's not necessary, Hugh. I'm scheduled tomorrow evening. I'll be here."

"Your dedication is admirable, but I'm afraid I'm going to

have to insist. The decision has already been made. Take tomorrow off, relax, and get some rest. Put all of this behind you," Hugh insisted.

"The board's decision isn't because of the horde of reporters sitting outside, is it?" Raymond asked.

"Of course not," Hugh said, then turned to address Hope.

"I'll tell you what, why don't you take a couple of days off."

Hope was about to decline a second time when Raymond placed his hand on hers and spoke up. "Actually, Hugh, that sounds like a great idea. She'll do it. But, I think that two weeks might be better. Yes, two weeks. That ought to be just about right." Hope looked at Raymond then to her sister. Faith shrugged then nodded and smiled encouragingly.

"Two weeks is a bit longer than I had anticipated."

"That's unfortunate, Hugh," Faith said, slightly forlorn as Raymond continued.

"I'm sure Hope's welfare is your foremost concern. Maybe Hope *should* discuss this with a counselor. I know an excellent one at Manhattan Medical or even Johns Hopkins. But, I'm sure that the publicity of Hope seeking medical attention elsewhere, because you wouldn't sanction it here, probably wouldn't sit well with the horde of reporters parked at the front door, or with Barclay Med. Two weeks," Raymond pushed.

"That's out of the question."

"I'm feeling slightly distressed myself," Faith chimed in. "I think that talking to the reporters might help."

"There's nothing you can tell them."

"I don't know about that. They might be interested to know that Barclay Med and its hospital's Administrative Director, who also happens to be my sister's ex-father-in-law, dismissed a doctor for personal reasons."

"All right, two weeks."

"That's with two weekends correct?" Faith asked, innocently. Hugh glared at Faith.

"Two week with two weekends would be fine."

"That's very generous of you Hugh. I'll make sure to mention it to my family's friends on the Barclay board."

Hugh looked stunned. "Yeah, you do that."

Before Faith went back to her duties, she pulled Hope aside. "Are you sure you're okay?" Hope nodded and they hugged each other warmly. "Good. Why don't you get away for awhile? I hear Crescent Island is darling."

"What do you know about Crescent Island?"

"Dennis told me all about it."

"You and Dennis?"

Faith nodded happily. "Me and Dennis."

They watched as Raymond came out of Hugh's office. The two men shook hands. "You know, he's really kind of unbelievable. Not at all like Nolan and the others."

"I know."

"Raymond was right, you could use a couple of weeks off. You've been a pain in the butt to live with for the last few days."

"I have not."

"Hope listen, I'm telling you this for your own good. Ever since you and Raymond went your seperate ways, you've been miserable." Hope opened her mouth to rebut but stopped. "You can't deny it. Whatever you and Raymond had lit a spark in you. He made you happy. It was nice having my old sister back."

"What do you mean?"

"You think I was too young to remember what happened?" Hope touched her scar and looked away. "Hope, for years you've been shutting people out of your life because of what our father and stepfather did. All men aren't like that. Raymond isn't like that."

"I know."

"Good, then do something about it."

"It's too late."

"It's never too late," Faith said. Raymond walked over as

Faith turned to leave. "Call me," she said, as she waved to Raymond and hurried down the steps to the fourth floor.

"Shall we go?"

"Raymond, thank you for everything. Two weeks off. Wow." She shook her head, elated. "But I need to use the time for myself. I think I might go away or something."

"Where?"

"I'm not sure."

"For how long."

"I don't know yet."

"Want company?"

She smiled and shook her head. He nodded. "Hope, I can't change the world for you. I wish I could, but I can't. Sometimes it's a dark, ugly, lonely and scary place for children and adults. I can't change that any more than I can change the horror you went through as a child. The only thing I can do right now is to love you with all my heart. And together, just maybe, we can change our small corner of the world. We can make sure that our children will never experience the pain and agony you suffered."

"Raymond."

"You have no faith in me. You don't trust that I'm not like your father and stepfather. And I don't know how to assure you that I could never hurt you. I would rather die than cause you pain. I love you. When you're ready to get through the pain, I'll be here for you. We'll survive this together. I'll be at home waiting for you." He stroked the scar on her face, then turned and walked away.

Twenty-six

Crescent Island was everything everyone had said it would be and more. At Louise's invitation, Hope stayed at Gates Manor. To Hope's surprise it was almost the size of her neighborhood.

The building itself was completely surrounded by hundred-year-old maple and oak trees. It was truly majestic. The stately, old house stood regal and dignified, proud and strong, resembling the prestige of its elder mistress.

The main section of the mansion was rectangular in shape, with an added semi-circular covered receiving area that protruded a good ten feet out into the red brick driveway. The covered section was held up by a number of white columns that eventually joined in with the huge pillars growing up from the wraparound white porch.

The building was pure-white with forest-green shutters and matching flower boxes at every window. The boxes overflowed with white impatiens and white geraniums. The sight was simply magnificent.

The wooden floor of the open porch was painted a cool, blue-gray color. There were several groupings of forest-green wicker furniture with thick, floral-patterned cloth cushions. Each seating arrangement boasted two or three chairs and a small table topped with a delicate wicker basket, brimming with fresh-cut flowers. Between each pillar was a huge hanging basket of red, yellow and orange poppies, trailing fuchsia, sweet peas, crimson geraniums and dazzling nasturtium

blooms, accented with tender English ivy. The effect was a
burst of color, separated by thick, white, stone columns accented by beautifully planted perennials and annuals.

Hope spent most of her time either on the receiving porch,
which was surrounded by white astilbe, or out back, on the
veranda by the pool.

It was early in the morning when Hope stepped out into the
large screen-covered deck that faced the garden areas and a
small portion of the bay. Her bedroom, rather Raymond's
bedroom, faced the gardens. She loved waking up to the brilliant sunrise and the sound of birds. She walked over to the
telescope and leaned down. She adjusted the settings and captured the close-up image of a bird in flight. She watched until
it disappeared from sight.

She sat down in the wicker chair beneath the miniature fig
and ficus trees. Planted in huge clay pots, they sat back
against the brick wall, behind a large display of flowerpots
filled with a colorful array of plants.

She stood and looked down over the iron rail and smiled as
she breathed in the aromatic scent of fresh flowers emanating
from the gardens below. She'd been there for almost a week,
but it felt as if she'd been there her entire life.

From her vantage point on the second floor she saw
Mamma Lou walking from the dock to the small cottage.
Hope opened the screened door, went downstairs and out onto
the patio.

Taking the brick path, she walked around the side of the
house to the scenic cottage. It was surrounded by towering
weeping willows, dwarfing its size to that of a miniature
dollhouse. It was a stark-white stucco building that was
tucked snugly between the varying green hues of several
weeping willows, magnolia and maple trees. A white, picket
fence encircled the front yard and continued around each
side, encasing a selection of colorful blooming flowers. The
heavenly scent of summer flowers encompassed the air. Two
large windows straddled the front door. They were framed by

open, white shutters and white flower boxes, filled with budding snapdragons and impatiens.

Hope came to the front door. It looked like it was right out of one of those old 1950s movies. It was one of those half doors that separated horizontally. The top half had several small pane windows and was completely open. The bottom half had raised wood panels, pushed together, but still slightly ajar. She leaned over the open top and called out to Louise.

"I'll be right out." Seconds later Louise appeared at the doorway with her basket filled with week-old flowers, having replaced them with fresh ones.

"Are you all packed up and ready to leave?" she asked, as Hope held the door open for her.

"Yes. Thank you so much for inviting me. It was exactly what I needed."

"I'm glad you enjoyed yourself and got some rest." They walked back up the path to a small area beside the vegetable garden. Louise dropped the wilted stems in a churner and began turning the crank. The flowers were immediately mulched.

"I have a small confession," Louise said. Hope looked at her oddly. "I'm allergic to almonds."

Hope was confused, but slowly understood. "You were matchmaking." Louise nodded. "Raymond and me?" Louise nodded again. "How did you know to come to the hospital? We'd never met before."

Louise confessed to eavesdropping on Hope's conservation with Faith the night of the play. Hope began laughing. "And you decided just like that I was right for Raymond?"

"You were exactly what Raymond needed and you still are. Now why don't you go back up there and find my grandson?"

As soon as Hope arrived home she busied herself with mindless chores, trying to keep her thoughts off Raymond. She remembered her sister's words and she knew Faith was right.

Raymond was different. He was nothing like their father or their stepfather. She knew it was also true that she had been miserable since she and Raymond had parted ways.

She decided to take a chance and give Raymond a call. She called the office and was told he'd taken a few days off and that she could possibly find him at home. She called his apartment. The machine informed her that he wasn't available. So she decided to drive over to his apartment.

Twenty-seven

The murky evening sky left a haze of film across the horizon. It had been a hot summer day and promised to be an even hotter night. The still, sticky air hung heavily as Hope made her way out of the city. Closely followed by thousands of commuters, she watched as towering skyscrapers sunk lower and lower beneath the horizon until they vanished from sight.

Congested to the point of feeling claustrophobic, the three-lane traffic bordered on madness.

It was early evening by the time Hope had finally left Manhattan. The sun was still high enough in the sky to make the view of the city from her rear view mirror sparkle in its radiance. The road in front of her was filled with congested traffic. She glanced up and adjusted the rear view mirror to see how far she'd come. Then she looked ahead to her future, somewhere northeast, toward Connecticut.

Her mind buzzed with Jimmy's remark.

She had just arrived at Raymond's apartment when she saw Jimmy in the lobby. "He's gone to Haven House," he told her. Hope immediately called Louise, who explained to her that Haven House was the name of Raymond's home in Connecticut. Fifteen minutes later, she was on her way.

Hope followed the map closely, referring to the detailed directions she'd gotten from Louise, until it became clear that she was lost. She'd been traveling all day. First, driving nearly four hours straight from Virginia and now a half-hour into this trip. Oddly enough, she wasn't at all tired. She was nervous.

She had absolutely no idea what she was going to say to Raymond when she saw him. The only thing she knew was that she needed to see and be with him. She wasn't even sure if he'd welcome her back. But she was hopeful.

Hope slowed the car to check the street sign, then made the appropriate turns, leading her, she hoped, directly into Raymond's waiting arms.

She traveled along the parkway of the southwestern shore, toward Connecticut. The coastline, dotted with numerous small lakes and ponds, was one long, wooded plain, occasionally broken by an inlet or small bay. It was nicknamed the gold coast, mostly because of its wealthy populace, generated from New York. Also, dozens of major corporations had headquarters in the surrounding Fairfield and New Haven Counties.

Hope drove through the quaint town of Stamford, excited that, according to the map and directions, she was almost there. Suddenly, enjoying the splendid scenery became secondary. She was too anxious about seeing Raymond.

The seemingly endless road narrowed to a single lane. Flat, rural fields that seemed to go on forever were broken up occasionally by a barn or farm. She passed a rundown shed by the side of the road. The once bright-red paint had faded to a dull wash of memories with painted flecks of muted color. Impatiently, she looked at the dashboard's digital clock, calculating that it would take just another half-hour.

Ray shifted the lawn mower into gear and crisscrossed a simple pattern, making sure that each blade of grass was properly cut. He adjusted the baseball cap lower on his head, then turned the steering wheel to make a second pass. He glanced back, satisfied with what he had accomplished. It wasn't capable of the precise cut and meticulousness of his usual instrument, the scalpel, but it would do.

Although he employed a full time gardener and small staff to care for the land surrounding his property, he often enjoyed the mindless exhaustion of something as simple as mowing the grass. It was a vast departure from the highly stressful intense surgical régime he followed daily.

He removed his sunglasses and squinted against the low-hanging sun. He speculated that he had at least another three hours of daylight. He decided to make another pass around the west side before grabbing a much-needed shower. After his last pass, Raymond drove the mower into the shed and walked back to the main house.

He peeled off his clothes and jumped into a hot shower that quickly cooled as soon as his thoughts strayed to Hope. Barely dry, he dressed and went back outside. He looked around at the pristine lawn and equally perfect landscape beyond. Like a magnet held secure by the memories of the past, this land would always draw him back.

Haven House was gently tucked between Stamford and New Haven, in the nestled refuge of the gateway to New England. On fifty acres of rolling green countryside, set against the backdrop of Connecticut's prime real estate, it stood secluded amid surroundings of pristine landscape and gently sloping terrain. Known for its privacy and quiet serenity, Haven House was aptly named as a sanctuary and safe haven to all who came.

Historically famed as a nineteenth century stationhouse on the *Railroad to Independence,* Haven's Manor, as it was once called, was a pivotal point in a long journey to freedom. Isolated and remote, it offered the perfect sanctuary to enslaved fugitives fleeing from all points south.

With the collaborative efforts of local conductors, under the guise of a lowly farmhouse dwelling, it offered protection and assistance to traveling passengers seeking shelter and aid. Albeit dangerous and punishable by death, those few harborers of the needy held fast to the rail system, giving comfort to the ailing and counsel to the lost.

Used as an integral cog to the destination of freedom, it stood as a vital portal until the last traveler was processed. Then finally, the gates to freedom, once opened wide, were discovered and laid to waste by the fire of hatred. With every inhabitant safely away, the fire consumed the main house and barn, leaving as a mark on history the hidden chambers used by newly freed men, women and children.

Now, over one-hundred and fifty yeas later, the hidden structure, in spite of everything, defiantly and unyieldingly maintained its place in history. Without apology it still proclaimed the will and determination of undaunted spirits that had traveled the rail to freedom.

The main house was eventually resurrected, rebuilt, and renovated. The property had been bought and sold numerous times before finally settling into its current owner's hands. With an eye toward historical ramifications, the property had been sanctioned as the treasured landmark it deserved to be.

Now, a panoramic vision of dreamlike perfection, Haven House was the epitome of freedom once again. This time it was the privately owned home and sanctuary of Raymond Gates.

The crisp scent of fresh-cut grass mixed with newly bloomed annuals filled the midsummer air. It was late evening, but the sky was still rich with summer's sunlight. The sun hung low in the western sky. The treetops, backlit by red, orange and purple, glowed with the last rays of daylight. Bright shafts of light slivered through the leaves, creating silhouettes of radiant splendor.

The usual bustle of daily activities had long since halted, leaving Raymond alone in the stillness of his thoughts. He gazed out over the distant land and inhaled deeply. He needed this. The rich solitude he often sought was found at Haven House.

With all of its historical references, he found it ironic that Haven House was still a sanctuary. At times, it had been his personal refuge allowing him to escape the turmoil of a hectic schedule or a particularly trying day. But, today he observed in reverence the struggles of the past, as he concentrated on the old structures across the lane.

The museum had been closed for renovations, so it was perfect that the foundation's building had been completed ahead of schedule. The grand opening of the Manhattan facility would coincide with the Foundation's annual awards ceremony.

He usually hosted the annual, overnight retreat and picnic for dozens of teens, honored for their willing spirit and courage in the face of astronomical difficulty. Each, with equally triumphant stories of overcoming adversity, was a recipient of the Haven Scholarship of Achievement. All college-bound seniors received a scholarship and a stipend for books and supplies. It was a welcome bonus to the joy of giving that Raymond relished.

Pleased by the distraction of the upcoming events, Raymond welcomed the semblance of normalcy. Like his work, it always grounded him when he was troubled. He thought about the name he'd finally chosen and smiled. It was perfect.

He hadn't heard from Hope in almost a week and a half. Although he'd left the ball in her court, he was beginning to wonder if that was the right thing to do. It hadn't occurred to him that she would cut off all communication.

Brandy walked up to Raymond slowly and stood by his side. He reached down and stroked the soft fullness of her hair.

She turned her face to his and nuzzled him warmly. Together they sat on the west side and watched the sun slowly begin to dip behind the trees. Tomorrow would be a long day of excitement and joy. At least he'd have his mind off of Hope for a while. Unfortunately, his thoughts strayed again, as memories of Hope drifted on the warm, jasmine-scented breeze. The feeling of loss shadowed his heart.

Hearing his name called, Raymond turned. He stood and walked back to the main house. Brandy followed. Madison stood on the porch and greeted him as he approached. "Hey,"

he smiled broadly and hugged her, "when did you get here?"
He spotted Kennedy walking up behind her, carrying her
overnight bag and computer. "Hey you," he continued to
smile. "Welcome." He reached out and gave her an equally
welcoming embrace.

"We drove up to keep you company before the gala opening tomorrow night. Tony had to stop in the city. He and
Dennis will be here in a few hours. Dennis is bringing his
new lady," Madison said, as Raymond gathered both sisters
to his sides and hugged them close.

"Well, I'm glad you came. I could use a little company.
How was your drive up?"

"Traffic was congested leaving the city."

"It usually is on the weekend. I really appreciate your
help this year. Having the awards ceremony in the city was
a lot more difficult that I planned, particularly with the new
building."

"Oh, no problem. We're delighted to help out." Madison said.

"The Foundation is truly a worthy cause. I sincerely hope
you finally came up with a name."

"I did."

"What is it?"

"Sorry, you'll have to wait for the unveiling."

"So, when do the festivities begin?" Kennedy asked.

"Tomorrow evening. Typically, members of the foundation
arrive early for a brief board meeting. What time are Dennis
and Tony getting here?" he asked.

"He said he'd be here around eight," Madison said as she
looked down to see Brandy slowly walking up the steps. She
smiled with delight. Brandy loped over to Raymond's side.

"Oh my goodness, who is this?" Kennedy asked, bending
down to greet Brandy.

Raymond bent down as well. "This is Brandy." He stroked
her long brown hair.

"She's beautiful. A sheepdog?"

"Yes, a Scottish collie."

"Look at her long hair. It's beautiful."

Brandy nuzzled her long, narrow muzzle between the two, and then nuzzled at Raymond's ear. They laughed as Brandy jumped up, knocking Raymond to the ground.

"She's excited. This is the most I've seen her jump around in a long time."

Kennedy stepped down from the porch and looked out, over the field and terrain. "Look at this view. This place is unbelievable."

Madison followed her sister down the steps. "It is incredible, isn't it?"

"It reminds me of home," Kennedy said.

"Wait until you get the fifty-cent tour. You'll never take the Underground Railroad for granted again."

Kennedy continued to look around, then spotted a cluster of old buildings on the far horizon. "Is that them? The cabins?" She pointed to a small series of dilapidated structures set off in the far distance.

Raymond turned to follow her sight of vision. "Yes. But why don't I get you settled, then we'll take a walk over there before it gets too dark."

"Are you kidding, no way! Between Mom, Dad, Madison, Tony, Dennis, and Mamma Lou, there's no way I'm waiting another minute. Forget the bags, I want a tour now."

Madison and Raymond laughed at her enthusiasm. Kennedy grabbed Raymond's arm and nearly dragged him toward the old structures. "We'll be back," Raymond said over his shoulder, as Kennedy broke out in a full run, threatening to beat him there.

Madison walked onto the porch and sat down in the rocking chair, watching as Raymond and Kennedy ran across the meadow. She shook her head, enjoying her sister's excitement at seeing the old structures. In all of Kennedy's success as a curator at the Smithsonian African Arts Museum, she was still wowed by the thought of a historic find of notable significance.

Madison ran her hands gently over her stomach. Apparently the drive was a bit more strenuous than she'd anticipated. As Raymond and Kennedy disappeared over the last mound, she decided to rummage through the kitchen in search of food.

Madison walked around the side porch and through the French doors that led to the rear of the house. She entered the mudroom, which was composed mainly of antique benches, a wall-sized, antique canning cupboard, and storage cabinets.

A closed and locked door, off to the side, led to a small, lower-level room. Now used to secure Raymond's wine collection, the small cellar, originally used to store perishables, had also been a shortcut to freedom.

Madison passed through the butler's pantry, a glass-enclosed, temperature-controlled mini-market of every imaginable luxury and necessity. From canned tuna and sardines to Beluga caviar and truffles, the smorgasbord of culinary delights was readily available to tempt the most finicky eater.

The sidewall was completely devoted to Raymond's ambitious library of cookbooks. Divided by a wall of smoked and beveled Plexiglas blocks, the brightly lit room led right into the main kitchen area.

The size of most New York apartments, Raymond's kitchen was a master chef's dream comes true. The design sense was influenced by an eclectic mixture of Mediterranean and Spanish styles. Satisfying culinary skills of varying levels, he had all the modern conveniences of a traditional kitchen as well as the contemporary restaurant effects as suggested by restaurateurs Colonel Wheeler and Dennis Hayes.

The first impression upon entering the massive space was that of astonishment. The room was brightly lit by skylights. Large windows along the outside wall flooded the airy space with light and fresh air.

The centerpiece, filling an entire wall, was the original sandstone-lined fireplace and cookery. Arching five feet across, the rustic alcove enabled easy access to a variety of temperature-controlled cooking.

Lining the room was a six-inch shelf that displayed a collection of vintage cooking paraphernalia. The center island, circled with high-backed, padded bar stools, was both functional and eclectic. It had a bi-level counter of cherry wood cabinetry, and marble, with inset tinted glass placemats. Hanging from cast iron circular hooks was an array of copper pots, pans, and cookery.

The floor, designed with slabs of terra cotta tiles stained with deep, rich wine, moss and earth tones, defined the space. Matching countertops, with a faux texture and gloss shine, added dimension to the already expansive space.

Madison opened the refrigerator doors and scanned the contents. It was packed with what Dennis referred to as must-haves for any well-stocked kitchen. Madison pulled out all the fixings and constructed a sandwich from turkey, Swiss cheese, spicy mustard and a pickle. She chose a bottled water, then went back outside and sat down on the porch.

Framed by the idyllic image of nature's perfection, Madison ate, sat, and rocked in perfect harmony. She'd always loved visiting Raymond. His warm wit and charming sense of humor was much like her husband's. Tucked away in the soft, reluctant shadows of dusk, Madison relaxed while munching on her sandwich and sipping the cool, refreshing water.

In the distance, Madison caught the briefest glimpse of a car. She stood and looked down the road, expecting to see Tony's jeep. She squinted against the musky evening; it wasn't Tony's jeep. The car, unfamiliar to her, continued up the circular drive, pulling slowly around to the front of the house. Curious, Madison walked the length of the porch as it wrapped around the side of the house. The car stopped just as she came down the front steps.

Although it had gotten late, the sun had not yet completely set. Deep, dusky hues of scorched-orange and warm-red fired the sky behind the hundred-foot-tall sycamore trees that lined both sides of the road. Hope had been driving for several miles before she noticed that she hadn't passed another house or car in over fifteen minutes.

She reduced her speed and glanced down at her directions. She decided that she had somehow taken a wrong turn and had wound up on the wrong road. She was just about to make a u-turn when she spotted a large, white sign a quarter of a mile ahead.

The sign read, *Haven House Museum,* and directed her a half mile down the road. She decided to continue to the museum in hopes of regaining her bearings. A few moments later she arrived at the entrance of Haven House Museum. The stone entrance had a chain across it with a small sign indicating that it was closed for the next few weeks.

From that vantage point, Hope saw a series of small, wooden buildings and behind them, a large white building. As she drove away she spotted another road leading to the large, white building. She decided to drive to the building and ask for directions.

She slowed down and glanced up at the black, iron gates. She put the car in reverse, blocking the entrance. She looked at the address she'd scribbled down on the small piece of paper, then back up at the gilded address on the front of the gate. They were the same. She shifted into drive and proceeded through the gates.

Hope turned the air conditioner off and rolled down the front windows. A soft breeze blew scented air through the window. It smelled of pine trees, jasmine, and fresh-cut grass. The immaculately cut landscape caught her attention immediately. Beautifully rolling meadows extended down the path on each side. The scenery was breathtaking.

Assuming the large white building was a bed and breakfast or a small hotel, she continued up the road. As she approached, she realized that it was actually an enormous private home.

Oak and pine trees, perfectly sculpted hedges and colorful

seasonal flowers surrounded the building. Bleach-white siding covered the entire house, except the bottom, which was constructed with beautifully carved, multicolored stone. Covered with huge, tinted windows and charcoal-colored shutters that matched the roof's shingles, the house was adorned with a wraparound porch.

Hope slowly steered her car around the circular drive. She watched as a lovely young woman came down the front steps to greet her. She instantly regretted her impulsive decision to drive to Raymond's house unannounced. The last time she went to Raymond's apartment, she'd received her own surprise: him walking out of the building with another woman.

What was she doing? What was she thinking? That was just it, she wasn't thinking. She'd let her desire to be with Raymond cloud her judgment. It didn't occur to her that maybe he had moved on and was now with another woman. After all, it was her idea to cool things off between them.

Hope looked at the woman as she approached. There was something vaguely familiar about her. She shifted the car into park, turned off the ignition, took a deep breath, and opened the car door.

"Hi, can I help you?" the woman said pleasantly, as she came around to the driver's side of the car.

"Hi. Yes. I hope you can help me. I'm not sure if I have the right address," Hope replied as she got out and closed the door behind her. "I'm looking for Dr. Raymond Gates," she said, realizing that she had definitely seen this woman before.

"Oh, right," Madison said, with surprise. "You must be from the foundation. You're in the right place. Raymond said that someone might be driving up early, but I presumed he meant tomorrow, in town. He stepped out for a few moments. He'll be back shortly."

Hope looked up at the massive house. "Is this his home?"

"Yes. Why don't you come in and wait inside. He shouldn't be much longer."

Hope grabbed her purse from the front seat of the car and

followed. Madison climbed the stairs and led Hope around the porch to the front door. She opened the door, inviting Hope inside. Hope's breath instantly caught in her throat. They stepped into the foyer. Madison stopped and turned around. "I'm sorry," Madison began smiling pleasantly, "I didn't introduce myself. I'm Madison Evans-Gates. I'll be helping out tomorrow evening."

"Nice to meet you Madison, I'm . . ." The telephone rang as she said her name. Madison quickly shook Hope's hand, then excused herself and hurried to the phone.

Hope looked around the spacious home in astonishment. This definitely wasn't the unfurnished, barren apartment Raymond used in town. She was stunned by the sheer magnificence of the home. Outside, the place looked like a palace; inside was like a mini-hotel. Hope looked around shaking her head in amazement. The only thing missing was a gift shop and bellman's stand. She had no idea Raymond was this affluent.

Hope continued into the nearest room. She peeked inside. Furnished to the hilt with designer and antique pieces, the inside was just as exquisite as the outside. Walking to the sitting room, Hope gazed around in awe.

It looked like a room for a glamorous movie set or from a sophisticated magazine layout. Every perfect piece was in its perfect place. From the beautifully polished, hardwood floors covered with Persian carpets, to the gilded antique chandelier with sparkling teardrop crystals hanging from the vaulted ceiling, everything was magnificent.

Architecturally superb, the crown, ceiling and chair rail molding, most likely the original trimmings, were painted white against the rich dark burgundy hue of the surrounding walls. Lavishly swaged drapery hung with meticulously pinched pleats at windows that offered a view that could have been a Monet landscape.

Hope walked around the room, touching everything in sight, from the textured-fabric tapestry of the sofa and settee, to the rich, buffed gloss of the antique coffee and side tables.

She eventually stood and looked up at the exquisite, Moorish tapestry. She reached to touch it but thought better of it.

Obviously an antique, it looked as if it had been woven just yesterday. Hope moved in closer. Thin colored threads interwove to create the brightly colored tapestry.

She stood at the large bay window just beyond the alcove and looked out at the landscape. Haven House was just as beautiful as Gates Manor on Crescent Island. Her thoughts staggered through images of Raymond. She silently prayed that he would still want her.

Raymond and Kennedy were laughing hysterically as they entered the rear of the house. Raymond stayed in the kitchen while Kennedy continued on, into the living room. She passed Madison, still on the phone, and found Hope standing in front of the window.

Hope turned around hearing someone behind her. She gasped, her mouth dropped open. This was the woman she had seen on Raymond's arm the night she had stopped by his apartment.

"Hi, I'm Kennedy Evans."

Hope took a second to ease her raging nerves. "Hi," she stumbled out finally. "I think I have to go."

"Wait," Kennedy said. "Didn't you just get here?" Hope nodded, not trusting her voice. "From New York?" Hope nodded again. Kennedy began to look at Hope oddly. "Can I get you a refreshment or something?"

Hope shook her head. "I have to go now." She turned to leave.

"Wait a minute," Kennedy began. "Don't you need to speak with Raymond?"

Hope was just about to turn and reply when she heard Raymond and Madison talking as they approached. She froze.

"Hope?" Raymond said.

Hope swallowed hard. Her heart pounded like a stamped-ing herd. She couldn't move. She couldn't speak.

"Hope?" Raymond repeated, his voice closer. He stepped in front of her, blocking her escape. "Hope?"

Hope turned around. "Hello, Raymond."

Madison looked at Kennedy as an uncomfortable awkwardness hung in the air. Both Madison and Kennedy spoke at the same time. They offered to retrieve their luggage from their car. They quickly dashed past Raymond and Hope and went outside.

"Hope." Raymond came closer and reached for her hand, but stopped himself. "Are you okay?"

"I have to go."

"No." Raymond stepped in front of her. "Hope, you came here for a reason. You came here to see me. Why?"

Hope shook her head. "I have to go."

"Hope, don't do this. Don't run and push me away again."

She nodded as a slow tear crept down her face. Raymond instantly gathered her up in his arms. Hope melted easily. She didn't care about Kennedy or Madison or anything else. All she cared about was that moment and Raymond's arms, holding and protecting her.

"Why are you here?"

"I—, I—, I—, " she began several times, her head bowed low, avoiding his questioning gaze. "I don't know."

"I think you do." Raymond tilted her chin upward. "I'm glad you came."

Hope looked up into his hazel eyes. His smile was all she needed. If she was going to make a fool of herself, it might as well be here and now. She reached up and pulled his neck toward her. She kissed him with all her might.

Madison and Kennedy returned from the car with their luggage. They sat the bags down in the foyer. They looked at Raymond and Hope standing in a solid embrace. Hope tried to step away, but was firmly held in place by Raymond.

"Hope, this is Madison, my cousin's wife and Kennedy, her

sister. Madison, Kennedy, this is Dr. Hope Adams," he stated proudly. Madison and Kennedy smiled and greeted her warmly.

Hope's emotions clashed as she sighed with relief. Raymond's cousin and Raymond's cousin's sister, reverberated over and over again in her mind. The connection was still clearing in her head when the door opened and two men and a woman walked in.

All heads turned as Tony, Dennis and Faith entered noisily, dropping their overnight bags down on the floor. Madison instantly went to Tony's side. They kissed lovingly.

"Faith?"

"Hope?"

The sisters embraced in a loving reunion.

Dennis shook Raymond's hand, grabbed Kennedy and kissed her brotherly. He grabbed Hope and embraced her warmly.

Raymond introduced and reintroduced everyone, then excused Hope and himself. Once outside, Raymond took Hope's hand as they walked around to the side of the house. A dimmed light cast deep shadows across the wooden floor. He guided Hope to the porch swing; they sat in silence.

Hope looked around in wonder. She'd never seen so much beauty in one place. "This place is incredible. Why do you ever leave?"

"Believe it or not, I have to go to work from time to time."

"But look at this place. It's incredible." Hope shook her head. "I'd never set foot in the city again."

"You'd miss it."

"No way. If I lived here, I'd never go back to Manhattan."

"I'm delighted to hear that. Come on, I'll show you around." Raymond grabbed a couple of flashlights as they walked the path together.

"I had no idea that you were a nutmegger."

Raymond nodded his head. "I moved to Connecticut several years ago. I was drawn to it by its proximity to New York and its quietness."

"I can see that. It's beautiful here." She continued to look across the meadow. "I passed a sign earlier stating that there was an Underground Railroad stop near here."

Raymond pointed in the direction of the old shacks. "It's over there, beyond those trees."

"Is this property connected to the museum?"

"Yes."

"You own a museum, too?"

"I'm more like a caretaker who happens to have it on the property. Are we going to dance around this all night?"

"Why do you do this to me?"

"Do what?" he asked with all sincerity.

"Make me feel like. . ."

Raymond stepped in close. "Feel like what, doctor?"

Hope took a deep breath and tried to step away. Raymond held tightly, refusing to let her go again.

"I feel like every fiber of my being dissolves the moment I see you. I feel like my body's on fire whenever you touch me." He touched her face with his finger as he continued. "I feel like there's no one else on the planet but you and me."

"I know that feeling, I know because I feel the exact same way. Know this, Dr. Gates. I'm a formidable adversary."

"Know it," Raymond smiled, then laughed mischievously. "I'm depending on it." He kissed her with all of the suppressed yearning inside of him.

Twenty-nine

Hope refused to open her eyes for fear that the magic would somehow, suddenly, dissipate into thin air. She laid there alone in Raymond's bed with a smile still plastered on her face. She had had the most wonderful time getting to know Raymond's family and friends.

Although politely shy at first, she and Faith had easily assimilated into the fold and were instantly accepted. With their upbringing so widely different, the four women marveled in their similarities and relished the differences that made them unique. It was a good feeling.

Madison and Kennedy, two from a set of triplets, were just like Hope and Faith, sisters of the heart and soul. Together, they talked for hours about growing up in their various locales and the outrageous experiences they'd encountered in their chosen careers.

Hope had relayed for the first time the assault she'd experienced in the hospital's parking garage. All three women listened intently, then cheered with solidarity and delight at Hope's victorious bravery. Then, to her even greater surprise, she found herself talking about her mother's death as Faith leaned in closer and they all four celebrated the life that was too short.

The conversation shifted and changed several more times before finally settling on Kennedy's recent trip to central Africa. As a curator at the Smithsonian's African Arts Museum, she told of her quest to secure a particular collection for an upcoming exhibition she was assembling.

Madison, barely out of her first trimester, relayed her tumultuous mood swings that had sent Tony scampering for cover on several occasions. Like any newlywed couple, they'd had growing pains, but devotion and, most importantly, their love, had seen them through.

Hope listened with particular interest. She'd been thinking a lot recently about Raymond's marriage proposal. She knew that they loved each other; she was just so afraid that it just wouldn't be enough to hold them together and that somehow she'd lose herself in the we of their union, as her mother had done.

Eventually the four stepped outside where the men had been. They sat out on the porch talking and stared up at the night sky. The heavens had performed the ultimate light show of brilliant stars and sparkling planets. Faith stood and looked through one of the weather-resistant telescopes.

A whole new conversation developed as Raymond and Tony talked about how they had spent hours looking up at the stars when they were on Crescent Island.

Raymond, sitting next to Hope, pointed out a bright red star, Betelgeuse, and its equal, Rigel. They were the two most prominent stars that made up the constellation, Orion the Hunter. Then he told the Greek myth of the great, giant hunter's love of Eos, the goddess of dawn, and his pursuit of the Pleiades. The hunter's eventual demise was at the hands of Artemis, Apollo's twin and goddess of the hunt.

Hope was amazed at Raymond's in-depth and informative telling of the ancient tale. As Tony continued, going into greater detail on Greek mythology, the outlay of the stars and planets, and their relationship to present day astrologers, she leaned in closer to Raymond.

"Is there anything you don't know and any question you don't know the answer to?"

"Just one."

Hope knew to what he referred. The last time he'd asked her to marry him in the chapel, she didn't answer. She still didn't.

Later, everyone had decided that a midnight snack was in order, so seven overly skillful cooks adjourned to the kitchen. In a humorous riot of madcap madness, they created a massive sandwich to be cut and equally divided. Of course, good intentions turned out to be anything but.

Lively disputes on ingredients, amounts, seasonings and condiments lasted as long as the sandwich making itself. Turkey was placed on one side, ham on the other, sweet spicy sausage on a single corner. Swiss, American and Provolone cheese was assembled and disbursed in Switzerland-like neutrality, as additional tomatoes and pickles topped one end, while mustard and mayo finished the other. Lettuce, no lettuce; peppers, no peppers; onion, definitely no onion.

Finally, with more sanctioned debates and disputed referendums than a UN commission, the layered masterpiece, of Dagwood-sized proportion was assembled, carved and eaten in enjoyable bliss.

They adjourned to the bedrooms. Raymond walked Hope to his bedroom and chastely kissed her at the door. He decided to sleep in one of the guest rooms. She watched as he walked down the hall and entered the last door on the left.

Hope sighed and snuggled deeper beneath the lightweight covering. Eos, the goddess of dawn had come too soon. If she lay there really still, and closed her eyes really tight, she could still see the millions of stars and hear Raymond's voice telling her about the different constellations.

She thought about the romantic Greek myth he had told the night before, about Eos, the goddess of dawn and the great, giant hunter, Orion. Forever in the stars, forever in love.

Suddenly she knew her answer, but she'd known it all along. She was just too afraid to let go and enjoy the great gift of love given to her. This was a new beginning for her and she intended to take full advantage of it. She sprang from the bed, showered, and hurried downstairs.

It was later than she realized. Madison, Tony, and Kennedy were already gone. Dennis was giving Faith a private tour of the museum. Raymond was sitting out on the patio reading a thick book on allergies and their catalysts.

"Good morning," she said.

"Good afternoon," he answered.

She smiled as he offered her brunch. She grabbed a cinnamon danish and nibbled. He placed the book back on the pile, poured her a cup of coffee, then picked up another book and began studying it. Hope walked over and smiled down at the now futile search. She closed the book. "Almonds."

"Excuse me?"

"Mamma Lou is allergic to almonds."

Raymond's mouth gaped open when he realized the complete scenario. "Matchmaking." Hope nodded and began laughing at Raymond's completely mortified reaction. He was so sure that Louise had nothing to do with their relationship, only to find out that she was instrumental at every point including the very beginning.

"How? When?"

Hope relayed the complete story Louise had told her about overhearing her conversation with Faith in the ladies' room.

"From the very beginning?" he asked, feeling completely dejected by his less-than-astute observational skills.

"Apparently," Hope said, still amused by Louise's ploy and Raymond's foiled reaction. He shook his head and surrendered easily. He had to give it to her, she was a master.

"So, any plans for today?" she asked.

Raymond relayed the events of the upcoming day and evening. The grand opening of the foundation's headquarters was going to be a comfortable, casual affair.

"Someone mentioned the foundation last night. Exactly what is the foundation and what does it do?"

"Its main function is to rescue disenfranchised children and teens, to afford them the opportunity to further their studies through education in the upper levels, most specifically in medicine. It was one of my mother's pet projects. My father already has a program like it in Baltimore in honor of her memory. It's called Ray of Joy."

"That's so wonderful. What's your program called?"

"It won't be announced until the official opening this evening." He looked at his watch. "So, you'd better get ready. We have to leave in three hours."

"I don't have anything to wear. I only brought an overnight bag."

"We'll stop in town and buy something, then change at the apartment. But first, I want you to see something." He stood and took her hand. Hope grabbed another cinnamon danish and a covered cup of coffee and was led across the meadow to a series of small buildings along the forest's edge.

"The museum?" He nodded. She paused and looked around like a child sneaking into the back of a matinee on a Saturday afternoon. "Is it okay?" she whispered.

"Hope, of course it's okay; it's my home." Raymond watched as she continued walking with added vigor. His heart sank at the mention of the words *my home.* He wanted so badly to say *our home.*

As they walked through the hidden passages and tiny holding rooms, Raymond described the particular details in all of their historical ramifications. Unpleasant in its presentation, it was the unvarnished truth of a history miswritten and often dismissed and shelved, as just one of those darker moments in time.

Windowless back rooms with wide plank floors were littered with cots, shackles, handcuffs, lashes, iron tools, maps and numerous other aged reminders of times past. A neatly placed basin and picture sat on an overturned crate beside a rocking chair and a smaller stool. Hope could easily imagine mother and daughter, or father and son, sitting there, awaiting their turn to race to freedom.

Several thickly stoned walls were scratched and etched with an artist's rendition of his escape to freedom and the family and friends he was forced to leave behind. Hope felt a silent awe as she dared to reach out and touch the past.

"This is merely one of many stations up and down the eastern coastline. No one knows exactly when the Railroad began, or ended, for that matter. The thirteenth amendment was signed in 1865, but it took years for freedom to truly saturate the states. Unfortunately, even now some African-Americans are enslaved by drugs, hatred and poverty."

Hope looked around as tears threatened. "The truth is so heartbreaking."

"No, it's heartening. We have to let our past inspire our future. And just like those brave souls traveling the Railroad all those many years ago, we have to go back and bring others out of the slavery of our modern shackles."

Faith and Dennis joined Hope and Raymond as they walked back to the main house in renewed strength. For the positive to be transformed from a negative was scientifically impossible, but they were ready to overcome the impossible.

Hope felt like a schoolgirl going on her first date with the high school football star. Her palms were sweating, her hands were clammy, and her brow was moist. She took one last look at her reflection in the car's side mirror. This is ridiculous. Why was she so nervous? She'd been to many such events like this. But never with Raymond.

She looked over as he easily maneuvered his car into the parking space in front of the brightly lit building. It was magnificent. The cast-stone façade and huge windows were truly a sight to behold.

The official opening was still forty-five minutes away. Raymond left her side to take care of last-minute details. Hope toured the facility and was impressed by everything she saw. As she arrived back at the main hall and reception area, she spotted Leanne Jackson by the front door. "Leanne? What are you doing here?"

"Dr. Adams!" Leanne ran over to Hope and threw her arms around her. "I hoped I'd see you tonight. Thank you, thank you, thank you."

Hope beamed at seeing Leanne so happy and relaxed. It was like seeing a brand-new woman. "How are your sessions with Charlene?"

"She's great. I can't tell you how incredible it was to meet someone like her. She told me that she actually went to jail for killing her husband after years of abuse."

Hope nodded. "It was eventually reversed on appeal as self-defense and she was released. But you're right, Charlene's a remarkable women."

"She really is. She told me that every day I have a choice to make with my life and that I'm in control. She's so dedicated and positive. I don't know if I'll ever be as strong as she is."

"You'd be surprised how strong you can be when it really counts." Hope spoke from experience.

"Sometimes I'm still afraid. But I'll call one of my new friends and I feel so much better. Sometimes they even call me for help. Can you believe it? Someone needs me?" A joyful tear of acceptance broke free and trickled down her face. "Thank you so much."

"I didn't do anything. You were the brave one. You took control of your life and refused to be a victim."

"One day at a time." She reached out and grabbed Hope in a warm hug. The pride in struggling to get her life back was a fight she was determined to win.

"So, what are you doing here?" Hope asked again.

"I work here."

"Here?"

"Yes, Dr. Gates hired me right after Wes was arrested. The building had just been completed when he hired me. I've been helping with setup." She looked around excitedly. "Isn't this place marvelous? I don't know what I would have done without him vouching for me in court. He told the judge that I was one of his assistants to help speed up the restraining order process.

"Maxine gave the court-documented proof of my husband's abuse and helped me file for divorce. She even found an apartment for me in one of her buildings. I don't know what I would have done if it weren't for you and Dr. Gates. He paid my rent for the first six months. He saved my life. You are so blessed to have a man like that in your life. Maybe someday I'll find someone just like him."

Hope was dazed by Leanne's joy. "Yeah, he is truly unbelievable."

"I have to go. I'm a working woman now. Thank you." She hugged Hope once more, then hurried off through the front doors.

Raymond walked up to Hope as she stood processing Leanne's new beginning, her new beginning, and Raymond's steadfast reliability. He was truly unbelievable.

"Hey, there you are," he came up behind her smiling and stole a kiss on her shoulder. He looked at his watch. "We're ready to get started. Are you ready to be the evening's hostess?"

"Yes," she answered.

"Good, let's go." He started to walk away but realized that Hope hadn't moved. He turned back to her.

She smiled and said, "Yes, Dr. Raymond Gates. I love you and I would be honored to be Mrs. Raymond Gates, Jr."

Raymond whooped loudly, grabbed Hope and spun her around. After several spins he set her down and pulled the ever present little, velvet box from his inside pocket. He placed the ring on her finger and kissed her tenderly.

The proverbial gates had been opened. And the masses stood at the front door awaiting the unveiling. Raymond made a short speech and pulled the cord, loosening the drape and unveiled the name for the first time, *Ray of Hope Foundation*.

Applause rang out as Raymond nodded to his father, uncle and grandmother standing in the audience. This was a very good moment, but not as wonderful as the moment Hope agreed to be his wife.

In nonstop momentum, the celebration was in full swing as word traveled that Hope and Raymond were engaged to be married. Faith, Dennis, Madison, Tony and Kennedy were all delighted and congratulated the couple as soon as they heard. J.T. arrived late, and at hearing the joyous news, passed Dennis a hundred dollar bill to pay off their wager.

Hope, true to her new designation was the perfect Ray of Hope Foundation hostess.

Raymond walked up beside Lousie and Otis. She reached up and kissed his cheek lovingly. "I'm so proud of you. Your mother would have been overjoyed."

Raymond smiled and looked around the massive facility. It had been a lot of work and a long time coming, but it was well worth it.

"Good job, Raymond," Colonel Wheeler stated proudly. "Great party."

"Thanks. I'm glad you could make it. By the way, Mamma Lou, I'd skip the marzipan if I were you." Louise burst with laughter. "Hope told you that I'm allergic to almonds, I see."

"What? You're what?" Colonel Wheeler exclaimed, his mouth gaped open. "Louise Gates, you had me buy you all those candy bars filled with almonds while you were in the hospital."

"Oops."

Epilogue

Crescent Island, Virginia

Raymond took Hope's hand and led her back to the main house. When they reached the pool she turned and looked back at the view. It was breathtaking. The still serenity of the water, the peace and quiet of nature, and the love of her life at her side. She was too happy for words.

"Hey," Raymond looked at her expression with concern, "are you okay?"

She turned to him. Emotion filled her. She never dreamed she could be this happy. "I'm just overwhelmed. Everything is so perfect. It's so wonderful to be back again."

"Again?"

"Yes, I came here for a few days after the attack in the parking garage. Mamma Lou and I got to spend some quality time together outside of the hospital. She's so special. You're so blessed to have her in your life."

Raymond raised Hope's left hand and kissed the sparkling diamond and its matching band of gold. "In our lives," he corrected. "Now I have two very special women in my life."

Hope threw her arms around her husband and kissed him until she could no longer breathe. The joy she felt was complete. They walked hand-in-hand back to the house. A soon as they entered, Raymond was immediately called to settle a battle between Tony, Dennis and J.T.

Family and friends were just beginning to leave as Hope

and Raymond entered. The reception was unimaginably beautiful. Having gotten married in a private ceremony, Mamma Lou had talked the newlywed couple into allowing her to throw the reception. She had truly outdone herself.

Hope looked around the living room, seeing a couple of familiar faces. "Maxine and Scott? Are you two together?" Maxine smiled at Hope then back up at Scott. His bushy moustache lifted into a humorous grin. "When did this happen? Where was I? Has hell frozen over and I didn't hear the rumor?"

Maxine laughed happily. "For some time now. Hope, if I told you once, I've told you a hundred times, you really must pay closer attention to the hospital gossip."

"I guess so."

"Your leaving to join the Ray of Hope Foundation was the topic of the latest rumor. But now I hear Nolan's denied application is all around. I guess Hugh didn't have as much pull with *Barclay Med* as he thought. I wouldn't be surprised if he retired real soon."

Hope looked from Scott's beaming face to Maxine's. "Nothing surprises me anymore." She hugged them both. "I'm so happy for you, Maxine."

Maxine winked. "We're gonna hang around for the rest of the weekend. I hear Crescent Island is fabulous. I can't wait to visit the historical freed-slaves' shantytown."

Hope nodded her head and almost burst with happiness. "Have a wonderful time." She watched as the happy couple walked out. She looked around for Raymond, but saw Faith and Dennis with their heads together, talking intimately in the corner.

Faith looked up. They smiled at each other. Hope nodded her approval; Faith mouthed the words, *thank you.*

When all the guests had left, the family sat around the family room, enjoying the last of an incredible evening.

"Well," J.T. began as he sat down on the sofa across from Madison and Tony, "it looks like your grandmother is finally out of grandsons with whom to play matchmaker." He moved a pillow so that Kennedy could sit down beside him.

Kennedy sat down and placed her glass of champagne on the coffee table in front of her. "I am so glad that Mom and Dad have never done that to us. The whole idea of someone planning and calculating your future behind your back is too strange for me. I'd be totally mortified."

Raymond and Hope sat on the cushioned window seat in their own loving world. He held his new wife even closer and nudged his chin into her the smooth of her graceful neck. "Oh, I don't know about that," he said with a smile wide enough to reach the moon. "I'm kind of glad that Mamma Lou decided to play matchmaker with us. I couldn't be happier."

"Ditto," Hope added. "There's definitely something to what she does and how she does it. There's no way that Raymond and I would have ever gotten together if it weren't for her superb matchmaking skills." Raymond nibbled at her neck and she giggled endlessly.

J.T. and Kennedy looked at each other and shook their heads in unison. "Better you than me," J.T. affirmed to Kennedy's exuberant nod and even more exuberantly said, "Amen to that."

Across the room, Tony reached down and stroked the side of Madison's newly swollen belly. "I have to go along with Raymond and Hope. There just might be something to Mamma Lou's matchmaking talent."

"I totally agree," Madison added, picking up her glass of iced lemon water to sip slowly.

"I'm afraid I'm also gonna have to agree with those folks," Dennis confessed, as he entered the living room and plopped down in the nearest chair. Faith snuggled right next to him. He wrapped his arm around her lovingly, took a long sip from his champagne glass and eased back comfortably. "They definitely have a point this time."

"Oh please, Dennis, not you, too," Kennedy began. "You can't really believe all that. Everything that happened with

Hope and Raymond was just coincidence. They were bound to meet at some medical gathering eventually. And Madison and Tony were just pure luck. They were all simply in the right place at the right time. Mamma Lou's so-called matchmaking skill had nothing to do with any of this. It was all just coincidence and random chance."

"Given the right circumstances, any happenstance meeting can seem like fate and fortune," J.T. added.

"I don't know," Dennis shook his head as he eyed the two loving couples longingly. "She's two for two. Tony and Madison, Raymond and Hope; you have to admit, her record is perfect so far. She's very good at this. Who knows," he added, more to Faith than to the others, "she just might be three for three this time—a tripleheader."

Everyone looked at Dennis in complete shock. "What?" echoed through the room.

Kennedy spoke up to respond. "You, the confirmed bachelor, matched up? Aw, Faith, say it isn't so."

"Now I know I've heard it all," J.T. added in utter disbelief.

"Not yet." Dennis instantly stood up and kneeled down on bended knee. He pulled a small velvet box from his pocket. He cleared his throat nervously. "Faith, would you do me the honor of becoming my wife?"

The room became silent as Faith gasped in stunned surprise. "Yes." A loud uproar of laughter and cheers rang out as they all jumped to their feet to congratulate the couple.

Faith, still in shock, held her finger out as Dennis slipped the ring on securely.

"Better you than me," J.T. said as he smiled appreciatively at the loving couples all around him. "I rather like being a bachelor and quite frankly, I intend to be one for a very, very long time."

"I agree with J.T. I don't think I'm ready for that step either," Kennedy said. "I think that the whole commitment thing is a bit scary. I like my life just as it is, thank you very much."

"I wouldn't get too comfortable with that idea if I were you," Raymond said as he and Hope looked out of the window. "You may not have a choice. Looks like Mamma Lou may not be finished with her matchmaking just yet. She just might be going into the matchmaker-for-hire business."

"What do you mean?" J.T. asked as everyone walked over to the wall of large bay windows.

They all stared out for a few minutes until J.T. asked, "Can you hear what they're saying? Who are they talking about?"

"Shh, no," Kennedy whispered as if they'd hear her inside the house.

"They can't hear us," J.T. said, still trying to read his parents' lips.

"They're making plans."

"They just mentioned your name."

"Whose name?" J.T. said.

"She said something about getting married."

"Who's getting married?" Kennedy asked.

All eyes were still on J.T., Kennedy and Madison's parents, Taylor and Jace Evans. They smiled and nodded knowingly to Louise and Colonel Wheeler. Louise returned their smiles and nodded in agreement. Then they all looked over at the house and waved at J.T. and Kennedy.

The brother and sister backed away from the window slowly. "Uh-oh," they said in unison. Instantly Raymond, Hope, Faith, Tony and Madison burst with laughter.

"Fifty dollars says Kennedy's the next one on the list," Hope offered first.

"I'll take that bet," Madison answered to Kennedy's amazement and open-mouthed gasp.

"Count me in," Faith added, sporting her shiny new jewel.

"Hey, wait a minute," Kennedy complained openly to the three women. "That's not fair, why me?"

"I think I'll take the long shot. A hundred says it's J.T.," Tony said, as J.T. nearly choked on his drink a second time.

"No way, not me," J.T. complained.

"Two hundred says it's J.T.," Dennis added as J.T.'s hardened stare turned into a warning threat.

"I'll take that bet," Kennedy said.

"Thanks a lot, little sister," J.T. said sarcastically, "but my money's on you for two hundred and fifty."

"I'll cover that bet," Raymond said, just before the room exploded into a boisterous discussion.

For the next few minutes bets and wagers circled the room as justifications, explanations and deductions caused several speculations to alter and change. Each wager raised the ante higher and higher. The stakes grew with each venture risked.

Louise, Colonel Wheeler, Taylor and Jace entered the room as voices raised and laughter rang out. With everyone talking at once it was impossible to hear and understand any one, definitive conversation.

"What's going on?" Louise asked, to the suddenly silent gathering.

Everyone turned to look at everyone else. "Who's next?" they all asked, as if on cue.

Dear Reader,

I hope you have enjoyed reading the story of Raymond Gates and Hope Adams. It was truly a labor of love and a joy to write. Your wonderful letters and e-mails said it all.

I am incredibly thankful for your continued support and dedication to my work. As for Mamma Lou's next matchmaking test, well, the bet is on. Will it be J.T., Kennedy, or someone else? The next story is already in the works. And believe me, the best is yet to come.

Also look for my next novel with BET Books, entitled *Reflections of You*. It's set on the tropical island of Puerto Rico and is hot, hot, HOT! You asked for a steamy romance, that's exactly what *Reflections of You* is.

I enjoy hearing from readers. Please send your comments to conorfleet@aol.com or Celeste O. Norfleet, P.O. Box 7346, Woodbridge, VA 22195-7346. Don't forget to check out my Web site at http://www.celesteonorfleet.com.

Best wishes,
Celeste O. Norfleet

ABOUT THE AUTHOR

Celeste O. Norfleeet, born and raised in Philadelphia, Pennsylvania, is a graduate of Moore College of Art & Design with a B.F.A. in fashion illustration. She has worked as an art director for several advertising agencies and now does freelance design for area businesses.

An avid reader and writer, Celeste has sold several novels to BET books. She is an active member of Washington Romance Writers amd Romance Writers of America and lives in Virginia with her husband and two children. She is blessed to have endless support of caring family and friends.